Also by Elaine Hankin

Flatmates
House of Secrets
Portrait of Rosanna
The Spanish Twin

LAWS ARE SILENT

'Laws are silent in times of war'
Cicero (Roman author, orator & statesman - 106 BC-43 BC)

Elaine Hankin

Published in 2013 by FeedARead.com Publishing – Arts Council funded

Copyright © Elaine Hankin

The author asserts the moral right under the Copyright, Designs and Patents Act, 1988, to be identified as the author of this work.

All Rights reserved. No part of this publication may be reproduced, copied, stored in a retrieval system, or transmitted, in any form or by any means, without the prior written consent of the copyright holder, nor be otherwise circulated in any form of binding or cover other than that in which it is published and without a similar condition being imposed on the subsequent purchaser.

A CIP catalogue record for this title is available from the British Library.

With grateful thanks to friends and family for their encouragement and help during the writing of this novel.

Cover design by Tom Hankin.

PROLOGUE

Padua 1939

The man held his breath. Something seemed wrong. Spinning around, he ran back to the square, stopping fifty yards from Dino's Trattoria where the students were still gathered. In high spirits, they seemed oblivious to the threat of war closing in on them. The waiter brought out more beers, side-stepping a couple of the students, who had embarked on a good-natured wrestling match. The onlooker chuckled, drawn back to his own time at university some ten years earlier.

The strains of a Benny Goodman melody reached him from a first floor apartment. He sniffed as the aroma of simmering garlic, tomatoes and olive oil enticed saliva to his mouth, reminding him that he hadn't eaten all day. Pushing aside his qualms, he turned to go home. What was he bothered about? This was just a typical Friday evening.

Suddenly, he was alert. There was a figure lurking in the shadows. And another, further along the road. Christ! He must warn them. From the cover of the shuttered shop windows, he tried to catch the students' attention, but they didn't notice his wild gesticulations. *Merda*, reckless youngsters! Why hadn't they distributed the tell-tale leaflets straightaway? Moistening his lips, he gave a low whistle.

One of the students looked up. Too late! A squad of blackshirts armed with batons and rifles, stormed towards the trattoria.

PART I

The solace of hatred.

One

Tuscany 1939

Shock churned his gut. With nausea rising, Count Vincenzo Di Tomasi dashed upstairs, reaching the toilet with seconds to spare. The bout of sickness passed. He kicked the door shut but his recently consumed dinner refused to remain in his stomach, and the retching began again. It was fifteen minutes before he felt stable enough to leave the bathroom.

His wife came out into the hall. 'You left the phone off the hook, Vincenzo,' she called up to him.

He wiped a handkerchief across his mouth, and managed to mutter, 'Sorry, Alice, I forgot to put it back.'

She laughed. 'Really, Vincenzo, you're getting terribly absentminded. Are you coming down for some coffee?'

Coffee! He needed something stronger than coffee.

'Hurry up, darling.' Alice's voice reached him again.

How was he going to break the news to her? How was he going to tell her that Enzo, the son who favoured her Anglo-Saxon side of the family, was dead?

They brought Enzo's body down from Padua in the small hours. Count Di Tomasi waited on the porch for the hearse's arrival, lines of sorrow etched on his features. Alice was too distressed to join him, but his old retainer, Matteo and his housekeeper, Grazia Elena, stood discreetly to one side, lending solemn comfort. Beyond the drive, the terraces were shrouded in the first mist of autumn, hiding their vines behind a gauze veil.

The pallbearers carried the coffin into the villa and set it down on a bier in the window recess of Alice's favourite room. Vincenzo stood staring at the cedar casket, finding it almost impossible to believe it contained his beloved son. He gave a start. A small hand had slipped into his. He looked down and saw his younger son, Beppe, standing next to him, dressed only in his pyjamas, his bare toes crunched up against the chill of the tiled floor.

'It's still the middle of the night,' gasped his father. 'Why aren't you in bed?'

'I heard a noise,' replied the little boy. He pointed at the coffin. 'Is Enzo in there?'

Vincenzo nodded.

'Will I ever see him again?'

'I'm afraid not.'

'I know he's dead.' Beppe's innocent tones trilled in the lofty room. 'But I want to see him just once more.'

Was it right for a nine-year-old to look upon his brother's corpse? Vincenzo knew Alice would be shocked. The English looked at death differently from the Italians.

'Please, Babbo.'

Reluctantly, he lifted the coffin's carved lid. Enzo lay cushioned on white satin, a defiant smile on his frozen lips. His hands were clasped across his chest, a silver crucifix laced between his fingers. Thankfully, there were no signs of the terrible injuries he had sustained.

Vincenzo thought back to the telephone call from the Commissioner of Police: the deferential condolences, the unsatisfactory explanation. A street brawl? No, he would never accept that his son had died like that. Ever since the call, his suspicions had been growing. Could Enzo have been murdered because of his political affiliations?

'Babbo!'

Vincenzo turned and beckoned. 'Come here, Son.' Sweeping him up, he held the little boy above the open coffin.

At that moment, the sun rose over the horizon, casting its glow on the young man whose life had been so cruelly snatched from him. It shone on his handsome face, highlighting the blond down on his chin. Beppe smiled through his tears and, pointing at the diagonal stream of light, said, 'That means Enzo's going to heaven, doesn't it, Babbo?'

His father nodded, certain now that it had been right for the boy to look at his brother's corpse.

The funeral took place the following day. It was a blustery afternoon, threatening rain. Everyone from the village came to the little church on the hillside. They stood in silence as Vincenzo and Alice stepped into the porch, then followed them inside to fill the pews and crowd the aisles. Throughout the prayers, Alice knelt beside her husband with tears streaming down her cheeks. To lend her strength, he reached for her hand and squeezed it.

Back at the villa, family friends and business associates came to pay their respects while Grazia Elena busied herself with the catering. Beppe stood between his parents to receive condolences. He looked self-conscious in a black suit run up in a hurry by the village dressmaker. Vincenzo would have preferred to have sent the little boy to bed, but he knew his son felt the need to stay with his parents, and say his last farewell to the brother he admired so much.

That night, aided by a sleeping draught, Alice fell into a deep sleep. Before going to bed, Vincenzo went in to see her. He stroked her blond hair, mulling over the decision he had made. He would send his wife and remaining son to stay with Alice's father in England. They would be safe there, beyond the reach of Mussolini's blackshirts.

During the weeks following Alice and Beppe's departure, Vincenzo spent the long lonely evenings thinking about the heated discussions he'd had with Enzo. His exceptional memory enabled him to recall one such conversation:

'You businessmen are all the same,' accused Enzo, jabbing a finger at him. 'You could change things; you could oust Mussolini and his henchmen. Why don't you do something about it instead of turning a blind eye?'

'What do you want, Son, anarchy, father against son, brother against brother?'

'It wouldn't come to that!'

He could almost hear the passion in his son's voice.

'But Papà, if the Communists had more backing, there'd be little bloodshed. There's growing hatred for the Fascist Regime; people want change but they're too lethargic to do anything about it.' Enzo had

thumped his fist on the glass-topped table making several petals from Alice's flower arrangement fall to the floor. '*We have to bring Mussolini down. For God's sake, Papà, can't you see, we must shake off the shackles of dictatorship before it's too late.*'

Vincenzo began to ask himself why he had dismissed his dead son's ideals as youthful rhetoric. He started to read up on communist doctrines and secretly bought left-wing newspapers and, as time passed, he became convinced that his son's death hadn't been the result of a disagreement between students. He wanted to make enquiries in Rome but, in the ongoing political climate, he knew his colleagues would be unwilling to express an opinion. At last, driven by the need to confide, he telephoned his school chum, Dr Stefano Amato.

'Be careful, my friend,' warned Stefano. 'Keep your suspicions to yourself. Italy is no longer a free state.'

'Do you think my fears are justified?' insisted Vincenzo.

'How do I know? I'm a medical man; politics is out of my sphere.'

'I can't let it rest.'

'You must, Vincenzo. Think of Alice and Beppe.'

'They're safe in England.'

'But you're not. Do you want to risk being arrested as a political agitator?' Stefano's voice became urgent. 'Trust no one, Vincenzo.'

Naturally, he hadn't mentioned his doubts to Alice. How could he suggest to her that Enzo had been murdered? Since her son's death Alice had vacillated between grief and sentimentality. He recalled a conversation they'd had shortly before her departure for England.

'Do you remember the evening we met?' she'd asked him.

'How could I possibly forget, my darling?'

'I didn't fall for you straightaway,' she confided, adding with a giggle, 'In fact, I thought you were a bit stuffy, always discussing business and politics with Daddy.'

He pretended to be wounded. 'Me, stuffy?'

She bit her lip. 'That is until I got to know you better.'

The recollection lured him back over the years to when her father, Robert McPherson-Corke, had been the British Ambassador to Italy. Following her mother's death, eighteen-year-old Alice had taken on the role of Ambassador's consort. Vincenzo smiled wistfully. How easily she had taken her place beside her father! She had proved to be a charming hostess with just the right amount of youthful naivety to capture the hearts of government officials, without raising too many dubious eyebrows amongst their wives.

They'd met at a British Embassy dinner party. For Vincenzo, it had been love at first sight. He couldn't believe that Alice would return his affection. He had never considered himself to be the handsome Italian stud. On more than one occasion, his looks had been compared to those of famous and infamous Roman emperors, whose busts lined the corridors of Rome's Palazzo Nuovo. His profile might be noble, but he was certainly not in the American movie star league. Clarke Gable he was not!

Alice, on the other hand, was a beauty. She reminded him of one of the heroines from the works of the English Eighteenth Century romantic poets. With her corn-coloured hair and Anglo-Saxon complexion, she had attracted a lot of attention from Italian men. Much to his surprise, after a whirlwind courtship, Vincenzo had won her heart.

On returning to Castagnetto with his new bride, the villagers had eyed Alice with suspicion. What was their count thinking, marrying a foreigner? But it wasn't long before they took her to their hearts, greeting the news of her pregnancies with excitement, celebrating the live births - first Enzo, then Beppe nine years later - lamenting the miscarriages, of which there were three. Last of all, came Isabella, the longed-for daughter who lived for only six months.

He shook his head to rid his mind of nostalgia. Alice was close to a breakdown. She was better off in England. He had always respected his father-in-law and knew he would be the best person to see his daughter through this difficult period.

In the new year, Vincenzo began badgering the authorities in Padua for the long-awaited police report on his son's death. Weeks went by with his letters remaining unanswered. Losing patience, he decided to go to Padua to ferret out the truth for himself.

He went directly to Dino's Trattoria, in front of which Enzo had died. It was a gloomy January morning, threatening rain. He went inside, took a seat at the bar and ordered an espresso and a calvados. The trattoria was busy. A buzz of voices rose against a background of military music coming from a radio on a shelf above the bar. Manning the bar was a balding, red-faced man, who found it necessary to cough into a grubby handkerchief with disturbing frequency. Suppressing his disgust, Vincenzo tried to encourage him into conversation, only to draw a blank.

For the next few months, he trawled the bars and cafés in Padua in the hope of discovering something useful. He questioned shopkeepers, stopped students in the street, and made enquiries at the hospital where Enzo had been taken. No one seemed willing to help. He toyed with the idea of asking for an interview with the Dean but decided that dragging the University into it might place other students in jeopardy.

He returned to Castagnetto one June evening to find Grazia Elena looking agitated. '*O Dio, Signor Conte.* The dear sweet countess phoned many times asking where you were. I didn't know what to tell her.'

A mixture of curiosity and reproof glinted in the woman's eyes. Her employer seldom stayed away from home for longer than a night or two; this time, he had been gone for a whole week.

Vincenzo's lips twitched with amusement at his housekeeper's gentle reprimand. 'Thank you, Grazia Elena,' he replied, 'I'll phone her back straightaway.'

'You'd better hurry, *Signor Conte,* the countess told me to prepare the bedrooms; she's coming home.'

'What?' Rushing to the phone, Vincenzo dialled the operator, drumming his fingers on the table until he was put through.

'Darling, where have you been?' demanded Alice.

'Forgive me, a*more*, I was away on business.'

'What business?'

'The annual review of last year's Cabinet Reserves.'

'That meeting's held in Milan; you usually only stay overnight.'

'It took longer this time, you know how tiresome these things are...' He rambled on about price controls, contracts. 'There's a lot of rubber-stamping these days.'

'It's lonely without you, Vincenzo. Beppe and I want to come home.'

'No, darling, you mustn't, this isn't a good time.'

'I miss you so much.'

Vincenzo's voice hardened. 'No, Alice, you can't come now. Mussolini's going to back Hitler. Things are happening here in Italy, unpleasant things. It's not safe for a foreigner.'

'Foreigner? But Vincenzo, I'm not a foreigner, I'm your wife.'

Vincenzo took a deep breath. He wanted Alice home more than anything in the world but he knew he must stop her. 'I'll come over to see you as soon as I can,' he replied. 'Maybe in a week or two…'

'Oh Vincenzo, come now.' She stifled a sob. 'I want us to be together again. It's been so awful without you. No one understands my grief…our grief.'

'Your father does,' Vincenzo replied gently.

'Yes, but…'

He cut in. 'You know I have a lot of responsibilities. There's the vineyard, darling, it doesn't run itself.'

'What's the matter with Matteo and that accountant fellow, Manzello, can't they look after it? For God's sake, Vincenzo, what do you pay them for?' retorted Alice, persuasion changing to anger.

He tried to reason with her. 'I need to oversee the vineyard and my other business dealings.'

Alice continued pleading with him until, at last, he succeeded in placating her. He thought about his younger son, imagining how difficult it must be for the boy to fit in to the English way of life. 'How's Beppe?'

'He misses you, Vincenzo.'

'He gets on well with his grandfather, I'm sure that helps.'

'Yes it does.' He heard a sigh judder in Alice's throat as she went on, 'Promise you'll phone every day and come over to Harrogate soon. Darling, I miss you so much.'

'I miss you too, Alice.' He wasn't sure whether she caught his reply because the line crackled noisily and went dead. He called the operator again only to be told that the lines to England had been cut. The next day, Mussolini declared war on Britain and France.

The official police report from Padua arrived shortly afterwards. Vincenzo read it three times, pacing the floor of his study, infuriated by the bureaucratic manner in which his son's death had been written off: "*Accidental death following a street brawl. Cause of death: a blow to the head.*" He screwed the piece of paper up in his hand and tossed it away. Enzo's injuries had been too extensive to have been sustained during a street fight. His son's friends would have intervened. The report was nothing more than a cover-up for an attack by an organised gang of thugs: Mussolini's blackshirts. He pressed his knuckles to his aching head as his suspicions took shape. Could Enzo have been involved with the partisans?

He stepped up his trips to Padua and one weekend in the spring his luck changed. Just before giving up for the day, he went back to Dino's, and sat at a table outside. He ordered *Pasta con i Bisi* with a half carafe of *Bardolino*. Halfway through his meal, he called the waiter on the pretext of asking for more bread.

'There don't seem to be many students about,' he said casually.

'They only come in the evenings,' replied the waiter.

'Do you ever get any trouble here?'

'Trouble! What d'you mean?'

'Between the students and the authorities?'

The man eyes narrowed. 'What's your interest in the students?'

Dangerous ground. 'Nothing really, except...' He paused. '...isn't this the haunt of that student who died in a brawl last autumn?'

This touched a nerve. 'I wouldn't know, *Signore*,' retorted the waiter. 'Sorry, I've got to go.'

'Just a minute, I heard the young man often came here.'

The waiter shrugged. 'Don't ask me, I haven't got much time for students.'

Vincenzo chuckled. 'Sure, I understand. They can be a nuisance, unruly, always spouting politics?'

The waiter's attitude softened slightly. 'That's right. I don't dabble in politics myself. Best left alone if you ask me.' That said, he made his escape before Vincenzo could question him further.

Vincenzo lit a cigarette and inhaled deeply. Once again, he'd drawn a blank, yet he felt convinced that somebody must know what had really happened. Maybe if he could find proof, he could approach the authorities in Rome.

He swore under his breath. '*Merda!* What am I doing? No one will listen to me.'

A couple of students walked past on their way to the university. Vincenzo gave licence to his imagination: saw youngsters debating their ideals; saw his tall, blond, headstrong son leading them on. The scene changed: now panic not zeal shone in the eyes of the students, now Enzo lay bleeding in the gutter.

He gave an involuntary shudder. Stubbing out his cigarette, he frowned with the realisation that he couldn't let go. Discovering the truth wouldn't bring his son back, but it might calm the turmoil in his troubled heart. Pushing back his chair, he slapped a handful of notes on the table and left the café.

'Wait, *Signore!*' The waiter appeared and, collecting up the notes, rushed after him.

'Thank you very much, *Signore.*' Then he lowered his voice. 'There's a meeting here tonight at 10 o'clock.'

Vincenzo looked at the man in surprise, but the message in his eyes was clear. Taking his cue, Vincenzo gave a nod of acknowledgement and went on his way.

He returned to Dino's Trattoria just before ten. He could see no sign of a meeting, but this didn't surprise him. A political gathering would not take place openly. The bald barman was on duty but there was no sign of the friendly waiter. Vincenzo ordered an *espresso* and kirsch, gulped down the drinks, and asked where the lavatory was.

'Through there.' The man pointed to an archway at the rear of the café.

Following his directions, Vincenzo went through the cluttered kitchen and looked around. The waiter who'd tipped him off saw him and gestured to a curtain in the corner. Pushing the curtain aside, he found himself in a small dark lobby. Directly opposite was a door. Voices reached him, but the words were indistinct. He felt uneasy. Who were these people? After his over generous tip, the waiter may have guessed he was wealthy and set him up. No one knew he was in Padua. They could easily rob and kill him. On the other hand, if they were members of the emerging Resistance Party, this could be his chance to discover what had really happened to Enzo.

Suddenly an arm encircled his neck. 'Mother of God, what's going on?' he gulped, clutching at his assailant's sleeve.

The arm tightened until his lungs screamed out for air and he felt his eyes bulge. With a jerk, his captor twisted his arm behind his back. The blood pounded at Vincenzo's temples while the pressure in his ears became intolerable. Desperate thoughts raced around his head: Dear God! Was it to be curtains without even the chance to ask a single question about Enzo?

The door flew open in front of him. The force at his neck eased, but a hand slammed into the small of his back, launching him towards the wall opposite. Air invaded his lungs. Gulping and spluttering he tried to brace himself for the forward pitch. His head cracked against the wall.

Two

Vincenzo came round to find himself in a small courtyard. He was slumped on a rickety chair, facing the wall. How long had he been out: seconds, minutes, longer? He lifted his head and blinked. The atmosphere was dense with smoke even though the courtyard was open to the heavens. Someone spun the chair around and he found himself looking into the glare of a flashlight. Blood trickled from a graze on his forehead. Four men confronted him.

'What were you doing in the lobby?' demanded the man with the flashlight. Vincenzo lifted an arm to shield his eyes. 'Speak up!' A hand sliced across his cheek, a working man's hand, rough and calloused.

'I was looking for the lavatory.' There was a disbelieving chuckle.

'Who are you?'

Vincenzo hesitated. It was clear these men would not be fooled. He abandoned the invented identity he'd thought up on his way to the trattoria, and replied, 'Di Tomasi.'

There was an intake of breath. 'You're related to Enzo Di Tomasi?'

'I'm his father.'

They fell silent. The man in charge studied him, and as Vincenzo became accustomed to the bright light, he was able to study him in return. He was tall with thick dark hair and had a piercing gaze. There was honesty about his manner, and instinctively, the count felt that he could be trusted.

'What the devil brings you here?' demanded the man.

Before replying, Vincenzo wiped the back of his hand across his mouth. 'I want to find out what happened to Enzo.'

'You know he died in a street brawl. Didn't you get the police report?'

'That was nothing more than a pack of lies.'

'What makes you say that?'

Vincenzo hadn't anticipated this much resistance. Surely, knowing he was Enzo's father, they would be prepared to hear him out. 'My son wasn't out looking for trouble. He was a serious student.'

One of the men gave a sniff and muttered, 'Those wealthy students are a bloody nuisance. They strut around the town bragging and throwing their weight about. They're always fighting.'

Here's the problem, thought Vincenzo, they only trust the working classes; they hold the upper classes in contempt. He felt a surge of vitriol. They were quick enough to accept help from those wealthy students when they needed it, weren't they?

'Enzo would not have deliberately picked a fight. He wasn't like that.'

'Huh, sons show a different face to their fathers.'

This was too much for the count. He turned on the man. 'You son of a bitch, are you trying to say he brought it on himself?'

'More than likely; hot-headed young aristocrat.'

'How dare you insult my son's memory.'

When the speaker gave a roar of laughter, Vincenzo's face darkened. '*Bastardo!*' he yelled and launched himself at the man, grabbing him by the throat and pressing his thumbs into his windpipe. His victim's hands flew up to claw at his assailant's wrists. The others rushed over and forced Vincenzo to let go. Incensed by the attack on their companion, they ploughed into him, punching him about the head and shoulders.

'Stop!' shouted the leader. Turning to Vincenzo, he gave vent to his anger: 'What the devil do you think you're doing? Have you got a fucking death wish?' Grabbing him by the shoulder, he shoved him back onto the chair.

As rational thinking returned, Vincenzo cursed the impulse that had led him to lose his temper. *Scemo*! How could he have been so stupid! The man had insulted him, but that was no reason to throttle the life out of him.

The man stepped towards him, but the leader's authority halted him. 'That's enough, Angelo! Leave the talking to me from now on.' Angelo retreated, still rubbing his neck.

They huddled in a group to discuss the situation, giving Vincenzo the opportunity to assess his chances. He could hear mumbled words: 'Infiltrator, filthy rich bastard, do away with him.'

He was trapped. The rectangular courtyard was no bigger than a prison cell. The door through which he'd entered was unlocked, but the men were standing directly in front of it. He glanced to his left. At the far end there was a wooden gate, presumably leading directly onto the street. Could he make a run for it? Did he *want* to make a run for it? He had come to ferret out information; if he left now, the chance could be lost to him forever. The men turned to face him.

'How do we know he is who he says he is?' demanded one of them.

The leader replied in a measured tone. "Well, Luigi, Enzo told us his father had been awarded the *Medaglia D'Oro* in the Great War. He said that he suffered a terrible stomach wound warding off an attack. His men escaped because of him. There'll be a scar.'

Vincenzo was taken aback. It touched him to learn that his son had bragged about his war record.

Luigi glowered and, addressing the leader, said, 'What are we waiting for, Guido? Let's take a look.'

They dragged him to his feet and, before he could protest, someone yanked open his trousers to reveal the cicatrix running from navel to groin.

There was a low whistle. 'That's some battle scar!'

The man called Guido raised an eyebrow. 'Satisfied? What about you, Angelo?'

Still scowling, Angelo nodded his head.

'Now we know you really are Di Tomasi,' said Guido. 'Tell us the truth. Why are you here?'

Vincenzo drew a handkerchief out of his pocket and wiped the blood from his forehead. 'I've told you, I have to find out what happened to my son. You must know something.'

Guido shook his head. 'Take my advice, *Signor Conte*, don't delve into your son's death, go back to your fat cat life while you still have the chance.'

Vincenzo's hackles rose. He raised his voice in accusation. 'You know what happened.'

'We know nothing,' replied Guido. 'Get out now and we'll forget this meeting ever took place.'

'No.'

'Give him a hiding and send him packing,' snarled Angelo.

'I'll go when I have some answers,' insisted Vincenzo.

The men shuffled their feet and even Guido looked as if he was losing patience.

Then the door opened.

'What's going on?' All heads turned towards the speaker. A small thin-faced woman stood in the doorway. Despite her lack of height, she wore an air of authority.

'Who are you?' she asked Vincenzo.

Inborn courtesy towards a woman dissipated Vincenzo's anger. 'Count Vincenzo Di Tomasi, *Signora*, Enzo's father.' He instinctively guessed that she would know who Enzo was.

Her expression gave no hint of her thoughts as he met her gaze.

'We can deal with this, Claudia,' said Guido.

'Not so fast. I want to hear what he's got to say.'

'But Claudia, if...' There was a rumble of protest.

The newcomer's voice cut icily through it. 'No ifs or buts, I want to talk to him.' She strode to the centre of the group. 'Sit down, everybody.'

Vincenzo couldn't suppress a smile. It seemed that Guido was only the second in command. This pint-sized woman was the real *capo*. Somehow she had managed to silence a group of hefty men. Although the atmosphere was still tense, Claudia's sober attitude helped to allay the men's hostility.

She sat down at the table between two of the men. Vincenzo found himself being pushed into a chair on the opposite side of the table between the other two. This pause in the proceedings gave him the opportunity to study her further. She was dressed in drab grey and appeared older than the men, a woman of his own generation or older. She cleared the debris of empty beer bottles and overfull ashtrays by sweeping her arm across the table in a semi-circle. A pair of candles stuck in

Chianti bottles flickered, making grotesque shadows dance on the walls.

She turned her attention to him. 'What brought you here?'

He gave her a potted version of his reason for coming to Padua and went on to tell her about his decision to send his wife and younger son to England. He explained how, following their departure, he had given a lot of consideration to Enzo's doctrines, finding to his surprise that, far from being poles apart, their views ran parallel. He finished with, 'If only I had realised this when my son was still alive.'

A couple of the men started muttering, but Claudia silenced them with a glare. 'Go on.'

'My wife's distress at Enzo's involvement in politics put pressure on me. You see, her loyalties were divided. Italy is her adopted country, but she's English-born.'

'I don't get it,' said Luigi, 'Why didn't you leave for England with your family?'

'I couldn't, Italy is my country.'

Luigi's lip curled. 'Huh, you mean you were afraid of losing everything: your property, your vineyards?' He added suspiciously, 'Didn't you have the foresight to stash something away in a Swiss Bank Account?'

Vincenzo gave a start. The man had hit on the truth. In the mid-thirties, alarmed by Mussolini's escalation to power and the rumoured atrocities carried out by his henchmen, he had begun transferring money to a strong box in Zurich.

'What's keeping you?' the speaker pressed on. 'You could be well out of this mess if you wanted to be.'

'I need to unearth the truth about my son's death.' Vincenzo scrutinized his listeners, trying to assess their reaction.

'You son was small fry,' sneered Angelo.

'I believe he gave his life for your cause,' retorted Vincenzo.

'How do we know you're on the level?'

'You'll have to trust me.'

Once more the men began muttering. Claudia lifted a mollifying hand. 'Let him finish.'

Guessing that she had an idea stirring, Vincenzo said impulsively, 'Let me join you. I've got useful contacts. I could get inside information … '

'What information?'

'Intelligence on the top brass: Ciano, Marinelli, even *Il Duce* himself.'

Guido frowned. 'Go on.'

'I'm a lawyer. I have a position of trust in their circle.'

'So?'

'I'm privy to their policies. I have access to dossiers on the prevention of public disturbance and civil unrest.'

'Bah, the man's all mouth,' snarled Angelo. 'Let's do him over and chuck him out.'

'He knows too much. Let's dump him,' said Luigi. The small wiry man seemed coiled, ready for action.

A dangerous type, thought Vincenzo. He looked at Claudia, knowing his fate rested with her. Even Guido's authority seemed to have evaporated in her presence.

'Violence is our last resort.' The woman frowned and went on, as if thinking aloud,

'On the other hand, if we let him go he might shoot his mouth off and come marching back with the blackshirts.'

A shudder of dread knotted Vincenzo's stomach muscles. What would it be like for Alice to lose her husband as well as her son? Desperation brought recklessness. Pushing back his chair, he stood up and shouted, 'Christ! Give me a chance. By helping you, my son won't have died in vain.'

The onlookers looked stunned by his outburst. Taking centre stage, he played his trump card: 'I could be of use to you. I have a photographic memory.' Encouraged by his audience's attention, he began spouting Mussolini's latest bombast word-for-word, mimicking his mannerisms.

A slight smile played at the corners of Claudia's mouth and he could see that, despite their antagonism, his performance had amused the men.

Claudia thumped her hand on the table and said, 'Enough! You, *Signor Conte*, can wait in the kitchen while we decide.'

As the door closed on the count, the men again began arguing among themselves. Guido had not joined in with the last spate of questioning because he felt certain that Di Tomasi was telling the truth. He had witnessed Enzo's brutal murder. He saw once more the dreadful scene. If only he had been able to warn the students. His own nephew had been one of them. He recalled how Enzo had aimed a right hook at Oscar's jaw before defiantly leaping onto a chair and scattering the tell-tale leaflets. The boy had deliberately drawn attention away from Oscar. Guido would never forget that act of selfless courage.

There was little physical resemblance between father and son: one dark and stocky, the other tall and blond. But he had recognised a steely determination in manner. The count's gift for mimicry had clinched it, a talent his son had inherited. On several occasions, in the company of his nephew's student friends, Guido had been amused to watch Enzo parody famous personalities. Clearly, both of them disliked pomposity and he wondered whether they had been aware of this shared irreverence towards public figures.

Claudia called the group to order and Guido spoke for the first time. 'I think we should give Di Tomasi a chance. We've seen evidence of his courage in battle. This courage was passed on to his son ... and with his Rome connections, Di Tomasi may prove useful.'

'Let's vote on it,' said Claudia.

Vincenzo waited in the kitchen, watching waiters hurry back and forth with plates of spaghetti and risotto. He wondered whether the kitchen staff was privy to the set-up in the courtyard.

'Scusi, Signore.' One of the waiters nudged him aside to open a cupboard.

The chef glowered at him. 'Keep out of the way.'

Then the door to the courtyard opened and Guido summoned him.

'Right, Count di Tomasi,' said Claudia as he entered.' You're on probation. Step out of line and you'll find yourself *persona non grata;* on the run, from both the *fascisti* and us. Understood?' Vincenzo nodded his agreement. 'You'll answer to Guido Ottone.'

She picked up her bulky canvas bag and went to the door, turning to say in a gentler tone, 'Sorry about your son, *Signor Conte*. Welcome to the Cell.'

As the door closed on the departing group, the count turned to Guido and made his demands. 'What really happened to my son?' he snapped.

'You've read the police report,' replied Guido.

'*Merda!* That was a cover up.'

'Dangerous talk, my friend.'

'I want the truth. You were there, weren't you?'

'What makes you think that?'

Vincenzo fixed him with an accusing stare. 'You were, weren't you?'

'You're a shrewd man, I'll give you that,' muttered Guido. 'Are you sure you want to know? A father should be spared these details.'

'I want to know everything.'

Guido focused on the memory of that terrible evening, describing the scene he'd witnessed. 'The students were in high spirits, drinking and joking. Claudia handed them some anti-fascist leaflets to distribute…Oscar took them from her.'

'Oscar?'

'My nephew.'

'Go on.'

'I told them to get moving but they were in no mood to break up the party even though it was getting late. I was on my way home when I saw a figure lurking in a doorway…'

'What did you do?'

Guido cleared his throat. 'I ran back to the café to warn the students, but when I reached the square …' He slowed to a pause…

'Well?'

'Are you sure you want me to go on?'

Vincenzo balled his fist. 'Don't try to humour me. I need to hear every last detail of my son's murder.'

'I signalled to the students but they were absorbed in Enzo's antics.' Guido gave a bitter laugh. 'Your son, the comic!'

Vincenzo frowned impatiently. 'What happened next?'

'A squad of blackshirts burst into the square. Enzo saw them.' Guido spoke faster as he described the scene. 'He snatched the leaflets from Oscar and aimed a right hook at his jaw. *Merda!* Some right hook! Oscar went down. The others panicked and took to their heels.'

'Why didn't Enzo make off too?'

'He acted impulsively. While Oscar was scrambling to his feet, he leapt onto a chair and tossed the leaflets into the air. They floated down onto the blackshirts, sticking to their leather batons, getting in their way. I've never seen such impudence. I heard him shout "Go, go!" to Oscar.' The scene was so graphic in Guido mind that he gave an involuntary shudder, just as he had done when the rifle butt had cracked down on Enzo's shoulder. 'I ran across the square and grabbed my nephew and shoved him around the corner, out of harm's way.'

'And Enzo?' The count's throat quivered as he gave a hard swallow. 'You let them beat my son to death?'

'There was nothing I could do.'

'You watched him die?' Vincenzo thrust out a hand and grabbed Guido's jacket, pushing him back against wall. 'Not good enough Comrade. Fill in the details. I deserve the solace of hatred.'

For a moment Guido held back. How easy it would be to lie to the count, to tell him that his son had been killed outright by a single blow. But he respected the man. He wouldn't insult him by suppressing the truth. He looked pointedly at the hand pinning him to the wall, then looked back.

Vincenzo withdrew his hand but his gaze bored into Guido. Could the man see into his memory? Guido wondered. Could he see the relentless blows, the stamping boots; hear the snapping of the ribs, the crushing of the skull? Was his stomach churning as his had churned when he'd seen a scarlet rivulet gush between the cobblestones, to swirl in a cluster of fallen leaves before flowing into the drain? Could he know that it was days before he was able to rid himself of Enzo's last terrible screams?

'He was knocked to the ground and beaten with batons and rifles. Your son was exceptionally brave,' he said quietly. 'He saved my nephew's life. Oscar's my sister's only child.'

Vincenzo's eyes became pinpoints of pain. 'Surely you could have done something?'

Guido shook his head. 'If I'd helped Enzo, all of us would have met the same fate.' He ran a hand through his hair. 'Young people see politics as a game. They believe they're invincible. Enzo was always at the forefront. I'm sorry but...'

Suddenly, the count swung round, brandishing his arm so violently that he sent a chair crashing to the floor. Striking the table, he shouted, 'You're *sorry,* is that all you've got to say? Your nephew got away with nothing more than a swollen jaw and a few bruises!'

'He was lucky.'

'And your sister - thankful to get her son back, huh! My wife lost hers.'

The two men faced one another across the courtyard and, in that moment, Guido sensed that a wrong move would provoke full-on aggression. But this time the count's anguish found release in profanity. Pacing the floor, he ranted and raved, his vitriol directed at Guido.

Guido withstood the verbal attack without flinching. When at last it petered out, he said calmly, 'You need rest, my friend; I'll give you a lift back to your hotel.'

'I'll make my own way.'

'Suit yourself,' replied Guido.

After Guido had left, Vincenzo sank down onto a chair, his head in his hands. The man had merely confirmed what he already knew. He had taken his anger out on Guido and, in the cool light of reason, he was grateful that his companion had not retaliated. Most men would not have been so tolerant.

He left the trattoria to collect his car, but the lights of a bar enticed him inside. One drink became two, then three, then he lost count. Two hours later, he stumbled out of the bar, realising through the fog in his brain, that he hadn't been so drunk since his student days. His stomach lurched and he vomited onto the road before staggering into a shop doorway and collapsing into a heap.

The rising sun woke him up and he struggled to his feet, blinking and gulping back the bile rising in his throat. Nausea and dizziness slowly cleared, bringing into relief the graphic details of his son's death. Nausea rose again, not from alcohol this time. Hatred against the regime consumed him. He punched the brick wall until blood poured from his knuckles, and for the first time, he was forced to admit that all men had their breaking point. He, Count Vincenzo Di Tomasi, was no exception.

A passer-by stopped and looked at him with concern. 'Are you all right?'

He glared back at the man, who hurried away. Overcome by exhaustion, he sank down onto his haunches. The sun rose higher, cars and trams began to fill the street. Going back to his hotel, he paid his bill and drove home.

From then on, Vincenzo spent more time at the Rome Headquarters, using his position as lawyer to the High Command, asking probing questions about *Il Duce's* projects. He hoped no one would notice his increased interest.

He deliberately distanced himself from his friends and, after several attempts to lift his spirits, they gave up, putting his withdrawal from society down to grief. Now that he had learnt what had really happened to his son, his taste for revenge had changed course. He saw that aiding the Resistance to bring down the Fascist Regime would do more good than trying to seek justice for Enzo through Mussolini's dictatorship.

'I know you're up to something, Vincenzo, and I don't want to hear what it is,' commented Stefano Amato, the only person to see through his façade . 'Just be careful. Watch your back.'

Vincenzo laughed this off. 'I've got nothing to hide. You'd know if I had any plans; you can read me like a book.'

Stefano gave a snort of amusement. 'Read you like a book! You're a tight-arsed bastard, no one can tell what you're thinking. That's what makes you such a good poker player.'

But Vincenzo knew that Stefano was right. In fact, his outward show of indifference contrasted very strongly with his inward zealousness.

In the early months, he fed the Resistance dates and locations of fascist rallies so that Claudia could organise disturbances to their greatest effectiveness. His memory for minutiae reduced the risk of the hecklers being caught.

Three

On his next visit to Padua, Vincenzo felt alarmed when he began to suspect someone was following him. Was this a tail from Rome or had his frequent visits to the town aroused interest locally? He tried to quash his suspicions, telling himself it was imagination. After all, there was enough intrigue and subterfuge in the air to foster such farfetched fantasies.

It was nearly curfew, but before returning to his hotel, he decided to put his fears to the test. He quickened his pace, turned into a side street and hid in a doorway. A tall figure with a cap rammed down over his ears, appeared at the corner, looking up and down the road. Stepping out from the doorway, Vincenzo grabbed his follower's arm, forcing it behind his back and yanking off the cap. A cascade of dark hair fell loose.

A woman! He was taken by surprise, and for a moment, relaxed his hold. The woman turned to face him. With her features twisted with anger, she wrenched herself free and darted into the road just as a patrol vehicle drove past. The wheels missed her, but the running board knocked her off-balance and she fell heavily to the ground. Instinctively, Vincenzo rushed to her assistance.

'Did Claudia send you?' he mouthed in her ear.

She gave an almost imperceptible nod as her anger switched to panic.

The vehicle stopped several metres ahead and an officer marched back towards them. Shoving the woman ahead of him into the doorway, Vincenzo pressed her against the wall and kissed her.

'What's going on here?' The policeman prodded Vincenzo with his baton.

'Sorry, Officer,' he said, turning away from the woman without releasing his hold on her. 'A lovers' tiff.'

"You shouldn't be out. It's after curfew.'

Vincenzo made a pretence of looking at his pocket watch. 'Is it that time already? All right, Officer, we'll be going home now.' Addressing the woman, he said, 'Come on, *amore,* time for bed.'

The man's manner softened. 'Don't let this happen again,' he said, adding with a chuckle, 'Otherwise I'll be forced to invite you both to spend a night in the cells.'

He turned and went back to the waiting vehicle. After it had driven off, Vincenzo loosened his hold on the woman. Glaring at him, she tried to move out of reach, but her ankle gave way and she gasped in pain. He caught her as she staggered against the wall.

'You've hurt yourself.'

'It's nothing. Let me go!'

'Not until you tell me why you were following me.'

'I wasn't following you.'

He gripped her arm firmly and said, 'Listen young lady, you're coming with me.'

'I'm not going anywhere with you.'

'You'll have to, you're injured. Lean on me, I'll support you. My hotel isn't far from here.'

'Damn you!'

'That's not very ladylike,' he replied, finding it difficult to hide his amusement. 'I hope you're going to behave yourself when we get to my hotel.'

'Let go of me. I'm not going with you,' she hissed.

'But you can't walk unaided.'

'Yes I can.'

'Oh really?' Vincenzo let go of her, but was forced to catch her arm when she stumbled. 'Don't be a fool, you've twisted your ankle. When we get to my hotel, I'll bathe it for you; then we'll have a talk.'

He helped her through the hotel lobby under the inquisitive stare of the night porter. As the lift whirred upwards, she pulled away from him, refusing his help when they arrived at the second floor.

Inside his room, he insisted on helping her into an armchair. He took off her shoe and examined her ankle.

'It's badly swollen.'

'I know,' she retorted.

'Take off your coat, and relax. I'll fill a bowl with cold water that should help to reduce the swelling.'

Still not trusting her, he went into the bathroom and ran the tap, half expecting to hear the door slam as she made her escape. But on his return, he found her slumped in the armchair with her head tilted on its backrest, her eyes closed. He took the opportunity to study her. Her features were strong, denying her conventional beauty. Her lips were full, her cheek bones finely chiselled, her brows heavy for a woman. He frowned, thinking of Alice's china doll features.

As he placed the bowl of water on the floor in front of her, she opened her eyes and looked at him. This is where her beauty lies, he thought as he gazed into their dark brown depths.

She wrinkled her nose. 'Is this really going to work?'

'I hope so.'

He crouched down and gently placed her foot in the water.

'Ouch!' she cried.

He looked concerned. 'It will feel better in a minute.'

'The water's bloody freezing.'

'I'll add some hot in a minute.'

Seconds later, she cried, 'Please add some warm water.'

He refilled the jug with warm water and poured it into the bowl. She plunged her foot back in and, after a few minutes, looked up at him, smiling. 'You're right, it does feel better.'

He'd been preparing a volley of questions for her but the smile disarmed him. She wriggled into a more comfortable position, spreading the towel across her lap.

'Who are you?' he asked.

'Livia Carduccio.'

'I guess you know my name.' She nodded. 'Did Claudia send you to spy on me?'

'Yes.'

'Why? I've kept my side of the bargain, given her lots of information.'

Livia tossed her head. 'Claudia's like that. She put a tail on me when I first joined. You need to prove your loyalty.'

'I thought I'd done that. Are you going to give me a good report?'

She smiled mischievously. 'I might.' She began drying her foot with the towel.

'How does it feel?' he asked.

'Much better.' Picking up her coat, she slipped it on whilst cautiously testing her injured foot.

'I'll see you home.'

She shook her head. 'There's no need, I only live round the corner.'

'What about the curfew?'

'Don't worry, I'll be careful.' She looked at him, searchingly, almost shyly, and said, 'Thank you for saving my life, Vincenzo.'

He joked off her gratitude. 'Saving your life? You only had a twisted ankle.'

Still she studied him and then, much to his surprise, she reached up and kissed him. Common sense told him to put a stop to the kiss straightaway, but it lasted longer than it should have done.

She drew away and limped to the door.

'I'll come with you.'

She clenched her fists. 'No!'

The force of her rejection surprised him. 'Why not?'

'I told you, I'll be all right.'

Puzzled, he watched her leave the room, but as the door closed after her, he had a change of heart. Snatching up his jacket, he hurried after her but she was already in the lift. He hesitated at the top of the stairs, wondering whether to run down and meet her on the ground floor. He heard the lift's cranky mechanism whirr to a standstill. What was the point? he shrugged. The woman was clearly used to looking out for herself, so why should he worry about her?

During the following weeks Vincenzo discovered that Mussolini was scheduled to address a rally in Florence. When he passed the information to Claudia, she immediately called a meeting at Dino's Trattoria.

Besides Guido, Bruno, Angelo and Luigi, Livia was also there. It was the first time Vincenzo had seen her since the evening at the hotel. Much to his chagrin, he experienced a frisson of excitement at seeing her again.

'This is great news, comrades,' declared Claudia. 'Now we can do something really effective.'

'What have you got in mind?' demanded Bruno.

'Assassination!' She took pains to annunciate each syllable separately.

Everyone looked stunned.

Claudia cleared her throat. 'I take it you're all in favour.'

There was a rumble of agreement.

'Thanks to our friend here ... ' Claudia nodded at Vincenzo. 'We have access to inside information.'

The men started to fire questions at her. She held up a hand. 'One at a time. Luigi!'

'What's it going to be? A rifle shot, a bomb?'

'We have to consider all angles.' She pointed at another of the men, 'You, Bruno!'

'Will other cells be joining us?'

Claudia shook her head vehemently. 'No, comrade, this is our baby.'

'What if we fail?'

'We won't.'

A volley of questions followed and, once again, Vincenzo was impressed by how well Claudia handled the men. But he wasn't happy about her determination to 'go it alone'.

'Are we ready for something as big as this, Claudia?' he asked.

She raised an eyebrow and sneered, 'Why? Can't you get more inside information?'

He ignored her slur and said, 'Don't forget, security will be very tight.'

After the others had left, he challenged her again. 'I still think we should have back-up, Claudia.'

'Are you questioning my authority, Vincenzo?' she snapped back. 'What's the problem, lost your nerve?'

His hackles rose. 'Of course not, but we haven't got enough time to organise this properly.'

Her eyes flashed. 'Don't piss me about, Vincenzo, are you with me or not?'

He wasn't going to admit that getting access to the Grand Council was going to be very risky. 'Of course I am, you've got my word.'

At his pledge of loyalty, Claudia's anger dissipated. She beamed at him and, taking a bottle of Vodka out of a cupboard, poured out two shots. 'In that case, let's drink to it.'

On the way home, Vincenzo experienced more doubts. He berated himself for having been swept along by Claudia's enthusiasm; he was beginning to understand what a power-hungry woman she was.

Getting into the Grand Council wasn't going to be easy. Only Mussolini's most trusted followers were allowed access. The dictator surrounded himself with 'yes men', men like Galeazzo Ciano and Marshal Eduardo Scarpone.

Fate played into his hands. He was in the building on the day the leader decided to call an impromptu meeting to finalise details for the rally. Ciano was out of town, Scarpone was tied up with important negotiations, and so were a number of others who were privy to the Grand Council. A young sub-lieutenant came to summon him to the conference.

He found Mussolini and several of his sycophants gathered over a map table.

Il Duce looked up as he walked in. 'Ah, Di Tomasi, I think you may be able to help with this project.' He placed a hand on Vincenzo's shoulder. 'Come, my friend, tell me what you think of this.' Spread out on the table was a street map of Florence.

Vincenzo couldn't believe his luck. Mussolini was asking his advice on the very project he was out to sabotage.

'You're familiar with the city of Florence, Di Tomasi, give me your opinion, strategically, where should we position the guards?'

The rest was easy. He knew the city well and he positioned marksmen in places which seemed secure, but which would, in fact, leave them vulnerable. However, at the end of the meeting, he got a shock: the rally had been brought forward by a week.

On leaving the building, he bumped into Marshal Scarpone, who was returning to his office. They nodded at one another in passing, then Scarpone hesitated. '*Eccellenza,* a word please.'

Vincenzo stopped in surprise. The marshal didn't usually bother with him. He was only interested in the higher echelons, those men who might influence his promotion.

'I was thinking about your dear wife?' he said jovially. 'The lady's English, I believe? Is she under house arrest?' He didn't wait for a reply but went on, 'If so, please let me know if there's anything I can do to make life more comfortable for her. Such a charming lady! I would hate her to suffer due to an accident of birth.'

'The countess is in England visiting her family.' Discussing Alice with this man brought an unpleasant taste to Vincenzo's mouth.

'Hmm! I suppose your sons are with her.'

Vincenzo's throat contracted. The marshal must know that Enzo was dead. Feigning innocence, he replied, 'My youngest son is with his mother but, as you may recall, my other son died last year.'

'Ah yes, a tragic accident. A street brawl, wasn't it?. These students… so irresponsible,' tutted the marshal. 'Why do you spend so much time in Padua these days?'

'I have business there.'

'Do you keep in touch with your son's friends?'

'Certainly I do.' The questioning had taken an unexpected turn.

The marshal raised an eyebrow. 'Don't tell me young lads of eighteen or nineteen are interested in an old goat like you.' He threw back his head and laughed. 'No offence meant, only you could end up causing a few tongues to wag.'

Vincenzo was on the point of giving a sharp retort, but at that moment, one of the marshal's subordinates called him away. Suppressing his anger, he reflected that it wasn't worth wasting time on such an odious individual.

As he continued along the road, recollections of the man's success story filtered through: the eldest of five brothers from a peasant family, Eduardo Scarpone had shown such promise in elementary school that the monks from the local monastery had taken over responsibility for his education. The boy was being coached for the priesthood, but having gained a taste for politics at university, he defied his parents and thumbed his nose at his benefactors to take, instead, a military path.

A memory stirred. Ah yes! There had been an unpleasant incident during the *Littorialia*, an annual contest, which encouraged bright students to secure a place in the fascist elite. Robert McPherson-Corke, British Ambassador to Rome at the time, had attended the award ceremony. During the reception, young Eduardo Scarpone had made a play for Alice, who had accompanied her father. The count had intervened. The young man had not taken kindly to an older man's interference. Vincenzo pursed his lips. Could Scarpone still hold a grudge after so many years?

He felt uneasy. Clearly Scarpone had kept himself abreast of his movements; perhaps the call to the Grand Council had been a test of his loyalty. There was no time to hazard a guess as to the outcome; he would just have to take a chance. He telephoned Claudia with the latest news about the rally.

'Brought forward, eh? That gives us less than two days, Vincenzo,' she said. 'You'd better come to Florence rightaway.' She gave him the address.

He arrived to find Claudia bursting with restless energy, eager to hear the full details of the forthcoming rally.

'Umm, yes,' she muttered, twiddling a pencil between her finger and thumb as she considered the information he'd given her. Without looking up from the map she was studying, she said, 'Pour some coffee, the kitchen's through there. Mine's black.'

He carried two steaming mugs back and set them down on the table. Stabbing a finger at a point on the map, she said, 'We'll rendezvous here.'

He noticed that her fingernails were bitten back to the quick and felt even more concerned. Claudia lived on her nerves, and she could be impetuous. He tried to point out the difficulties. 'It's risky, we need more time, Claudia.'

She refused to listen. Nursing her mug of coffee between cupped hands, she insisted, 'This is our big chance, Vincenzo, we can't let it go.'

He spent a sleepless night worrying about the flaws in Claudia's plan, but he knew that Scarpone was getting suspicious, and this could be his last chance to get hold of the necessary information.

On the appointed day, Vincenzo arrived at the meeting place to find Claudia leaning over the table, finalising details. Luigi was servicing a rifle with a long-range sight.

'Need help?' he asked.

'Keep out of the way,' snapped Claudia.

'Where do I come in?' he demanded, affronted by her dismissive tone.

'You did well, comrade, now get off home, there's a good fellow.'

His anger rose but he knew this was not the time to get into an argument, so he left the building and headed for a bar. The streets were heaving. The atmosphere was filled with anticipation as the crowd surged towards Piazza della Signoria, where Mussolini would shortly begin his pontificating. Most people were treating the rally as a day out.

He ordered an espresso and schnapps, wondering whether Claudia had decided his use to the Cell had come to an end. Then, through the window, he saw something that made his pulse quicken. Two cavalrymen were cantering along the road, close to the buildings, searching through the crowds. Had they got wind of the plot? Galvanized into action, Vincenzo left the bar and elbowed his way through, memorising the route Claudia and her squad planned to take.

Il Duce's supporters chanted as they waved banners and flags. No one took any notice of the cavalrymen. Vincenzo stared around him. He shouldered his way through towards the palazzo pinpointed on Claudia's map. He looked at his watch. Time was running out.

He reached the door of the building and tried the handle. It was locked. He yanked at the door chimes, peering through the metal grille covering a small window in the door. The hallway was in darkness. More mounted officers came into view and it occurred to him that, although the authorities knew about the plot, they might not know where the assault would come from. Somehow, he had to stop the operation before it was too late.

A military band struck up. Squawking pigeons soared into the sky. He looked up and saw Guido at a first floor window. He was in position, unaware of the danger he was in. Vincenzo thumped on the door but the noise in the street drowned out his hammering.

Whipping out his handkerchief, he scribbled a message on it: 'Abort -- get out! V.' A mother pushing a pram tried to edge past him while her toddler sat happily sucking milk from his feeding bottle. Vincenzo snatched the bottle out of his hand. The child let out an ear-piercing yell; the mother gasped in shock.

'Thanks,' he muttered as he tied his handkerchief around the bottle.

The woman came to life. With a shriek of fury, she tore at Vincenzo's sleeve. He shook her off. Indignant, she cried out to the people around her. Nobody heard her. He launched his makeshift projectile through the open window and turned to apologise to the woman, but the crowd surged forward, sweeping him along into Piazza della Signoria. Above the square, flags and banners fluttered in the breeze, the band played louder. Vincenzo felt mesmerised. Here were the zealots, the dictator's most ardent followers. With their arms raised in the fascist salute, their chants echoed from historic building to historic building.

A deafening roar rang out as a short thickset figure mounted the dais. The crowd pitched forward. A shot rang out. A second's silence, then a collective gasp. Spectators twisted and turned, screaming in terror. Soldiers fired above the heads of the crowd.

Vincenzo watched helplessly as the giant surge of humanity began to recede in a tidal wave of panic. More shots! More screams! Women and children were pushed to the ground.

The cavalry cantered forward into the crowd, their horses' hooves trampling on the unfortunates who chanced to fall. Vincenzo managed to stay on his feet. The retreating crowd rounded the corner from Piazza della Signoria into the narrow street he'd left only minutes earlier.

As he brushed past the building into which he had lobbed his message, a random thought darted into his mind. Had the woman been able to push her child to safety? He hoped so.

Carried along by the throng, he eventually reached the building that Claudia had set up as the Cell's headquarters. He loped upstairs to the second floor to find her frantically gathering pencil-marked maps together.

'Give me a hand,' she barked, scooping up a heap of documents from the table and shoving them into a metal bin. Striking a match, she dropped it into the bin.

She rushed to the door, expecting him to follow her. Vincenzo hesitated as the flames rose dangerously close to the side of the wooden table.

'Come on, what are you waiting for?' she shouted.

'How did they know?' he muttered.

'Good question,' retorted Claudia.

Four

They regrouped in the hills above Fiesole. Claudia summoned everyone around a trestle table.

'We could be holed up here for days,' she announced. 'Food and water will be rationed. Keep your heads down.'

Then, with a wave of her arm, she dismissed most of the men, indicating for Guido, Bruno, Angelo and Vincenzo himself to remain.

'What went wrong, Claudia?' demanded Bruno.

'I don't know, but we're going to find out.'

Vincenzo felt uneasy. Suspicion could fall on him. He was, after all, in a perfect position to betray them.

'Did you get my message, Guido?' he asked.

Guido nodded. 'Thanks for that.'

Bruno spoke. 'That trigger-happy little *stronzo*, Luigi Silone, made things worse. Never will obey orders.'

'He needs watching but he can be useful,' said Claudia.

'You should have kept him out of this operation.'

'He knows the city inside out.'

Guido shook his head thoughtfully. 'He's unreliable.'

Claudia persisted, 'He's useful.'

As they talked, Vincenzo saw that Claudia hated being proved wrong. Pig-headed and arrogant, she was just as dangerous as Luigi.

Bruno looked around. 'Where is the little bastard? I haven't seen him since we came up here.'

Claudia shrugged. 'He's probably sloped off somewhere.'

'Stop worrying about that little shit,' snarled Angelo. 'He's no snitch. I guarantee he wasn't the one who tipped us off.' His gaze shifted to Vincenzo. 'This is the first time we've been let down.'

Bruno cracked his knuckles as he leant forward. 'Better go and look for Silone.'

'Wait!' Livia strode out from the surrounding trees.

'What is it, Livia?' Claudia sounded irritated.

'You're wrong about Silone.'

Claudia's mouth tightened. 'Don't interfere.' Pointing at the men, she snapped, 'Go and find him.'

Vincenzo was struck by the way the women interacted. Claudia handled herself coolly but he could see that Livia's intervention had riled her.

Guido, Angelo and Bruno disappeared into the trees. Vincenzo followed them. Glancing back, he saw Livia straddle a chair, her elbows folded on its back. She watched them go, a mocking expression on her face.

Alerted by raised voices, Vincenzo returned to the camp to find Luigi being manhandled into the centre of a circle of men. The man's squinty eyes darted around as he was nudged towards a hole in the ground.

Claudia pushed her way to the front. 'A night in the bear trap might loosen your tongue,' she snarled.

So Claudia had accepted that Luigi could be the leak, thought Vincenzo. This took the pressure off him, but he wasn't sure they'd got the guilty man. Livia didn't seem to think so, and for some reason, he felt she was right.

He watched as Luigi was shoved down into the hole. A sturdy plank of wood was placed over it and, on top of that, a large boulder. He could hear Luigi's shout of protest gradually become a plea for mercy.

The men began to erect tents. Someone lit a fire and it wasn't long before an appetising smell rose from a pot over the embers, reminding Vincenzo that he hadn't eaten properly for over forty-eight hours.

Plates of risotto were handed around and the men ate voraciously, mopping up the sauce with crusty bread. Livia joined them briefly, only to slip away as soon as she had finished eating.

Someone brought out an accordion and started playing. One of the men began to sing, others clapped their hands in time with the music. Some lay on the ground, chewing tobacco or smoking, their hands resting behind their heads. Vincenzo began to relax. The group seemed satisfied that Luigi Silone was the turncoat.

Claudia walked over and pointed to one of the tents. 'That's yours,' she informed him.

Vincenzo woke up next morning to overhear Claudia and Guido discussing the prisoner. When they moved out of hearing, he got up and made his way to the centre of the camp to find Bruno dragging Luigi Silone out of the pit.

Claudia marched over and began interrogating the little man. 'Why were you trying to leave the camp yesterday?' she demanded.

'My boy's sick; I needed to get home,' he stuttered.

With a look of scorn, Claudia continued questioning him, asking the same questions over and over again. Luigi refused to change his story.

'Hold on a minute!' Livia strode into the middle of the group, speaking with such conviction that everyone, including Claudia, turned to listen. 'It's true, his son is sick.'

'How d'you know?'

Giving a final draw on her cigarette, Livia dropped the butt, grinding it into the earth with her heel.

'I heard him mumbling about it the day before we started out on this ill-conceived venture. His boy's gone down with diphtheria.'

Claudia frowned and addressed the prisoner. 'Is this true?'

Luigi nodded. He seemed incapable of speech.

'Why didn't you tell me?'

'I thought I could take part in the operation, then make off home,' he whimpered. 'How was I to know it would all go wrong?'

'You shouldn't have tried to leave the camp without telling me.'

Sensing sympathy, Luigi gained courage and grunted, 'I was afraid you wouldn't let me leave.'

Claudia gave a contemptuous sniff. 'You're a fool, Silone, you could have got yourself into real trouble.'

Livia looked triumphant. 'I told you, he wasn't the informer.'

'Then who is?' asked Guido.

'He's over there.'

Livia threw out her arm, and all heads turned to look at Vincenzo. His stomach lurched. She was accusing *him*. Barely thirty seconds had elapsed. It seemed like a lifetime. Livia strode purposefully towards him. She drew level. All at once, he realised her gaze was fastened on the man standing behind him.

'You!' she screeched. 'Angelo Bernadini, you're the maggot in the woodpile.'

The onlookers gasped as she brushed past Vincenzo to confront the bald-headed man. Angelo looked as astounded as everybody else, but Vincenzo was close enough to detect a glimmer of alarm in his eyes.

'What rot! I've been with the Cell for over two years, you can't suspect me.'

Claudia recovered her composure. 'Show me proof!' she demanded.

'I've been watching him. He's got some interesting friends.'

'What d'you mean?'

'Bacello.'

'Franco Bacello?'

'The very same.'

Vincenzo knew Bacello's reputation. He was a prominent member of the local fascists, one of Mussolini's keenest devotees.

'We've only got your word for that,' rejoined Claudia.

Vincenzo watched fascinated as the scene unfolded: Claudia was unwilling to admit that Livia could be right. Livia drew a photograph out of her pocket.

'Will this convince you?' she said, handing it to Claudia.

Angelo began to get restless. 'That means nothing.' He pointed at Vincenzo. 'What about him? He only came into the Cell recently; he mixes with the top brass in Rome. He could be your turncoat.'

'Question him!' interrupted Livia, stabbing a finger at Angelo's chest. 'Search him!'

Claudia snatched back authority. 'All in good time. I'll handle this, Livia. Bring him to my tent, Guido.'

'Not so fast!' For a heavy man, Angelo moved with surprising speed. Fastening his arm around Livia's neck, he dragged her back towards the woods. In his free hand he clutched a knife. Several of the men made a move towards him. He retaliated by placing the knife to her throat. 'Keep back!'

Vincenzo watched with growing alarm. All at once, he realised that Angelo's gaze was fixed on the men he knew, the men he'd lived and worked with over the months. He'd overlooked the man standing nearest to him.

Reaching out, Vincenzo snatched the big man's wrist, twisting it sharply. The knife loosened from his grip, enabling Livia to wriggle free. Vincenzo moved swiftly. As the knife began to slip, he caught the blade with his left hand, wresting it from Angelo's grasp. It gave the men time to pounce on Angelo and drag him away.

Blood dripped onto the ground. As Vincenzo rummaged in his pocket for a handkerchief, Livia rushed over to him. 'Use this,' she said, starting to strip off her shirt.

Claudia scowled. Events had taken control out of her hands and she didn't like it. 'No need for that, Livia,' she said. 'Guido, fetch some bandages. You took a stupid risk, Vincenzo.' The reprimand carried a hint of respect. Then she surprised him by revealing a softness in her character. Turning to Luigi, she said, 'Get off home to your son, but make sure you're not picked up.'

Guido frowned at her.

'He knows all the back streets, Guido, they'll not take him.' She addressed the men. 'Put Bernardini in the bear hole. I'll question him later.'

But the afternoon's events had incited the men. They were out for blood.

'Why waste time on a trial? Let's sort him out now,' shouted one of the men.

Claudia shook her head. 'We'll go about this properly,' she replied.

'Action! Action!' The men started to punch the air.

'String him up!'

Livia's voice rose above the meleé. 'Shoot the goddam traitor!'

Vincenzo looked at her, shocked by the exultant smile on her face.

Guido moved to Claudia's side, lending their leader support. Claudia held up her hands. 'Enough! There'll be a trial tomorrow morning.'

Still the men continued to chant. Vincenzo began to feel anxious. They were raising enough noise to attract attention. Something needed to be done. Claudia must have come to the same conclusion.

She shrugged. 'If this is what you want, so be it. Everybody assemble here in an hour's time. Take the prisoner away, Guido. Now quieten down.' With her face set grimly, she stormed off.

The men cheered and Livia snatched off her cap and threw it in the air. The excitement subsided and Vincenzo watched mesmerised as she strode away. On reaching the trees, she turned to smile directly at him.

The men dispersed, leaving Vincenzo hoping that this turn of events would change their attitude towards him. He went to sit down on an overturned tree, staring at the ground between his feet. A voice startled him. He looked up to see Guido Ottone standing at his side.

'Smoke?' he said, offering a cigarette packet to Vincenzo. 'The Florence operation was doomed to failure. It was too rushed; typical of Claudia. She's stubborn, won't listen to reason.'

'Why is she in charge?'

Guido shrugged. 'She's done a lot for the Cell, taken risks, the men respect her. In a way, because she's a woman, she has more control over them. By the way, did you know that both Livia and I have been shadowing you? Claudia's orders of course.'

'I knew about Livia, but I didn't spot you.'

Guido laughed. 'I've had more experience than she has. You're in the clear now, my friend.' He thrust out a hand. 'Shake on it?'

Vincenzo took the proffered hand. The clasp was strong and he knew, instinctively, that this was the start of a lasting friendship.

The men watched silently as Angelo Bernadini was hauled out of the bear hole. Their excitement had cooled, leading Vincenzo to hope that the prisoner would get some semblance of a trial.

'Over there.' Claudia was determined to take charge this time.

Vincenzo was convinced she would insist on a trial despite the men's incitement for on-the-spot punishment. Confinement to the hills was playing on their nerves. They wanted action, something to relieve their frustration at the failure of the mission. Now they had someone to blame. The chill of foreboding sent a shiver down his spine. He glanced again at Claudia. Surely she wouldn't go through with execution without a fair trial?

The big man's terror was apparent. He was trembling violently and although he opened and shut his mouth several times, no words came out. They tied him to a tree. Several times, he slumped down and had to be supported. Finally, desperation revived his powers of speech. 'You've got it all wrong,' he screamed. 'I'm no traitor.'

The bile rose in Vincenzo's throat. 'Stop!' he shouted.

All heads turned in his direction. Claudia's eyes blazed. 'Keep out of this, *Signor Conte*.'

'Let him plead his case,' protested Vincenzo.

'After what he did to you?' scoffed Livia, pointing at his hand.

'Let him defend … '

His words were cut short as a hand clamped over his mouth. He felt his arms being pinned behind his back and, out of the corner of his eye, saw Guido's warning look. He gave up struggling when Guido muttered, 'For God's sake, don't make matters worse.'

Livia sidled up, an enigmatic smile playing at her lips. 'Is this too much for your sensibilities?' she mouthed.

Claudia called for a blindfold, her henchmen took their place, rifles at the ready. This is an elaborate hoax, thought

Vincenzo, they wouldn't dare shoot. Suspicions would be aroused in the nearby villages. Or would they? After all, it was the pigeon shooting season; gunshots were frequently to be heard shattering the silence of the countryside.

The riflemen took aim. Vincenzo sensed Livia stiffen. He cast her a sidelong glance and realised she was actually enjoying herself. He held his breath, waiting for Claudia to give the signal. A volley of shots rang out. Livia let out a hiss. The onlookers pressed forward. Angelo's body gave a final twitch and slumped forward.

A moment of silence; then Claudia said, 'We're on the move tomorrow. Thank you for coming.' She might have been bringing a routine meeting to a close.

For the rest of the day, Vincenzo kept his distance from the others. Fortunately, he wasn't involved in burying Bernadini's body. That would have tested his self-control to the limit. His hatred of the man was no less than that of his comrades and he didn't doubt that he was guilty, but the manner of the sentence was unacceptable. He gave a mental shrug and told himself that the deed was done and it was best to let matters rest. Nevertheless, he felt ashamed of himself for not having protested more vigorously. He thought of Enzo, wondering what he would have made of this event. Would such a youth -- an idealist with little experience of life -- have been able to stomach such callousness? No, his brave, idealistic son would have stood up for the prisoner, demanding a proper trial.

He went for a walk, returning after dark, enticed back to the camp by the glow of the fire and the smell of food. He collected his plate of pasta and beaker of coarse red wine and went to sit on his own. The men had recovered their spirits, some exchanging jokes while others played poker. The accordionist squeezed a lively tune out of his instrument. It was as though nothing untoward had happened. They were going home tomorrow, what was there to be glum about?

Vincenzo went to his tent. It had been a long day, and despite his troubled thoughts, he fell into a deep sleep. He woke with a start. Somebody had entered the tent. God! He should have been on his guard.

'Shhh!'

For the second time in less than 24 hours, a hand fastened over his mouth. But this was not a calloused paw, tinged with the smell of tobacco. Recovering from shock, he blinked and by the dim glow of the camp fire's dying embers reflected through the tent, his gaze met that of Livia's. She slipped off her coat and lowered her naked body down beside him.

'You saved my life again today, Vincenzo. Are you going to make a habit of it?'

She staved off his astonishment by firmly clamping her mouth to his. He should resist. He loved his wife. Alice was his life. But Livia's sensuality, her amorality, quashed decency. She had plotted her campaign of seduction cleverly, planning to surprise him during the hour of deepest sleep, robbing him of choice.

An hour later, she left his bed, wrapping her trench coat over her nakedness and creeping back to her own tent on bare feet.

It must have been a dream. With the first stirrings of consciousness, Vincenzo tried to brush aside the events of the night before. Pulling on his trousers, he crawled out of his tent to find the men packing up their gear. Following their lead, he dismantled his tent but when he came to roll up his bedding, Livia's perfume wafted up from the blanket. He was struck by a mixture of emotions. Pleasure quickly followed by embarrassment. What an easy target he had been!

He looked around, but there was no sign of Livia. Her tent had been dismantled along with the others. She wasn't a woman to waste time. She had probably left the hillside at first light. A sense of disappointment took him by surprise. He went to look for Claudia.

'So you're off now,' she said conversationally.

He nodded. 'I'll keep up surveillance in Rome, but I'll have to be careful.'

She stopped her packing and smiled at him. 'I know. You've done well, Vincenzo. It didn't work this time but I'm planning something big down in Rome. Guido will be in touch.' She clasped his arm. *'Buona fortuna!'*

Five

A few hours later, he arrived home to be greeted by an agitated Grazia Elena. She gave a gasp of concern when she saw his bandaged hand.

'*Signor Conte*,' she cried. 'What have you been up to?'

'A minor accident,' he replied.

She looked him up and down reprovingly. 'There have been a lot telephone calls. Marshal Scarpone phoned several times asking if you were in Florence. I told him I didn't know where you were.' She hesitated. 'It would be most helpful, *Signor Conte*, if you'd let me know where you are when you go away.'

Vincenzo gave a grim smile. So Scarpone was interested in his whereabouts! That didn't bode well.

'On the contrary, Grazia Elena, it's better if you don't know,' he replied.

He immediately regretted his words. Grazia Elena was no fool and her loyalty was beyond question, but he feared for her safety. His equivocal reply was enough to tell her that he had not been missing on regular business.

He tried to recapture normality. 'I could do with a hot bath. In the meantime, a drink and a smoke would be nice?'

She bustled off and the count went upstairs, his tread heavy. He felt a sense of failure. In the company of the others, he had been swept along on a tidal wave of excitement but, with hindsight, it was obvious that Claudia's plan had been ill conceived. They were lucky to have escaped with their lives. He felt he was partly to blame. To have seen Mussolini lying dead in the gutter would have been sweet revenge for Enzo's death.

He paced the floor of his study, trying to justify the Cell's conduct. He always came up with the same anomaly: what was the difference between Angelo Bernardini's execution, without trial, and the blackshirts' unauthorised clubbing to death of a young student? Neither victim had been given the opportunity to defend himself.

He took a cheroot from the silver cigar box on his desk, lit up and reflected that without Livia's provocation, Claudia might have delayed Bernadini's punishment until he'd been given a fair trial. The younger woman had incited the men into seeing their leader as weak. To regain her credibility, Claudia had been forced to carry out the execution. He experienced a frisson of revulsion. Livia was a dangerous and ruthless woman.

Death didn't shock him. He had seen it at close quarters during his army days. He recalled his enthusiasm when, after university, he had joined the Cavalry Regiment. Traditionally, the family had military connections carried on by the eldest son. Vincenzo had welcomed the prospect. Army life gave promise of adventure and travel. Going into combat changed his perspective. Plotting death and mayhem from afar was one thing, looking into a man's eyes whilst running him through with a bayonet, was another. He completed his term of service, earning that prestigious medal along the way, then resigned. His father was disappointed, but he accepted his son's decision.

Grazia Elena was pleased to have him home. She went about her work humming happily to herself. 'The place is too quiet without the family,' she confided. 'If only the dear sweet countess hadn't departed for England!'

Vincenzo gave a wry smile. 'The countess would have been imprisoned, or at best, kept under house arrest,' he reminded her.

Grazia Elena gasped. '*Madonna mia!* The countess, imprisoned!' She shook her head vehemently. 'It would never have come to that.'

He missed his wife's light-hearted chatter, her fumblings on the violin. She was an able musician but she always attempted pieces that were beyond her. Sometimes, she would get annoyed, throw down the instrument and flounce out of the room. When this occurred he and Beppe would exchange a conspiratorial smile. This empathy with his younger son was something he had not shared with Enzo. There had always been a division: Alice and Enzo, he and Beppe. He reflected that had their last child, Isabella, not died in infancy, Alice would at least have had the comfort of a daughter.

The papers said that the war was progressing in Hitler's favour. But he didn't trust the press. Mussolini's propaganda alarmed him. A keen amateur radio buff, one evening he discovered it was possible to tune into the British World Service and from then on, he was able to get a clearer idea of the war's progress. Tuning into a foreign station was an offence of the highest order. He made sure Grazia Elena and Matteo had left the house before tuning in.

Lack of contact with the Cell was frustrating. After three months he tried phoning Guido only to discover that Dino's had been closed down. Concern for his fellow members grew. Had they dispersed or had they been wiped out?

A visit to Rome made him even more uneasy. He found himself constantly checking over his shoulder, convinced that Mussolini's sycophants were watching him. He tried to revert to his old routine, to forget about the Resistance until one autumn morning, when Guido telephoned him.

'Claudia's transferred to Ferrara,' he informed Vincenzo. 'She'll be in touch.'

'Is the Rome project to go ahead?'

'Patience my friend,' admonished Guido. 'You'll get your chance to be a hero.'

'I heard the trattoria's been closed down.'

'Yes, everyone's gone to ground.'

'Livia?' Her name slipped off his tongue before he could stop it.

'She vanished after the Florence shambles. I've not seen her since.'

Vincenzo's throat contracted. 'Could she have been picked up?'

Guido gave a laugh. 'Picked up? Not that one, she's a wily bitch. She's gone off before; she'll turn up again.'

Vincenzo frowned. Despite his mocking words, Guido's fondness for Livia had shone through. Anxious to get off the subject, Vincenzo said, 'I'll keep my eyes open. But there's much to do here on the estate. I've neglected my affairs for too long.'

Vincenzo hadn't exaggerated when he'd said his business affairs needed attention. At the law practice, there were some legal matters which needed clearing up. For some time, his partner, Giacomo Tobino, had been urging him to settle them. But above all, the vineyard was suffering from neglect. Grazia Elena and Matteo had done their best, but he did not completely trust his accountant, Raimondo Manzello. For a small town bookkeeper, Manzello was doing very nicely, and Vincenzo couldn't help wondering whether he was creaming off some of the profits from the estate. He decided to double-check the figures.

After pouring over the accounts for several hours, he discovered why the books didn't balance. The doctored figures were cleverly hidden but, when he challenged Manzello, the man's nervous fidgeting enforced his suspicions.

'I should prosecute,' he told the man. 'But in these difficult times, I have no wish to make your family suffer more than they need to.' Manzello looked puzzled. His employer went on. 'You'll soon be receiving your call-up papers. If I find out that you've tried to wriggle out of conscription, I'll have no compunctions about filing my complaint with the police.'

It was an empty threat. Vincenzo knew he would never go to the police since it could draw their attention to him, which was the last thing he needed.

Old Matteo stood by the water tub scratching his head as he watched Manzello leave, reminded of Grazia Elena's observation two days earlier. '*Il Signor Conte* will see through his cunning ways, mark my words.'

When the old man joined her in the kitchen at lunchtime, Grazia Elena was ready to gloat. 'What did I tell you? I always knew that *cafone* was up to no good,' she said as she rubbed floury hands down her apron.'

Matteo kept silent. Privately, he felt uneasy. Manzello was not a man to cross. He had a foxy manner, and once, on a rare visit to Arezzo, Matteo had seen him coming out of the Fascist Headquarters in the company of Commandant Petronelli, who was known to be one of Mussolini's bootlickers.

Time passed, but Vincenzo heard nothing more from Guido. There were rumours of skirmishes in the Veneto Region, where blackshirts were rounding up Jews and dissidents and carting them off to Germany. He listened to these reports with growing alarm, unable to believe that this could be happening in his country, to his people.

Although he missed his wife and son, he also missed the coarse yet good-natured banter of his partisan companions. And he couldn't help thinking about Livia. Was she safe? Had she left the Cell for good? Would he ever see her again?

During a visit to Rome shortly after dismissing Manzello, he ran into Scarpone.

'Di Tomasi, we haven't seen much of you lately, is everything all right?'

Vincenzo tensed, suspicious of the marshal's concern. 'I've been too busy with my vineyard to get down to Rome,' he replied.

'Don't tell me you're obliged to run your own estate?'

'I'm short staffed.'

'Ah yes, I heard. You had trouble with your accountant, I trust you'll be prosecuting him.'

Vincenzo gave a jolt. How the devil did Scarpone hear about Manzello's dismissal? 'I've decided not to press charges,' he replied quickly.

At that moment, one of the marshal's staff approached and Vincenzo was able to make his escape. He returned to Castagnetto still baffled by the incident. Twenty-four hours later, Scarpone's secretary telephoned ordering him to report to him urgently.

The next day, he drove down to Rome, puzzling over the summons. Could it be about his connection with the Resistance? Months had elapsed since his last contact with Guido. He concluded it must be something to do with his dismissal of Manzello. Perhaps Scarpone was going to insist that he press charges.

To his surprise, the marshal's secretary informed him that her boss had been called out of town. Vincenzo felt angry at the waste of time. What was Scarpone up to?

On his way out of the building, he met a couple of high-ranking party members, who invited him to lunch. It crossed his mind that they could be a plant. He pulled himself up sharply. Was he getting paranoid? The table talk was largely of Italy's invasion of Greece, the Africa assault and Mussolini's increasingly high profile. Vincenzo kept his contribution to the conversation at a minimum.

In the evening, he ate a lonely dinner in a small trattoria in Trastevere before checking in to his usual hotel. The receptionist smiled at him. 'Good evening, *Eccellenza*, welcome.'

He returned her greeting and couldn't resist a mild flirtation with her. 'You're looking prettier than ever, *Signorina*? Has your boyfriend proposed yet?'

She blushed and showed him the ring on her left hand. 'We're going to be married on his next leave.'

'Congratulations!'

'Thank you, *Eccellenza*.'

'Have you been busy down here in the capital?'

She threw up her hands. '*Signor Conte*, the hotel's full all the time.'

'Is my usual first floor room available?'

She bit her lip and studied the Register. 'I'm afraid not, an important church dignitary and his entourage have taken up the entire first floor.' She looked up anxiously to determine her client's reaction to this news. 'I hope you don't mind, but we've had to put you in Room 44. It's on the second floor.'

'It can't be helped. I'm only staying for one night anyway.'

She looked relieved and apologised again. 'I'm so sorry for the inconvenience, *Signor Conte*.'

It had been a long day. What he needed now was a hot bath and a comfortable bed. He went to the bathroom and turned on the bath tap. The pipes gave a noisy rattle but only a trickle of tepid water came out. Wartime! He leant forward and, in the mirror, saw a world-weary, middle-aged man with grey streaks in his hair and worry lines around his eyes. He'd aged since being separated from Alice and Beppe. What a mess everything was! What had made him associate with that bunch of disorganised dissidents? Thinking about the Cell, brought back

Livia's image. Despite his resolve to forget all about her, her memory intruded on his thoughts just as surely as her physical presence had intruded into his tent that night in the hills above Florence. Self examination -- there had been plenty of time for that -- had revealed that he'd found her seduction flattering. What had prompted such an attractive young woman to seduce him? He was old enough to be her father. Another notch on a whore's bedpost, he thought bitterly.

He was about to get into bed when he heard a tap on the door. It was after eleven-thirty; late for an uninvited caller. Had that conniving rat, Scarpone, had the cheek to send someone to question him at this time of night? He dismissed the idea as absurd. It was probably one of the hotel staff checking on the blackout blinds. He pulled on his bathrobe and went to the door. 'Who's there?'

'Open up, Vincenzo. It's me, Livia.'

He gave a start of surprise, hesitating before letting her in. His mind raced. She was the last person he had expected. With mixed emotions, he opened the door. Livia brushed past him, pushing the door shut behind her.

'You took your time.'

'What are you doing here?' he demanded, hardly trusting himself to look at her.

She threw back her head and laughed. 'That's not much of a greeting. I thought you'd be pleased to see me.'

'You surprised me,' he replied. Pleased? He wasn't sure. 'Why are you here?'

'I had business in Rome so I thought I'd look you up.'

'How did you know where to find me?'

She tapped the side of her nose with her forefinger. 'I have my ways.'

'Where have you been hiding out all this time?'

'Here and there.'

She dumped her bag down beside the bed and loosened the belt of her coat. He felt puzzled. Surely there was a purpose to her visit. As she took off her coat, he noticed that she'd lost weight.

She smiled at him and reached out a hand to stroke his cheek. He drew away, not trusting her. What had made her seek him out after such a long time? It was over a year since the assassination attempt.

'You shouldn't be here. It's dangerous!'

With a toss of her head, she threw her coat onto a chair. He felt uncomfortable. She wasn't behaving like a casual visitor.

'How did you get hold of my room number?'

'I sneaked a look at the register.'

'I hope nobody saw you.'

'Of course they didn't. What do you think I am?'

'Deliver your message, Livia, and get out of here.'

'Message?'

'Claudia's message?'

Livia burst out laughing. 'Claudia hasn't given me a message.'

'Why else would you come here?'

'Darling, this is a social visit,' she whispered, edging closer and sliding a hand inside his bathrobe.

Her touch made his skin tingle but, this time, he was wide awake. Her presence filled him with alarm. She was beautiful, desirable, he wanted to strip off her clothes and make love to her.

She ran her tongue over her lips. 'Don't you want me?'

He thought of Alice. She loved him; she trusted him. Grasping Livia's arm he thrust her from him. 'Stop playing games.'

With a pout she shook off his hand, and when she made no move to leave, he swept up her coat and threw it at her. 'Get out!'

She caught it, and went to the bed as if to collect her bag. Instead of picking it up, she dropped her coat on the floor and flopped down onto the counterpane.

Vincenzo realised that he was faced with a dilemma. Clearly, persuasion would get him nowhere, but if he threw her out, she might cause a scene in the corridor. Should he call the manager? He quickly abandoned the idea. Livia had the upper hand; she could easily turn the tables on him.

'Nice hotel,' she remarked. 'Nothing but the best for Count Vincenzo Di Tomasi, eh?'

His anger erupted. 'Enough, Livia! Get out of here. Go home!'

'Home?' she said. She sat up and repeated, 'Home! Where's that?'

'Go back to where you're staying?'

'I've nowhere to go and I haven't got any money.'

Vincenzo frowned. The woman was trouble. He had to get rid of her. Picking up his wallet, he took out a wad of notes, flicking them in front of her face. 'Go and find yourself a room for the night in another hotel.'

This produced an unexpected reaction. Springing up from the bed, she knocked his hand aside, her eyes blazing. 'Damn you, Vincenzo, keep your bloody money, I'm not leaving until the morning.'

He felt confused. Was she putting on a performance? Had he wounded her pride or was she afraid of something? 'What's this all about, Livia?' he asked.

His restrained tone calmed her. She said quietly, 'If I leave here at this time of night I could be picked up by those Nazi-loving blackshirts.'

'Nonsense!' he snapped. 'As I recall, you didn't mind venturing out after curfew when we were in Padua.'

'That was different,' she retorted. 'Things have changed. I could find myself being carted off to Fòssoli.'

Fòssoli? Vincenzo was puzzled. What was she talking about? Fòssoli was an internment camp for foreigners.

She stooped to retrieve her coat and bag, muttering, 'Thank you very much, *Eccellenza*. I was banking on your help, a bed for the night at least. I didn't ask for money. Why did you treat me like a prostitute?'

He was filled with contrition. She had never asked for money; she might be amoral but she wasn't a whore. 'Maybe I was a bit hasty,' he muttered. 'You can stay.' She turned round slowly, her mouth clamped shut as if to curb her emotions. Was that fear in her eyes? 'I insist, Livia.' This was madness. He should send her away. 'I don't know how you're going to get out of the hotel in the morning.'

She slumped heavily into the armchair. 'Don't worry, I'll leave early, mingle with the night staff when they go off duty.'

'Have the bed; I'll sleep in the chair.'

She didn't protest. Peeling off her clothes, she climbed into bed.

'I hope you won't be too uncomfortable, Vincenzo. Take the top blanket.'

He snatched it up and fumbled his way back to the armchair. Livia's presence filled the room, reminding him of the night in the hills when she'd crept into his tent. He desired her more than any woman he had ever known.

He twisted and turned in the armchair until he heard her whisper huskily, 'Come in to bed with me, Vincenzo, then we might both get some sleep.'

He shuffled across the room in the dark. She threw back the bed covers, placed her arms around his neck and drew him close. Her hair brushed his shoulder, her breath teased his cheek. Slipping under the sheet, he felt the warmth of her flesh, soft yet firm, vibrant with youthful energy, and he knew he was embarking on a dangerous road.

Their lovemaking bore none of the desperate haste of the previous occasion. This time, Livia showed herself to be a tender, yet passionate lover. As they separated, she whispered throatily, 'I'm falling in love with you, Vincenzo.'

A scuffle in the corridor woke them in the small hours. 'You've got the wrong man, *commissario*,' cried an indignant voice. 'Check the room number. I'm an innocent businessman.' A thud, a moan. The voice again, less protesting; more pleading: 'Check your records, I'm a paid-up member of the Party, a loyal citizen … '

Muttered expletives, then, 'Shut him up for God's sake!'

A frantic plea: 'This is a mistake. Let me go, I'm innocent!'

Vincenzo leapt out of bed and ran to listen at the door. Livia joined him. The stomp of boots made them jump back in alarm. There was more shouting, more cursing. The metal lift gate clanged. The intercom rang. With a sinking heart, Vincenzo answered it.

'*Signor Conte*, get out quickly!' It was the friendly receptionist. The line went dead.

Vincenzo knew the layout of the hotel. The fire escape had been damaged during the bombing. From the second floor there was no way out except by the main staircase. Livia rushed to his side.

'What are we going to do?' she whispered anxiously.

'They might search the rooms. Go out onto the balcony.'

'Like this?' she shrieked. She was wrapped in a sheet from the bed.

Scooping up her clothes, he thrust them into her arms and shoved her through the *Persiani* into the cold night air. 'Put your clothes on out there.'

'It's freezing.'

'Shut up, Livia!' He closed the *Persiani* without securing them.

They'd be back for him. He was certain of that. A mad idea had dawned on him. Going to the mirror, he inspected his reflection, then reached into his pocket and put on the spectacles he had been prescribed, but never wore. After a quick check around, he picked up his briefcase and left the room. Less than five minutes had elapsed since the corridor scuffle. It seemed the *commissario* hadn't yet discovered his error. His mouth was dry, his palms sweaty as he made his way downstairs. A group of blackshirts stood in the foyer with their backs to him. They were gathered around their commanding officer who was studying the prisoner's identity papers.

What luck! Vincenzo glanced across at the reception desk and saw the white-faced receptionist staring at him. She gave a nod. Following her gaze, he headed for the dining room where an emergency exit led out to a side street.

A shout rang out from the lobby. 'There he is, that's the man we want!'

He was done for! They seized him roughly and frog-marched him back to the *commissario*. Feigning outrage, he made a play of resisting his captors knowing it was a useless gesture. The falsely accused businessman stood in the centre of his interrogators, trembling and bumbling incoherently.

'Let that fool go,' shouted the *commissario*. Turning his attention to Vincenzo, he said with mock respect, 'Good morning, count, I'm sorry to get you up so early but I have to ask you to accompany me to Headquarters.'

'What's this all about?' demanded the count, continuing his charade of naivety.

'My orders are to escort you to Headquarters, *Eccellenza*,' rejoined the official.

Vincenzo stood his ground. 'And where have these orders come from?'

'I'm not at liberty to say.'

The count gave a curt laugh. 'Come now, *commissario*, surely I've a right to know who wants to see me.'

'I'm only following orders.'

He argued for a few more minutes, hoping to give Livia time to make her escape, but he could see the *commissario* was getting irritated. Now that the mistake had been rectified, he was anxious to get away.

Vincenzo gave a nod. 'Let's get it over with.'

The inquisitive guests who'd been drawn from their rooms to witness the fracas quickly dispersed, shaking their heads and tittering nervously. Vincenzo glanced towards the reception desk and registered the frightened expression on the face of the receptionist. She had tried to warn him; no doubt she had deliberately given the blackshirts the wrong room number; she had pointed him towards the emergency exit. He hoped she hadn't put herself in danger. And Livia? Had she managed to escape? His heart gave a lurch. He should have forced her to leave instead of succumbing to her charms. The memory of their lovemaking was bittersweet. Had she meant what she'd said: that she was in love with him? With these thoughts flitting across his mind, he resisted the temptation to look up at the second floor balcony, as one of the policemen escorted him to a waiting car.

Six

Vincenzo had been to the Fascist Police Headquarters on a number of occasions, but he had never entered the premises under escort. By day, the place was buzzing with activity, at two o'clock in the morning, it was eerily empty. His imagination played tricks on him. Not far away stood Castel Sant'Angelo. Only a century earlier, prisoners would have been taken from this very *palazzo* to end their days in that forbidding edifice overlooking the Tevere. That couldn't happen now of course, but what of those stories of prisoners being transferred from Rome to Berlin and thence to a concentration camp. He shook his head to rid his mind of such ridiculous fantasies. He wasn't under arrest. This was nothing more than an interview.

He followed the *commissario* into the building, passing between two guards. Their footsteps rang out deafeningly in the vast entrance hall as his escort led him to a large desk, clear of paperwork save for a leather-bound register.

'Please sign here,' said the *commissario*, handing him a pen. Vincenzo felt uneasy. Why the formality if this was to be a simple interview? The *commissario* was courteous in the extreme. As Vincenzo finished signing, he said, 'I'm terribly sorry *Eccellenza*, but my orders are to search your briefcase.'

'You're welcome.' Had the officer been given explicit orders or was he just being facetious?

The officer seemed to sense his resentment and offered further apologies. 'Orders from above, you understand, if it were up to me … '

'Quite so.' Vincenzo could hardly bring himself to reply. This fawning made him quiver with irritation.

With a propitious smile, the *commissario* made a cursory inspection of the contents of the briefcase and handed it back. 'I'll try not to keep you waiting too long,' he said. 'Is there anything I can get for your *Eccellenza*, a coffee perhaps?'

'No thank you.'

He gave a salute, swivelled on his heel and marched off, a white-gloved hand on the hilt of his ceremonial sword, his spurred boots echoing on the tiled floor. He was a small, stout man and Vincenzo couldn't help thinking how absurd he looked against the splendour of his surroundings.

The hallway struck cold. Vincenzo suppressed a shiver, acknowledging that by night, for the sake of economy, the building was left unheated. It was only dimly lit but there was sufficient light for him to admire, once again, its stuccoed ceiling and marbled columns. Marble benches lined the walls and above the splendid staircase with its carved balustrade rose a Renaissance cupola, decorated with gold leaf.

A large clock ticked away the minutes. From his position, Vincenzo could see the sentries. Once the *commissario* had departed they relaxed and leant against the wall; one lit up a cigarette. Clearly they did not expect any more disturbances.

From time to time, he heard a door open and shut but no one called for him. Why didn't he just walk out of the place? He heaved a sigh, realising that this was not an option. The guards may have taken a breather but they were still on duty.

An hour went by, then another. Vincenzo began to get restless. Had they forgotten him? He dismissed this possibility. It was more likely that Scarpone was deliberately trying to make him sweat. His back began to ache. There was no backrest behind the marble bench. He stood up and paced the floor thinking about Livia, praying that she had made her escape. She had seemed different, less self-assured, jumpy. He wondered what had happened during the intervening months to make her so nervous.

Feeling stiff and chilled, he decided to explore one of the corridors leading off the vestibule. If challenged he could always say he was looking for the lavatory. The corridor was even darker than the hallway. All the doors were locked except for one. This one opened into a narrow, sparsely furnished room, which had a small barred window high up in the wall. The shutters were open and the first faint hint of dawn gave some light.

The noise of movement reached him from an adjacent building. He froze. A man's voice shouted an order, followed by a shuffling of feet; then the sound of a slap and a woman's scream. Someone was being interrogated. His heart missed a beat. Had they taken Livia? The possibility made him choke. Another scream, a plea for mercy! He rushed to the window and gripping the bars, hauled himself up to see out. Another terrified scream. *O Dio!* What were those fascist pigs doing? The woman's voice rose, imploring. It wasn't Livia, it couldn't be. Livia would never beg. No, she would shriek her defiance back at them. He loosened his grip on the iron bars and dropped into a crouching position, his knuckled fists pressed to his forehead. God, don't let them take Livia! All at once, he felt a hand on his shoulder. Straightening up, he spun around to come face to face with one of the guards.

'What are you doing here?' the man demanded.

'Looking for the lavatory.'

The guard's eyes narrowed, but after a moment's hesitation, he decided to believe him. 'This way,' he said and led him to a bathroom further along the corridor.

On returning to the hallway, Vincenzo sat staring at the wall opposite. Why had they picked him up? Had they discovered his allegiance to the Resistance? Over and over again, he kept telling himself that Livia had got safely away. This must be a separate issue; something that could be sorted out quickly? But why was Scarpone keeping him waiting so long?

The guard had chosen to stay with him. He may have believed his story about the lavatory, but he wasn't going to take any chances. At last an official appeared at the head of the staircase and called out an order. The young soldier sprang to attention and saluted.

'Follow me, *Signor Conte.*'

Vincenzo glanced at the clock and saw that it was nearly six am. He had been there for four hours. His temper erupted. Damn Scarpone! He would file a complaint against the man.

He followed the official up the stairs, into Scarpone's office. The marshal got up from behind an enormous desk and came towards him, a convivial smile on his handsome face. 'Good of you to come,' he said, ignoring the fact that Vincenzo had been given no choice in the matter. 'Sit down, please.' He continued with polite niceties. 'How are you? Have you heard from your wife? How's business?'

'Enough! What's the meaning of this? Why am I being detained?' demanded Vincenzo.

'My dear fellow, I do apologise for the wait. It's been a long night. Unfortunately, something urgent cropped up ... ' He spread his hands. 'It had to be dealt with immediately. I'm so sorry. Can I offer you a whisky, a cognac, a coffee?'

Fury consumed Vincenzo. 'I shall make sure *Il Duce* hears about this,' he retorted, ignoring the offer of a drink.

'My friend, forgive me. I know how inconvenient this has been. I've deprived you of a good night's sleep. My humblest apologies! Now, tell me, *Eccellenza* are things going well on your estate?'

'Very well,' replied the count, curbing his anger as he realised that to continue showing outrage would only serve to prolong the interview.

'I understand you've been short-staffed since you sacked your accountant.' Vincenzo felt puzzled. Why was the fellow so interested in the running of his estate?

All at once, Scarpone's manner changed. Leaning forward, he rested his elbows on the unblemished green blotter on his desk and rammed his knuckled fists together. Friendliness had vanished. The arrogant brown eyes scrutinised the count's face. Vincenzo met his gaze, knowing that he was at last about to find out why he'd been summoned.

'There have been reports, reliable reports, *Signor Conte*, that you've been involved in subversive activities.' The marshal paused. 'The Regime doesn't tolerate dissidents. We *deal* with them. You've been spending a great deal of time in the North. Have you got friends up there?' The man's lip curled. '...of the female persuasion?'

Vincenzo felt sweat gather on his brow. Livia! Did Scarpone know about her? Had they picked her up?

He tried to control his alarm. 'I have friends all over the country,' he retorted. 'Not to mention business associates in Milan, Bologna and Florence.'

'And Padua?'

'Padua too! Does that make me a suspect?'

'I understand you've been taking an active interest in politics lately.'

'I've always kept myself up to date.' It was getting more and more difficult to keep his voice even.

'That's what your housekeeper said when we searched your villa.'

'You searched my villa! On whose orders?'

'We have the right to search anybody's home if suspicions are aroused.'

'I have nothing to hide.'

Scarpone pressed his fingertips together beneath his chin. His thin mouth twitched mirthlessly as he muttered, 'Subversive material was found in your study, *Signor Conte*.'

Vincenzo suppressed a moment of panic. He had been careful not to leave anything that could be construed as controversial lying around. Was Scarpone making wild accusations or did he have hard evidence? If so, such evidence must have been planted. All at once he understood. This was down to that conniving accountant fellow, Raimondo Manzello. He recalled his surprise when, on mentioning the incident to Scarpone, the marshal had taken such an interest in his dismissal of the man. The disgusting little sneak must have decided to take his revenge. Who else would have had the opportunity to plant subversive material in his study?

Scarpone opened a drawer in his desk and took out a sheaf of papers. Slamming it down on the desk, he said, 'These were found hidden inside a copy of Dante's *'Inferno'* on your bookshelf.' He produced a book. 'By the inscription, I see that it was given to you by your father when you were a boy.'

'It was, but I know nothing of those papers.'

The marshal picked up one of the sheets and tossed it at Vincenzo. 'Well?' he said, easing back in his chair and stretching out his long legs. 'If *you* didn't hide the papers, someone else must have done so. Who do you think it could have been?'

Vincenzo thought quickly. 'One name springs to mind: Manzello. You're right, I should have prosecuted the fellow. He must have planted the papers. Destroy them! You must know I would never touch such stuff.' Confidence returned. Scarpone could not keep him in custody on such flimsy evidence. He felt jubilant: Livia's name had *not* been mentioned. Relief made him reckless. He made as if to stand up. 'Well, you're a busy man so now we've cleared up this matter, I'll be on my way.'

'*Ahimé*, if only it were that simple!'

Vincenzo fought down his impatience. Why was Scarpone prolonging the interview? He watched him twist a gold signet ring round and round his little finger. All his nails had been cut short, save for the one wearing the ring. This one was long and pointed: the peasant's scratching nail!

Scarpone noticed his focus on the ring. Getting up from his chair, he walked round to the front of his desk, and stood towering above the count. 'I'm afraid that won't do, *Eccellenza*. We know that Manzello can't be responsible. He's been sent to the Eastern Front.'

A hush fell on the room while Vincenzo took in this piece of news. The only sound was the squeak of Scarpone's polished leather boots as he started to pace up and down.

Suddenly, he stopped pacing. Jabbing a finger, he shouted, 'You know something about this, don't you? If the material isn't yours, it must belong to someone else in your household. If it's that housekeeper of yours, don't bother trying to shield her.'

This was the last thing Vincenzo expected. 'That's impossible,' he retorted. 'She's a simple country woman with no interest in politics.'

'Nevertheless, I shall be looking into her background. Has she always lived in your village?' Vincenzo was worried now. It had never occurred to him that the marshal would use Grazia Elena as bait. But Scarpone had done his homework. He went on, 'She's Italian by marriage; her father was Polish. Let's bring her in for questioning. He pressed the intercom button on his desk. '*Borroni!*'

'Stop!' shouted Vincenzo, springing to his feet. 'Grazia Elena Polaski-Gallo cannot be involved in anything of this nature. You can't arrest her ... '

Scarpone ignored the outburst and continued to issue instructions.

'You can't do this,' protested Vincenzo. 'The woman's done nothing wrong.'

Scarpone raised a quizzical brow. 'Someone's got to be held responsible.'

Hatred filled Vincenzo's heart as he stared at the jubilant man in front of him. 'All right, I admit it. The papers are mine. Cancel the order.'

'You admit it?' The marshal's jubilance grew. With a beam of triumph, he pressed the intercom again and countermanded the order.

Vincenzo remained silent. Scarpone had won. What would happen now?

'Have you anything further to add, *Signor Conte*?'

'Nothing,' replied Vincenzo, knowing that to protest would only make matters worse. He couldn't let Grazia Elena bear the brunt of these false accusations and, whatever the future held for him, he was now confident that the woman he'd heard screaming under interrogation in the adjacent building had *not* been Livia.

'You do know what this means, don't you? We can't afford to let troublemakers roam free, especially people in a position of authority. We can't allow your political affiliations to influence others.'

Scarpone studied his prisoner. The count looked drawn. It must have seemed a long wait downstairs in the dark cold vestibule with only his thoughts for company. He frowned. If only the man weren't so composed! He wanted him to cower.

He caught a glimpse of himself in the glass doors of the lofty *credenza* behind the count. Vanity superimposed irritation. He was a handsome man, who enjoyed female company, and he had never found it difficult to seduce any woman he desired; his lips curled - except for the lovely Countess Alice Di Tomasi. Would she have succumbed to his charm or would he have had to force himself on her? What a pity her husband had packed her off to England before the incarceration of foreigners. He turned back to the prisoner. Curse the man! Curse the aristocracy! He hated them all. It was easy to be successful when you were born into money.

He cleared his throat and smoothed a hand down the front of his immaculate uniform. 'You'll be taken back to your hotel where you will remain until arrangements for your future can be made. There will, of course, be a guard outside your door at all times. You may telephone your housekeeper to instruct her to pack a suitcase with some clothing.' Picking up the copy of Dante's '*Inferno*', he handed it to his prisoner. 'You may take this and you may wish to have some other books boxed up. You won't get much entertainment where you're going.'

'You'll take no action against Grazia Elena Polaski-Gallo?'

'You have my word.'

As he watched Di Tomasi being escorted out, Scarpone's thoughts winged back to his childhood: never enough to eat; inadequate clothing; a family of nine crowded into a tiny hovel, too cold in winter, too hot in summer. As the eldest, he had taken full advantage of seniority, snatching the best of a poor lot from his younger brothers and sisters. At the village school, his good looks and quick intelligence had brought him to the notice of a visiting cardinal, who had recommended his transfer to the monastery. It hadn't taken him long to learn how easily he could manipulate the monks even if this necessitated the granting of certain favours. After all, it had got him what he wanted in the end. He'd made it into Mussolini's hierarchy.

Seven

Vincenzo spent the next two days in his hotel room. He saw no one except the guard. When the chambermaid brought his meals, the guard brought it in and withdrew from the room without uttering a word. On the third day there was a change of guard. This man was younger and less hostile so Vincenzo tried to engage him in conversation.

'This must be a boring job for you,' he said.

'Could be worse. At least I'm out of the rain.'

'Yes, the rain hasn't let up all day.'

'It's supposed to clear up tomorrow.'

'I could do with a smoke,' remarked Vincenzo. 'Could I go down and buy some cigarettes at Reception?'

The man shook his head. 'Can't leave my post,' he replied. 'Otherwise I'd go myself. Tell you what, I'll ask the chambermaid to bring some when she comes with your dinner.'

The ploy didn't work and Vincenzo wondered what he would have done if the man had left him unguarded. Would he have been able to get out of the hotel unnoticed? To escape from Rome would be dangerous, and to find Livia would be well nigh impossible.

He spent hours resting on the bed thinking about Livia, only to nod off momentarily, and wake up perspiring. His throat felt dry, his limbs weak. Was he starting a cold or was his condition down to lack of fresh air and sleep?

Early the next morning, the *commissario* came to see him. 'Time to go, *Signor Conte*,' he announced.

'Where to?'

'You'll find out soon enough.'

Vincenzo's heart leapt in hope. Perhaps Scarpone had decided to let him go. After all, the evidence against him was flimsy to say the least. But the *commissario*'s next words killed that hope.

'You're going to be put out of circulation for the duration of the War.' He gave a not unfriendly smile.

'What d'you mean?'

Ignoring his question, the *commissario* went on, 'There are some who would jump at the opportunity to get away from the mayhem. Don't worry, it won't be for long. The war will be over by this time next year. Collect your things.'

They took him to the railway station in a police car, where the station master was waiting for him. A porter took his suitcase and a sturdy trunk out of the boot of the car, trundling them onto the platform on a trolley. Vincenzo recognised Grazia Elena's hand in his packing; judging by the weight of the trunk, it was loaded with books. He smiled to himself, wondering which volumes Grazia Elena had chosen. She was not an educated woman and, in the case of foreign literature, she would have been incapable of distinguishing between French, English and German.

He watched while his belongings were loaded into the luggage compartment of a waiting train.

'This way, *Signor Conte*, I'm afraid it's only third class,' said the *commissario*, handing him over to a heavily-built, scruffily dressed policeman with a disagreeable manner.

Vincenzo climbed aboard. The carriage was narrow and dirty with the odour of old tobacco smoke lingering in the air. They were going south, which meant he wasn't being taken to Fòssoli. He'd heard rumours of bad conditions at the camp and, recalling Livia's fears, experienced a moment of panic. Had she got safely away from the hotel?

Passengers boarded and left the train as they drew into the local stations: bustling mothers, bothersome children, blue collar workers returning from night shift. He tried to identify their location but all station names had been blanked out. As they got further into the country, the going got even slower. Commuters were soon replaced by peasants bringing with them caged hens, growling dogs, and in one case, a nanny goat. The smell in the carriage became almost intolerable.

'What's your name?' he asked his minder.

'Why d'you want to know?'

Vincenzo shrugged. 'I've got to call you something.'

'Giorgio Basso.'

'Well, Sergeant Basso, why don't we move into first class? At my expense, of course.'

Basso's reply was to the point. 'Not fucking likely.'

The afternoon wore on and Vincenzo tried to take a cat-nap, but the narrowness of the wooden seat and the continual stop-start of the train made sleeping impossible. He didn't feel well, and longed for a good night's rest.

'Where are we going?' he asked again.

'I'm not allowed to tell you.'

By late afternoon, the wintry sun had all but disappeared. Shadows cast a dull greyness over the barren landscape, its monotony broken by the occasional village. The train drew into a station and Basso stood up.

'Have we arrived?' asked Vincenzo.

Basso nodded, ushering his prisoner off the train and into an ill-lit waiting room. A porter followed with their luggage. Most of it belonged to Vincenzo since Basso carried only a small cardboard attaché case secured by a scratched leather strap.

'Are you from these parts, sergeant?' he asked conversationally. When the man didn't reply, he went on, 'You may as well tell me our destination now we've come this far.' The enquiry fell on deaf ears.

Why the secrecy? Vincenzo shivered in the damp, unheated room. Could he be destined for an Internment Camp? Despite his exhaustion, his troubled mind persisted in trying to unravel impossible riddles. Had Scarpone been involved in Enzo's murder? Had he been arrested because the top brass feared he was getting too close to the truth? Or was it simply that the marshal wanted to settle an old score?

He glanced at his companion's reflection in the waiting room's grimy window and saw that, for a few unguarded minutes, he was taking a catnap. Here was his chance. He could make off across country, maybe hitch a lift back up north. Too late! His minder gave a shuddering snore, jerked his head up and blinked, squinting with relief at seeing his prisoner still sitting opposite him.

The unanswerable questions flooded back. Trains came and went, but Basso made no move to board any of them.

Vincenzo's spirits sank, but he tried to look on the bright side. An enforced period of inactivity could be advantageous. He had planned, on retirement, to write a social history of the Italian people. What was to stop him starting this project now? The hustle and bustle of the big city would be forgotten; in the quiet of the countryside, he would have time to gather his thoughts and put pen to paper.

Hunger gnawed at his stomach. He hadn't eaten since the evening before and wartime had closed all the station kiosks. To make matters worse, Basso brought out a crusty roll, which he proceeded to gobble up hungrily, following each bite with a gulp from a flask. Vincenzo patted his pocket for a cigarette, then remembered that he'd run out. He couldn't recall the last time he'd enjoyed one of his favourite Havanas.

All at once, Basso shook him by the shoulder. 'Our train's in.'

Vincenzo blinked. He must have dozed off after all. The carriage into which they climbed was no better than the one on the other train. Its ill-fitting windows rattled as it gained speed; cold air rushed in through the cracks. Vincenzo could stand it no longer. He got up and tried to wedge the window shut. Jolted out of semi-consciousness, Basso leapt up and launched himself on top of him. They finished up on the floor, tussling like schoolboys.

'*Merda!*' burst out Vincenzo when at last he managed to regain his feet. 'I was only going to fix the window.'

'How was I to know that?' snarled Basso. 'You could have been about to jump for it.'

'At this speed! You must be joking.'

'In future, leave the window to me.'

Clearly, Basso was embarrassed by his over hasty reaction. He yanked the window up and wedged a folded piece of cigarette packet into the gap at the bottom. Returning to his seat, he stretched out full-length with his legs crossed at the ankles and his hands clasped behind his head.

Vincenzo took the opposite seat, following Basso's example. The window remained closed until the train hit a bend when it began to slide slowly down again, allowing the cold air to whistle through the compartment. Basso didn't bother to stir himself to close it.

Sleep came at last and Vincenzo was surprised to see daylight streaming in when he next woke up.

For the first time, Basso volunteered a few words. 'Not far now.'

Getting to his feet, he gave a stretch. Vincenzo smothered a snort of disgust. The carriage stank of sweat and stale cigarettes. He felt ill, his back ached, his limbs were stiff and he was afraid he had the beginnings of a head cold. Beyond hunger, he ran his tongue across cracked lips, longing for a long drink of cool water.

The train slowed down, grinding to a halt at the end of the line. Basso ordered him along to the luggage compartment where, between them, they hauled down his suitcase and trunk.

'*Ciao amico!*' A humpbacked man shuffled over to them. Basso's mood changed. He grinned cheerfully, joking with the hunchback in a dialect unintelligible to the count. They led him to an old lorry, heaving his luggage onto the back of it. Going round to the driver's cabin, Basso ordered Vincenzo to get in, and when he didn't move quickly enough, he gave him a sharp dig in the ribs.

'Get in!' he snarled.

All three squeezed into the front of the lorry, with Vincenzo in the middle. After a couple of tries, the hunchback managed to coerce life out of the engine and they set off towards the outskirts of town. Civilisation was left behind as the road dwindled to nothing more than a pot-holed track, bounded on one side by a rocky overhang, and on the other, by barren terrain scattered with semi-cacti undergrowth.

The driver produced a flask. With his gaze fastened on the uneven road ahead, he thrust it across to Basso ignoring the prisoner seated between them. Basso slurped from it, spluttered and belched before handing the flask back. They talked across him in their guttural dialect which, save for a word here and there, Vincenzo couldn't understand.

The hunchback lit up a black cheroot, spitting the end out of the window. He sucked and chewed on it, occasionally wiping a globule of spittle from his chin with the back of his hand. From time to time, he would swivel his head round and exhale a thick spiral of fumes into Vincenzo's face. At last, the lorry jolted to a halt beside a small outcrop of rocks.

'On foot from here,' announced Basso.

They climbed out of the lorry and Vincenzo found himself being jostled round to the tailpiece. He looked up at the steep slope and wondered whether he had the strength to go on. His cold seemed to be developing into something more serious, a touch of 'flu perhaps?

The hunchback, a man of no more than five foot three, muttered through blackened teeth, pointing to the trunk. Basso took charge. Pulling the suitcase down, he shoved it at the count and said, 'Take this. Me and Alfonso will carry the trunk.'

'Where are we?'

'Ginosola,' came the curt reply. 'Bit different from Rome, ha?'

His escorts started up the track, carrying the crate of books between them, stopping periodically, to change sides, complaining under their breath. Vincenzo followed them, his step heavy with fatigue, stopping when a fit of coughing stole the air from his lungs. Towards the top of the track, the ground flattened out to a plateau. He saw that it led to a scattering of windowless crofts built into the hillside.

The trio continued for a further hundred metres up a rough, steeply sloping road, where they took a left turn along another track until they came to some rough steps hewn into the rock face. They turned left again at the top, walking on the craggy roofs of the houses below. Thus, they continued zigzagging upwards for five hundred feet until Basso and Alfonso stopped to deposit the trunk outside one of the houses. The door opened and two women appeared.

Basso said, 'This is widow Donna Bonelli and her daughter, Santina.'

'Benvenuto, Signor Conte,' said the women in unison.

Vincenzo blinked and dropped the suitcase beside the trunk. He opened his mouth to return the greeting but his head began to reel, and he was forced to reach for the jagged rock wall to stop himself from falling. Sweat broke out on his forehead, and he began to tremble uncontrollably.

Through a mist, he saw the widow dismiss Basso and his companion. Rushing over to him, she hoisted his arm across her shoulder, and dragged him inside the dwelling where between them, the two women managed to help him onto a narrow bed.

Clucking hens and a strong smell of cooking woke Vincenzo. He was in darkness. He reached out a hand and touched a cold damp wall. Stretching out the other hand, he touched another wall. The narrow mattress on which he lay creaked as he moved. For a moment, he panicked. Was he in a prison cell?

Slowly, details of the nightmare journey returned. He pushed off the bedcovers and started to sit up but weakness forced him to collapse back. A few minutes later, he sat up again, more cautiously this time. Swinging his legs to floor, he sat holding the edge of the bed, his knees almost scraping the wall, whilst his eyes became accustomed to the gloom. The coldness of the uneven stone floor struck his feet and he realised in alarm that he was wearing an old-fashioned nightshirt made of coarse material. Where were his clothes? He tried to remember how he had come to be undressed, but failed.

Getting unsteadily to his feet, he lurched towards a narrow strip of light on the floor and fumbled his way through a heavy curtain hanging over a doorway. He found himself in a square living room, the door to which gave directly onto the street. Although this was wide open, very little daylight penetrated the room due to an overhang of rock above the low doorway.

There was no one about. Hitching back the curtain, he fixed it to one side and inspected the bedroom. It was no more than ten feet by six and apart from the bed there was only an old table and a straight-backed wooden chair. A search of every inch of the tiny room failed to reveal the whereabouts of his clothes, although it did bring to light a half-full chamber-pot, which he could not recall using during the night. He sat down on the bed, heavy with fatigue. Was this to be his home for the foreseeable future? A bout of coughing left him breathless. He ventured back into the other room to continue his inspection of the house. It didn't take long. The dwelling was no more than a cave carved out of the mountainside. The walls were solid rock, as was the floor and the ceiling.

A massive bed dominated the room. It was high off the ground and he could see that the women's possessions had been stored beneath it. To one side, a wood-burning range served as a stove for cooking and heating. He remembered Basso alerting him to these chimney outlets during the climb up the hill the evening before. The aroma, which had woken him up came from a huge iron pot on the hob. He went to lift the lid, only to hurriedly drop it. Using a cloth, he lifted the lid a second time and saw pieces of cabbage and onion bubbling in a colourless liquid. His heart sank. Were things so bad here that they couldn't even afford rabbit or pigeon pie?

A further look around revealed a woodworm riddled table and four chairs set on a threadbare rug. The polished surface of the table and the presence of a lace doyley in its centre brought a smile of respect to his lips. Clearly Donna Bonelli took pride in her humble dwelling. A spotless marble slab served for the preparation of food; beneath it, an assortment of pots, pans and crockery were neatly stacked. A battered tin bath hung on the wall. He soon discovered that there was no running water, but a jug of water had been left on the marble slab. He removed the cotton kerchief covering it and poured himself a drink. Hunger pangs stabbed his stomach, and he knew that even the widow's cabbage soup would taste like a delicacy in his present need for nourishment.

Glumly, he took in the conditions of his internment. Scarpone had chosen well. How he must be laughing! Books and writing materials were going to be of little use in this hovel. A labour camp would have been less frustrating. Enforced inactivity was the worst punishment his inquisitor could have meted out.

A sound startled him. He turned round and came face to face with the two women. The widow spoke but, in his befuddled state of mind, he couldn't understand her. She repeated her words more slowly, enquiring after his health.

'A little better, thank you,' he replied, feeling embarrassed clad only in the baggy nightshirt.

'Did you sleep well?'

'Extremely,' he assured her,

'We want you to be comfortable here, *Signor Conte.*' She certainly seemed eager to make him welcome.

'*Signora*, where are my clothes?' he enquired politely.

She barked an order at her daughter, who bowed her head and scurried off, returning within minutes carrying his clothes over her arm. Proudly, her mother took them from her.

'Here are your clothes, *Signor Conte!*' she declared. 'Santina has taken good care of them, washed away all that nasty dust from your journey. Look!'

When she held them up for inspection, Vincenzo couldn't hold back a gasp of dismay. His white Egyptian cotton shirt had been passably ironed but he knew that his suit, cut by a Savile Row tailor just before the War, was ruined. He took the clothes, thanking the women profusely in an attempt to cover up his consternation. They nodded their heads, clearly delighted to have been of service.

Donna Teresa herded him into the back room, announcing that a meal would soon be ready. In the semi darkness of the bedroom, he examined his appearance. The trousers were well above his ankles, the jacket tight across his shoulders, the sleeves barely reached the middle of his forearms. He wondered where his suitcase was. This would contain the spare clothes he had asked Grazia Elena to provide. The jacket was too uncomfortable to wear so, despite the chill in the air, he took it off before re-joining the women.

Chunks of fatty pork had been added to the cabbage broth. In his absence, the widow had placed a chequered cloth over the table. Its heavily starched edges stood out like a ballerina's tutu. Donna Teresa gently nudged him into a chair, saying, 'Please make yourself comfortable, *Signor Conte*. Buon appetito!'

The two women stood watching him, hands clasped over their stomachs.

"Please join me,' he said.

Donna Teresa looked mortified. Pressing a hand to her bosom, she gasped, '*No, Eccellenza*, Santina and I will have ours later, after you've finished.' She puckered her brow encouragingly. 'Please eat up.'

He couldn't help reflecting that a couple of years ago he would never have considered inviting these women to join him.

What a radical change his association with the Resistance had made to his outlook!

The woman placed a hunk of crusty bread and a carafe of water on the table, the daughter brought a glass. He picked up his spoon and began to eat. The women continued to watch him. From time to time, he smiled his approval of the meal. They nodded and smiled back. He noticed that they both wore black skirts. The widow's was mid-calf length with a matching long-sleeved blouse, the girl wore a similar skirt but her blouse was short-sleeved and pale blue. Each had an apron tied around the waist. The mother's was light grey but her daughter sported a colourful flowery number, which hinted at a touch of rebellion in her character.

The broth was as tasteless as it was colourless but Vincenzo was grateful for anything, although he wondered whether a better menu, with the addition of wine, could be arranged if he offered her more than the pittance Basso had negotiated.

The simple meal rejuvenated him and he decided it was time to make a few enquiries about the village. Donna Teresa seemed reluctant to talk. He assumed she had been given clear guidelines as to her duties

'Where does Basso live?' he asked.

'Sergeant Basso!' Donna Teresa spat out the name with undisguised scorn. 'He doesn't live in Ginosola. He's from Matera.'

'Can I get to see him?'

She shrugged, making it clear that she was unwilling to have anything to do with the surly go-between.

'Very well, if I can't get to see Basso, perhaps you can direct me to the Town Hall.'

Donna Teresa didn't reply, but her daughter sprang forward and said importantly, 'It's up the hill; I'll take you if you like.'

'Thank you,' he replied and they left the house together, with the widow frowning after them.

Outside, chickens pecked at a scattering of seed, a skinny cat lay close to the house, fast asleep. Across the road, a goat was tethered to a stake. It looked up dolefully before continuing to nibble at the few tufts of grass that had managed to grow between the rocks. The climb was steep. The view to their right gave onto rows of terraced roofs descending to the gully. Beyond it, a barren terrain stretched as far as the eye could see.

To the left, more crude habitations had been excavated from the rock face. The doors to these primitive habitations stood open -- vast gaping mouths shrieking their anguish out to the horizon. Black-clad women went about their daily business with resignation etched on their faces. There was no lightness in their step, no joy in their manner.

Santina stepped out briskly, her head held high, a gleam in her eye. As they passed, the women stopped what they were doing and stared, whispering once he and Santina had passed by. He heard the words: *Rome, dissident, nobleman.* One young woman even gave a little curtsey as he passed her.

By the time they reached the centre of the village, Vincenzo was panting for breath. The girl didn't seem to notice. The village square was dominated by an elaborate fountain. No water flowed from it and, by the look of the verdigris on its bronze centrepiece and the rust stains on its marble surround, Vincenzo suspected it had been out of use for some years. He noticed that it had been built in commemoration of those lost in the First World War. Cleaned up, it would have been an illustrious monument; neglected, it spoke of the abject despair of the down-trodden population of Ginosola.

Santina pointed: 'Look, the Town Hall's over there.' Then, as if afraid she had over-stepped the boundaries of her mother's authority, she turned and fled.

It was mid-afternoon and there was no one about save for a couple of old men sitting outside a run-down bar. They glanced up briefly, but quickly lost interest in the newcomer and resumed their conversation.

Vincenzo walked across to the main entrance and rang the bell. No one came. He tried again and, after the third try, began to wonder whether the place was, indeed, occupied. The paint-peeling shutters were closed. Hearing a sound behind him, he turned to face a young man dressed in the grey uniform of a postman. He was pushing a bicycle and carried a postbag over his shoulder. Doffing his cap, he stammered, 'There's no one here on Tuesdays, *Eccellenza,* try again on Friday.'

'Thank you,' replied Vincenzo. The man doffed his cap again and started walking away. 'Wait! Can you tell me the mayor's name and where he lives?' he asked.

Flattered by the important visitor's attention, the young man leant his bicycle against the wall and said conversationally, 'He lives in Ginosola di Sotto, only comes to this village twice a week. Not much happens up here.'

Vincenzo already knew that. 'How do I get to Ginosola di Sotto?' he asked.

The postman removed his cap and scratched his head. 'It's a long walk, *Eccellenza*.' He didn't add, *for the likes of you*, but Vincenzo caught the inference.

'I'd like to go there. Will you take me? I'll pay you.'

The young man looked surprised, thought about it, then, nodded his head. 'All right, tomorrow morning after I've finished my deliveries.'

'Where shall I meet you?'

'I'll come to Donna Teresa's.'

Vincenzo smiled grimly to himself. It hadn't taken long for everyone in the district to learn where he was staying.

'What's your name, son?' he asked.

'Gianni Pasolini. *Signor Conte*.'

'Good, tomorrow then, Gianni!'

After the postman had cycled away, Vincenzo went into the bar and ordered a cognac. The bartender had a wary look in his eye. He slid the drink across the counter and held out his hand for money. For a moment, Vincenzo was floored. He hadn't given a thought to money when he'd left the house with Santina. He'd only had time to snatch up his ill-fitting jacket and sling it around his shoulders. What had the women done with his wallet when they'd washed his suit? He felt in his trouser pocket and, with relief, discovered his small leather coin purse. He handed the bartender a handful of coins and, gulping down the cognac, left the bar.

Although the return was down hill, Vincenzo was utterly exhausted by the time he reached the widow's house. The cough, which had eased during the course of the day, returned with a vengeance and immediately after his meagre meal of rolls -- no longer fresh from the morning bake -- filled with goat's cheese and a side salad of fennel washed down with a glass of coarse red wine, he made his excuses to the two women and went to bed. He heard them chattering in the adjoining room. He had still not discovered where his suitcase and chest of books had been stored, but he was too weary to bother with such things. Tomorrow would do. Besides, how could he make use of his books in this God forsaken hole? The prospects were bleak. He fell asleep dreaming about Livia, only to wake in the middle of the night, panicking that she had been picked up.

Eight

As promised, the next day Gianni Pasolini arrived to take him to Ginosola di Sotto. The widow and her daughter watched their departure with undisguised curiosity. Donna Teresa didn't raise any objections, but Vincenzo could see disapproval in her eyes.

He felt tired, having spent the night in fitful sleep due to his troublesome cough. He stumbled down the uneven track behind the young man, a skinny individual full of pent-up energy, who spoke in rapid bursts preceded by spells of nervous throat clearing.

'Hmm...it's quite a long way, your Excellency but the weather looks promising. Hmm, I don't think it's going to rain today, the sky always gets overcast like this at this time of year.' He stopped to check that Vincenzo was keeping up with him.

'I'm most grateful to you, Gianni,' gasped the count.

They reached the gully and turned left, continuing along the road southwards. Rain would be a blessing, thought Vincenzo as he stopped to rest after another fit of coughing. The morning breeze had gathered momentum causing dust to swirl up into their faces. Gianni seemed oblivious to this inconvenience and, gaining confidence in the presence of his distinguished companion, kept up a stilted monologue, giving his impressions of life in New York, a city to which he had never been and was never likely to go. It seemed that the Big Apple was an obsession of his brought about, Vincenzo learned, because his cousin had emigrated to the United States some years earlier and made a fortune.

Mayor Nando Rubaldi had been forewarned of his visit. He was a short stout man with sleekly greased black hair, a pencil-thin moustache and darting eyes. He greeted Vincenzo pompously, carelessly dismissing Gianni.

'Hmm, what, what t ... t ... time shall I come back for you, *Eccellenza*?' the postman enquired nervously, the confidence gained during their one and a half hour walk, evaporating in the presence of the mayor.

'Later, my boy ... say, five o'clock,' replied Rubaldi impatiently.

'It will be getting dark by then,' the boy protested, but he was ushered out without a second hearing.

The mayor invited his guest into the parlour. 'Make yourself at home, *Eccellenza*.' A mountain of cushions obliged Vincenzo to perch on the edge of a dark red velour sofa. 'My wife will be joining us in a few minutes.' Raising an enquiring brow, Rubaldi went on, 'You will of course be staying to lunch?'

'I don't want to put you to any trouble,' protested Vincenzo. 'There must be a restaurant in the village. I can go there.'

'I won't hear of it,' declared the mayor.

At this moment, the door burst open and Donna Luisa Rubaldi made her entrance. Her husband was slightly-built compared to his spouse. She filled the doorway, her emerald silk dress billowing out over her hips. Vincenzo suppressed his amusement. She reminded him of a sailing ship propelled forward by a following breeze. Her hair had been carefully coiffured, and Vincenzo wondered how she had managed to get to the beauty salon in time for his visit. Did she always take this much pride in her appearance? With ring-clustered hand outstretched, she waltzed across the room on her surprisingly small feet.

He took his cue, dutifully kissing her hand. '*Enchanté, Madame*, I apologise for calling on you at such short notice.'

She gave a high-pitched giggle. '*Eccellenza*, the mayor and I are honoured by your visit.'

The next hour was filled with inane conversation about the wonderful shops in Rome's Via Condotti, about the couple's memorable honeymoon visit to Paris a decade earlier and a detailed description of the charitable works the lady of the house performed for the wayward girls in the area, of which it seemed there were many.

Donna Rubaldi glanced at the clock on the mantle-piece and exclaimed, 'Time for lunch.'

Picking up a hand-painted china bell from the table beside her, she rang it vigorously. The door opened and a maid appeared. She was very young, no more than fourteen. Wearing a black dress with a crisp white apron tied around her waist, she curtsied timidly and looked towards her mistress for instructions.

The latter rose to her feet, clasped her hands together, and twittered, 'Will you accompany me to the luncheon table, *Eccellenza?*'

'My pleasure *Signora*,' replied Vincenzo.

Donna Rubaldi slipped her arm through his and led him on tiptoe across the marble-tiled hall floor. On reaching the dining-room, she ushered him to a chair at one end of a rectangular rosewood table opposite her husband, and then took her place between the two men. Throughout the meal, she swivelled her head from side to side above her ample bosom, reminding him of one of Donna Teresa's pecking hens, as she nodded in agreement with everything the two men discussed. Despite her earlier romantic visits to Rome and Paris, Vincenzo doubted whether she had any inkling of what was happening in the these cities now. Tucked away in this remote corner of the peninsula, the mayor's consort reigned supreme. What happened elsewhere didn't interest her.

The tediousness of his hosts' company was made bearable by the spread they had taken the trouble to lay before him. The maid ran hither and thither doing her best to please, spilling the soup in her over-zealous handling of the ladle and, later on, accidentally jogging Vincenzo's elbow so that his coffee spilled over into the saucer.

Rankled, Donna Rubaldi chastised the girl, shrieking, '*Stupidina!* Go and fetch a clean saucer for his Excellency.'

Vincenzo sprang to the maid's defence. 'It was my fault,' he protested, whereupon the poor girl burst into tears and fled from the room. She returned with a clean saucer, which she slid onto the table beside Vincenzo, not stopping to remove the original one, before turning tail and making off again.

Donna Rubaldi's mouth fell open and she started to call the girl back, but Vincenzo calmly switched the saucers over and, with a smile, began talking about his accommodation with the widow Bonelli, tactfully leading the conversation around to the purpose of his visit. The mayoral pair, relieved that he hadn't taken offence, hung onto his every word. When he described how Santina Bonelli had, out of the kindness of her heart, seen fit to wash his Savile Row suit, *Podestà Rubaldi* threw up his hands in horror. 'We can't have this,' he exclaimed. 'Leave it to me, *Eccellenza*, I'll sort out some first-class accommodation for you. Why, I'm sure *Signora* Caterina Vazzano would be only too pleased to help out.'

His wife butted in breathlessly. 'The poor woman's struggling to make ends meet, she'd be glad of the extra money. What with her husband away and having to look after that pathetic son of hers ... '

Her husband cut her short. 'There's no need to go into that, my dear.' He rose to his feet and walked around to where the count sat, saying confidently, 'Don't worry, *Eccellenza*, your problem is solved. I'll speak to Donna Caterina first thing tomorrow morning.'

The journey back to Ginosola di Sopra was exhausting. Uphill, on a road strewn with potholes and boulders, it was sometimes difficult to see the way in the fading light, even though Gianni had had the foresight to bring a lamp with him. Vincenzo felt he would never make it to the top. Donna Rubaldi had suggested that he stay the night with them, but he was anxious to get back and find out what the well-meaning widow had done with his personal possessions.

The deterioration in his health was beginning to give him cause for concern, but he knew the trip to Ginosola di Sotto had been worthwhile. The lower village was larger with proper houses, running water and electricity. Once he had moved in with Donna Vazzano, he would get over this influenza-like illness.

Vincenzo woke up next morning to the sound of raised voices. He struggled out of bed, pulled on his clothes and went to see what all the fuss was about. A crowd had gathered in front of the house, with the widow Bonelli taking centre-stage. She stood akimbo, her head thrown back. She was shouting angrily. The hunchback, Alfonso, stood facing her, equally irate.

Vincenzo went to stand behind the widow's daughter, who was lurking on the sidelines. 'What's going on, Santina?' he asked.

At the sound of his voice, the girl gave a start and muttered nervously, 'Alfonso's come to take you down to Ginosola di Sotto, *Eccellenza*.'

Vincenzo was astonished. He had not expected the mayor to act so quickly. He was even more astonished to see that his suitcase and trunk of books had already been loaded onto Alfonso's handcart. Where had his precious belongings been stored? Under the present circumstances, it seemed unlikely he would ever find out.

Still unaware of his presence, the protagonists continued their battle until Alfonso, tiring of the widow's tirade, turned his back on her, gripped the handles of the cart and started shuffling away. Donna Teresa's verbal abuse exploded into physical attack. She ran after him, and began pounding the hump on his back with clenched fists. This brought her daughter to life. Rushing after her mother, she screamed, '*No, Mamma, no!*'

But nothing was going to deter the widow, who continued her onslaught, urged on by the watching neighbours. Vincenzo decided it was time to intervene. 'Stop!' he shouted at the top of his voice, whereupon the assembled company turned in his direction. 'What's going on, Donna Teresa?'

The woman stopped remonstrating and closed her mouth. Jutting out a defiant chin, she walked back and announced, '*Eccellenza*, this idiot has confiscated your belongings. He's taking them down to Ginosola di Sotto. He says the *Podestà* ordered it.'

'That's right,' replied Vincenzo.

The widow looked deflated. '*Per carità!* What's the matter, haven't I looked after you properly?'

'You've looked after me extremely well, *Signora*, but I need a place to display my books and a desk at which to write.'

The woman wrung her hands and croaked, 'But *Eccellenza*, you can use the front room; my daughter and I will move into the back room.' She swivelled her head towards the girl standing at her shoulder. 'We don't mind, do we, Santina?'

'Of course not, Mamma,' agreed the daughter.

Vincenzo took a quick glance at the onlookers, neighbours of the widow, and realised that for the sake of Donna Teresa's reputation he would have to lie. 'That is very kind of you but you see, *Signora*, my eyesight is very poor and I need a good, strong light by which to read.'

Alfonso spoke up. 'Hurry up, *Eccellenza*, his honour the mayor is expecting you.'

Vincenzo grasped at the opportunity to extract himself from the situation. 'I'm sorry, *Signora, Signorina*,' he said, smiling first at the widow and then at her daughter. 'But the decision is out of my hands. I'll be back to see you both very soon and don't worry, you'll not be out of pocket. I'll compensate you for the loss of rent. Thank you both very much for your hospitality.'

Alfonso again gripped the handles of the cart and started trundling it down the hill. Vincenzo followed him.

Podestà Rubaldi met them at his front door and, after polite enquiries as to his well-being, he escorted Vincenzo to a house at the far side of the village. Alfonso followed behind with the handcart.

Donna Caterina Vazzano was very different from Donna Teresa Bonelli. She greeted him courteously and beckoned him into the house, pointing out the advantages of the accommodation in a businesslike manner. The first floor back room was large and airy with a narrow balcony overlooking the barren landscape. It gave access via a steep flight of stone steps, to a strip of land behind the house. The room was spotless, the furniture sparse, but Vincenzo knew at once that it would suit his purpose. The double bed was covered by a pale blue bedspread, a large desk was fitted against one wall, above which there were several empty shelves. On the marble-topped dressing table, a pristine white towel and a bar of soap had been laid out beside a bone china jug of water. The floor was tiled and there was a small brightly-coloured rag-tied rug placed next to the bed.

Much to Vincenzo's embarrassment, the *Podestà* took it upon himself to discuss terms, haggling with the widow over the rent. Realising there was no way he could halt the bargaining,

Vincenzo allowed things to proceed, determined to put the matter right once the mayor had left. The latter eventually departed after much handshaking and declaration of goodwill, leaving the count with his new landlady, who invited him to join her in the front parlour for an aperatif.

This social drink gave him a chance to rectify the question of the rent and, although Donna Caterina made a pretence at protesting, he could see that she was relieved to be paid a fair amount for the accommodation she was offering.

'You see,' she explained. 'Until eight years ago, my husband and I owned the village hairdressing salon. It was a good business and we lived well.' She heaved a sigh. 'The trouble started after the birth of our son. My husband wasn't satisfied with his life here, he wanted more. He emigrated to the States, promising to send for me and the boy as soon as he'd found a job and somewhere to live.'

'What happened, *Signora?*'

She shook her head sadly. 'He hasn't sent for us yet, but he will one day.' She paused. 'I couldn't manage the salon on my own, partly because of my son ... well ... he needs special care. In the end I had to sell the business. A couple from Matera bought it, and now I work for them as an employee and ...'

'They don't pay you very well?' finished Vincenzo. He wondered whether she had been responsible for Donna Rubaldi's hairdo.

Donna Caterina nodded. Abruptly, she changed the subject, saying, 'I serve lunch at one o'clock. Will that suit you?'

'Perfectly.'

She smiled and said, 'Very well, I'll get back to the salon. I expect you'll want to unpack. If you need any ironing done, please let me know. You can leave and enter via the back staircase. There's no need to come through the house if you don't want to.'

Vincenzo thanked her and watched her leave, finding it difficult to imagine why such an attractive woman had been deserted by her husband. He went upstairs and unpacked his clothes guessing, by the untidiness of the packing, that his suitcase had been subjected to a search by the authorities before being handed over to him.

Grazia Elena had chosen wisely: a pair of serviceable trousers, a warm Harris Tweed jacket, three shirts, some underwear, a spare pair of shoes and a scarf and gloves. Tucked deep into the pocket of the trousers, he found a letter. Whoever had riffled through his suitcase had missed it. Her handwriting was childish, her spelling full of mistakes, but Grazia Elena wrote that she and Matteo would do their best to keep the villa and the vineyard running smoothly. He was glad he had, long ago, set up an arrangement with his bank for a monthly stipend to be paid to the pair, plus a reserve for emergencies.

At one o'clock he went downstairs for lunch. The table was covered by a floral tablecloth with three bowls of steaming soup and crusty rolls placed on it. A boy, his back to the door, was already seated at the table. He looked around at the count's arrival. Vincenzo managed to stifle a gasp of shock. The boy's features were dominated by a hideous leer. The expression, however, was not intentional. He had a hair-lip so badly deformed that it reached to his nostrils. His hair was jet black, his eyes deep enigmatic caverns. His heavy brows seemed fixed in a bad-tempered frown.

Donna Caterina introduced them. Placing a hand on the boy's shoulders, she said, 'Say good day to the count, son.'

The boy bowed his head obediently and muttered a greeting before snapping open his roll and proceeding to immerse a hunk of bread in his bowl of soup and conveying it to his horrendous mouth, dribbling most of the liquid back into the bowl. Donna Caterina invited Vincenzo to sit down, before taking the third chair herself.

The soup was excellent, the bread fresh, a far cry from the meals he had endured with Donna Teresa. A plate of *Spaghetti ai Carciofi* followed, a dish, which Donna Caterina explained, originated from her home province of Calabria. Her son scoffed down his food with amazing rapidity, finishing before either of the other two were half way through their meal.

He glanced enquiringly at his mother, who said, 'You may leave the table, Rocco.'

Pushing back his chair with a rasping sound, the boy got up and loped to the door without uttering a word.

Donna Caterina made no move to leave the table, and Vincenzo sensed her need for conversation. She smiled shyly at him.

'He's a good boy, a little slow perhaps. And that deformity isolates him from the other children in the village. They jeer at him.' She wiped a tear from the corner of her eye. 'My husband couldn't take it.'

'Is that why he went to the States?'

'Partly. You see, I don't come from Ginosola. I was born in Catanzaro. When I was seventeen, I came here to visit my aunt, and I met Paolo.' She lifted her head proudly. 'He was the most sought-after young man in the village. I'll show you a photo.'

She pushed back her chair and went to fetch a silver-framed photograph from the dresser. Handing it to him, she said, 'Look, *Signor Conte,* isn't he handsome, my Paolo? We married within the year; my dowry enabled us to open the salon. It did well, but Paolo wanted more. He was ambitious. You see, his brother-in-law had made good in New York.'

Ah, thought Vincenzo, Gianni's cousin!

'Paolo was convinced that if Carlo could do it, then so could he.'

'Did he have any luck?'

Donna Caterina lowered her head, leading Vincenzo to guess that she was weighing up her reply, unwilling to show her husband in a bad light. Lifting her face to meet his gaze, she went on almost apologetically, 'These things take time. Besides, I know he wouldn't think of sending for us until he was established.' She hesitated, then went on, 'After Rocco was born, Paolo changed. He became discontented, couldn't wait to leave here. It was the shame, you see, he couldn't bear … he couldn't bear Rocco's affliction.'

'He couldn't accept his own son?' The words slipped out, words that Vincenzo immediately regretted.

The woman shook her head and sat down again. 'You have to understand what it's like here. In Lucania things are different. For a man like Paolo, the disgrace was too much. Rocco's condition strengthened his yearning to emigrate. He said they could do something for him in America. They have wonderful medical facilities, miracle cures. For months he put money aside for the fare. It wasn't until later that I learned he'd mortgaged the business so that he'd have money in hand to start up over there. He wrote home a lot at first, saying how well he was doing and how much he missed me, but gradually, his letters became shorter and scarcer.'

'Does he still write to you?' ventured Vincenzo.

'The last time was over a year ago.' She rose to her feet, and with a toss of her head, put an end to the conversation. 'It's because he's working so hard; he hasn't got time to write; he'll send for us one day.' Collecting up the dirty dishes, she added in embarrassment, 'I don't know why I told you all this.'

Vincenzo watched her perform her chores, her movements flustered. He guessed that her reason for confiding in him was due to inherent loneliness. Clearly, Donna Caterina was better educated than her neighbours, many of whom were illiterate and could provide little in the way of stimulating conversation for a woman of her intelligence.

Vincenzo went upstairs to his room and flopped onto the bed, his mind in turmoil. Watching the boy had brought back memories of Enzo and Beppe. How his youngest son must have grown! Youngsters of that age had spurts of growth. And what of Alice? How was she faring? Thank God he'd got the pair of them out of Italy before his arrest!

Despite the pleasant, airy room and the relief at having found suitable lodgings, Vincenzo found it difficult to sleep. He tossed and turned all night, feeling nauseous, waking at two in the morning to find his sheets soaked with sweat. He struggled to sit up, trembling uncontrollably as he reached for the carafe of water Donna Caterina had left on the bedside table. He took a sip and sank back onto the pillow, utterly exhausted.

A tap on the door woke him just as he had drifted off again.

'Come in.' His words came out as a mere whisper.

Donna Caterina entered the room, gasping in alarm when she saw him. The pottery jug of steaming water she had brought chinked against the marble-topped dresser as she set it down. Hurrying across to the bed, she placed a cool hand on his forehead and muttered, 'Malaria.'

'That's impossible, I haven't had malaria since I left North Africa.'

'Malaria,' repeated Donna Caterina with conviction. 'I've seen it many times. In summer it's rife in these parts.'

'But this is winter.'

'Once you've had it, it can recur at any time,' she explained.

Still Vincenzo wasn't convinced. 'It's influenza,' he argued. 'A day in bed will see me fit again.'

The days that followed might have been a dream. At night, he felt himself to be in a vacuum. His head throbbed. Nausea, thirst and a terrible shivering racked his body. He knew more blankets had been piled on top of him but they were of little use. On the third night, this changed. While he was tossing and turning with his limbs trembling uncontrollably, he felt the soothing caress of a woman's hand on his forehead and a kiss on the lips.

The next morning, he woke up and realised that he was no longer shivering. The nausea and headache had gone. Slowly, he began to recall the incident of the kiss which had occurred during the turning point to his recovery. Had it been a dream?

Donna Caterina came to check on him, rushing to his side to ask how he felt.

'Much better, *Signora*,' he replied.

'I'll bring you some broth,' she said. 'Now that you're no longer delirious I must fatten you up. You've lost so much weight, *Signor Conte.*'

She left the room leaving Vincenzo feeling puzzled. Could Donna Caterina have kissed him? He made up his mind to question her when she brought the broth.

He tried to be tactful, saying casually, 'There seemed to be a lot of people coming and going while I was ill. Was this part of my delirium or did it really happen?'

'The doctor came, but he's not much use; drunk most of the time. Father Pietro paid a visit … '

Vincenzo gave a gasp of feigned shock. 'He didn't come to administer the Last Rites, I hope!'

Donna Caterina frowned. 'We thought you were close to death.'

'We?'

'The mayor, his wife, the doctor too.'

Vincenzo gasped in alarm. Had the whole village come to gaze upon him in his delirious state?

She went on, 'Then Xavia came with her herbal mixtures. She brought a quinine concoction and I must say, you have recovered since I gave it to you. People say she's a witch; the village girls go to her for love potions...' She gave a sanctimonious sniff. ' ... but I don't hold with all that.'

'Who else came?'

'No one.'

Vincenzo fixed his gaze on Donna Caterina convinced, when she lowered her eyes that she was keeping something from him. He had to know the truth. 'I was under the impression that someone ... oh, never mind.'

'Go on.'

'That someone kissed me.'

Donna Caterina's eyes widened. 'That's impossible,' she exclaimed in astonishment. '*I* was the only person to come and go freely ... *Signor Conte,* you don't imagine ... ' She clapped a hand to her mouth and stepped back.

Feeling stupid, Vincenzo could only offer his apologies. Donna Caterina collected up his empty bowl and left the room. From the other side of the door, he heard mumbled words and wondered to whom Donna Caterina was relating the incident. Seconds later, a figure appeared in the doorway.

'You!' he croaked.

Nine

Vincenzo blinked, unable to believe his eyes. Livia walked over to the bed, a smile hovering at her lips. 'So you've decided to rejoin the land of the living,' she said.

His brow cleared. 'It was *you*!'

Drawing up a chair, she sat down next to him. 'Of course! You needed comfort. Did you think it was Donna Caterina doing her Christian duty?' She threw back her head and laughed. 'I told her I was your sister.'

'What?'

'It was the only way she'd let me into your room.'

'What brought you down here?'

'Can't you guess?'

'Claudia sent you.'

She shook her head. 'You fool! I came to see you. Our last encounter was cut short, remember? You don't seem pleased to see me.'

'I am,' he protested. 'But you're taking a risk coming down here.'

'Rubbish! Who's interested in what goes on in this godforsaken hole?'

Livia's disregard for danger confused him. In Rome, she'd seemed nervous. What an enigmatic woman she was!

'Someone from the village could grass on us. Informers are well paid,' he persisted.

Livia gave an amused chuckle. 'I think not. You're something of a celebrity around here. The villagers admire you.' She raised her eyebrows in the mocking way he found so irresistible. 'A War hero!'

'What are you talking about? They don't know anything about me.'

'Your medals. Your housekeeper packed your medals and your commendations. It didn't take Donna Caterina long to spread the news.'

Vincenzo couldn't help smiling. Grazia Elena was proud of his accomplishments.

'How did you find out where they'd sent me?' he asked.

'It was easy.'

'D'you know someone in the Ministry?'

'Maybe.'

'Maybe? What does that mean? Either you do or you don't.'

'It's not important, I'm here, that's what counts.'

Angered by her attitude and frustrated by his own impotence, Vincenzo lost his temper. He grabbed her wrist and gave it a sharp twist. She cried out in pain. 'Stop it! Stop or I'll scream. Do you want to bring Donna Caterina running in here?'

'Tell me!'

'Let me go!'

'Only when you tell me.'

'All right.'

He released her arm and she drew away, rubbing her wrist and muttering sulkily, 'If you must know, it was the big man himself.'

For a moment, he thought she meant Mussolini. 'Not ... ?

'Yes, the handsome Scarpone. I knew he was in the habit of sending political prisoners down south, but I didn't know the exact location.'

Vincenzo was horrified. He'd been worrying about Scarpone arresting Livia. Now, it seemed, she had offered herself to him on a plate!

'How did you make contact with him?'

'Through mutual friends,' she replied evasively.

'Scarpone doesn't give away information for nothing.'

Her eyes flashed. 'Maybe he does.'

Vincenzo drew a deep breath. 'Did you sleep with him?'

'Stop interrogating me.'

'Well, did you?'

'What if I did? All men are the same once you get them between the sheets.' Her retort was like a slap to the face. He was outraged even though he knew her scorn was induced by shame. 'He turned out to be quite amusing.'

'What d'you mean?' He could hear himself speaking but it sounded like a character in a stage play. Why was he feeling jealous? He'd only been with the woman a couple of times. 'Surely you didn't fall for that bastard's charm?' he gulped.

'He was a perfect gentleman.'

'It's a well-practised guise; you haven't seen the other side of him.'

'He wants to see me again,' she announced petulantly. 'You never know, I might extract information from him. It could prove useful now that you're out of the picture.'

'No!' Vincenzo's voice rose in alarm. 'I forbid you to see him!' The words were out before he could stop them. It was as if someone else had taken charge of his brain, making him say things he didn't want to.

Livia's eyes narrowed mischievously. 'You're jealous?'

Vincenzo tried to cover up angry embarrassment. 'Don't be ridiculous.'

Reading the warning signs and mindful of her sore wrist, Livia leapt away from the bed, knocking a chair over. Beyond his reach, she challenged him, 'In that case, why do you care what I do? I shall see Scarpone again if I want to and there's nothing you can do to stop me.'

He pounced on her words. 'No Livia, don't play with fire.'

'I don't know why you're getting so worked up; we have to take risks in this business.'

'I don't want you getting hurt.' There it was again, this show of concern for her when he didn't really give a fig. He felt as furious with himself as he did with her.

She pursed her lips. 'So you do care?'

'Only because you're a member of the Cell.'

The argument was sapping Vincenzo's strength. He said irascibly, 'Listen to me, Livia, Scarpone isn't a man to cross. He's cruel, he's vengeful, he's extremely dangerous. God knows what he'll do if he finds you down here with me. You must leave at once.'

'Leave?' she retorted. 'I've only just arrived. I'll leave when I'm good and ready. And as for Scarpone, I've tackled lower life than him! If it's your own skin you're worried about, don't fret, he has no idea I've got any connection with you.'

'*Idiota!* I'm not thinking about myself. It's you who'll bear the brunt of his anger. How long do you think it will take him to put two and two together? You think you're clever but, believe me, the marshal will outwit you.' Vincenzo felt the sweat rise on his forehead. He'd heard tales of Scarpone's cruelty: the beating, the maiming. The man had no respect for human life. The only thing he was interested in was furthering his political career.

'I can handle Scarpone; it'll be easy wheedling information out of him.' Tilting her head to one side, she said slyly, 'You *are* jealous, aren't you? Umm, I suppose he is an attractive man. Some girls would give their eye-teeth to go to bed with him!'

She was playing games, taunting him. 'Shut up, you little minx,' he snapped.

Fighting weakness, he struggled out of bed. Livia gave a gasp of dismay and launched herself at him, forcing him back onto the pillows. He tried to push her off but, to his amazement, she cried out, 'Let me stay, I love you, Vincenzo.'

Astounded by her emotional outburst, he relaxed his guard. She leant forward and kissed him fiercely on the mouth. He felt her front teeth bite into his lip, drawing blood. It brought pain, pain that he wanted to feel forever. She drew away and sat on the edge of the bed, staring into his eyes. Her unblinking gaze seemed to penetrate to the depths of his soul.

Suddenly, he came to his senses. 'Get out of here, go at once,' he shouted. Guido was right. She was trouble. Common sense told him to send her away.

'You can't get rid of me that easily,' she retorted.

'Go!'

She didn't move. Infuriated, he brought up his hand and slapped her across the cheek. She slipped off the bed onto the floor, a look of astonishment flickering across her face. Vincenzo was mortified. How could he have done that to her? The other man inside him wanted to cry out: *I'm sorry, my darling, I don't know what got into me. I love you too.*

Livia stood up, brushed down her rumpled clothing and said coldly, 'If that's what you want, I'll leave first thing tomorrow.' Wiping a trace of blood from her mouth with the back of her hand, she left the room.

Exhaustion claimed Vincenzo. He slept for hours. It was dark when he woke up and he found himself replaying the scene with Livia. How could he have allowed her to incite him to anger? She meant nothing to him. She was nothing but a tramp, an arrogant rebel who invited trouble. He'd seen her at the campsite provoking Claudia, flirting with the men. Why had she followed him down to Lucania? He shuddered remembering that he'd almost shouted out *I love you*!

He threw back the covers and got out of bed, holding on to the bedpost for a few seconds to steady himself. Once he was sure of his balance, he went across to the mirror and gave himself a critical inspection. He looked like a vagrant with several days' growth of beard. His cheeks were hollow, his eyes sunken pits. What on earth did a girl like Livia want with a man nearly twice her age? Was she after his money? Was she impressed by his title? He couldn't stop thinking about her. What was her background? Why hadn't she returned to her family during this fallow period? He realised the only thing he knew about her was her name and that she came from the Trentino region. Shuffling back to the bed, he lay down again and, closing his eyes, forced himself to think about Alice. But it was no good: Alice's fresh-complexioned charm was always superimposed by Livia's exotic allure.

Livia stayed. Worn down by her insistence, Vincenzo reluctantly agreed that she could stay on for a while. They kept up the pretence that she was his sister, but they both knew that Donna Caterina wasn't fooled.

Up in the hills above Florence, Vincenzo had caught only fleeting glimpses of Livia; she had lived like a man, donned men's clothing and behaved as bravely as any of her male companions. Here, in this barren land simmering with suppressed sensuality, Livia discarded her masculine attire and put on a peasant-style skirt and blouse, leaving her lustrous hair to fall loose to her shoulders. When he first saw her moving gracefully across the room in flat ballet pumps, swinging her hips and humming to herself, it was all he could do to stop himself from crushing her in his arms.

'Where did you get those clothes?' he asked.

'From Donna Caterina.' She twirled around in front of him expecting flattery, but he deliberately held back.

The two women vied with one another in aiding Vincenzo's recovery and, although Donna Caterina begrudgingly agreed to fix up a truckle bed in a corner of the kitchen for Livia, she made it plain that her presence was tolerated rather than welcomed.

Residing in a household with two strong-minded women and a boy with behavioural problems was far from peaceful. The women often bickered, mostly over trivial matters. Donna Caterina, although well-educated, had a southern mentality and was inherently deferential to the male gender. Also, despite her scorn of Donna Xavia's miracle potions, Vincenzo knew that she covertly consulted the seer for news of her errant husband, never losing faith that one day Paolo would return.

Livia, on the other hand, had a modern outlook. He was sometimes shocked by her outspoken opinions, although he understood that, during the twenties and thirties, under American influence, attitudes in the affluent north of the country had changed dramatically. Livia had been born into a world of suffragettes and flappers. The outbreak of war had done her a favour, enabling her to cast off feminine apparel and extend her emancipation by mingling with her male counterparts on an equal footing.

Things came to a head towards the end of the second week. Returning from a stroll around the village, Vincenzo heard the women arguing.

'I won't have it, I tell you.' Donna Caterina's voice rose shrilly.

'I thought you'd be glad; this way I won't be under your feet all the time.'

'You came here uninvited pretending to be his sister; I made you welcome, gave you board and lodging. Is this how you repay me?'

'I pay well over the odds for your so-called board and lodgings.'

'I charge a fair rent.'

'For what? A makeshift bed in the kitchen and a bowl of onion soup for lunch!' Livia's tone became even more petulant. 'Anyway, it's too late, I've already done it.'

Good God! What had Livia done? He'd heard enough. Let the women fight it out between them, probably it was only another one of their minor disputes. He withdrew unnoticed and made his way around to the back of the house to go up to his room via the outside staircase. As soon as he entered he knew what the argument was about. Livia had moved her truckle bed up into his room. While the bed was installed in the kitchen, Donna Caterina could continue to keep up the pretence that Livia was his sister; moving the truckle bed upstairs declared to the world that the visitor was his lover, and that she condoned the relationship. Such exploits were frowned upon by the villagers. Of course, everybody knew they went on, and nobody cared, so long as they went on behind a curtain of respectability.

A keen observer of human behaviour, it hadn't taken Vincenzo long to realise that status meant everything to Donna Caterina. She had been flattered when her home had been chosen to accommodate him, nursing him back to health had been a privilege. She deeply resented Livia's arrival. With a sigh of resignation, he understood that this was not a disagreement that would fizzle out. He would have to appease both women before things got worse.

He went back downstairs to find that in his absence, the argument had become even more heated. Neither woman noticed him.

'*Puttana!*' screamed Caterina. 'The count's too good for a whore like you. To think I took you in, lent you my clothes!'

'Your clothes!' spat Livia in response. 'A bundle of rags. In Turin and Milan they'd be ridiculed. Short skirts are in vogue, or haven't you noticed?'

They faced one another, hands on hips, cheeks flushed. Across the room, Rocco stood by the fireplace, the disfiguring leer on his face enhanced by his look of alarm.

'*Puttana!*' Caterina shouted again. 'Give me back my clothes.'

Livia gave a hoarse laugh. 'Here, take your disgusting garments. I don't want them.' Without giving a thought to the watching child, she pulled off the blouse and threw it at her opponent, then wriggled out of the skirt and kicked it across the room. Rocco let out a howl and started stamping his foot, swaying his body and beating the air with clenched fists.

Appalled by the scene, Vincenzo stepped in. 'Livia,' he shouted. 'Think of the boy, cover yourself at once.'

'*Madonna!*' Donna Caterina flew across the room and grasped her son's wrists in an attempt to calm him down. But he was a big boy, strong for his age and he fought her. His bellows grew even louder as he began to twist and turn until he was in danger of throwing himself onto the open fire. Vincenzo rushed to Caterina's aid. It took all his strength to restrain the boy, whose howls now changed to deep-throated sobs of frustration as he tried to free himself. During his struggles with Rocco, Vincenzo caught a glimpse of Livia standing unashamedly half-clothed, staring at them, as if mesmerised.

'Livia,' he yelled. 'Get out of here!' She came to life and ran out of the room.

It took another five minutes for Vincenzo and Donna Caterina to calm Rocco. The mother was distraught.

'He hasn't been this bad for ages,' she gasped. 'The last time was when we had a letter from his father. He misses Paolo; a boy needs a father figure.'

Vincenzo gave a start. The words, spoken casually, carried a profound meaning for him. Was it guilt? Beppe was far away in England without his father.

Once Rocco was settled, he went upstairs to find that Livia had put on the working trousers she had worn in the hills above Florence. She ran towards him as he entered, her arms outstretched, an expression of contrition on her face. He brushed her aside, in no mood to respond to her charms. With drooping shoulders, she sat down on the edge of the bed, reaching for the corner of the coverlet and twisting it between her fingers like a child fondling a comforter.

'I'm sorry, Vincenzo,' she whispered.

'What were you thinking of?' he demanded.

'I only wanted to be close to you but that stupid ... ' She paused, then overcome with indignation, went on, ' ... stupid woman with her prudish notions didn't want me to sleep up here with you.' She threw out her hands. 'I ask you, what right has she to sit in judgement, with her reputation?'

'What are you talking about? Donna Caterina's a respectable woman.'

'Huh!' rejoined Livia with a return of her customary spirit. 'She pretends to yearn for her missing husband, but that doesn't stop her ogling other men.'

'What d'you mean?'

'Oh Vincenzo, are you blind? Can't you see she's making eyes at you?'

'What nonsense!' he retorted rather more hotly than was necessary.

'It's not nonsense. You like her too, don't you?'

'She's a good woman, *simpatica*,' he said emphatically. 'Why did you deliberately make her angry?'

Livia sprang to her feet, smacked the flat of her hands against his chest, pushing him backwards to the desk. 'So you *do* care for her. I knew it,' she hissed.

Her cheeks were flushed and her entire body shook with emotion. Never had she looked more desirable. Vincenzo fought down the urge to crush her in his arms.

'Stop it, Livia!' he cried, pushing her from him. 'You must leave.' He began to pace the floor in an effort to sustain his determination. 'You must leave at once,' he repeated.

Her eyes blazed. 'If I leave you'll never see me again. It will be for good, *for good*, do you hear me?'

'Yes, I hear you, so what are you waiting for. Go!' Get rid of her, he told himself. She represented all the things he hated in a woman. She was unpredictable, challenging, stubborn. She did things that shocked him, said things that appalled him. She allowed her emotions to dominate her life, rode roughshod over anybody who got in her way.

'How can you use me like this, Vincenzo? How can you be so cruel?' Clearly she wasn't going to leave without saying her piece. Launching into a vitriolic attack, she grew more and more hysterical.

He grabbed her wrists and tried to calm her but she shook herself free, and balling her fist, punched him fiercely on the shoulder. When he didn't retaliate, she spun around, snatched up his keys from the desk and drew them savagely down his left cheek. Astounded, he slapped a hand to his face as globules of blood began to appear.

'*O Dio*!' she cried, jumping back, horrified at what she had done.

Shocked into silence, they glared at one another. Vincenzo felt as if the world had come to a standstill. No one else existed except Livia and him. Recovering, he grabbed her arms and shook her. She seemed drained of strength. Pulling her to him, he held her close while she sobbed into his collar, her tears mingling with the blood from the scratches on his face. 'Livia, *amore*, you know I love you, only you,' he whispered.

She looked up with red-rimmed eyes. 'Truly?'

'Of course.'

Blinking back more tears, she murmured, 'Oh Vincenzo, I can't live without you. I think of no one else. I want to be with you always.'

'I want that too.' He spoke sincerely although he knew that the realisation of such a dream was impossible.

With ill-concealed disapproval Donna Caterina agreed to allow Livia to sleep in Vincenzo's room on the condition that she was discreet, and always came in through the house, never taking the outside staircase to the room. The weeks went by and Vincenzo's intentions to start work on his book were shelved. Every day the couple went for walks in the hills, talking, always talking: exchanging unfulfilled dreams, confiding fantasies. He told Livia about Alice and Beppe. 'I love my wife,' he told her. 'I'd never leave her.'

She gave a careless shrug. 'I wouldn't expect you to. In wartime, you have to live for moment.'

'Tell me about your parents,' he said.

She grinned. 'Rita?' He ultimately learned that she always referred to her mother by her given name. 'Rita's a vain woman. She fancies she looks like Wallis Simpson. Can you imagine that? She follows the latest fashion and smokes from a long cigarette holder.'

'What's your father like?' asked Vincenzo.

'A stick in the mud. Boring as hell.'

It flashed across Vincenzo's mind that Livia's father would almost certainly be about his own age. A sobering thought!

He started getting up to his old tricks, amusing Livia with his mimicry and practical jokes. Her reaction was very different from that of his wife. Although charmed by his efforts at impersonation, Alice could never quite come to terms with his love of playing the fool. 'Oh do stop, darling,' she'd urge, her colour deepening with the first signs of irritation puckering her brow. 'Somebody might be watching.'

Livia suffered no such inhibitions. His every antic left her convulsed with laughter. She would often collapse into a chair holding her sides, crying, 'Stop, stop, Vincenzo, I've got a stitch.'

At night they made love feverishly, waking in the early hours to taste love again. With Alice, he had always been the one to take the lead. Their lovemaking had been tender and unhurried. She had never refused him, yet he knew in his heart that more often than not her response was driven by duty rather than desire. No such sense of obligation prompted Livia's response. Invariably, she initiated their coupling, teasing him beyond the bounds of control. Her body had become as familiar to him as his own. He knew what thrilled her, he knew what troubled her.

Afterwards, they would talk for hours. He would never have believed that he could open his heart so freely to another living soul. Much as he cared for Alice, such moments of intimacy with her would have been unthinkable. Yet Livia always managed to surprise him. He couldn't make up his mind whether he found her mood changes irritating or enchanting.

He had no idea how long his exile would last. News of the War's progress trickled down from Rome, but for the most part, it was as if the region were on another planet, and although there were occasional losses amongst the conscripts from surrounding areas, Ginosola seemed almost untouched by the conflict. Food was in short supply but near starvation was no novelty to these people. The villagers lived from hand to mouth now just as they had done for centuries. Donna Caterina managed well enough due, Vincenzo suspected, to a contact in the black market. She could certainly afford to pay over-the-top prices on account of the extra money he gave her.

One morning, Livia shattered his euphoria by announcing airily, 'I'm going back to Florence.'

He couldn't hide his dismay. 'No Livia, not yet.' Only weeks ago, he'd told her to leave, now he was begging her to stay.

'I must report back,' she replied. 'Claudia may have an assignment for me.'

A knot tightened in Vincenzo's throat. He wanted to shout, *don't go!* But he knew she was right. Snatching her wrists, he squeezed them. 'You'll come back?'

She gave a yelp. 'Vincenzo, you're hurting me.'

He took her in his arms. 'I'm afraid for you, take care.' Why was he being so calm and reasonable? Driven by a wild and futile hope, he begged, 'Quit the Resistance, stay here with me.'

Livia drew away from him, looking shocked. 'What are you saying? Give up the fight, let those fascist pigs win? Have you lost your nerve?'

Shamed, Vincenzo shook his head. 'No. All I'm asking is that you don't take chances. We've everything to live for, *amore*.'

Livia's expression softened. 'I know that,' she murmured, reaching out a hand and caressing his cheek. 'I'll be back.'

'The Fuhrer's influence is stronger than ever,' muttered Vincenzo as if talking to himself. 'I don't trust those brutes.' Images of the barbaric acts the Nazis had perpetrated on French partisans rose in his mind.

'Neither do I and I don't trust the *fascisti*. Mussolini has started rounding up Jews and sending them to Fòssoli …' She stopped short as if she'd said too much.

Vincenzo was staggered. Fòssoli was an internment camp, a halfway house for foreigners awaiting repatriation. The cold hand of fear clutched at his heart. Until now, he hadn't believed the rumoured atrocities taking place in the camp. With a flash of horror, Alice's image sprang to mind. Thank goodness he'd got her out of the country before things got this bad.

He grasped Livia by the arms, 'Don't leave. Wait until Guido sends a message from Claudia.'

A haughty look glanced across her face. 'Don't you trust me? You think I'll slip back into my old ways.'

'Of course I trust you,' he protested hotly. But he didn't trust her; that was the trouble. He was afraid she'd take unnecessary risks but, most of all, he was afraid she'd be unfaithful.

She started packing her things, moving rapidly, giving him only a cursory kiss on the cheek before dashing off to catch the bus. It was only after she'd gone that he understood how cleverly she'd manoeuvred the situation. With a show of arrogance, she had wiped away tears, thus avoiding a crushing separation. Vincenzo felt hollow inside. It was as if she had died. It was even worse than the shock of Enzo's murder.

PART II

My name's not Joe.

Ten

Harrogate 1940

Beppe Di Tomasi sat by the bay window of the sitting room, watching his English cousins shooting at one another with toy rifles. He made a mental calculation. It was August and he'd been living in Harrogate for over six months, yet he still hadn't got used to the English way of life.

His mother, Alice, came into the room. 'Why don't you go and play with your cousins?' she suggested.

He scowled. 'They don't like me.'

'You won't make friends with them if you don't make an effort, Beppe.'

'Why should I?'

Alice came to sit beside him on the window seat. Her crêpe de Chine dress rubbed against his bare knee. To avoid meeting her gaze, he studied her feet, slim and elegant in high-heeled, peep-toed shoes. She started talking, urging him to join his cousins, but he wasn't listening.

'Beppe, don't ignore me.'

He looked up then. 'Sorry, Mamma.'

Her blond hair swung as she looked down at him. It was done up in a funny snood thing. It would make a good fishing net, he thought.

She twisted her solitaire diamond ring round and round her finger; it was loose because she'd lost weight. He'd heard his aunt and uncle urging her to eat more. With him, she alternated between over-protectiveness and disregard, and he instinctively knew that disregard occurred when despair at the memory of Enzo's death overwhelmed her.

He hated the way his Yorkshire-born Uncle Arthur and Aunt Thelma kept a constant vigil over him. They disapproved of his mother's lack of interest, they couldn't stand her moods. All at once, Alice reached out for him, hugging him tightly and, as she pressed his head against her bosom, he felt as if he'd returned to babyhood. To his chagrin, tears rushed to his eyes; tears of joy at her show of affection mixed with tears of shame at his show of weakness.

She stroked his dark hair and murmured, 'Beppe, how I miss your brother!'

He froze. Why did she always go back to Enzo? It was as if she were the only person in the world to miss him. Didn't she realise that he missed Enzo as well? Her tears dampened his collar.

He wriggled free and stuttered, I think I'll go out to play after all, Mamma.'

When he got outside, twelve-year-old Ronald tossed him the third rifle, the one he and nine-year-old Leslie didn't want because it was dented.

'Come on Beppe, you can be a hun,' he called out. Then, he corrected himself, 'No, I meant, an eye-tie. We've cornered you. Go down on your knees and beg for mercy.'

Ronald and Leslie hooted with laughter while Beppe stood there quietly, hating them. His silence made them even more scornful. They charged at him with their sham rifles, willing him to run away, but he stood his ground, his own rifle held firmly out in front of him and when the younger boy came too close, he thumped him over the shoulder with it.

Leslie sank to the ground, curled himself into a ball and howled while his brother dashed into the house, screaming for their mother. White with anger, Beppe threw down his toy rifle and stomped away.

At the sound of the scuffle Alice rushed to the window in time to see Beppe storm out of the gate.

Ronald's accusations reached her from the hallway. 'Mum, mum, come quickly. Come and see what Beppe's done to Leslie.'

Then, she heard Thelma's shrieks of indignation. 'What? Oh my God! That vicious foreign child's gone too far this time.'

She watched Thelma march across the lawn with Ronald at her heels. They both crouched over the sobbing Leslie. She couldn't hear what they were saying, but their gesticulations were all too clear. Should she rush out and plead her son's case? She shuddered at the thought of facing Thelma's self-righteous finger-pointing. Instead, she ran upstairs to her room. Her cheeks were flushed with shame. She'd sent Beppe out to play with those unruly little beasts and when they'd taunted him and he'd retaliated, she hadn't had the decency to go to his defence.

Sinking down onto the bed, she rocked back and forth with shame. Tears streamed down her cheeks, leaving rivulets of mascara. She felt wretched, but despair twisted shame into indictment. It was Vincenzo's fault. He shouldn't have sent them to Harrogate. Surely, in wartime, it was better for families to stick together. They could have remained safely concealed in the depths of the Tuscan countryside, coping with food shortages and power cuts. Did Vincenzo think she'd lost the ability to cook and budget just because she'd been a lady of leisure since their marriage?

She clenched her fists. How she hated living in England! She'd spent most of her childhood travelling abroad from diplomatic post to diplomatic post with her parents; England had never been her home. The tears poured down her cheeks. Here, in Harrogate, her brother and sister-in-law behaved as if Enzo had never existed. Even her father no longer spoke his name. It was Vincenzo's fault, he shouldn't have forced them to leave Italy. There was a knock on the door. Alice gulped back her sobs and crept over to listen.

'Alice, are you in there? Come downstairs and see what that vicious son of yours has done. My poor Leslie's black and blue…Alice, answer me!'

Alice pressed her back against the wall. She saw the door handle turn and held her breath, hoping that Thelma wouldn't look behind the door when she poked her head into the room. Leslie's frantic yells carried up the stairs and Thelma retreated, muttering, 'The bitch must have gone out.'

Alice heaved a sigh of relief. So Beppe had dodged them! She went to sit at the dressing table mirror and dabbed the mascara stains from her cheeks. Twisting open her lipstick, she puckered her lips then paused. She would make it up to Beppe. She would pay him more attention. Her gaze fell on a silver-framed photograph. She picked it up, kissed Enzo's image and, uttering a smothered wail, clutched the photograph to her breast.

Beppe ran along the lane, muttering to himself about how much he hated England with its neat little houses and busy roads. He smothered a sob as he remembered his Tuscan home. A sprawling villa in the country, it had belonged to his father's family for generations. Far away from the sound of car horns and the trundle of trams, it had grown randomly as, first the east wing then the west wing, were added. He bit his lip as he made bitter comparisons.

In Harrogate, his cousins barged uninvited into his bedroom, messing with his things, making fun of the books he read.

In Castagnetto, he could hide in his tree house. He gave a smug smile. Ronald and Leslie wouldn't disturb him there; he would fight them off with the wooden sword old Matteo had carved for him.

With a jerk of nostalgia, he recalled that the tree house was really Enzo's. Matteo had built it and, after Enzo had outgrown it, it had passed to him. He still missed Enzo even though, in recent summers, his brother hadn't had much time for him, shooing him away with, 'Go away, you little brat! I've got better things to do than play cops and robbers with a kid like you.'

A knot of pain formed in his chest as his fickle mind played a trick on him, bringing back the unforgettable scene, which he'd tried so hard to erase from his memory:

Babbo's choked words: *'Terrible news, son, the worst... ...your... your brother's dead.'*

Mamma slumped on the floor, arms wrapped around her body, rocking and wailing.

His own shriek of denial. *'Mamma, Enzo isn't dead, is he?'*

Mamma's sobbing plea: *'Why Enzo, why him?'*

But worst of all:

Mamma's shriek of rejection when he'd tried to rush into her arms: *'Go away, Beppe!'*

The knot of pain tightened. What had he done wrong? Why had she pushed him away? He sniffed back more tears.

Mamma had always praised Enzo. He stopped abruptly, a devastating question exploding in his mind: what if he, not Enzo, had been the one to die! Would she have cared?

A woman pushing a perambulator nearly collided with him. 'Look where you're going, you careless boy,' she snapped.

'Sorry,' he mumbled, and hurried on to the corner shop to buy a gobstopper with a penny he'd found in his pocket. Sucking the gobstopper lifted his spirits and he dawdled back, kicking a pebble in and out of the road. There was no one about when he got home so he went up to his bedroom to read a book.

He forgot about the incident with his cousins until later that evening when his grandfather took him aside and spoke to him in Italian.

'You know what you did to Leslie was wrong, don't you Beppe?'

'I don't know what you mean,' he replied, genuinely mystified.

'You hit your cousin.'

Memory returned. 'Oh that! But Grandpa, he deserved it.'

'Maybe so, but you'll have to get used to your cousins' teasing if you're ever to fit in here. They'll soon lose interest if you don't retaliate.'

'I don't want to fit in.'

The kindly man brushed a hand over his moustache. 'Beppe, my son, Italy has joined Germany in the War. This is very difficult for you, but remember, your father sent you here to keep you safe. For his sake, you must try to settle down. In September you'll start at the same school as your cousins.' The old man gave a sigh. 'You're a clever young man so I know you'll have no trouble with your lessons. You're far cleverer than either of your cousins ... " He gave his grandson a conspiratorial wink. '...far cleverer than me.'

'No, Grandpa, not cleverer than you; you know loads of things, you've travelled the world, you speak lots of languages ... I'm not nearly as clever as you,' protested the boy.

'You will be one day. Promise me, you'll do your best. Once this awful war is over, you'll be able to go home to Italy.

You've got a great future ahead of you. You must try hard for your father's sake.'

Looking wistful, the boy nodded; then breaking into English, he said, 'I miss Babbo so much, he makes me laugh. D'you know, Grandpa, he can do a cracking take off of Charlie Chaplin?'

At hearing his grandson's trip into schoolboy slang, the old man raised an amused eyebrow. 'I see you're quickly picking up the language,' he chuckled.

September and school came around all too quickly. Beppe was resentful at being forced to study the English curriculum.

'Beppe, hurry up, you don't want to be late for your first day,' said his mother. 'And don't forget, you'll be called Joe.'

'My name's not Joe, it's Beppe.'

Alarmed, Alice shook him by the shoulders. 'Listen to me! You're Joe from now on. People won't accept you with an Italian name.' She hugged him so tightly he could barely breathe. As he wriggled free, she went on, 'You're going to be a sensible boy now, aren't you Beppe. Oh...' She clapped a hand to her mouth and giggled. '...I mean Joe.'

He burst out laughing. 'You see, Mamma, I'm not Joe. I don't want to be English. Why can't we go home to Italy?'

'Don't be silly. You know we can't go home. Really, you are so obstinate.'

The boy experienced a glow of pleasure during this moment of intimacy with his mother. She *did* care about him after all!

Then she spoilt it by adding, 'Your brother would have had more common sense.'

At that moment, Robert McPherson-Corke came down the stairs and asked, 'What's all this about?'

Beppe pulled away from Alice's feverishly plucking hands as she tried to button up his blazer, and ran to his grandfather.

'Grandpa, I don't want to be called Joe,' he cried.

The old man sat down on the stairs and pulled his grandson onto his knee. 'Son, I explained the reason. You know, sometimes we have to do things we don't want to do. Your headmaster decided that because of the War it would be sensible to anglicise your name to Joseph Thomas. Your mother calls herself Mrs Thomas now.'

Beppe shook his head, frowning. 'I don't want an English name.'

Robert smiled patiently and waited. The boy's head drooped sulkily, but he knew he couldn't disobey his grandfather. He respected him too much. He looked into the old man's periwinkle blue eyes, aware that the laughter lines were getting deeper and said, 'All right Grandpa, if *you* say so.'

The boy's first few weeks at Monksmede School were a nightmare. It took him a long time to get used to being called Joe, and he was often teased about his foreign accent. Ronald boarded, but he and Leslie were day pupils. Although the younger boys were the same age, Leslie was placed in Alpha and Joe in Beta because the headmaster thought that difficulty with the language in the early days could hold Joe back.

The trouble started after half term when his mother and his aunt and uncle were called up to the school to discuss their sons' progress. He learnt about the interview when he accidentally overheard his uncle and aunt discussing it later that day.

'I've never heard anything so outrageous,' declared his Aunt Thelma. 'Moving Joe up to Alpha and our Leslie down to Beta! How can Joe be more advanced than Leslie?'

'You can't get away from the fact that Joe's a bright lad,' said Arthur. 'Look how his father excelled at University!'

'But he can't even speak English properly! It's all wrong, he and his mother should have stayed in Italy where they belong. They've disrupted our lives. If it weren't for the fact that this house will be ours one day, we'd be better off moving into a place of our own instead of lodging with your father.'

Joe's heart convulsed, contrasting emotions churning in his chest. Yes, Italy was exactly where he'd like to be; nonetheless it was a shock to learn that his Aunt Thelma was so anxious to get rid of him. He held his breath and pressed his ear to the door.

'As for the changes at school, I think we should complain,' grumbled Thelma.

'Complaining will do no good,' argued Arthur. 'There's no point in Leslie staying in Alpha if he can't keep up with the rest of the class. Don't worry, my dear, we'll get him coached.'

'Arthur!' screeched his wife. 'You're missing the point. That irritating little foreign brat is proving to be cleverer than our boys. It's untenable!' She didn't stop there. 'Your sister practically ignores him. She leaves me to sort out his uniform, and make sure he has a hair cut. I don't think she loves the child at all!'

'Leave Alice out of it!' snapped Arthur.

'Joe!'

The boy swivelled round guiltily at the sound of his grandfather's voice and burbled, 'I didn't mean to eavesdrop, Grandpa.'

Robert smiled and said amiably, 'Come here lad, let's have one of our chinwags before you go off to bed.'

Leslie never did catch up at school, and to make matters worse, the following September, Joe skipped a year. This infuriated Thelma, who didn't bother to hide her indignation.

By 1942, all things foreign were frowned upon, but by then, Joe had completely lost his accent. He had learnt the value of discretion and never revealed that he was half Italian.

They never heard from Vincenzo. In the early months when Alice rushed to answer the telephone, he'd been close on her heels until, one day, he caught a glimpse of his grandfather eyeing them sadly.

'Babbo isn't going to phone, is he, Grandpa?' he asked.

Robert shook his head. 'No, my boy, he can't. Your mother doesn't want to believe the lines have been cut.'

'Do you think Babbo is all right, Grandpa?'

'Of course he is.'

'Do you think he misses us?'

'I'm sure he does.'

As war dragged on, Alice stopped talking about Vincenzo, fixing instead on memories of her first-born child. She frequently brought Enzo's name into the conversation. Thelma and Arthur would cast one another long-suffering glances.

'Joe's doing very well at school,' observed his grandfather at dinner one evening.

'Yes, but it's a pity he isn't as good at sport as Enzo was.'

This pressure on the old man to praise Joe's accomplishments further antagonised Thelma, who became increasingly testy. Joe's antipathy towards her doubled. 'I'll show her,' he told himself indignantly, 'I'll do better than Ronald and Leslie.' He could cope with his aunt's snide remarks by secretly planning ways to retaliate, never actually putting his plans into practice of course, but it was his mother's offhand attitude that cut the deepest. How could he win back Alice's affection?

That year Joe and Leslie joined Ronald as boarders at Monksmede. Due to his high grades, Joe spent most of his time with students some two years his senior, boys who had reached puberty with all its accompanying trials and tribulations. Because of this, he had no close friends.

At school, Leslie and his pals taunted him, shouting, 'Swot, swot!'

While at home, his aunt accused him of being sullen.

His grandfather saw what was going on, but felt unable to intervene. He knew that a more extrovert boy would have rebelled, but Joe was not as boisterous as his cousins nor as confident as his brother had been. With a sigh, the old man acknowledged that his grandson was a prisoner of his own personality.

It wasn't long before casualties of the War became a fact of life. At Monksmede, Joe noticed pupils disappear, returning to school a week later, looking subdued. He learned to ignore the incident, and to allow the grieving boy to wear the proverbial *stiff upper lip*.

He discussed the progress of the War with his grandfather.

'Monty's Army's taken Tripoli, Grandpa,'' he cried when the news hit the headlines in January 1943. 'That means the Allies will take Tunisia, then march into Italy. The War will soon be over.'

'Yes, Son, it's excellent news,' agreed Robert, although he was less confident about a swift end to the conflict.

'Babbo will be all right, won't he, Grandpa? I mean, once the Allies learn about his English connections, they'll ask him to help re-form a government, won't they?'

His grandfather smiled and nodded, unable to bring himself to destroy the boy's expectations.

May 1943 saw the surrender of German and Italian troops in North Africa. The Eighth Army advanced towards Sicily. Joe followed the news keenly. He'd heard rumours of Germans destroying farmland and confiscating villas. He couldn't bear the thought of them marching through his beloved Tuscany.

'The Yanks will drive the Huns out of Italy, won't they, Grandpa?'

'Of course they will,' replied his grandfather.

All at once, the boy experienced a surge of frustrated anger, and shouted, 'I hate the Huns.'

Clenching his fists, he spun round and ran out of the room, slamming the door behind him.

Eleven

At Half Term Joe went home to Harrogate determined to win back his mother's affection and to prepare them both for the longed-for reunion with his father. Alice wasn't at the door to greet him. Pushing aside his disappointment, he went to look for her and found her sitting in the summer house. He stopped in the doorway studying her as if for the first time. She was beautiful: pale and delicate looking, not dark and heavy-featured like his Italian relatives. Enzo had taken after her. No wonder she had loved him so much!

On seeing him, she looked startled and the Wedgwood tea cup from which she was drinking clinked against its saucer. Joe experienced a pang of anguish. Surely his arrival was no surprise, she must have been expecting him.

'Hello Joe,' she said dully.

He went over, kissed her cheek and sat down beside her. Now that he had reached his teenage years talking to a woman, even his mother, made him feel self-conscious, and for a moment, he was at a loss for words.

Alice smiled weakly but made no attempt to ease his awkwardness. At last, he said, 'How are you, Mamma?'

'How should I be?'

It's that time of the month, he thought to himself, she's probably suffering awful stomach cramps. His father had sometimes warned his sons: 'It's a bad time of the month for your mother, boys, treat her kindly.' At these words, Enzo would give him a wink, and he would wink back without having the remotest idea what the fuss was about. Now he understood.

Determined not to be put off by his mother's lack of interest, he tried to reassure her. 'The War's going to be over soon and we'll be going home.'

When she didn't reply, he felt even more uncomfortable. Enzo would have known what to say. He would have cracked a joke and made her laugh. In desperation, he dredged his mind for something to talk about, settling on wistful reminiscences of their life in Tuscany.

All at once, she turned on him. 'Stop it, Joe, stop it! Stop yapping on about your father and the vineyard. What's the good, the War may be coming to an end but nothing...' She shook her head wildly and spat out the words, '... nothing will bring Enzo back to life.'

Convulsed by sobs, she sank back in her chair. The outburst disturbed Joe. He clenched his fists to quell the welling tears as he felt again the shock of rejection. 'But Mum, you still have me,' he whispered.

'Yes, Joe, I still have you.'

The words were hollow, intended to make him leave her alone. He got to his feet and backed away. 'I'll go and unpack. See you at dinner.'

At Christmas, the thirteen-year-old received an excellent School Report. He arrived home in good spirits, convinced that his mother would be waiting for him and that, at last, he was going to win her approval. But his hopes were quickly dashed.

'Your mother's gone out,' his Aunt Thelma informed him curtly.

Swamped by disappointment, he slunk away, the Report screwed up in his hand. As he climbed the stairs to his room, all hell broke loose downstairs. He heard Thelma ranting and raving about Ronald and Leslie's poor results with Arthur making vain attempts to appease her. Joe looked back and met his grandfather's gaze. Robert winked at him.

Later that evening, his grandfather came to his bedroom and, putting an arm across his shoulders, said fondly, 'Well done, lad. What did I tell you? What's it to be, Oxford or Cambridge?'

Joe reddened. 'Steady on, Grandpa, I've still got to get my Higher School Certificate.' He hesitated then ventured apprehensively, 'Do you think Mum will be pleased with me?'

'Why, my lad, she'll be delighted!'

But his grandfather's reassurance did not convince Joe, particularly when Alice failed to return before bedtime. He found her at the breakfast table next morning. She looked up from her coffee cup and smiled. 'Joe, darling, I'm so sorry I wasn't here when you got home. Grandpa's told me about your excellent Report. Well done!'

These words of praise should have gladdened his heart but somehow the gingerbread had lost its gilt. 'Thanks, Mum,' he muttered.

Alice's trips away from home began in the spring when Arthur and Thelma threw a party to which they invited a number of their London friends. She was particularly taken with the Kennards, a gregarious couple from Chiswick.

The day after the party, she asked her sister-in-law about them. 'Johnnie and Betsy?' exclaimed Thelma. 'They're Arthur's friends! Johnnie's a retired Group Captain. He was invalided out of the Air Force with heart problems. His dicky ticker doesn't stop him leading an active life. Betsy's from South Georgia.' She clicked her tongue. 'Betsy doesn't look after him properly. Americans are not as fussy as we are.' Thelma stopped rubbing margarine into a bowl of flour with her fingertips and gave Alice a quizzical glance, clearly puzzled by her interest in the Kennards. It wasn't often the two women stopped to chat.

'Go on,' encouraged Alice.

Thelma resumed her pastry-making. 'Their house is always spilling over with recuperating service personnel.'

'That sounds praiseworthy!'

'Praiseworthy?' Thelma frowned her disapproval. 'I think it's all rather gruesome, some of them have horrible wounds: amputations, dreadful burns and things.'

'Does Betsy help nurse them back to health?'

Thelma shook her head. 'Oh goodness no. They only take in people who are on the mend.'

'A sort of informal convalescent home?' suggested Alice.

'I suppose you could call it that.'

Thelma drizzled water into her pastry bowl and went on, 'They invite all sorts of people into their home. *I* wouldn't like it. Soldiers and airmen who've nowhere to go while they're on leave, even total strangers.' She sucked in her breath. 'I've heard they throw some really wild parties.'

'What fun!' giggled Alice. 'Tell me more.'

For the first time in months, Alice found herself taking an interest in people outside her immediate environment. Until now, she had immersed herself in nostalgia, recalling the days of her youth when, after her mother's death, she had helped Robert host Embassy functions. After Joe had gone away to boarding school she had found she could discipline herself to leapfrog back over the years and draw on earlier, carefree recollections. When Joe came home for the holidays, she found herself again beset by sad memories. He looked nothing like Enzo, yet he reminded her of her dead son.

She had always found Arthur and Thelma dull and set in their ways. The farthest distance from home that Thelma had travelled was to Scotland and Arthur's interests did not extend beyond the War situation and the cricket scores. Unlike her, he had not yearned to travel the world with his parents, and he had missed being called up because he had turned forty-six when war broke out. Alice had much in common with her father, but Robert was now approaching his eightieth birthday and showing signs of slowing down. Father and daughter no longer had the animated discussions they once had and the humdrum life in the Harrogate household was sending her deeper into depression.

After her conversation with Thelma, Alice decided to take action. She telephoned Betsy with the intention of using the excuse of asking her for a recipe she'd mentioned.

'Hello, honey, how lovely to hear from you.'

'I hope you don't mind me ringing you, Betsy, but it's about…'

'Mind? Why, honey, I was going to phone you. How about coming down to Chiswick to spend a weekend with me and Johnnie? We'd jest love to see you again.'

This was just what Alice had hoped for. 'Oh, Betsy, that would be wonderful. Are you sure it wouldn't be too much trouble?'

'Trouble? Of course not. Come down next weekend.'

After she had put the phone down, Alice realised she hadn't needed to use the excuse of the recipe.

The occasional weekend soon became a regular fortnightly feature. Much to Thelma's annoyance, she even went there during the boys' school holidays. She knew she was being unfair to Joe, and this tore at her conscience, but his awkward attempts to please her only seemed to give an extra twist to the bitter blade of loss. In Johnnie and Betsy's lively company she was able to put aside her grief.

Betsy praised her handling of the recovering soldiers. "Alice, sweetie, the guys jest love you.'

This made her feel better. Surely it was important to lift the spirits of the men who were fighting to save the country!

As she got to know the Kennards better, her affection for them grew. Once, when she expressed admiration for their hospitality, Johnnie coughed self-consciously and rumbled in reply, 'Just doing my bit for the War effort, m'dear.'

She learnt that Betsy was some twenty-five years younger than her larger-than-life husband and that they had met when Johnnie was on a visit to the States. 'It was love at first sight, honey,' explained Betsy, going on to describe the easy-going South Georgian luxury she had given up in order to marry her Englishman and move across the Atlantic.

'What kept you here when war broke out?' Alice asked her. 'You could have gone back to the States.'

'What?' cried Betsy, throwing up her hands in mock indignation. 'Johnnie and I would never desert a sinking ship.'

Alice loved the Kennards' optimistic approach to life. At first, she felt sad that they had never been able to have children of their own, but on getting to know them better she realised that Betsy and Johnnie were, in fact, surrogate *mom* and *pop* to all the young service men and women who invaded their home.

Betsy never seemed to take anything seriously. When Alice asked her whether she was troubled by her husband's disregard for his heart condition, she shrugged and drawled, 'There's nothing I can do about it, honey, he won't listen to me.'

Alice met Peter Winstanley at the Kennards' on her second trip to London. A Squadron Leader with a record number of flying hours chalked up, he was tall, good looking and witty. His contempt for his own safety sent shivers down her spine; his anecdotes of near-misses -- told amusingly with tongue in cheek -- brought tears of laughter to the eyes of his listeners although, as time wore on and she became more involved with him, Alice's tears became tears of concern.

The day after their first encounter, they bumped into one another in Fortnum and Mason.

'We meet again,' he said softly.

A smile lit up her face. 'Peter, how lovely to see you!' She knew she looked fetching in a slim-fitting pastel blue linen suit. Her high-heeled shoes were fashionable, her shapely legs clad in black market silk stockings. Thank goodness her straight-laced brother didn't know about them! She gave a perplexed frown. 'I thought you were going back today.'

With a slight bow, he took her by the elbow and guided her out of the path of other shoppers. 'Not until this evening. Would you care to join me for a cup of tea? Lyons Corner House isn't far from here. With a bit of luck they might have one or two cakes left.'

Alice glanced at her watch. There was still time before her train departed. A lock of blond hair had managed to escape from under her navy straw hat, which was tilted rather saucily over one eye. 'Yes, thank you, that would be nice,' she replied, telling herself that there was nothing wrong with having a cup of tea with a man she found amusing. After all, it couldn't go anywhere, could it?

He led her to the restaurant where they found a table by the window. The waitress appeared in her smart black dress and white apron. 'What can I get you, Sir?'

'Tea for two please.' He smiled engagingly at the waitress. 'And cakes, if you've got some tucked away under the counter.'

The waitress blushed and replied, 'I might be able to find you a piece of Madeira cake.'

Alice experienced a tremor of excitement. What a charmer this man was! She was pleased to be seen in his company.

Peter broke into her thoughts. 'You know, I spent the whole of yesterday evening wondering how I could get to see you again, and here you are. The gods have been kind to me.'

His flattery pleased Alice, but she pretended indifference. In fact, she had been very much aware of his interest in her. It had been a lively dinner party with good conversation and a great deal of laughter. At one moment, Peter's focus on her face had unnerved her, bringing the colour to her cheeks when the woman seated beside him had jokingly called him to task when he failed to respond to a question she'd put to him.

'I should very much like to get to know you better, Alice. Tell me about yourself. Where do you live?'

'Harrogate,' she replied. 'I live with my brother and sister-in-law and my father. It's quiet at the moment, but things liven up when the children break up from school.'

'Children?' He raised an enquiring eyebrow.

'My own son and my brother's two boys.'

'And your husband?'

'He's... he's... ' Should she divulge that she was married to an Italian?

'With the Eighth Army?' prompted Peter.

'No... '

Peter's eyes narrowed and he tapped the side of his nose. 'It's hush-hush.'

She let it go at that, hoping that he would not find out the truth from Johnnie or Betsy. To avert his attention from her own background, she asked him about his. His reply was straightforward. 'Born in Wales, parents both dead, one widowed sister with two children.'

'Are her children young?'

'Five and seven. Gwyneth's husband was killed at Dunkirk.'

'How terrible,' murmured Alice. 'How does she manage without your parents to help her? I've been so lucky having Daddy take care of me and... Joe.' Just in time she remembered not to call her son Beppe. Dangerous ground again. To steer him away, she asked, 'Have you ever been married?'

Peter shook his head. 'You could say I'm married to flying. It's my life.'

'Were you a pilot before the War?'

'I've been flying since I was seventeen.'

'So you've got twenty-twenty vision?'

He laughed and pointed across the room. 'I would be able to see the perfection of your face from way over there.'

She blushed at the compliment. It triggered a warning signal. This man was too ready with the sweet talk. He winked and her blush deepened. He was only poking fun at her! All at once, his mood changed. Becoming serious, he leant over the table and took her hand. 'Look Alice, I've got five hours to kill before I report back to my Squadron. Help me fill the time, please.'

Taken aback, she stared into his grey eyes, then shifted her gaze to her wristwatch and saw that her train left in twenty minutes. There was, of course, a later train. She felt she ought to say 'no' and started to withdraw her hand, but he squeezed her fingers. 'Please say 'yes' Alice. God knows where I shall be this time tomorrow.'

For a fleeting moment, he dropped his guard and she saw apprehension in his face. 'All right,' she whispered, her voice trembling slightly.

It was a balmy afternoon and they walked in Kensington Gardens, admiring the flowers, watching the ducks on the Round Pond. The easing off of the bombing had brought a few stalwart families back to the capital and one or two uniformed nannies paraded their charges in expensive baby carriages. At six they made their way to the Ritz, ordered g&t's and sat in the bar.

'I wish I didn't have to leave,' he said.

'What time's your train?'

'Not until nine. We could fit in dinner.'

'I ought to go home.'

'Are you worried about what your family will think?'

Alice shook her head.

'You feel disloyal to your husband?'

'A little. I haven't heard from him in ages. I've no idea where he is or what he's up to.'

'*That* hush-hush?'

She gave a non-committal shrug.

'Well,' he said, dolefully. 'I guess you've decided you've had enough of me.'

'Oh no!' The words burst out before she could stop them.

Triumphantly, Peter got to his feet and held out a hand. 'In that case, I know a nice little restaurant just round the corner from here. Let's go.'

They were half way through their meal when the Air Raid Siren sounded. The restaurant began to clear. Peter looked at her enquiringly, 'Do we run for cover or do we stay?'

His disarming smile made her brave. 'Let's stay and finish our meal,' she said.

But a few minutes later, a loud explosion shocked them. Peter placed a steadying hand on the table to stop it rocking. 'Come on, let's go. This is too close for comfort.'

Snatching up her bag, Alice sprang to her feet. Although her trips to London had been punctuated by the occasional air raid, she hadn't experienced the heavier bombing. Peter grabbed her hand and they ran all the way to Leicester Square Underground Station, her heels clattering as they launched themselves down the steps.

'In here, you two,' called a Warden, pushing them onto the crowded platform.

Peter led her between canoodling lovers and family groups. At last, they found a space where they stood, shoulder to shoulder, leaning against the wall. The bangs continued intermittently. 'Don't be scared,' whispered Peter. 'We're quite safe down here.'

Despite Peter's reassurances, Alice felt nervous. Harrogate had remained fairly unscathed throughout the bombing. In fact, apart from the disappearance of luxury items and the scarcity of a number of essentials, her life had barely been affected.

The outbreak of war had not caused separation from Vincenzo, Enzo's death had. She was convinced that had their son not been killed, she would still have been living happily in Tuscany with her husband. Enzo's death had driven a wedge between her and Vincenzo, bringing an end to their marriage. She would never understand how he could accept Enzo's death with such forbearance. Why hadn't he ranted and raved and shown his emotions as the Latin races were supposed to. She blamed her husband for her own negative feelings. When they'd married she had adored him, his charm and good looks had completely swept her off her feet; throughout the births and deaths of their babies, she had clung to him for support, yet when the worst tragedy of all had occurred, he seemed to have forsaken her.

As she sheltered with Peter in the dingy tube station, these emotive memories infiltrated her mind and swam around aimlessly before floating away. She felt touched by them, yet remote from them. Reading about them in a book would have made her cry, yet the impression they made would have been banished in the flicker of an eyelid. Thus it was now. This moment is real, she told herself, everything else is meaningless. She listened to the hubbub of voices, the crying of children, the coughs and the sneezes; she blinked at the cigarette smoke swirling about her. Adjacent to them, a couple tucked into cod and chips out of newspaper. She passed her tongue across her lips, almost tasting the salt-and-vinegar flavour.

'Are you all right?' asked Peter.

Startled out of introspection, she gasped, 'Yes thank you.'

Peter's breath was warm on her cheek, his fingers firm in hers. What could be more real than this? It felt perfectly natural when he draped an arm round her shoulders. A pleasurable tremor ran down her spine.

'Are you feeling cold?' he asked, turning to look into her eyes.

'No!' The single word escaped almost soundlessly through her semi-parted lips, a negative response that had nothing to do with the temperature. She knew what would follow, but could do nothing to divert it.

His arms tightened around her, his lips closed over her mouth. She could taste the Players he'd just stubbed out. The sleeve of his uniform was rough against her neck; it smelt coarse and earthy. The abruptness of the embrace sent her spinning back to when she was a young girl, to when she'd experienced her very first kiss. A clumsy advance by one of the pupils from the adjacent boys' school, it had been nothing more than a gesture of defiance against the black-habited sisters. Now, as then, guilt made the kiss all the more exciting.

Someone pushed past them, making her stumble. Her head bumped against the tiled wall, her straw hat became dislodged. Instinctively, she put up a hand to catch it, bringing an abrupt end to the kiss.

'I'm sorry, I shouldn't have done that,' gasped Peter.

She tried to look disapproving, but failed. The All Clear sounded, saving her from further embarrassment. Everyone turned towards the exit, those on the floor scrambling to their feet, parents rounding up their offspring and their belongings.

'It's almost time for my train,' said Peter as they reached street level. 'Can I see you again?'

'I sometimes come down to stay with Johnnie and Betsy, I expect we'll meet up there.'

'I do hope so.' Their encounter seemed about to end formally when, all at once, he pushed her into a shop doorway and hugged her so tightly that she felt as if her ribs would snap. Again, his mouth sought hers and she found herself responding. He released her as suddenly as he had embraced her and strode away without word. Alice leant against the shuttered shop doorway. The fierceness of his embrace and the turmoil of her own emotions leaving her breathless.

Twelve

At first, Robert was pleased that his daughter was getting out and about again. 'I'm glad to see you enjoying yourself, darling,' he told her. You're still young, you need to have fun.'

'She certainly knows how to have fun,' muttered Thelma. Addressing Alice, she went on, 'I only hope you'll stay home during the school holidays this time and keep an eye on that son of yours.'

Robert jumped to his grandson's defence. 'Joe's no trouble.'

'And Ronald and Leslie are, I suppose!' retorted Thelma, always ready to take offence. She wouldn't let the matter rest. 'It's not easy having three boys run amok for six weeks. You *must* be here, Alice.'

'Don't worry, I will be.'

But Alice didn't keep her word, and even during the holidays, she continued her visits to Johnnie and Betsy.

'You don't mind keeping an eye on Joe do you, Daddy?' she'd say, knowing full well that her adoring father found it difficult to say 'no' to her. She felt guilty, but managed to appease her conscience by telling herself that Joe was happy in his grandfather's company. As for Thelma -- she wrinkled her nose impishly -- hadn't she always taken a perverse delight in antagonising her sister-in-law?

Alice had always been close to her father. At the age of 11, tears and tantrums had coerced Robert into keeping his daughter with him instead of sending her to boarding school with her older brother. This had resulted in her education being somewhat fragmented due to the many moves Robert had been required to make during his career with the Foreign Office. She had attended school in a number of capital cities, acquiring a motley collection of skills, which included a smattering of knowledge on most subjects and a useful command of a number of foreign languages. When her mother died suddenly, these skills were to stand her in good stead.

Eventually, Robert spoke to her about her trips to London. 'It's getting dangerous, darling, the Jerries will step up their bombing again. I wish you'd stay at home. Johnnie and Betsy are welcome to spend a weekend up here in Harrogate with us whenever they like.'

'Don't be silly, Daddy, I'm perfectly safe. Johnnie's got an Anderson shelter in the garden. He won't take any chances.'

Robert raised an ironic eyebrow. 'Not take chances, Johnnie! That's not what I've heard. Why the old codger has always thumbed his nose at danger!'

Her father describing Johnnie as an old codger so amused Alice that her indignation immediately vanished. Robert was twenty years older than Johnnie. She ran over and gave him an affectionate hug. 'Stop fussing, you silly old ex-Ambassador, I'll be all right.'

So Alice's trips to London continued. She met many young servicemen, received numerous offers but she kept all admirers at bay. The only man who interested her was Peter Winstanley. The afternoon they'd spent together was etched on her memory. Had it meant as much to him as it had to her? She'd glimpsed him a couple of time since then but only when their paths had briefly crossed: she on her way in to see Betsy and Johnnie, he on his way back to camp. She almost gave up hope of meeting him again until, one evening, he walked in on a dinner party at the Kennards.

'Peter, what a pleasant surprise!' Jumping to her feet, Betsy rushed over, planted a kiss on his cheek and called out, 'Johnnie, pull up another chair.'

'Don't let me disturb you, I only popped in to say *hello*,' protested the new arrival.

'Join us for a bite to eat,' insisted Betsy.

He shook his head. 'I won't hear of it. I mustn't take up your rations.'

'There's plenty, please sit down.'

'I'll have some coffee with you,' he replied, pointedly dragging his chair nearer to Alice's.

In the eyes of the guests Peter was a hero. They bombarded him with questions, and he answered them in his disarming way, making the men laugh and the ladies blush.

Alice had more cause to blush than the others. Whilst talking, he slipped his hand under the table and touched her thigh. She should have been outraged; instead she felt thrilled. If Vincenzo had taken such a liberty during the early days of their courtship, she would have slapped his face. She cast a glance at Peter and behind the surface bonhomie saw stress.

'Let's have some music!' Betsy's drawl broke into her reflections.

Johnnie got up and put a record on the gramophone. 'Who likes Cole Porter?'

Responding to the lyrics, Alice experienced a rush of exhilaration. This is wartime, she thought. *Anything goes!*

Betsy busied herself serving coffee; the attention of the guests was diverted. Peter took advantage of the moment of privacy and shifted his weight to draw nearer to the table. Alice felt his shin brush hers. He leant closer and whispered, 'Are you staying here tonight?'

She shook her head.

'Where then?'

She named her hotel.

'I'll meet you there in an hour.'

It was neither a question nor an order. It was as if their secret tryst were a foregone conclusion. She gave an imperceptible nod and, turning to the man next to her, engaged him in conversation. Closing her hand over Peter's, she dug her nails into the back of his hand. Anything to stop the utter delight of his covert caresses which were threatening to destroy her composure and shame her.

He took the hint and, in his turn, began flirting with a young wren opposite him. Alice's emotions were put to the test. Against common sense and prudence, she knew she was poised on a slippery slope. Yet she knew also that she couldn't resist.

'The Allies are doing so well in France and Belgium, it won't be long before we can sleep safely in our beds again,' her table companion said.

'Yes, it's good news,' replied Alice, her head half-turned towards Peter. Out of the corner of her eye she could see the girl opposite responding to his flattery. She felt a stab of jealousy.

'Is your husband an army man?'

'Er, sorry, what did you say?'

'Is your husband in the army, Mrs Thomas?'

'Oh, yes.' What was wrong with a half-truth? Vincenzo had served as a Cavalry Officer in the Italian Army during the 1914-18 Conflict.

She thought the evening would never end. Peter left first. As soon as it was decently possible, she took her leave, politely declining Betsy's offer of a bed for the night.

'It's very kind of you but I've booked into a hotel not far from here,' she insisted. 'I mustn't take up room in your house. You have other guests to consider.'

This was true. Betsy accepted her refusal graciously, but added, 'It's early yet, honey, can't you stay a little longer.'

Alice smiled and shook her head. 'I've got a bit of a headache. I'd like an early night, you don't mind do you?' She gave Betsy a hug and a peck on the cheek, and made her escape.

It was only when she got out into the street that the image of Vincenzo rose in her mind. Dark and good-looking, he'd bowled her over when they'd met. Did he miss her? Had he found himself another woman? Her husband enjoyed female company and despite his outwardly calm composure, she knew he was a passionate man. Such troubling thoughts provoked guilt. *What am I doing?* she asked herself. Coming to a halt, she turned around and began retracing her steps, but Peter's face rose to obscure Vincenzo's. With a tortured cry, she turned again and ran the short distance to the hotel.

Peter was waiting for her in the foyer. She rushed straight into his arms. Smiling, he disentangled himself. 'You'd better collect your key from Reception.'

They took the lift to the first floor and, on reaching her room, Peter unlocked the door and pushed her back onto the bed. He stepped away and frowned. 'This *is* what you want, isn't it, Alice? If you're not sure, not ready, I'll leave.' She found herself trembling. Was it what she wanted? 'I mean it, darling, you only have to say.'

She closed her eyes for a fraction of a second, then murmured, 'Stay!'

His gaze seemed to sear into her soul. 'Time's running out,' he whispered as he pressed his lips to hers and pushed her gently onto her back. She had to respond, couldn't help herself. No time for shyness, for modesty, for convent-cloaked reminders of hell's damnation. The rights or wrongs of what she was doing would have to be faced later.

She slept in his arms, stirring in the early hours when he made love to her again. Waking several hours later, she found he had gone. A rose lay on the pillow beside her. She smiled and held it to her lips. How had he come by it so early in the morning, before the florists were open? Ah yes, Betsy's rose bush would have one less bloom today than yesterday! She sniffed its scent -- strong and sweet -- careful of its thorns. Her conscience would need no pricking, it demanded atonement without reminder.

From then on, she saw Peter as regularly as his terms of duty would allow, living from one visit to the next. The sight of his tall figure in the air force blue uniform coming towards her made her heart leap, driving away lingering misgivings. The cycle was always the same: anticipation, ecstasy, remorse. She would return home with her features set in an implacable expression, a defence against Thelma's poorly masked disapproval. But it was the two people who loved her the most who bore the brunt of her penance. In the case of her father, it took the form of bad-temper, with her son, neglect.

Back at school, Joe continued to do well during the Spring Term. Excelling in maths, English, foreign languages and the sciences, he also had the draughtsman's ability to produce complex drawings, accurate in every detail. Yet his mother seemed unimpressed by his achievements.

Joe racked his brains for a way to endear himself to her. He'd already tried taking an interest in sport, but physical activities were not his forte. He was destined to be an academic and no amount of effort would endow him with good coordination or an eye for the ball. Laughed off the football pitch and carried off the rugby field, he gave up on contact sports, sticking instead to playing a passable game of tennis and making a fair effort at cricket.

Music, however, was something he had enjoyed since early childhood. He thought wistfully of the old wind-up gramophone his grandfather had left behind for him when he'd retired from the diplomatic service. It was probably still in the tree-house unless Babbo had thought to bring it into the house.

Then he remembered how his mother used to play the violin. Since their arrival in England, she had not taken the instrument out of its case. Surely, it would please her if he were to take up a musical instrument; it might even encourage her to take it up again herself. The next day, he went to the music master and asked whether he could learn the violin.

'Good idea, Thomas,' replied the master. 'Come back this afternoon at four-thirty, I'll sort out an instrument for you.'

Joe mastered the reading of music with comparative ease and soon learned to produce an acceptable melody. This success encouraged him to keep practising. He kept the lessons a secret from the family. At the end of the Spring Term, the music master advised him that if he were to carry on he would need to ask his mother to buy him a violin. 'I'm sorry, Thomas,' he explained. 'But the instrument you're using might be needed by a new pupil.'

Joe was crestfallen. 'Can't I take it home for the holidays?' he begged. 'I'll bring it back safely next term. I'm sure my mother will let me borrow hers when she's heard me play.'

'So your mother plays too?'

Joe blushed. 'She used to.'

The music master looked thoughtful, clearly keen to encourage a promising pupil but hesitant about bending the rules. 'I suppose that's where you get your musical talent from,' he said at length. 'Very well, I'll make an exception and let you take the instrument home. I think your mother may be in for a surprise.'

Joe returned to Harrogate for Easter armed with the violin case. This gave rise to a great deal of taunting from his cousins. At sixteen, Ronald had reached the age where, if he wasn't on the sports field giving vent to his energy in physical activity, his mind was focused on the latest piece of *skirt* he fancied, usually a pupil from the nearby girls' school, or one of the barmaids in the village pub. Leslie was equally obsessed with the opposite sex except that, in his case, the lusting and sniggering were done on the quiet in the company of his adolescent pals. Joe had no such interest in the female sex, refusing to join in these after-hours exchanges about conquests his peers claimed to have made, feeling disgusted at talk of masturbation.

Arthur met the boys at the station and drove them home in his Wolseley. Joe rushed into the house, carrying the violin.

'Where's Mum?' he asked his Aunt Thelma after giving her the mandatory peck on the cheek.

'She's not here,' replied his aunt. 'She'll be back tomorrow.'

He didn't have a chance to ask where she was because his cousins rushed in and their mother turned her attention to them. After dinner that evening, he questioned his grandfather.

'Where has Mum gone?'

'London, son,' replied Robert.

Joe looked alarmed. 'Isn't it dangerous down there, Grandpa?'

'She'll be all right, your mother is visiting her friends in Chiswick. It's good she's getting out and about again, don't you agree?'

Joe wasn't so sure. Grown-ups did strange things. Why would Mum risk going to London? Surely it was safer to stay in Harrogate. He experienced an irrepressible surge of anger, and shouted, 'No, I don't, Grandpa.'

He pushed past the old man to run upstairs to his room, bitterness crowding his mind. Why couldn't Mum have been here to greet him? What was wrong with him? Why didn't she love him? He dredged his memory for an answer. He'd always been obedient, not like his brother who had taken pleasure in defying authority. An image sprang to mind: Enzo being ticked off by their father, Mum hurrying to his defence, the deserved ticking off evolving into to a row between their parents. It was all too clear now. Enzo had enjoyed stirring the waters. He tried to thrust the unwelcome vision from his head. It sullied his brother's memory.

After two days Alice came home. One glance at her face and Joe lost his resentment. She looked radiant. He loved her so much. It would be wonderful once the War was over and the three of them could be together again. He thought about his father a lot, avidly reading the newspapers, following news of the German retreat through Lazio. He worried when he read that Hitler's army had systematically destroyed Tuscan farmlands and vineyards en route to the North. He didn't discuss this news with his mother for fear of upsetting her.

Her eyes lit up when he told her about the violin lessons. 'Darling, Beppe, you must play for me after dinner tonight.'

Her enthusiasm brought a broad smile to his face. He ran upstairs to his room to practise. Had he at last hit on something that would please his mother? That evening, Alice failed to appear at the dinner table.

'Where's Mum?' he asked his grandfather.

'Your mother's gone out *again*,' snapped his Aunt Thelma before Robert had time to reply.

'But she...' Joe didn't finish the sentence because his Uncle Arthur got annoyed with Leslie, who was noisily slurping his soup.

Thelma immediately jumped to her son's defence, ranting at her husband to leave the boy alone. There followed a slanging match between his aunt and uncle about how children should behave at the table. Throughout this angry discourse, Leslie's brother, Ronald adopted his best table manners in order to win his father's approval, nodding his head in agreement every time Arthur managed to get a word in edgewise. Robert McPherson-Corke kept a tactful silence, and Joe concentrated on trying not to slurp his own soup.

Alice was missing for most of the Easter vacation. Whenever Joe did manage to pigeonhole her and mention the violin, she always found an excuse. 'Sorry, Joe, must dash, got to get this letter in the post,' or 'I must just make a phone call.' When he was bold enough to ask her who she was phoning, her reply was evasive. 'Friends, darling, just friends.'

He returned to school without having played his violin for her and, in consequence, much to his music master's disappointment, he gave up the lessons.

On her next visit to Chiswick, Alice was surprised when Betsy took her aside for a girly chat.

With a smile of complicity, her friend wagged a finger in her face and said, 'You crafty pair, no one's guessed you know, except me that is. How long has it been going on?'

'What do you mean?' Alice blushed despite her efforts to appear unconcerned.

'You and Peter of course. Stop playing the innocent, sugar, you can't fool your old friend.'

Alice looked sheepish. 'I don't know how you found out, Betsy, we've been so careful. Please keep it to yourself.'

'My lips are sealed.' Taking Alice's hand, Betsy exclaimed. 'Is it serious, do tell?' Her friend's directness floored Alice. 'Well, is it?'

Alice bit her lip. She had never thought about the depth of their relationship. Peter was not a serious person. He joked a lot, a little too much sometimes. She could never pin him down and she wondered whether she would ever want to.

She shrugged her shoulders. 'Of course not.'

Betsy seemed relieved. 'That's just as well,' she said. 'Despite his charm, Peter's not that reliable. Johnnie says he's got a death wish, but I wouldn't go as far as that.'

'A death wish?' Alice was horrified.

'The guy takes chances. He's highly decorated; he's gotten a lot of ops under his belt.' Betsy wrinkled her brow with concern. 'Don't get too fond of him, honey. Johnnie says he'll be lucky if he reaches his thirtieth birthday.'

This last remark took Alice's breath away. So Peter was still in his twenties! She'd guessed he was younger than she was, but not by ten years.

She went home, pondering on this information, feeling rather foolish. How could she have allowed herself to fall for a mere boy? Betsy's revelation nagged at her for days until, finally, she came to a decision. She would tell Peter she couldn't see him any more. A shiver coursed through her as his image rose in her mind. It was going to be so hard. She balled her fists, digging the nails into her palms. How had she allowed things to go this far? The affair must end: for Peter's sake, for Vincenzo's sake, for Joe's sake.

But how would Peter react? Would he try and win her back? Her eyes filled with tears. She wouldn't be able to resist if he protested. And if he didn't protest? Why, that would be even worse. She thrust a knuckle into her mouth to stem the tears. Thelma mustn't see that she was upset.

She paced the floor racked with indecision until an idea struck her. Why tell him face-to-face? She would write him a letter. It was cowardly but, to soften the rejection, she would give him a parting gift. Yes, that was it: a parting gift. And she knew just the thing. She would send him a book, a very special first edition, one she held dear. That way, there would always be a link between them.

Coming to a decision made her feel strong, but she needed to bolster this strength, so she rang Betsy and arranged to see her the following weekend when she knew Peter would be on duty. She wanted Betsy to know that she, not Peter, was the one to end the affair. She would tell her about the letter she planned to write.

On Saturday, as she was leaving, her father called her back. He looked concerned. 'Don't go, Alice, it's dangerous. There are rumours about a deadly secret weapon Hitler's thought up. He might decide to try it out on London.'

Alice put down her overnight bag and turned to face him. 'I'll be all right, Daddy. Johnnie's place hasn't suffered more than a broken window or two.' She gave him a hug, fondly kissing his wrinkled cheek. 'You worry too much. Besides, I promise this will be my last trip for a while.'

Robert's expression brightened. 'I'm glad to hear it.'

'And Daddy, when you phone Joe at school this weekend, give him my special love. I know I've neglected him lately.'

'Of course I will, my dear.'

She checked her watch. 'I must hurry, my train leaves in 20 minutes.' Picking up her bag again, she went out, stopping briefly to give her father a final wave before getting into the waiting taxi.

Betsy greeted Alice with an affectionate hug, saying in her warm Southern accent, 'Come in, honey. Johnnie's out and I've gotten some of the WVS gals here. The Home Guard have taken over the Boy Scouts' hall so we have to meet here.'

Alice followed her friend into the sitting room, nodding at the occupants. Like a piano chord, there was a succession of chinks as Betsy's Worcestershire teacups were restored to their saucers. All eyes turned in her direction. She apologised profusely. 'I'm so terribly sorry to disturb you. Please don't let me hold up your meeting.'

The stern-looking, middle-aged matrons quickly made it clear that they had no intention of letting her arrival hold up their meeting. Returning to their notebooks, they took up where they had left off, sticking rigidly to their agenda.

Even Betsy's offer of more tea and carrot cake failed to distract them from the matter in hand. The green-uniformed ladies were polite but businesslike.

'Thank you dear, no more tea for me.'

'Such nice cake, Betsy, you must let me have the recipe.'

The clearing of a throat. 'Let's get on, ladies, time's getting short.'

Alice sipped her tea and listened, with amusement, to the suggestions put forward. With planning like this, she thought, these women could win the War all on their own.

After they'd departed, Alice said, 'I hope you don't mind me descending on you without warning, Betsy.'

The American woman patted her arm with scarlet-tipped fingers and drawled, 'Of course not.' Her brown eyes lit up with excitement. 'As a matter of fact, I was going to call you after the meeting.'

Alice raised an eyebrow. 'Were you?'

Betsy went on. 'Honey, have I got a surprise for you! I couldn't wait for the meeting to finish. Guess what?' She paused dramatically. 'Peter's here.'

Alice gave a jolt. This *was* a surprise, a surprise she wasn't prepared for. Her plan of action had gone wrong. She almost panicked. Would she have the courage to break it off with Peter face-to-face?

But Betsy's next words drove these troubled thoughts from her head. 'Don't be alarmed, babe...he's been wounded.'

A cold shiver shot down Alice's spine. 'Wounded? How bad is he?' she gulped.

'Not too serious, little more than a scratch really, a superficial ankle wound. The medic says he'll make a full recovery, just needs rest ... ' Betsy hesitated. ' ... and affection, and since the bombing seems to have eased off a bit, we invited him here to recuperate.'

Fleetingly, Alice remembered her father's warning about Hitler's latest invention. Perhaps Betsy hadn't heard about it. No, it was more likely she chose to ignore it.

'Where is he?'

The American drawl penetrated her emotions. 'It could have been so much worse. He managed to fly the plane back across the Channel, crash landed in Kent.'

'A crash landing? My God!" Alice was half way upstairs by now. 'Which room?'

'Front bedroom but...'

The rest of Betsy's words were lost to her. She needed to see him for herself, to know he was all right. She burst into the room, stopping abruptly just inside the door. Peter was sitting in an armchair by the window, his plastered lower leg resting on a large Egyptian leather pouffe, the one Alice recognised as having been brought up from Johnnie's study.

'Darling!' She flew across the room and fell to her knees beside him, sobbing into his shoulder.

He eased her away, smiling wryly. 'My word, what a show of emotion!'

'You could have died,' she wept.

'Not me, sweetheart, didn't I say I was indestructible?'

'You must take more care, Peter.' She knew she was spouting nonsense. How could he take care when he was flying a Hurricane, playing cat and mouse with the enemy?

His smile spread into a broad grin. 'Do you think I deliberately court danger?'

'Stop making fun of me. I shall be more worried than ever from now on.'

'I've got nine lives, eight more to go.'

'Don't be facetious.' The tears began to stream down her cheeks.

'My injuries aren't serious, darling, just uncomfortable.'

Alice hugged him tightly.

'Ouch! Did Betsy mention the wound in my shoulder?'

She drew back in alarm. 'Not that as well?'

'It's nothing much, but I *am* a little tender.'

'Darling, I'm so sorry.'

He reached for her hand. 'Give me another hug but make it gentle.'

Laughing through her tears, she stroked his face until they drew close again and their lips met.

'I've missed you so much,' he whispered. 'Will you stay?'

'Yes of course, provided Betsy and Johnnie don't mind.'

'That's wonderful. And don't worry, in a few days I shall be back on my feet and we can go out and paint the town.'

Alice was touched when Betsy insisted on serving them dinner in Peter's room. With a wicked smile, the American said, 'You two need some time alone together.'

Alice found herself blushing. Betsy's openness shamed her. Her thoughts flew to Vincenzo. How shocked and hurt he would be by her infidelity! She stamped on her conscience. In wartime, you had to live for the moment.

'What's the matter?' asked Peter.

'Nothing, darling, nothing at all.' Remembering the book, she added impulsively. 'I had a present for you but I didn't bring it because I didn't know you were going to be here. I'll send it to you.'

'How exciting, what is it?'

'Wait and see.' She didn't add that it was originally intended as a parting gift.

The days sped past. Peter recovered sufficiently to go out, albeit on crutches, as far as The City Barge on Strand-on-the-Green. The be-whiskered landlord, a former WWI pilot, was friendly and encouraged Peter to regale his audience with tales of daring escapades, pre-war of course, since he was not at liberty to discuss his operational flights over France and Germany. The walls of the pub were plastered with posters. *Walls have Ears* and *Careless Talk costs Lives* reminded patrons to be on their guard. During the course of the evening, others joined them at the bar to listen to his anecdotes, which became more outrageous as time wore on. Alice longed to have Peter to herself, but knew that for an hour or two this wasn't to be.

They returned from the pub and let themselves into Johnnie's house. The Kennards were out. Normally, Johnnie would assist Peter upstairs; this evening the task fell to Alice. They had both drunk a few g&t's and, by the time they reached the top landing, they were laughing helplessly. Peter leant against the wall. 'Now I know what it's like to be an old man,' he grinned. 'And to prove that I'm not, I shall make love to you tonight despite my injuries.'

She bit her lip. 'But Peter, you can't, can you?'

'We'll see.' Taking her by the hand, he limped into the bedroom, stopping just inside the doorway to kiss her. They drew apart as the Air Raid Warning sounded.

'Damn!' exclaimed Peter. 'What rotten luck! There hasn't been an air raid for over a week. There's nothing for it, we'll have to go down to Johnnie's shelter.'

Alice frowned. 'Do we have to? It may not last long and it's taken us half an hour to get up here. The All Clear will have gone off by the time we get you downstairs again.'

'That's true, but *you* must take cover, darling. I'll stay here."

She clung to his hand. 'No Peter, you said yourself that you've got a charmed life. I'll stay, your luck will protect both of us.'

He gave her a gentle push. 'Go down to the shelter, sweetheart, please.'

'No!' she retorted. 'Not without you.'

He pushed her again and said harshly, 'I'm telling you to go.'

Alice stood her ground. 'I won't.'

'Please, darling,' he begged. She shook her head and backed to the bed. 'Very well,' he said, 'I'll come too.' She didn't move. He got angry. 'Come on, Alice, stop playing the fool.'

She ignored him. Sinking down onto the bed, she began to unbutton her blouse. Still angry, he reached for her hand but she countered by pulling him off-balance. He fell onto the bed beside her. She entwined her arms about his neck, drawing him down and kissing him.

As he responded, she fleetingly thought about the resolution she'd made only days earlier. It was no good. There was no way she could disentangle herself from this man. He was her reason for living. He had brought her back from the abyss when life without her adored first-born child had seemed unbearable. A searchlight lit up the room.

Alice gave a start and gasped, "We haven't closed the blackout.'

'Don't worry, the house is in darkness,' Peter reminded her.

He made no further mention of taking shelter, but set about undressing her before loosening his own clothing. She could smell the Brylcreem he used on his dark hair, the scent of her own Amami Setting Lotion. His touch was feather gentle on her body, his breath like a breeze on her cheek.

Against a star-speckled backcloth, Alice gave herself to her lover, losing all sense of time and space, immersing herself in a passion that blinded her to danger. Peter's face flickered in and out of view as searchlights performed pirouettes across the room. His words of endearment harmonized with the anti-aircraft's ratatat, the former soothing, the latter burgeoning towards momentum. A crash of symbols! She gasped.

'Don't worry, that was over Hanwell,' muttered Peter.

His closeness reassured her. Nothing could touch them. Their love would shield them. Fulfilled, they drew apart to lay side-by-side on top of the eiderdown. She felt pleasantly warm, her skin not yet chilled by the cool night air. The explosions had ceased, the ratatat had faded.

Another searchlight hit the window, bringing the contents of the room into relief. Normality had returned. Alice took in all the details: the painting of a highland stag hanging on the wall opposite; the silver candlesticks on the mantel shelf; the brass lamp in the shape of a female nude. *Very Betsy* she thought with an amused smile. Dear kind Betsy, so caring and protective, what a pity she had never been able to have children! She squeezed Peter's hand and he turned to face her. Her heart swelled with happiness. After the war, she would sort everything out. She would leave Vincenzo and come to live with Peter. Maybe it wasn't too late for her to bear him a child, a brother or sister for Joe. Joe would like Peter.

'I love you so much, my darling,' she whispered.

His lips parted in reply but a steady drone drowned out his words. She felt his body stiffen beside her. The drone cut out.

Thirteen

The Headmaster called Joe into his study. Placing a hand on his shoulder, he said gently, 'Your grandfather's here to see you, my boy. He has something to tell you.'

Joe's spirits soared. His father had been in touch! He knew he would. But when Robert McPherson-Corke entered the room, his face was ashen and the boy knew the news wasn't good.

The Headmaster walked round from behind his desk. 'I'll leave you alone. If you need me, I'll be along the hall.'

'What is it, Grandpa?' Joe burst out as soon as the Headmaster had shut the door. 'Have you heard from Babbo?'

Robert shook his head. Taking his grandson's hand in his, he said gravely, 'I'm afraid I've got terrible news for you, my boy -- the worst.'

With a jolt, Joe recalled his father's words when he'd broken the news that Enzo was dead -- *notizie terribili, figliolo, le peggiori* -- words in a different language, but identical in meaning to those of his grandfather.

'My papà! He's not ... ?'

'Not your papà, Joe, it's your mother. She went to visit her friends in Chiswick ... ' Robert's words began to trail away. 'There was an air raid, a direct hit, no survivors ... '

Joe squeezed his eyes shut in disbelief only to be confronted by the image of a visit to the pictures a week earlier when the Gaumont Pathé News had shown a film of the latest raid on London. His treacherous mind conjured up the cruellest of images: *Air Raid Wardens and police picking their way through rubble searching for survivors*. Was Mamma laying at the bottom of such a crater, buried beneath tons of debris, her limbs askew, her beautiful face smashed and bleeding? He recalled his lack of interest and impatience as the newscaster's voice had droned on; all he'd wanted was for the big film to start.

He clenched his fists and shouted his denial. 'She can't be dead, she can't be dead!'

Robert clasped him to his chest, muttering, 'She didn't suffer.'

'What was she doing in London?' sobbed Joe. 'You told her not to go there.'

'Visiting her friends, Group Commander Kennard and his wife. I expect you remember them.'

'I *do* remember,' muttered Joe bitterly. How well he remembered! Since meeting them he had seldom seen Mamma; now he would never see her again.

'Your headmaster said you can come home for a few days.'

Joe pulled away from his grandfather. 'Do I have to?'

Robert looked dismayed. 'I thought you'd want to. There's the funeral ... ' He paused, his eyes tormented. 'But I suppose you could come home just on the day of her funeral if that's what you want.'

Comprehension dawned: the old man needed him. 'No, Grandpa, I'll come home now,' he muttered, his face reddening as, for a fleeting second, he entered the complicated world of grown-ups where you were expected to read between the lines, to guess what the spoken words *really* meant. Yes, he would go home because although his mother had not cared for him, she had loved her father dearly. It had been a reciprocal affection, a father-child closeness for which he himself yearned. He would go home, less to grieve for his mother, more to give comfort to his grandfather.

On arriving in Harrogate, his Aunt Thelma fussed over him. She had never been so kind. He wanted to tell her to *shove off* but respect for his grandfather kept him polite. He took refuge by withdrawing into a kind of trance, responding when addressed but not really taking in what was said to him. The grown-ups were busy: arranging the funeral, writing to Alice's friends, contacting the solicitors.

'Will Babbo come to the funeral?' he asked his grandfather, knowing this was impossible.

Robert shook his head. 'We can't contact him during wartime, you know that.'

Joe was utterly dismayed when his aunt took on the task of disposing of Alice's clothes. He wanted to intervene, to tell her to take her hands off his mother's personal belongings. One day, he caught her tucking a couple of Alice's dresses into her own wardrobe.

Thelma must have sensed his presence at the open bedroom door. Turning to meet his gaze, she drew herself up straight, and muttered primly, 'There's no point in wasting perfectly good clothing.'

Throwing discretion to the winds, Joe was about to launch a verbal attack at her when his cousin, Leslie, pushed past him beseeching his mother to sort out a squabble he was having with Ronald. Grim-faced, Joe clenched his fists and stalked along the corridor to his own room, telling himself that Thelma couldn't wear the dresses anyway. She was much too fat.

Shortly after the funeral, came the reading of the Will. Joe gleaned from the mutterings going on around him that this was causing problems due to the unknown whereabouts of his father. It seemed that, on her return to England, Alice hadn't bothered to re-write her Will. This caused furore because, not only was the document drawn up in Italian, it left everything to Vincenzo, which meant that the money had to remain in trust until such time as Vincenzo got in touch. In the interim, Joe received nothing.

One evening, soon after he had gone to bed, he heard raised voices from the sitting room. He got up and crept to the top of the stairs to listen. Thelma's outraged tones were audible as she argued with his grandfather: 'But Robert, why should you pay for Joe's education? Let him leave Monksmede and go to the local school.'

His grandfather's reply was too quiet to hear.

Thelma again, dragging in her husband this time. 'I think it's insufferable, don't you, Arthur? It's *your* inheritance your father wants to fritter away. What about Ronald and Leslie, doesn't their future count for anything? I wouldn't mind, but Joe's a foreigner.'

His grandfather's next words reached him loud and clear. 'There's no argument, Thelma, until we can sort the finances out, I shall pay Joe's school fees. It doesn't matter to me what you think.'

'But it's not fair. What about his father, Vincenzo thingummy? Why should we suffer just because he wants nothing more to do with his son? Once the War's over, I've no doubt he'll claim Alice's legacy quickly enough.'

'It's his to claim,' retorted Robert.

'Ah, yes, but will he bother to reclaim his son?'

Joe's heart convulsed. It had never occurred to him that his father might not come for him after the War. Suppose Thelma was right! He'd been pinning his hopes on a reunion with Babbo. With Thelma's cruel words ringing in his ears he spun around and dashed back to his room, where he threw himself onto the bed and burst into tears. His mother had despised him, did his father despise him too?

A week later, he returned to school. Surprisingly, his cousin Ronald made a point of speaking to him in a kindly manner. Leslie, however, continued to jeer at him. Despite the fact that he had all but lost his accent, his youngest cousin made relentless fun of him, calling him *ice cream Joe*. He reminded himself of his grandfather's words of consolation: 'Only another year, Joe, and you'll be in the Upper Sixth, well away from those immature boys and their silly teasing.'

This was true, but the prospect of transferral to a dormitory in another part of the building made him feel uneasy. At fourteen, he would be living with sixteen and seventeen-year-olds, boys who were nearly men. He wasn't ready for that. Academically he was top of his class but, emotionally, he was immature.

He passed his end-of-year exams with flying colours, excelling in English literature and languages. In Latin he achieved the highest marks ever recorded at the school. His grandfather was justly proud of him. His uncle congratulated him, but his aunt made no comment.

School broke up for the summer vacation. Joe prowled about the house and the garden not knowing what to do with himself. Sometimes he went on lonely walks or caught the bus into York simply to get away from the over-bearing presence of his Aunt Thelma and the constant bickering between his cousins.

At first, he sought his grandfather's company but Robert had aged since the death of his daughter. He was no longer the upright, energetic man he had been, and when Joe suggested going for a stroll together, he invariably declined, saying he preferred to stay indoors and do the crossword.

Most of the time, the three boys were left to their own devices. Joe missed his mother. Despite her neglect of him during his formative years, he had known that she was there. Her footsteps had echoed on the staircase, her perfume had lingered in the air, her voice in comparison to Thelma's had been soft and persuasive. Why hadn't she loved him when he had loved her so much?

One afternoon, when his aunt was out, he sneaked into her old bedroom only to find the place unrecognisable. All Alice's knick-knacks had been cleared away, her tasteful pale blue striped wallpaper stripped off and the walls re-papered with rose-patterned paper. A bright pink satin eiderdown covered the bed with velvet cushions piled at the headboard. Not a single thing of his mother's remained. He felt nauseous with rage. Disposing of Alice's clothes had been bad enough, transforming her bedroom was sacrilege. Feeling betrayed, he went in search of his grandfather.

'Whatever's the matter, Joe?' asked his grandfather, alarmed by the sight of the boy's chalk-white face.

'What have you done with Mamma's things?' he burst out angrily.

Robert had only just woken up from an after lunch nap. He blinked and said, 'Your Aunt Thelma had the room redecorated and changed into a guest room.'

This explanation didn't satisfy Joe. 'What did she do with Mamma's ornaments and pictures?' he asked.

The old man smiled and said reassuringly, 'Don't worry, my boy, they've been safely stored in the attic. You can go up there and take a look if you want to, but be sure to leave everything the way you found it if you don't want to make your Aunt Thelma angry.'

'Thanks Grandpa,' cried Joe, racing away.

The attic ran the entire width of the house. The floorboards creaked as he crept across them but he was pleased to find that the beams were high enough for him to stand upright. The first thing he found was Alice's violin. He opened the case and stroked it lovingly, the tears welling in his eyes. Maybe one day he would be able to bring himself to play it.

He gave a sniff, drew his cuff across his face and turned his attention to the contents of her trunk. It was covered in dust and cobwebs. Inside, there were gifts from his father, snapshots of himself and his brother and a silver-framed studio portrait of his maternal grandmother who had died long before he was born. There were also mementoes from Alice's travels abroad: a silk shawl from Spain, a pair of Dutch clogs, an embroidered Tirolian bodice. What was this? He opened up a small article carefully wrapped in tissue paper. A baby's pink bonnet! Isabella's! He could just about remember his little sister who'd died of meningitis when he was four. After her death, all the baby paraphernalia had vanished. Yet Mamma had kept this small memento. He felt touched, wondering what it would have been like to have had a little sister. He rewrapped it and placed it back in the trunk, thankful that his grandfather had managed to rescue these special items from Thelma's grasping hands.

Delving deeper into the trunk, he found some dance band records, Harry James, Victor Silvester, a sheaf of sheet music, a large photograph of Isadora Duncan, a yellowing copy of *The Times* reporting the sinking of the *Titanic* and, at the very bottom, a pile of books. This surprised him because although he had often seen his mother flipping through fashion magazines, he had never seen her reading a novel.

Most of the books were romances, either in English or in Italian. They didn't interest him. He accidentally dropped one and it fell open. Out of curiosity, he started reading. His eyes widened. This was no ordinary romantic novel. He flipped back to the cover. It said: *Romance in Ravenna* by Delia Sargent. That seemed an innocent title. It was just a silly romance. He was about to put it back in the trunk, when the book jacket slipped off and he saw to his amazement that the real title of the novel was *Lady Chatterley's Lover*. He nearly dropped the book again. He'd heard of D.H. Lawrence. At school, the English professor had urged his pupils to study Lawrence's First World War poetry: *Look! We Have Come Through*, presumably to encourage patriotism during the present conflict. However, he hadn't mentioned Lawrence's novels.

Joe held the book in his hands. How had such a novel come into his mother's possession? A distant memory surfaced:

He's crouching on the stairs, peering through the banister rails as his parents entertain dinner guests from America. They're laughing and drinking, trying to outdo one another with risqué anecdotes. Someone mentions the name of a book. The men chuckle, the women titter. His mother gives a giggle: 'The latest Lawrence? I believe it's scandalous. Hasn't it been banned here and in the States?' The diners fall silent, then one of the guest says, 'Banned but not unobtainable, my dear Alice, a few copies were printed privately a year or so ago. Guess who managed to get hold of one?'

Joe couldn't remember what happened next. Probably Grazia Elena had chased him back to bed.

It was beginning to get dark. Joe replaced his mother's belongings in the trunk and fastened shut the lid. Shoving the copy of *Lady Chatterley's Lover* inside his shirt, he left the attic, blushing to the roots of his hair when he came face-to-face with his Aunt Thelma coming into the house. She was loaded with shopping bags.

'Give me a hand, Joe,' she said.

Praying that the book wouldn't slip down from inside his shirt, he helped her carry the bags into the kitchen.

She looked at him sternly. 'You're covered in cobwebs, have you been upstairs in the attic?'

He nodded awkwardly and mumbled, 'Grandpa gave his permission.'

Thelma's nose twitched. 'I hope you left it tidy.'

'Of course I did, Aunt Thelma,' he replied and hurried away before she could question him further.

He read the book under the bedcovers at night. It aroused a mixture of emotions. If he had discovered it amongst his father's belongings, he would have given an amused chuckle, but to think that his adorable, genteel mother could have chosen to read such eroticism filled him with horror. He recalled her trips down to London, the spring in her step, the brightness in her eyes when she returned home, her inability to shrug off the big city ambience. Finding the book made him see his mother in a different light. He felt guilty for having discovered it, ashamed on her behalf, but at the same time, excited by his discovery. He couldn't let go of the book. To begin with, he had intended to flip through it and return it to the trunk, but weeks went by, and it remained hidden in his room.

During the holidays, he'd seen little of his cousins. They liked to go out, spending money indiscriminately. He frequently heard them begging their indulgent mother for extra pocket money. He didn't know how much pocket money they got and he didn't care, being only too grateful for the small monthly allowance his grandfather gave him. It wasn't much but he rarely spent all of it.

The last week in August brought a heat wave and he spent time in the garden resting in a hammock slung between two trees. He became more daring and brazenly re-read the book within its false cover. One afternoon, while he was reading, Ronald sidled up to him.

'I say, Joe, I suppose you couldn't lend me half a crown?'

Feeling annoyed, Joe said, 'Why don't you go and ask your mother?'

Ronald started to cajole and, to get rid of him, he put his hand in his pocket and drew out a coin. 'I've only got a florin; here, take it?'

'Thanks.' Ronald snatched the money and started to amble away. Then he turned back. 'I say, what's that book you're so engrossed in?'

'Eh, nothing,' replied Joe.

'Let's see.'

Joe tried to steer his cousin's interest away from the book. 'It's a silly novel I picked up.'

'It can't be *that* silly, you were awfully wrapped up in it.'

'It's nothing, really. If you don't mind ... '

'Stop being so secretive,' insisted Ronald. 'Let me see what it's called.'

Joe held the book up with its fake title.

'For God's sake, what a fairy! Fancy reading that rubbish. You should try *Fanny by Gaslight*. Where have you got up to? Are you sure you can manage the long words?' taunted Ronald.

Infuriated, Joe swung off the hammock and launched himself at his cousin. Taken by surprise, Ronald crashed to the ground and the two boys wrestled in the grass, rolling over and over, beating at one another with clenched fists.

'Hey, what's going on?' Leslie appeared on the scene. 'Can anyone join in?'

Ronald managed to extricate himself long enough to point at the abandoned book and shout, 'The book, Les, get the book.'

Leslie picked it up and ran into the house. With a mighty thrust, Ronald pushed Joe off and, springing to his feet, chased after his brother. Joe let out a howl of rage. He was done for. The consequences of its discovery rose ominously. If his aunt and uncle found out about the book he would never hear the last of it; his mother's name would be irreversibly tarnished. And Grandpa! The discovery would destroy him.

It didn't matter what any of them thought of him for reading banned material; what did matter was the fresh inscription inside the book, written in his mother's handwriting. It said: *To Peter, my dearest love, yours forever, Alice – June '44.*

Joe raced into the house in pursuit of his cousins, bumping into his grandfather in the doorway.

'Hey, what's the hurry, Joe?' exclaimed Robert, side-stepping just in time.

'Sorry, Grandpa,' he called back as he headed for the stairs. Guessing that his cousins had gone up to Ronald's bedroom, he swung round the newel post at the top and skidded along the corridor to launch himself at the door. It was locked. Angrily, he hammered on the door panel, but all he got in return were jeers. He tried to calm himself. If he behaved as though it really didn't matter, maybe his cousins would lose interest.

'Suit yourselves,' he called out. 'Only, you'll be the ones in trouble if your father gets to see that book.'

More jeers, more snorts of laughter. Joe shuffled away knowing there was nothing he could do. With any luck, his stupid cousins wouldn't notice the inscription inside the fly leaf or, if they did, they wouldn't recognise its significance. He left the house and went for a walk.

For several days nothing happened. Once or twice he was tempted to demand his book back, but common sense told him that the less fuss he made, the better. Ronald would eventually tire of the whole thing and return it to him.

It was Aunt Thelma who found it. One morning, she set about the task of getting her sons' things ready for their return to school. Joe had always sorted out his own kit but Ronald and Leslie were lazy and relied heavily on their mother to make sure that everything was ship-shape. It transpired that Ronald had hidden it in with his school books. The first Joe heard of it was when she came storming downstairs to her husband, the offending volume in her hand, her face contorted with indignation.

'Arthur,' she screeched. 'Look at this piece of filth I've found amongst your son's belongings!'

'What's that, my dear,' came her husband's unconcerned response.

'Arthur!' she screeched again. 'For goodness sake put that newspaper down and look at this.'

The culprits heard her stomping feet and looked at one another nervously.

'Come on, Les, let's scoot!' muttered Ronald and the two brothers headed for the door.

'Wait a minute!' called out Joe. 'Hadn't we better stay and face the music?'

'It's your bloody book, you can carry the can,' came Ronald's retort.

'It was in with your school things.'

'I shall swear *you* put it there.'

Joe stayed where he was. For him, taking the blame for reading such a *piece of filth*, was secondary to the fear that Aunt Thelma would notice the hand written inscription inside the front cover. He crept to the sitting room door and listened.

'It's just a book,' said Arthur, trying to pacify his wife.

'It's disgusting, just take a look at it. There, *that* page!' Through the crack in the door, Joe saw Thelma hand the book over, her finger jabbed at the offending page.

'Um, yes, I see.' His uncle raised a quizzical eyebrow. 'Well, my dear, boys will be boys.'

'What's going on, Joe?' Robert McPherson-Corke appeared at the youngster's shoulder.

On hearing mention of her nephew's name, Thelma jerked round and snapped at him. 'I suppose you've read it too, Joe.'

'I don't know what you're talking about, Aunt Thelma,' he replied, his cheeks burning as Robert nudged him into the room.

Arthur showed his father the book. 'Young lads are bound to get their hands on such rubbish. It's all part of growing up, don't you agree, Dad?'

Robert nodded as he flipped through the pages. 'I can't see much harm in it,' he agreed adding, to appease his daughter-in-law, 'But I'll take charge of the book and perhaps you could have strong words with the boys, Arthur.' His eyes twinkled. 'You can start with Joe.'

Joe intervened. 'Please Grandpa, can I...' he stopped, his courage failing him.

'Can you what, Joe?'

'Can I take the book and put it away somewhere safe? I promise I won't read it.'

Thelma's eyes widened at his audacity. Sucking in her breath, she gave a hiss which was reminiscent of a punctured balloon, and shrieked, 'Can you do what?'

Joe realised his mistake at once. By placing importance on the book he had drawn his grandfather's attention to it. Robert frowned sternly. 'Certainly not,' he snapped.

Without another word the old man left Joe to face his uncle's reprimand, which took the form of a half-hearted telling-off, interspersed by histrionic outbursts of exasperation from his aunt.

At last the boy escaped and ran upstairs to his room, throwing himself onto the bed, and bursting into tears of impotent anger.

Later that day, Joe guessed by his grandfather's expression that he had read the inscription. The old man said nothing, but he gave his grandson a penetrating stare over the dinner table. Joe wriggled uncomfortably, wishing the floor would open up and swallow him. The only consolation he could find was that his aunt, uncle and cousins had failed to notice the inscription.

The next day, the three boys returned to school. Robert saw them off, standing on the doorstep, a stooped figure, cloaked in despondency. Usually, before Joe went back to school, his grandfather spent some time with him, giving words of encouragement. This time, he deliberately avoided any opportunity for intimacy.

'Goodbye, Grandpa,' he said, shaking the old man's hand.

'Goodbye, Joe.'

Miserably, he clambered into his uncle's car, glancing back as Arthur drove off, to see Robert go up the steps into the house, his head bowed, his shoulders hunched.

The boys didn't go home for Half Term because Arthur and Thelma were invited for a week's holiday by friends in the Highlands of Scotland. They stayed at school with those children whose parents lived abroad. Joe hoped their grandfather would pay them a visit, perhaps take them out for the day, but he didn't. Consequently, he spent a lonely week, reading, going for long walks and worrying about Robert.

Christmas loomed. It would be the first one since his mother's death and he dreaded the prospect of Aunt Thelma's contrived merriment. On previous Christmases spent in England, with her father's encouragement, Alice had managed to snap herself out of depression long enough to make the day enjoyable.

On the twentieth of December, Arthur drove up in his Wolseley to collect them. He seemed to Joe to be even more distracted than usual but neither Ronald nor Leslie paid any attention to this because they spent the entire journey home squabbling over a Dan Dare comic. Joe couldn't believe how infantile they were. He sat between them in the back of the car -- they had each grabbed a window seat -- trying, unsuccessfully, to catnap.

As soon as Joe saw his grandfather, he understood his uncle's uneasiness. The old man's health had gone downhill since he had last seen him. He greeted his grandsons as affectionately as ever, but the old sparkle had disappeared. After a brief enquiry as to their wellbeing, he departed to his study, shutting the door behind him. Joe unpacked his suitcase and put his clothes away, then went downstairs and knocked at the study door. There was no reply. He knocked again. Normally, he would have left it at that, but on this occasion, intuition told him something was wrong. Tentatively, he opened the door and went inside.

Robert McPherson-Corke was slumped over his desk, his arms flung out in front of him. Fear clutched at the youngster's heart as he crept across the room. The old man's head was turned towards him; the watery eyes, once so startlingly blue, were wide open. An ink bottle had overturned as he'd fallen and some of its contents had splashed the side of his face, giving the effect of a bruise. Fighting down the bile rising in his throat, Joe ran to find his uncle.

'What's the matter, Arthur?' called out Thelma when she saw her husband hurrying after Joe to the study.

'It's Dad, Joe thinks he's had a heart attack.'

The three of them rushed to Robert's side and Arthur lifted his father's head. Turning to his wife, he muttered gruffly, 'He's gone, I'm afraid. You'd better call the doctor.'

Thelma raised her hands in exasperation, muttering almost inaudibly, 'Tch, why did he have to die here? Why here, and at Christmas?'

Arthur looked mortified. 'For God's sake woman,' he shouted, roused to confront his wife for one of the few times in his life. 'Just do what I ask you. Call the doctor.'

For Thelma, this unexpected display of assertiveness was tantamount to a slap on the face. Clamping her mouth shut, she swivelled around and hurried out into the hall to make the telephone call.

'Joe, run and fetch a damp face flannel please.' Puzzled, the boy did as his uncle asked him. Returning, he handed the flannel to Arthur, who said, 'Now, could you give me a hand, I need to move your grandfather a little.'

Joe hesitated, wondering what he intended to do. Then he understood. He wanted to close the old man's eyes and wash the ink off his face. He went to Arthur's assistance and, as he attempted to lift the dead weight of his grandfather's upper body, he saw that buried beneath his chest was his mother's book, open at the title page.

'Can you manage, Joe?' asked Arthur anxiously. 'I know this must be awfully upsetting for you.'

The boy nodded, touched by his uncle's concern. When the washing procedure began, he surreptitiously slid his left hand under Robert's chest and retrieved the telling book, sliding it to the edge of the desk so that it fell silently onto the rug by the dead man's feet. He nudged it gently out of sight with his toe.

Thelma rushed back into the room. 'What on earth are you doing, Arthur?' she cried.

'Just tidying things up, my dear. Now, I think we'd better go and break the news to the boys. Did the doctor say what time he would get here?'

'In about twenty minutes,' replied Thelma, hastily casting a backward shudder at her father-in-law's corpse before leaving the room. 'Joe, come out of there and close the door behind you. It's unhealthy to hang around a dead body.'

'Ronald, Leslie!' called out Arthur. 'Come downstairs for a minute please. I have something to tell you.'

Joe stood listening, impressed by the way Arthur had taken charge. He could see that his uncle was as distressed as he was over the old man's death.

After Ronald and Leslie had been ushered into the sitting room with the door closed behind them, Joe tried to gather his wits together. The coast was clear; he could retrieve the book. He began to tremble. Helping his uncle handle his dead grandfather was one thing, sneaking back in to fumble under the desk between Robert's feet to find the book was another. But the alternative was unthinkable. He couldn't risk his aunt and uncle reading the inscription. Taking a deep breath, he crept into the study, ran across the room and dived under the desk to retrieve the book. Shoving it under his pullover, he raced out of the room without looking at the corpse.

His heart thumped fiercely. What luck he had spotted the book in time! Tomorrow, he would burn it in the garden incinerator. No one else would ever read his mother's give-away inscription, he alone and his dead grandfather would be the only people privy to her secret. But as his emotions began to quieten, elation changed to shame, then shame to grief as he relived the past hour. Tears welled. Grandpa was dead. That kindly old man, who had been his mainstay throughout the terrible years of his enforced sojourn in England was no longer there for him. From now on he would be obliged to face Ronald and Leslie and his awful Aunt Thelma without his grandfather's backing.

Running feet and loud sobbing from outside his room startled Joe. He recognised Leslie's frenzied howl, an echo of Thelma's, and felt sickened. Ronald and Leslie had never shown their grandfather any love or respect. Behind his back, they had mimicked his old-fashioned manners, jeered at his reminiscences, sniggered at his failing memory and, more latterly, scoffed when he had been obliged to pause half way upstairs to catch his breath.

Ronald's heavy footsteps followed close on the heels of his brother. 'Stop making such a fuss, Les,' he taunted. 'Grandpa was an old man, it was about time he snuffed it.' Their mother called out, 'Leslie, my poor baby, I had no idea you were so close to your grandfather.'

Joe sat up straight, hating what he was hearing. Snatching up his pillow, he folded it over his ears. He didn't want to listen to any more, he didn't want to be party to such hypocrisy. Thus he remained until darkness enveloped the room. Rocking to and fro, he gave way to grief, just as he had done five years earlier when his devastated mother, shattered by the news of Enzo's death, had seemingly forgotten her younger son's existence.

The days that followed were a living nightmare. Ronald carried on as if nothing had happened. Leslie followed suit, only occasionally remembering he was supposed to be grieving. He would then put on a display of abject mournfulness, a performance dramatic enough to grace the boards of a Greek theatre. To *bring him out of himself,* Thelma indulged her younger son unashamedly, insisting on an excess of jollity and, on Christmas Day, she made herself tipsy on Rum Punch and Mulberry Wine. Thankfully Arthur, genuinely saddened by his father's demise, put a stop to his wife's over-indulgence by packing her off to bed early. He then set up a quiet game of cards with the boys. Joe willingly acquiesced; anything to curb the staged merriment of the evening! Ronald and Leslie joined in with bad grace until, at ten o'clock, Arthur decided it was time for bed.

Fourteen

Robert McPherson-Corke CBE was buried on New Year's Day 1945. The funeral was well attended since he had been a prominent figure in the Foreign Office, narrowly missing out on a knighthood due, his daughter had once proclaimed, to the untimely outbreak of war. Joe stood beside his uncle to receive the many tributes to his grandfather. For the occasion, despite clothes rationing, dark suits had been procured for the three boys. Ronald complained that his was too tight, whilst Joe found himself catching his heel in the trousers which were too long for him. Leslie, on the other hand, who at the same age was taller and a lot tubbier than his Italian cousin, fitted in to his suit rather well.

Thelma stood between her sons, a matronly figure in deepest black. Her veiled hat bobbed up and down as she murmured sob-stifled thanks for condolences offered, replying, 'I must keep up a brave face for Arthur's sake.' Dabbing a lace-edged handkerchief to her eyes, she would wrap a comforting arm about Leslie's shoulder and add, 'And for my boys.' Fortunately, she didn't notice the smirk this produced from her favourite offspring, nor did she see him stick out his tongue at Joe while the latter was dutifully shaking hands with one of the visiting Foreign Office officials.

At last the whole dreadful business was over, and with a feeling of relief, Joe returned to Monksmede. Anything to get away from Aunt Thelma's beady eye and his cousins' constant squabbling. The only good thing that came out of the painful episode was the shared sorrow with his Uncle Arthur, a sorrow which brought them closer together.

Until Robert McPherson-Corke's Will was read, Joe did not think about his future. Despite the fact that he didn't get on with his aunt and his cousins, he saw their home as his home, at least until the time came for him to return to his beloved Italy. It didn't occur to him that, with his grandfather's passing, circumstances would change.

Thus, he was taken by surprise when his uncle called at the school and arranged to take him out for lunch. Even more surprising was the fact that Ronald and Leslie were not invited to join them.

'Well, lad,' said his uncle once they were seated at a window table in the village restaurant. 'I expect you're wondering what this is all about. As you know, your grandfather's Will was read last week.' Arthur unfolded his napkin and carefully placed it on his knees. 'He's left you well provided for. Your remaining time here at Monksmede is secure.'

'I thought my mother left funds for my education,' replied Joe, looking slightly puzzled.

'So she did, so she did,' agreed Arthur. 'But it wasn't enough, your grandfather subsidized it.'

'I didn't know that.' The boy twisted his hands nervously. He didn't want to talk about his grandfather; the memory of his gruesome discovery in the study was still too fresh.

'I must admit the Will surprised me,' went on Arthur. 'It seems that with an uncertain future ahead of you ... ' He broke off and studied his fingernails, clearly unwilling to embark on a subject he knew to be disquieting for his nephew. 'Hmm, it seems your grandfather was concerned that ... ' Again he hesitated, looking increasingly uncomfortable.

Joe leant across the table. 'Yes?'

Arthur took his time replying. Clearly this interview was as difficult for him as it was for the boy himself. He went on, 'In his wisdom, your grandfather has left you a substantial sum of money to see you through university, plus his house.'

'His house! But surely it's now yours,' burst out Joe in astonishment.

'There is a proviso. We, that is, your aunt and myself are to be allowed to live there until Ronald and Leslie have finished full-time education, after which it becomes your property.' As Joe started to protest, his uncle lifted his hand to silence him. 'But you cannot dispose of it until the present conflict ends and

... ' He gave a hard swallow. ' ... until it's been proved that Vincenzo is no longer with us.'

Joe frowned. What did that mean? Was his uncle suggesting that his father wouldn't want to see him after the War? It didn't bear thinking about. The boy gulped as Arthur's next words clarified the situation.

'Should Vincenzo have survived and ... ' Arthur reached out and gave Joe's hand a consoling pat. ' ... I've no reason to doubt that he hasn't, it is assumed you will want to return to Italy; in which case, under the terms of your grandfather's Will, the house will revert to me. Of course, if something *has* happened to your father, you will probably want to stay in England. Please Joe, be assured that your Aunt Thelma and I will always give you our utmost devotion.'

Joe stared at his uncle in silence. All at once, the room began to spin. What was Arthur trying to convey to him -- that in the event of his father's death he would be tolerated by their family, bearing in mind that he would have the power to turn them out into the street? Throwing his napkin down onto his untouched meal, he jumped to his feet and ran to the cloakroom, where he vomited into the wash-hand basin.

The boys were nearing their end of year exams when the War finished. Ronald and Leslie greeted the news jubilantly, rejoicing along with their peers, making stupid jokes about the *jerries*. Fortunately, since the War with Italy had finished earlier and with less tabloid coverage than the German offensive, Joe was spared his cousins' taunts about the cowardly *eyeties*. The end of hostilities meant so much more to him than it did to them. Reunion with his father beckoned. He tried to imagine the scene: the joy at seeing one another again. He bit his lip uneasily. How would Babbo react to the news of Mamma's death? Blood seeped from his lip as his teeth dug deeper. The book! He experienced a twinge of guilt. He had never quite got around to getting rid of it. Whatever happened Babbo must never find out about the book! He found it difficult to keep his mind on his studies, but with exams looming he knew he must make an effort. He wanted Babbo to be proud of him. Gradually the consequences of peace dawned on him. Oxford or Cambridge were no longer on the agenda; he would go to an Italian university. He was fluent in both English and Italian. Maybe, he'd go to the one his brother had attended.

He was dubbed a wet blanket by his peers, who kept up the momentum of victory for days on end. Secretly, his heart thumped wildly, and he found it all but impossible to concentrate. He would sit for hours mulling over events in his mind, the open maths book in front of him, his science formulae fumbled through at the last minute, his essays scribbled off late at night by the light of a torch.

At home, since the reading of the Will, his Aunt Thelma's attitude had switched from bitter recrimination to keen interest in everything he did. She greeted him with hugs and kisses, she enquired as to how his studies were going, even praising his achievements despite her own sons' mediocre results. This sham affection irritated Joe even more than her earlier fault-finding. He longed to shout: *Stop toadying up to me, you stupid woman, your home's safe.*

Despite the lapse in his studies, Joe gained good exam results. Next term he would join his older cousin in the Upper Sixth. Leslie lagged behind, a poor third to his cousin and brother. Neither academic nor sporty, the boy resorted to misbehaviour and his despairing parents were frequently called up to the school by the headmaster. To make matters worse, he somehow managed, by bribery and corruption, to get hold of more sweets and sticky buns than were good for him, resulting in a crop of acne, and an increase in girth, exacerbated by lack of exercise.

In the Autumn, Arthur began making enquiries about Vincenzo. He kept his nephew informed, telephoning the boy with regular updates. Italy was in turmoil and records had not been kept up-to-date. The Christian Democrats with their regime of *low politics* came to power ousting the Communists who had risen with such success, aided by the Resistance, during the concluding months of the War. No-one trusted anyone, and to obtain information from outside the country was well nigh impossible.

Towards the end of Term, Arthur paid Joe a visit. Again, he took him to the village restaurant for lunch, and again, Joe sensed that his uncle had news that he didn't want to hear.

'I'm sorry, lad,' he began. 'But there's no way of breaking this gently; I've heard through the Foreign Office that your father is *missing presumed dead.*' He reached across the table and clasped his nephew's hand. 'I'm so sorry.'

Joe snatched his hand away. 'Sorry,' he snapped. 'Sorry for me, or sorry because this means you won't have a home to live in in a couple of years' time?'

Arthur's mouth dropped open and he withdrew his own hand. Regaining his composure, he said quietly, 'Is that what you think of me, Joe?'

Joe experienced a stab of shame. Of course he didn't think that, but a stubborn streak refused to let him apologise. It pained him to see the hurt in his uncle's eyes, yet he felt incapable of rectifying the situation.

This time, it was Arthur who brought the meal to a speedy conclusion. Not bothering to order dessert, he called for the bill and drove Joe back to school in silence. He dropped his nephew off at the gates of Monksmede, barely saluting him before driving away. The boy felt terrible. The news about his father had devastated him, but he hadn't meant to offend Arthur. The words had slipped out unintentionally and now, he would give anything to take them back. He sloped into school, shoulders hunched, hands in pockets, to be met by one of the house masters, who reprimanded him for slouching.

After the ticking off, he hurried up to the empty dormitory and sank onto his bed to stare down at the floor, unable to cry, unable to confide in anybody. Study became his salvation. During the following months, he seldom raised his head from his books. In July 1946, at the age of 16, he matriculated with brilliant marks, winning a place at Oxford.

With his place at Oxford secure, Joe went home for the summer to prepare himself for university life. He was eager to continue his studies but the prospect of becoming an undergraduate filled him with trepidation. Ronald and Leslie didn't help.

'You'll be a laughing stock,' sneered Ronald. 'In their first year all those chaps think about is sex and booze. You won't fit in with your puritanical outlook. They don't like goody-goodies you know.'

'Yeah.' Leslie smacked his lips in delight. 'They'll probably make you their mascot, get you cleaning up after them when they've puked.'

'The scouts do that,' protested Joe with vehemence lacking conviction.

Ronald grinned and went on, 'You'll be a go-between, made to deliver love-notes.' He turned to his brother. 'Hey, Leslie, do you think one of their floozies will take pity on him and offer him a bit on the side.'

'He wouldn't know what to do,' came Leslie's retort.

The brothers guffawed cruelly, barring their cousin's way when he tried to leave the room. 'One or two of those chaps might turn out to be fairies,' chortled Ronald. 'Gosh Joe, you'd better watch out, specially when you go in the showers.'

'Yeah,' agreed Leslie. 'A weedy little thing like you wouldn't stand a chance.'

This last insult cut Joe to the core. He was, indeed, underdeveloped. His cousin, Ronald was an able sportsman and, at almost nineteen, stood a head and shoulders taller than both Leslie and Joe. Leslie was thickset; a lazy boy, he continued to pile on the pounds by stuffing himself with fattening snacks despite his mother's mild admonition.

'Shut up, both of you,' shouted Joe, barging past Ronald and racing upstairs to his room.

Throughout the summer, there was no getting away from his cousins' taunts, and although Joe put on a brave face, their teasing left him feeling more than a little apprehensive. He was only sixteen; most of his companions would be eighteen or older and he knew he would feel out of his depth. Thus, when his uncle suggested that he take a year off before taking up his place at Oxford, he was only too ready to concur.

'I think you're a bit young for university as yet, Joe, but given a year, you'll be ready,' advised Arthur. 'And this way both you and Ronald will be setting off on a new life at the same time.' This reference to his cousin was because Ronald had failed his highers and needed to re-sit them. 'Of course you won't have your cousin for company.' He went on in a resigned tone. 'I'm afraid it looks like a red brick university for Ronald. In the meantime, I've fixed you up with a junior post in my office. I'm sure Alice would have approved.' He stretched out a hand to touch Joe's shoulder but quickly withdrew it, and the youngster realised that his rejection of his uncle's sympathy a few months earlier might have been forgiven, but had not been forgotten. 'Your mother would have been proud of you, Joe.'

Fifteen

Joe's duties at his Uncle Arthur's office with the Harrogate Borough Council proved to be little more than those of messenger boy, tea maker and general factotum, but the typists and the office clerks were friendly, and he began to enjoy himself. He particularly liked one girl. Her name was Patricia and she was several months older than him. She was a pretty blond with a charismatic nature. The other typists made a point of befriending her if only to stake their place amongst the boys, who were attracted to Patricia's bubbly personality. When the occasional catty remark was flung in her direction by a disgruntled colleague, she was always able to disarmingly sidestep it with her easy-going manner, thereby cementing her popularity with her co-workers. Joe was smitten. He idolised her from afar. In his eyes she could do no wrong. He compared her favourably with his mother; in fact she was even more of a paragon than Alice, for Patricia did not brush him aside as Alice had done.

The first time he was invited to go to the pub with his colleagues after work, Joe declined. The truth was, he was so surprised he took the easy way out. The next time, however, he went with them. He became part of the group, listening to and laughing at their banter even though he seldom contributed to their conversation.

On one occasion, because he had missed his usual bus home, and had to wait an hour for the next one, he found himself alone in the pub with Patricia. It was a Friday night and the others had gone on their way.

Feeling tongue-tied at being left to hold the fort on his own, he searched his mind for something interesting to say, but could only come out with, 'Are you going out tonight, Patricia?'

She wrinkled her nose. 'My boyfriend's ditched me.' Joe was surprised. How could any sane young man discard someone as lovely as Patricia! 'Oh it's all right,' she went on when he grunted his sympathy. 'I wasn't keen on him. It's ... ' She stared down at her small feet which were encased in black patent shoes.

'Yes?'

Her voice took on a bitter tone. 'I don't want to go home because my mum's fancy man's coming round and I hate the sight of him.' On seeing Joe's startled expression, she went on, 'My dad was killed at El Alamein.'

'I'm sorry.'

She shrugged off his sympathy, asking, 'Are your parents alive?'

'They're both dead.'

Her eyes widened. 'How awful for you! At least I've still got my mum, even if I don't like the company she keeps.'

'It's not so bad,' he hastened to assure her.

'You look foreign,' she said. 'And someone at work said you speak Italian.'

For a moment Joe was taken aback. As far as he was aware the only person in the office who knew about his Italian background was his uncle. He gave a mental shrug. If it were common knowledge, what was the point of denying it. He found himself telling Patricia about his mixed parentage and his father's vineyard in Tuscany.

'Gosh!' she exclaimed. 'I bet you lived in one of those posh villas with balconies and swimming pools.'

'It wasn't all that posh,' he protested. 'It was quite simple really, tucked away in the countryside.'

She dimpled. 'Don't be modest. What other secrets have you got up your sleeve?'

'None!' Joe protested hurriedly.

'I can't understand what you're doing in a stuffy office with the likes of us.'

'What d'you mean?'

'Well,' she said, 'It's obvious you could do far better. You ought to be at technical college or even university with your brains.'

Joe was totally nonplussed by the unexpected flattery. 'As a matter of fact, I've got a place at university next year,' he admitted.

'Thought so, which one?'

He tried to smother his embarrassment. 'Oxford.'

Patricia looked impressed, but suddenly her mood changed. With a merry laugh, she cried, 'Come to the pictures with me; there's a good film on at the Regal. It's called, *Notorious*.' Her face lit up expectantly. 'Come on, don't worry, I'll pay for myself. Only it's got Cary Grant and Ingrid Bergman in it. You'll love it.'

Thus began Joe's first association with a member of the opposite sex. The pair went to the cinema together, they went ice-skating, they joined a ballroom dancing class, yet their friendship remained platonic. Apart from Patricia's frequent declaration that he was her very best friend and her occasional affectionate peck on his cheek, she showed no indication that she wanted their relationship to go further. For his part, Joe was too shy and too much in awe of her, to venture beyond the parameter she had set.

But at night, in the privacy of his bedroom, he dreamt of a time when she would be his. He knew she dated other boys, but he wouldn't let himself picture her with them. He fantasized about what it would be like making love to her. This wasn't easy since he had no experience, and could only call on his imagination. He simply knew that he would do anything for her and when Leslie, home for half-term, saw them out together, he came close to causing his cousin a serious injury for her sake.

'Hey *Ice cream Joe*, where did you pick that one up?' sneered Leslie when he got home.

'She's a colleague from work,' he replied, having noted with a twinge of satisfaction, the envy in his cousin's tone.

'A work colleague! What were you doing at the cinema?'

'We're good friends, that's all.'

'Huh, I've heard that before. What on earth does she see in a patsy like you?'

'Leave off, Les,' said Joe, beginning to get riled.

But Leslie never could read the warning signs. He pressed on: 'I get it. She's a pro. How much does she charge to spread her legs?'

This was too much for Joe. Swinging a right hook, his fist made contact with his cousin's jaw and it was more by luck than dexterity that the latter managed to swerve aside. It did, however, bring a halt to Leslie's insinuations. Rubbing his chin, he stomped off grumbling, 'Touchy, aren't we?'

Joe's friendship with Patricia continued for another eight months until, one summer evening as they left the Palace Cinema, she made her devastating announcement. 'I won't be able to see you like this any more, Joe.'

'What d'you mean?'

Her eyes shone. 'I've been dying to tell you; something wonderful has happened.'

'What?' demanded Joe.

'Don't frown like that.'

'I'm not frowning.'

'Yes you are.'

'Go on, what wonderful thing has happened?'

'We'll still see one another in the office,' she stalled.

'What are you talking about? Have I done something to upset you?'

She tapped his arm lightly and giggled. 'Really, Joe, you are a silly billy, 'course you haven't done anything to upset me. You're my very best friend, you know that.'

Joe's heart beat like a drum. Why wouldn't she come out with it? 'It's your mother, she disapproves of me,' he croaked.

Patricia seemed to think this very funny. 'How can she disapprove, she's never even met you.'

'Maybe she doesn't like you seeing someone who's half Italian.'

'What makes you think I told her?'

'Well, did you?'

'Of course not!'

He spoke more harshly than he intended. 'Well, come on then, tell me what this wonderful thing is.'

She pouted and turned her head away. "You've spoilt it. I'm not sure I'm going to tell you now.'

Angered by her prevarication, Joe pushed her into a shop doorway. 'What's going on?' he demanded.

Patricia bit her lip, tears welling in her eyes. 'Like I said, we can still be friends ... ' She looked down at his hands clasping her forearms and said, 'You're hurting me, Joe.'

'Sorry.' He let go of her, but barred her way. 'Why can't I see you any more?'

She gave a sniff and replied sulkily, 'What are you getting so worked up about? After all, you're going off to Oxford in September.'

Joe experienced a tweak of conscience. This was true. He could hardly expect her to hang around for him when they would only be able to meet up once in a blue moon. His mind raced. He'd drop out of university. He'd stay in this job, close to Patricia. He opened his mouth to speak but Patricia shoved him aside with, 'Let me pass.'

As they continued along the road, he kept trying to find the words to tell her that he'd flunk out of university but somehow he couldn't. She stomped ahead of him, her head held high and, on reaching the bus stop, said in a choked voice, 'You haven't even asked me why.'

'I did,' he protested. 'But you wouldn't tell me.'

She shot him a sidelong glance and said, 'Promise you won't get cross again.'

Joe gave a swallow. 'I promise.'

Miraculously, her mood swung to one of bubbling excitement. Taking his hands in hers, she cried, 'Guess what? I've met this really gorgeous boy called Roger.'

Was that all? Joe's spirits lifted. Patricia was always enthusing over new boyfriends. They usually lasted for about two weeks.

She went on, 'Roger wants to get engaged. Fancy that, Joe. Me engaged!' Engaged! This was different. Joe couldn't register what she was saying. Patricia didn't notice his preoccupation as she rushed on with her confidences, describing the romantic way Roger had proposed. 'Of course, we'll have to wait a while before we can get married. After all, we've got to save up. Weddings cost money and I can't see mum coughing up much towards it.' She stopped abruptly and stared at him. 'Joe, what's the matter, aren't you pleased for me?'

'Of course I am.' Her scrutiny forced his attention back to her. 'It's just ... well, such a surprise.'

'I've been seeing Roger for quite a while, you know, three weeks at least.'

Three weeks! He wanted to point out that three weeks was no time at all but somehow his tongue had become cleaved to the roof of his mouth and he couldn't utter a single word.

Her eyes became dreamy. 'Roger and I knew at once that we were right for one another.'

The rest of her words faded away. He heard them but they made no sense. 'And he's just bought a motor bike so we can go to all sorts of places,' she enthused. 'I love riding pillion. 'Course it's not a Norton or anything like that but Rodg says he's going to get one of those next year.' All at once, she clutched his sleeve. 'Why don't I take you along to the jewellers and show you the ring Roger's picked out for me?'

'I mustn't miss my bus,' protested Joe feebly but it was no good. He was too shocked to decline the invitation. She dragged him along the road and made him press his nose against the barred window to peer at a diamond ring resting on it's satin cushion at the back of the display.

After she had oohed and aahed over it, they parted company, Patricia tripping her way home happily unaware that she had broken her best friend's heart.

The remaining weeks before his departure for university, were the most miserable of Joe's life. He met up with Patricia in the office every day. There was no avoiding her. He stopped going to the pub after work, thinking up lame excuses for his absence. Even though she talked endlessly about Roger, Patricia was as bubbly and flirtatious as ever. The boys still adored her, the girls envied her.

In September, Joe began making preparations for Oxford. To his surprise, Aunt Thelma took an interest in his wardrobe, advising him on how to eke out his clothing coupons and joking about the girls he might meet. 'Only studious girls get to go to Oxford,' she quipped. 'Girls who will prefer an egg-head, like you.' Joe took this teasing with good humour although he couldn't help wondering whether his aunt had an ulterior motive for the softening of her attitude towards him.

However equivocal his aunt's behaviour was, an unexpected incident made him realise that Arthur was truly fond of him. On the day of his departure, his uncle left the office early to see him off.

They stood awkwardly on the platform waiting for the train to come in. Joe was tongue-tied. His uncle tried to make small talk, but eventually dried up. At last, the train steamed into the station, emitting its acrid steam. Joe climbed in and Arthur handed up his luggage. The door slammed between them. Lowering the window, Joe leant out and shook his uncle's hand. 'Thanks for coming to see me off, Uncle Arthur.'

Arthur seemed bewildered. Squeezing Joe's hand tightly, he mumbled, 'I'm really proud of you, Joe.' He shook his head as if in disbelief. 'Merton! Such a famous college. What a pity your parents aren't here to see this day!' Tears glistened in his eyes, as he went on almost inaudibly, 'I'll miss having your around, son.' Joe was touched. Arthur had never addressed him as *son* before. Was this a slip of the tongue or wishful thinking?

On reaching Oxford, he had no time to feel nervous. First Year arrivals were greeted in noisy confusion. Second Years consulted clipboards and roared directions at dazed new boys. At last, Joe located his rooms. He climbed the stairs to the second floor, dumped his suitcases down on the threshold and took a deep breath. The door was flung open. A stocky, ginger-haired young man stood facing him.

'You must be Thomas?' He thrust out a freckled fist, gripping Joe's hand with surprising strength. His welcoming grin brought colour to an otherwise pallid complexion, pale blue eyes lit up with interest. 'Enter the hallowed halls!' With a sweep of his arm, he gave a mock bow.

Joe nudged his luggage into the room, closing the door behind him.

'I'm Batts, Batts by name, bats by nature. Charlie Batts.'

'Nice to meet you, Batts,' replied Joe, warming to his cheerful room-mate.

Charlie led him into the bedroom. 'I've bagged the bed by the window,' he said, wrinkling an enquiring brow. 'First come, first served.'

Joe chuckled. 'It's fine by me.'

'I haven't met our Scout yet but I gather he's called Wilkins. What's your subject, mine's Geology?' He had a habit of jumping from one sentence to another without pausing for breath.

'Mediaeval History.'

'My word, that's a grim choice,' observed Charlie. All at once, he spotted the new gramophone Joe had bought with his last pay packet. 'What's that?'

'I like to listen to music in the evenings,' explained Joe.

Charlie began unpacking his bags, bringing out tennis and squash racquets. 'What sort of music, swing, jazz?'

'Classical mostly.'

Charlie slapped a hand to his forehead. 'Christ, don't say I'm to be bombarded with Wagner and Mahler, Joe Loss is more my style.'

'I promise not to play that stuff when you're around,' replied Joe, guessing that to admit to being an opera fan would not help get him off on the right foot.

Being landed with Batts as a room-mate proved fortunate for Joe. Charlie's gregarious nature guided him through his painful inaugural days at Oxford. At lectures, Joe cut a lonely and self-conscious figure in his gown and mortar. Gradually, however, he got used to the protocol, accustomed to traffic in the city centre coming to a halt when *gentlemen in subfusc* crossed the road; able to read the implied reprimand in their Scout's eyes when one of his *young gentlemen* committed a misdemeanour.

His room-mate was often in trouble. Unable to keep his opinions to himself, he was frequently obliged to pay the Warden's penalty: chanting grace in Latin prior to the evening meal and then knocking back a couple of pints of beer without pausing for breath. Charlie seemed well able to cope with such a punishment but Joe, unaccustomed to heavy drinking, was grateful that for once his lack of communication skills protected him from a similar fate.

Joe made rapid progress with his studies, his enthusiasm bringing him to the attention of lecturers. Although encouraged by Charlie, he nearly always declined to join his companions in drinking sessions or outings with the local girls. Patricia's image was still prominent, the shock of her engagement to Roger still raw. Occasionally, she wrote to him: rambling letters on scented notepaper in her untidy scrawl, signed with a flourish and a kiss. Each time one of her letters arrived, he resolved not to reply, but in the end, fear of losing touch with her altogether, drove him to send a cursory note with the excuse that study kept him too busy to write more.

Early during his second year, he was staggered to learn that she planned to visit Oxford. She gave him no time to reply, and he knew it would be unthinkable not to meet her off the train. He was unclear as to what her message implied. Was she coming alone or was the lucky husband going to be with her? Nervously, he went to the station.

He bought a platform ticket and waited for the train to come, scouring the alighting passengers for Patricia. At last he saw her and waved, relieved to see that she was on her own. She waved back and fairly flew down the platform, overnight bag bouncing on her arm, blond pony-tail flying out behind her. She dropped the bag at her feet and flung herself into his arms, hugging him with genuine affection. He hugged her back, holding his breath in wonderment. Her cheek against his felt like silk, her hair smelt of fresh lemons. She was still panting slightly from her dash along the platform so that when she spoke her words were tremulous, as if driven by emotion.

'Oh Joe, it's so good to see you!' She pressed her forefinger to his chin and, widening her eyes in the delightful habit he remembered so well, asked, 'Have you missed me?'

'Of course I have,' he breathed.

Other passengers jostled past them, edging Patricia out of his embrace. She smiled and went to pick up her bag. Joe took it from her. 'I take it you're staying overnight.'

'I've booked in at a b&b, I hope it's not far from your digs.'

'Didn't Roger want to come with you?' he asked uneasily.

Patricia giggled. 'Guess what? He's had to go down to London this weekend, that's how I've been able to get away.'

Her voice rose in excitement. 'I've been saving up for this for ages.'

'Do you mean Roger doesn't know you've come to Oxford?'

She shrugged a shoulder. 'Does it matter? This is such an adventure, Joe.'

Joe frowned. 'Yes, it does matter.'

She pouted. 'I don't see why.'

'It isn't right, Patricia, you ought to go home. You should have told Roger what you were planning to do.'

She looked furious and burst out, 'Don't be so old-fashioned, I'm staying and if you don't want to spend the weekend showing me around, then I'll look around by myself.' Biting her lip, she looked up at him, her eyes welling with tears. 'Don't spoil it, Joe.'

Joe felt nonplussed. She was as beautiful as he remembered. More beautiful: marriage had given her a certain maturity, filling out the skinniness of her arms and legs, lending a fullness to her breasts. Her complexion was as flawless as ever, her eyes as bright. He loved her still and, for a split second, felt angry with her for turning up out of the blue to inflict the bitter-sweet pain of loss upon him once more.

She broke into his thoughts. 'Well, are you going to help me find my way to my digs or not?'

Patricia's arrival coincided with a spell of clement weather. Responding to her assumption that he would be at her beck and call throughout her stay, Joe skipped lectures for the first time since his arrival at Merton.

As they strolled along the street the following morning, he searched for something to say, still overwhelmed by shyness. 'How are things in the office?'

'I don't know.' She gave a laugh. 'I forgot to tell you, I don't work there any more.'

He looked surprised. 'Where do you work?'

She tilted her chin proudly and replied, 'I'm a sales assistant in the lingerie department of Marks & Spencer's.'

'Oh!' Then realising that a more enthusiastic response was expected, added, 'Well done!'

Turning her attention to their surroundings, she squeezed his arm and asked, 'Are there any big stores in Oxford? Oh Joe, this is so exciting, you must take me to see all the sights, introduce me to your friends, show me where you live.'

'I don't know about that,' he mumbled.

He felt confused. He didn't want to share her with anybody, let alone other undergraduates with their waggish humour; on the other hand, he was proud to be seen with such a beautiful young woman. The choice, however, was not to be his. That afternoon while they were strolling by the river, they bumped into Charlie Batts who was jogging along the towpath. Joe cursed himself. He had forgotten that, having been selected as first reserve for the Boat Race crew Charlie regularly ran beside the river in order to improve his fitness. On seeing them, he stopped short in surprise. Doubling over he stopped to regain his breath, his hands clasped on his thighs, perspiration dripping from his brow. Charlie was rarely at a loss for words, but on this occasion, much to Joe's relief, exercise had robbed him of the ability to utter a saucy quip.

Forced into introduction, Joe said, 'Patricia, this is my roommate, Charlie Batts.' He turned to Charlie. 'Patricia's a friend from Harrogate.'

Patricia dimpled, and disregarding the sweatiness of the runner's hand, held out her own for him to shake, saying, 'Nice to meet you, Charlie.'

Straightening up, the red head stared into Patricia's eyes, admiration apparent in his own. 'The pleasure's all mine.' He shot a glance at Joe. 'You crafty bounder, Thomas, how d'you manage to keep this cracker under wraps for so long?'

Patricia's dimples deepened and she made no attempt to disengage her hand from Charlie's.

For something to say, Joe remarked, 'Patricia's only here for a couple of days.'

'Then we must make sure she enjoys herself,' rejoined Charlie. 'See you back at base, old boy. We'll make plans for tonight. Super to make your acquaintance, Patricia.'

With a flourish of his hand, he stepped between them and continued his run.

'He's nice,' said Patricia.

'Yes, he's a good chap,' replied Joe.

Anxious to change the subject, he took her arm and led her to the water's edge, pointing out a pair of swans which were gliding gracefully towards them.

Joe intended to take Patricia to a quiet restaurant that evening, but Charlie put paid to his plans.

'Must make sure your girlfriend enjoys her stay in Oxford,' were his words of greeting when Joe went back to his rooms to change.

'She's not my girlfriend.'

Charlie cast him a disbelieving glance. 'Oh yeah?' He went on enthusiastically, 'We've organised a party for her.'

This was the last thing Joe wanted. 'Aren't you on the wagon?' he protested. 'I thought partying was out until after the Boat Race.'

Charlie gave a grin. 'One slip won't hurt.'

Joe searched desperately for an excuse. 'Patricia's a bit shy,' he lied. 'She might not feel like going to a party where she doesn't know anybody.'

'She didn't seem shy to me. Ring her up and ask her.'

'I don't have the number,' protested Joe, hoping this would put an end to Charlie's plans. It didn't.

Going to the door, Charlie called out, 'Wilkins, got a minute?'

The scout appeared at the bottom of the stairs. 'Yes Sir, can I help you.'

'Look up the telephone number of the...' Charlie turned back to Joe. 'Where's she staying?'

Reluctantly, Joe supplied the information. 'The Isis.'

'The Isis Boarding House. Make it snappy, there's a good fellow.'

The scout quickly returned with the information, giving Joe no choice but to make the telephone call. He couched the invitation in careful terms. 'We're invited to a get-together this evening, but it could be a bit boring for you because you won't know anybody. I'll say *no* and we can go to that restaurant I told you about.'

'Wait a minute!' cried Patricia. 'I'll know you, and Charlie. Oh Joe, it sounds fun, much more fun than eating on our own. Let's go.'

'Are you sure you want to?'

'Why, don't you?'

'Umm ... '

'Joe,' she trilled down the line. 'Sometimes, you can be such a wet blanket!'

The party was only the start. Much to Joe's exasperation, the two days of Patricia's visit were swallowed up in a merry-go-round of activities. He soon saw that Patricia hadn't lost her talent for charming people: the young men found her attractive and exciting, their girlfriends found her friendly and funny. Despite his disappointment at not spending time with her on his own, Joe was gratified to find that she seldom strayed far from his side, behaving as if she were *his* girl, not someone else's wife. At one point during the course of the first evening, he noticed she had removed her wedding ring, but a surfeit of alcohol soon blotted out this disturbing observation.

On the evening of her departure, he accompanied her to the station. The train was waiting, giving little time for long-drawn-out farewells. Joe felt choked to see her leave. Patricia, easily moved, turned to him with tears in her eyes. Clutching his hand, she gasped, 'I've enjoyed my visit so very much, Joe. It's been lovely seeing you, and your friends are really nice. I must come again. You do want me to, don't you?'

'Of course, I do,' he stammered although, behind his joy, lay the reality that she was married to another man. He glanced down at her hand and saw that she had put her wedding ring back on.

The train made *getting ready to go* noises and, before he had realised what was happening, Patricia reached up and fastened her arms around his neck, kissing him firmly on the mouth. 'Oh Joe, I do love you,' she whispered as they drew apart.

'I love you too.' There, he'd uttered the words. He meant them. Did she?

The guard's whistle blew amid the final slamming of carriage doors. Patricia climbed in, and wound down the window.

Leaning out, she called,. 'I'll come again soon. Promise you'll be here for me.' His reply was drowned out as the train steamed out of the station.

He wasn't sure how long he stood on the platform after the train had left. A porter walked past. 'You've got a long wait, the next one's not until ten o'clock, guv'nor.'

Abstractedly, he thanked the man and, as if in a trance, walked the length of the platform out into the street. How dreary and cold everything seemed. Patricia had brought a hint of spring; with her departure, winter had returned.

Common sense told him to put a stop to the relationship before it got out of hand, to write to Patricia and tell her to stay away. But in his heart, he knew he couldn't do that. Seeing her again had reawakened his love for her. He was no longer the adolescent in Harrogate to be teased and toyed with; he was a man now, and he knew exactly what he wanted. If necessary, he would give up everything for the girl he loved.

PART III

Ten Bells

Sixteen

Lucania 1942

As spring blossomed Vincenzo started taking long walks in the countryside, stopping to chat to farmers and labourers as they worked in the fields. Gradually, he became accustomed to their manner of speech, even finding himself adopting the dialect. He frequently spent the evening with Donna Caterina and, before long, he found himself telling her of his grief at losing Enzo, knowing that she would understand his heartache. In her turn, she reconfirmed her loyalty to her husband and he realised that Donna Caterina yearned, not for a lover for herself, as Livia had suggested, but for a father for her son. If she could have had one without the other, such was her devotion to her unfortunate offspring that the choice would have been in favour of the father figure. Livia was never mentioned; it was as if her five-week sojourn had never taken place.

The short *mezzogiorno* spring soon gave way to the intolerable heat of summer. The temperature soared; the desolate, moonlike landscape fell away to the dazzling horizon, beyond which another world existed. Only sub-tropical plants were hardy enough to thrive. Vincenzo found their beauty breathtaking, but like Livia, the joy of their existence was short-lived.

He never stopped thinking about Livia. But he could never be sure of when or if she would return. The days were monotonous. He rose at five, walked for an hour across the rough terrain to return before the sun became too fierce. He spent the rest of the day in his room writing, only venturing out again at sunset to join the farm labourers who gathered in the square to discuss football, war and politics while their wives prepared the evening meal.

Donna Caterina met her lodger's application to his life-long dream with enthusiasm, attending even more keenly to his needs, chastising Rocco for making too much noise.

'Don't fret, *Signora,*' insisted Vincenzo. 'The boy must play. He doesn't disturb me.'

Sometimes, Rocco would knock at his door. The Count would invite him in to sit and watch him assemble his notes. At first, the boy sat quietly without uttering a word. Gradually, however, he gained confidence and started asking questions. It wasn't long before Vincenzo realised that Rocco wasn't slow at all, that his monstrous appearance masked a quick intelligence. He mentioned this to his mother, who shrugged her shoulders and said, 'What use is a good brain if people turn away in horror?'

'Have you heard from your husband lately?' Donna Caterina shook her head. The sadness in her eyes tugged at Vincenzo's heart. 'There must be something that can be done,' he said. 'It's outrageous that the boy can't be helped.'

At night, sleepless and alone, the tragedy of Rocco's affliction began to prey on Vincenzo's mind. He wondered how much it would it cost to send the boy and his mother to the States for an operation? The Americans had made enormous advances in the field of medicine, and once the War ended, it might be possible for mother and son to make the journey across the Atlantic.

Autumn brought more hardship: less food on the table, more young men from the community lost. By now, Vincenzo had been accepted by the villagers, who began seeking his advice. By default, he found himself elevated to the position of magistrate, giving counsel on local issues. At first, he shrank from the responsibility, preferring to be left in peace to continue with his writing. Gradually, however, he came to see that, as a neutral arbitrator, his word settled many a minor dispute which might otherwise have developed into an on-going feud between neighbours.

From time to time, Livia came visiting. Her arrival brought joy tinged with pangs of anxiety but it made the severe winter bearable. He was plagued with doubts. What had she been up to? Who had she been with? Jealousy of her imagined lovers prompted him to talk to her about breaking parole and returning to the capital. She laughed him off, insisting that it was too dangerous, that Scarpone would find out and re-arrest him. The mention of the marshal's name brought further suspicions, but when he grilled her, she resolutely denied having been with him.

Months passed, until one day in mid-June, she arrived unannounced, coming to his room via the outside staircase, explaining that she wanted to avoid a confrontation with Donna Caterina. They made love with frantic haste, as if the end of the world was on the horizon. Afterwards, Vincenzo got up and studied his sleeping lover, his gaze devouring her naked body. He knew she was tired, could see that the past few months had been difficult for her. He turned his attention to his papers but found it difficult to concentrate. A little later, he heard her stir and after a few minutes, she came to stand behind him as he sat at his desk.

'Hello, darling!' She sat down on his lap and gently fondled the nape of his neck. 'What are you thinking about?'

'Oh dear, Livia, I feel cut off down here. Tell me what's happening up there in the north?'

She pulled a face. 'Can't you forgot about the War for five minutes.'

He felt exasperated. 'It's all right for you, you're in the thick of it. You know what's going on, but I'm stuck down here in the middle of nowhere. I might as well be on the moon.'

'Sorry,' she said. 'The truth is, things aren't going well with the Cell. Claudia's losing her grip.'

'What makes you say that?' Knowing how much the two women despised one another, he wondered whether Livia was being fair to their leader.

'She's organised nothing more than a foray here and there. 'She doesn't seem to be in control any more.'

'Have the Germans advanced very far?'

'They're all over the north. They're supposed to be our allies but they've carried out awful atrocities in France; carted innocent people off to Germany. They're moving down to Rome.'

Her words alarmed him. He gasped. 'But I heard that British and Americans are gaining ground in North Africa.'

She frowned and said bitterly, 'If they move into Sicily, Italy will capitulate and the country will become a bloody battleground between opposing forces.'

She was right. The future looked grim, but somehow they would have to live through it. She slept fitfully for the rest of the night, tossing and turning in his arms, muttering in her sleep although he couldn't make sense of her words. The next morning as she got ready to leave, he questioned her. 'What were you talking about in your sleep, *amore*?'

She shrugged off his question. 'The War, everything.'

It wasn't the reply he was looking for but she refused to give him a direct answer. His jaw tightened. 'I'm coming back to Rome with you.' Opening the wardrobe, he began throwing clothes onto the bed.

'No.' Clutching his shirt front, she cried urgently, 'What about Scarpone? He'll throw you in prison.' She glanced at the clock. 'I must hurry, the bus leaves in five minutes.' She turned and swept up the rest of her belongings, ramming them into her bag.

He twisted her round to face him. 'I'll catch the next bus and join you.'

She shook her head vehemently. 'Be patient, Vincenzo. Wait a week or two. I'll get word to you, I promise.' She kissed him briefly and ran down the staircase to board the bus just as it was about to leave.

Weeks passed without a word from Livia. Vincenzo's alarm grew when news filtered through of the Allies' landing in Sicily. The villagers gathered around their wireless sets, listening anxiously to the scratchy voices of the newsreaders. Just as Livia had predicted, the population was being squeezed from both sides: their purported comrades in arms -- the Germans -- were pushing down from the north; the British and Americans were pressing up from the south. He felt sick with worry. Was Livia caught up in this mayhem? If only she would contact him!

A plan began to take shape in his mind. Apart from the hunchback's dilapidated lorry and the mayor's Fiat, the twice-a-day bus was the only means of transport in and out of the village. Asking for help from either Alfonso or Nando Rubaldi would be futile. But house arrest entailed a prisoner reporting to the Prefecture once a week. In the early months, Basso had escorted him on this regular bus trip to Matera, but once the sergeant realised his charge had no intention of breaking parole, he relaxed his guard, and for over a year, Vincenzo had been making the trip alone. He decided he had no alternative than to abuse this trust and make his escape from Matera on the next Parole Day.

A twist of fate delayed Vincenzo's departure. As he was preparing to leave, he heard a disturbance in the street. Hurrying to the window, he saw Rocco and another boy facing one another, scowling angrily. A crowd had gathered as the confrontation became even tenser. It didn't take Vincenzo long to see that a girl was involved. Rocco's opponent had taken his unkind taunts one step too far by ridiculing him in front of the girl.

The girl stood timidly to one side, a clenched fist pressed to her mouth. All at once, Rocco, a big boy for thirteen, launched himself at his opponent who, unprepared for the assault, fell at the first blow. To his alarm, Vincenzo saw Rocco move in, and start to batter him about the head and shoulders while the other boy yelled for mercy.

Vincenzo didn't waste time. Running out into the street, he found Donna Caterina trying to separate the boys by squeezing herself between them. With a surge of anger, Rocco shoved his mother aside, and once again laid in to his cowering victim. The sight filled Vincenzo with horror. Rocco was doing to his schoolmate what the blackshirts had done to Enzo.

For a second, the boy's gaze caught his. Was it defiance or pleading in his eyes? Vincenzo didn't wait to find out. Grabbing him by his shirt collar, he dragged him away. Rocco made no great effort to free himself. Twisting his head round, he looked into Vincenzo's face and the Count saw an expression of gratitude flash across his features. He understood then that by hauling him away, he had not only managed to avoid a terrible outcome, but he had enabled the boy to save face.

Donna Caterina herded them back to the house, her cheeks flushed, her limbs trembling. She slammed the door shut against the prying eyes of neighbours and set about tending to Rocco's cuts and bruises. The boy shoved her away. Thrusting his knuckled fists in the air, he chanted, '*Bravo Rocco, bravo Rocco!* Look how clever Rocco is!'

His mother wrung her hands in agitation; the tears streamed down her cheeks. Turning to the Count, she cried, 'What am I to do? Rocco's not normally a vicious boy, what's come over him?'

Vincenzo understood the woman's dilemma and believed her. On earlier occasions he'd witnessed the boy's outbursts of frustration which were always directed against himself; this was the first time he had directed violence towards somebody else. He visualized the bleak future Donna Caterina faced, the difficulties she would have to surmount. This incident had established Rocco as an individual to be reckoned with, but driven too far, he could turn into a bully. Vincenzo felt certain that the boy's facial disfigurement could be helped by specialist surgery. Donna Caterina and her son deserved a better life. It seemed unlikely that her husband would ever contact her again. He glanced at the pair as he left the kitchen. The boy was sitting on a chair grinning triumphantly; his dismayed mother was kneeling on the floor beside him clutching his hands and weeping. He resolved to contact his Zurich Bank as soon as possible, and make a deposit in her name for use when the war was over.

The episode resulted in his administration as a magistrate being called into service. The father of the other boy demanded a hearing and it took all of Vincenzo's diplomatic prowess to resolve the matter. The curiosity this unofficial court case prompted brought a renewed surge of interest in Donna Caterina's esteemed lodger so that he suddenly found himself flooded with complaints needing his jurisdiction, many of which were clearly contrived. It took several days to sift through the genuine ones.

On the next Parole Day Vincenzo was ready. Before leaving, he put a wodge of notes into an envelope and left it under the water jug for Donna Caterina to find. This would have to suffice until such time as he could arrange a more substantial donation.

After months of inactivity, it was exciting to be on the move again. His heart raced as he boarded the bus. He recognised most of the passengers. They were regulars heading for Matera on market day. His briefcase was bulging with his manuscript. He had left the rest of his belongings at Donna Caterina's, confident that she would store them for him.

At the bus terminus he made his way to the Prefecture, walking casually, determined not to draw attention to himself. The clerk greeted him cheerfully, signing him in as usual. 'Nice day, *Eccellenza*,' he observed. 'It's going to be a hot one.'

'Yes indeed,' replied the Count, conscious that the other appeared to have taken note that he had chosen to wear a jacket despite the soaring temperature.

He was thankful the market was in full swing. This meant the mid afternoon train would be packed, making it easier for him to lose himself in the crowds. But he had several hours to kill before he could safely make his way to the railway station. He bought a newspaper and spent an hour in the park, reading it from cover to cover. The news wasn't good: intensified bombing over major cities; fierce hand-to-hand fighting between British and Italian troops in Sicily.

When stall-holders began packing up, he mingled with the departing shoppers as they made their way to the station. It was crowded with animals as well as people. Piles of caged chickens cluttered the platform; a bearded nanny goat chewed at the ribbons of a toddler's sun bonnet; a stooped old man squeaked his wheelbarrow along the platform. Black market-toting opportunists elbowed their way through the crowd, one of them kicking aside a mangy cat which was sniffing at his wares. Hens clucked, dogs barked, toddlers bawled, mothers shrieked, while a banjo-playing beggar supplied musical accompaniment to the cacophony.

The train pulled in and he found himself being jostled forward with the mass. All at once, he felt a hand clasp his shoulder. 'Not so fast, *Eccellenza*.' He turned and met his custodian's black-eyed scowl.

Without thinking, he threw off the man's hand and thrust his way onto the train. The mass closed in behind him blocking Basso's path. He willed the train to pull away quickly giving him a sporting chance, but a scuffle further along the platform held things up. Basso battled his way through and, this time, there was no escape. Taking Vincenzo's arm, he manhandled him off the train.

Seventeen

'How did you know?' asked Vincenzo.

'Briefcase, jacket,' sneered the other. So the friendly clerk at the Prefecture had been alert!

They drove him to the Police Station where, after relieving him of his belongings, Basso took delight in locking him in a cell. With time to reflect, he wondered whether Scarpone would be informed of his attempted escape or whether the matter would be dealt with locally. He hoped the latter. Surely one misdemeanour over eighteen months could not warrant severe punishment: a day or two in the cells perhaps!

Basso woke him the following morning at six to take him to see the Chief of Police. The chief's words surprised him. 'You're leaving within the hour, Di Tomasi.' No deference to status from this man! He jabbed a finger at Basso. 'Make sure his possessions are returned to him before he boards the train, sergeant.' Vincenzo's hopes rose. Was he being released?

The sun streamed through the carriage window. Vincenzo tried pulling down the blind but it came away in his hand. He dropped it onto the floor and toed it under the seat. Basso, sitting opposite raised an amused eyebrow. Encouraged by this show of friendliness, Vincenzo asked, 'Where are you taking me?'

'All prisoners of conscience are being transferred to the capital."

'On whose orders?'

'Marshal Scarpone issued the orders two days ago.'

'So this has nothing to do with my arrest yesterday?'

Basso shrugged.

Vincenzo smothered a curse. If he'd left a week earlier as he'd originally planned, he would have got clean away!

Basso made it clear he was in no mood to talk. Pulling out a newspaper, he started reading but Vincenzo realised he was still watching him. The merest movement brought his penetrating black eyes swivelling around in his direction.

They left the train at Potenza, and much to his embarrassment, Basso produced a pair of handcuffs, fixing one to his own wrist and snapping the other onto Vincenzo's.

'This isn't necessary,' he protested hotly. 'I'm not likely to make a run for it.'

'You tried it once.'

There was a two-hour wait for the Rome train and Vincenzo soon understood why his captor had insisted on the handcuffs. Basso folded his arms and closed his eyes. Within minutes, his head dropped forward and he began to snore. Vincenzo couldn't follow his example. His mind was too busy trying to figure out his fate. Transfer to a closed prison was the most likely prospect.

The sound of an approaching train jolted Basso back to life. 'We part company here,' he said, unlocking the handcuffs. He sounded almost sorry.

Vincenzo's hopes rose again. Could this mean he really was being released? But when the train pulled in, he saw that it was no ordinary train. It was entirely composed of goods wagons. The wagon doors slid open.

'Go on then,' said Basso, giving him a shove and tossing his briefcase and jacket in after him. The door slid closed, a whistle blew and the train set off again. Vincenzo recovered his balance, picked up his belongings and looked around. There were about a dozen men in the wagon. One man made room for him. Some occupants squatted on rolled-up bedding, others sprawled on the floor, smoking or gazing into space.

As the train gathered speed, sunlight flickered through the wagon's slatted walls like a magic lantern show, striking across the features of the men opposite to fleetingly reveal a bearded profile, the whites of a pair of eyes, the outline of a down-turned mouth.

The stench of unwashed bodies and stale tobacco told Vincenzo that his companions had been travelling for some time. He began to feel nauseous. The man next to him struck up a conversation. 'Where've you come from?'

'Matera.'

'Been there long?'

'Eighteen months.'

'What did they get you for?'

'A trumped up charge of … '

'Oh yeah!' One of the men began a slow hand clap, others joined in.

The first man chortled, held up a staying hand and said. 'Leave off.' Turning back to Vincenzo, he said, 'They're all trumped up. Conscientious objector, me! Dodged them for a year, they caught up with me a month ago. Picked me up for petty theft.' He held up a pocket watch between thumb and forefinger. 'Me, a pick-pocket, I ask you!'

'*Merda!*' Vincenzo slapped his hands to his pockets. 'What else have you snatched from me?'

His companion grinned broadly. 'You haven't got anything else worth taking. Here!' He returned the watch and drawing out a packet of cigarettes, lit one up before handing the rest back to their rightful owner. It was the packet Vincenzo had bought in Matera the day before. 'I think you'll find everything back in place. Check if you don't believe me.'

'You're good!'

They shook hands and when Vincenzo looked down to check on his signet ring, the other man gave a sly wink. 'Don't worry, that's me done for today.'

'Do you know where we're headed?' he asked him, for despite the fellow's shady background, he had taken a liking to him.

'Civitavecchia if I'm not mistaken.'

Vincenzo's heart sank. This was a tight-security prison north of Rome. What a mess he'd made of things! If he'd stuck to his original plan, he could have got away. Leaning his head back on the carriage wall, he took a long draw on his cigarette and blew a series of smoke rings up to the ceiling, smiling at the memory of how this trick used to amuse Beppe. For a brief second the reek of cheap tobacco became the satisfying aroma of a fat Havana, the briefcase resting on his knee, a wide-eyed little boy.

He drew on the cigarette again, reminded that Beppe would now be approaching his thirteenth birthday.

Most of the men dozed off, lulled by the train's rhythm, only to be jolted awake when the train came to a shuddering halt. Vincenzo shifted his position in an attempt to ease his stiff limbs.

'Nearly there,' announced his travelling companion. 'We'll ... '

He was cut short by the ratatat-tat of gunfire. Shouting broke out and the doors of the wagon slid open. The prisoners leapt to their feet, clutching their belongings defensively in front of them.

'Out! Get a move on!'

Vincenzo looked around in confusion. The man shouting orders was not in uniform. Urging the prisoners out, he told them to run and hide in the nearby copse. Rolling and scrambling down the embankment, the escapees dived for cover before the guards on the train had time to open fire. Another man was waiting for them among the trees.

'Split up,' he muttered. 'You're all on your own now.' His gaze searched the faces of the escapees until he saw Vincenzo. 'You!' he shouted. 'This way.'

Vincenzo followed the man along a narrow track deep into the woods. They came to a clearing where several men with rifles slung over their shoulders were standing in a circle. He recognised one of them.

'My God, Guido Ottone!'

The two men embraced.

'Good to see you, Vincenzo,' said Guido.

Bruno and Luigi came forward to greet him, then much to his surprise, Livia ran out from the trees.

'Vincenzo!' she cried, flinging her arms around his neck and kissing him, while the men discreetly melted back into the trees leaving them on their own.

'What happened? Why didn't you contact me?'

'I couldn't, it was too dangerous. Besides, we got wind of Scarpone's new orders and decided this was the safest way of releasing you.' She took his hand. 'Come on, we've got to get going.'

'Where to?'

'Shhh! Keep your questions till later.'

She led him through the trees until they came upon a small dell thick with brambles. Livia thrust her way through, pushing aside loose branches to reveal a dilapidated motorcycle. 'Give me a hand,' she called.

Vincenzo raised an eyebrow. 'Does it work?' It looked too old to be of any use.

She frowned impatiently. 'Of course it does. Stop wasting time.' They cleared the motorcycle and pushed it out of the dell up to a stubbly track. 'I hope you know how to ride this thing?' He didn't miss the gleam of mischief in her eye.

He climbed on the bike, finding to his surprise that the engine started at once. Livia swung a leg over the pillion behind him, gripping him tightly round the waist, the briefcase wedged between them. The sounds of gunshots had diminished, and with the setting sun casting a golden glow over the landscape, mayhem seemed a long way off.

'Get a move on,' she shouted. 'They'll be scouring the area soon.'

When they reached the road, he turned north but Livia dug him in the ribs. 'Go south,' she yelled.

'Why? It's safer to head north.'

'No,' she shrieked, 'We've got to go back to Rome.'

'What?'

She kicked him in the shins, but he ignored her and accelerated. To his astonishment, she clapped her hands over his eyes. He veered off the track into a field, stalling the engine.

'Idiot!' he shouted. 'What are you doing? Do you want to get us killed?'

'We've got to go back to Rome, to Monte Mario.'

'Scarpone's men will be looking for me. What's the matter with you, Livia?' He re-started the engine. 'We're going to Castagnetto.'

'What makes you think they won't look for you there?' she sneered. 'In any case, some things are more important than *your* safety.'

'Ah,' he said, killing the engine again. 'Claudia's orders. What's up? What's the plan?'

'I can't tell you yet.'

'Why not?' Vincenzo was getting very angry. He couldn't understand what she was up to. 'We're not going anywhere until you tell me.'

'Damn you, Di Tomasi, if you won't take me then I'll hitch a lift.' She got off the bike and started striding along the road.

'Livia, wait'!' He dumped the bike and ran after he. 'We'll make for my village. I've got friends there, they'll hide us. '

Livia's eyes blazed. 'Rome first,' she said, not slowing her stride.

He didn't like being pushed around. Gripping her arm, he pulled her to a halt. 'What's going on?'

She looked up at him and he was surprised to see tears in her eyes. 'Please, Vincenzo, I have to go to Rome. It won't take long, then we can go to Castagnetto.'

She was so upset, he felt unable to refuse. 'All right.'

'Thank you Vincenzo.' She reached up and kissed him on the mouth. 'I'll tell you what this is all about when we get there.'

They walked back to the bike and climbed aboard, setting off with a roar. The road was theirs. With petrol in short supply, vehicles were few and far between. The going seemed easy and Vincenzo began to relax.

He was never sure what caused the collision. Maybe he was over-confident, disorientated from the train journey and the events following it. All at once he felt Livia's arms tighten around his middle. She screeched a warning into his ear. But it was too late. A powerful motorcycle emerged out of the gloom. Vincenzo served, slamming on the brakes, his lightweight footwear scraping the road. The bike careered onto the verge before crashing into a hedge. It was only by gripping the saddle tightly between his knees that he was able to stop himself from being thrown off.

It took him several seconds to regain his equilibrium. A knot of panic rose to his throat as he realised that Livia was no longer seated behind him. Swinging himself off the bike, he stumbled along the verge afraid of what he might find. She was lying face down on the grass, her arms flung out in front of her.

'Livia!'

She moved her head and looked at him, a dazed expression in her eyes. Blood streamed from a cut on her forehead.

'*Madonna!*' he croaked. 'Are you all right?'

She sat up with a groan. 'No bones broken. The foliage saved me.'

Relief flooded over him. He helped her to her feet, pulled her to him, burying his face in her black hair, and murmuring incoherent words in her ear. She winced and pushed him away. 'Be careful, you're hurting me.'

They stood wrapped in a trembling embrace, recovering their senses. All at once, Livia came to life. She pointed at the other bike, which had skidded down the road before slewing to a halt. There was no sign of the rider.

In his concern for Livia, Vincenzo had completely forgotten the other motorcyclist. 'You wait here; I'll take a look,' he said, urging her gently into the cover of the hedge, and running back to where the other bike had ended up. All at once, a figure stumbled out of the darkness.

'Get down!' yelled Livia.

Her shriek of warning was drowned out by the sound of a gunshot.

Vincenzo recoiled. One moment the man was stumbling across the road, the next, he was sprawled on his back on the tarmac, blood forming a halo around his head. He stared at the body, fixated. Livia ran to join him. A revolver dangled from her hand.

He gave a gasp. 'What the hell!'

Dropping the revolver, she threw her arms round his neck, croaking, 'That was close.'

He pushed her away. 'Close! What are you talking about? The man was coming to speak to me.' He couldn't believe she had opened fire.

Her eyes widened. 'He was going to kill you.'

'Don't be ridiculous, Livia.' Throwing off her arms, he stalked over to kneel down beside the prone figure. '*Stupidina!* How could you... ' The words died on his lips as he lifted the man's arm and saw his 7- round Glissenti. The safety catch was off.

Livia rushed to his side. 'What did I tell you?'

'You could have disabled him,' was all he could bring himself to mutter.

'My God! Is that all the thanks I get. Don't you realise, it was you or him?'

All at once, she began to shiver. Vincenzo's anger changed to shame. He shouldn't have shouted at her. She had saved his life. She was weeping into a handkerchief now, trying to stifle her sobs. Turning from him, she started to walk away. He hurried after her and took her in his arms.

'I'm sorry, *amore*.'

He was stunned, and ashamed of his outburst. Livia's accuracy of aim had astounded him. Where had she learnt to shoot like that? He felt a knot of nausea rising to his throat. How could she have done this? If his army days had taught him one thing, it was that to kill a man, even in self defence, was akin to destroying a piece of one's own soul. It was a terrifying experience.

He led her to the side of the road and made her sit down on the grass.

'Have you got a cigarette?' she asked.

He lit one for her and she took it from him with trembling fingers. It was completely dark now, and he began to feel anxious. Shaking off stupor, he glanced up and down the road. It was deserted. He ran back and picked up the revolver. Then he bent down and dragged the motorcyclist over to the verge. A search of his pockets revealed that he was a 26-year-old First Lieutenant of the *Bersaglieri* Cyclist Regiment seconded to round up escaped prisoners on behalf of the Civatavecchia *Carabienieri*. Vincenzo gave a hard swallow. The man would have had orders to shoot on sight. Livia's quick reaction had indeed saved his life. He saw that the dead man was about his own height and build and an idea dawned.

He picked up the soldier's bike and found that it seemed to have escaped serious damage. A broken headlamp didn't matter. He signalled to Livia, who joined him.

'We'll use this bike; it's twice as powerful as the other one. I'm going to swap clothes with him, but you'll have to help me undress him.'

She had recovered her composure, but he noticed the cut on her forehead was still bleeding.

'Let me take a look at that.' Taking a handkerchief out of his pocket, he gently dabbed the wound. 'You can ride sidecar if you like.'

'I'll ride pillion,' she retorted, snatching the handkerchief from him and tying it round her head. 'Stop fussing and get on with the job.'

Vincenzo gave a grim smile. It seemed that Livia was her old self. The man's boots were half a size too small for him but more suitable for riding a motorcycle than his own lightweight shoes. While he was changing, Livia went in search of his briefcase.

As they continued towards Rome on the more powerful bike, Vincenzo tried to convince himself that Livia's errand wouldn't take long. Once she had done whatever it was she had to do, they could go on to Castagnetto where he would get his old friend, Dr Stefano Amato, to take a look at the wound on her head. Thinking about Castagnetto brought a surge of homesickness. He longed to move back into his villa, but he knew that Scarpone might look for him there. But back on his own territory, friends would hide them until things had cooled down.

All at once, he felt Livia tug at his waist. 'Can we stop for a minute,' she yelled in his ear.

He drew to a halt by the side of the road. 'What's the matter?'

'Call of nature,' she said, climbing off the bike.

She looked pale and drawn. 'Don't you feel well?' he asked.

'I'm all right, just shut up and let me find somewhere to go.'

She pushed her way through a hedge and disappeared. He climbed off the bike and paced up and down, concerned about her. Several minutes later, she staggered through the hedge wiping the back of her hand across her mouth. 'Come on, what are you waiting for?'

'You look awful, Livia,' he said.

'Thanks a lot. That's just what a woman wants to hear.'

'I didn't mean ... Look, if you're not feeling well, let's rest for a while.'

'All right, just ten minutes.'

She reached into her pocket, drew out a packet of cigarettes and offered him one.

He took it, lit up and asked, 'Where did you get these?'

'Our dead friend had no further use for them.'

The cigarette seemed to restore her spirits, if not her state of health. Stubbing out the butt, she climbed back onto the pillion, impatient to be off again. He tossed his own cigarette stub to the ground, stamped on it and got on the bike. As they roared off again, he felt a rush of exhilaration. It was as if he had regained his youth. Here he was, riding a powerful motorbike with the wind whistling past his face and a beautiful girl riding pillion behind him.

Half an hour later, they reached the city outskirts and Vincenzo reduced speed. The streets were quiet, giving a false sense of security. It was while they were driving along Corso Vittorio Emmanuele that the stillness was broken by the screech of sirens. Then, they heard the drone of low flying aircraft. Livia clamped her arms more tightly round his waist as he fought to correct a skid after avoiding a pothole. All at once, there was a deafening explosion. The building ahead of them crashed to the ground and pieces of concrete hurtled up into the air. There was another detonation, forcing Vincenzo to brake as shrapnel skittered towards them. He slapped a hand to a cut on his cheek and turned to Livia. She was unhurt but her eyes were wide with fear.

'We've got to find shelter,' he shouted.

'No!' she shrieked. 'Keep going.'

He couldn't understand. She was clearly terrified, yet she wouldn't give up her mission.

'Look!' he said, starting to get off the bike. 'We can take cover over there.'

There was yet another explosion, and people began running from their homes to head for the air raid shelters. Vincenzo was spurred into action. Whatever happened, they had to get out of the direct line of fire. Shifting into gear, he squinted into the dust filled street and drove on. The bike jolted around masonry and scorching debris to emerge onto an undamaged section of road. Vincenzo accelerated and they shot forward, tyres screeching.

Panicking civilians ran blindly across the road in front of them, vehicles and bikes filled the streets as people tried to make their escape from the city centre. Forced to stop at a road junction, Vincenzo's stomach muscles tightened when he saw a member of the *Carabinieri* coming over. Would his stolen uniform pass the test?

'Where are you heading, *Tenente*?' asked the man.

'*Aquila*,' he replied, his own voice echoing strangely in his ears. Would the man notice his agitation?

The officer looked surprised, but he waved them on.

'We got away with it,' whispered Livia.

But for how long? thought Vincenzo. Looking for cover, he slowed down to scour the neighbourhood.

Livia snatched at his arm. 'What are you doing?' she screamed.

'Looking for shelter.'

'Keep going," she shrieked.

He lost his temper. '*You* may have a death wish, Livia, but I haven't.'

'Think again, Vincenzo.'

He heard a click and felt something cold against his skin. Livia was holding a revolver to his neck. *Merda!* Where had it come from? The one she'd used to shoot the motorcyclist was safely tucked into his belt. Then he remembered: she'd rifled the dead man's clothes. She wouldn't use it, surely she wouldn't shoot him. But a sideways glance at her unyielding expression told him she was in deadly earnest. Her eyes wore a hard glint, her high cheek bones made her look gaunt. His mind whirled. Was getting to Monte Mario *that* important to her? Suddenly, he understood; her errand was personal. It had nothing to do with Claudia or the Cell. In that split second a multitude of thoughts raced across his mind. He owed his life to Livia. If completing the errand was important to her, then it was important to him too! He thrust the bike into gear and accelerated. Livia lowered the revolver.

They crossed the river under the rat-tat-tat of shells. Army vehicles raced across in both directions sounding their horns but Vincenzo pressed on, focusing on the façade of St Peter's, which stood starkly outlined against the brightly lit sky. On the far side of the river, Vincenzo rode close to the Duomo walls, trusting that the Vatican City wouldn't be a target. At last they reached Viale delle Medaglie d'Oro and started the ascent to Monte Mario.

Halfway up the hill, Livia snapped, 'Stop! Turn off here.'

Vincenzo brought the motorcycle to a halt in a cobbled cul-de-sac. Livia clambered off the bike, and ran across the road to disappear through a door in a high wall. He read the inscription above the door: *Il Convento di Santa Maria della Pietà*, and felt puzzled. What business had she here? In his mind, he replayed her evasive replies to his earlier questions, but couldn't come up with an explanation. He got off the bike to stretch his legs, and stood staring at the scene below. Dante's Inferno! Fires lit the streets, smoke rose in swirls against the orange-red sky. His thoughts shifted to his wife. London had suffered like this. But Alice and Beppe were safe in Harrogate. Thinking about Alice brought a rush of conscience. How could he have let himself become involved with Livia? These thoughts made him angry. Where the devil had Livia got to? All at once, the door opened and she stumbled out. He rushed towards her, and tried to take the bundle she was carrying.

'Be careful!'

Vincenzo gasped as he felt something stir in his arms. Pulling the covering blanket apart, he met the bewildered gaze of a young child.

Eighteen

Rome

In a bunker beneath the city, Marshal Eduardo Scarpone sat at his desk mulling over the night's events. Not only had he lost almost fifty prisoners off the train from Lucania to Civatavecchia, but the Americans had chosen this very night to inflict their heaviest raid ever on Rome. The ground beneath his feet trembled, reminding him that the worst was not yet over. He frowned angrily. An hour ago, a dispatch rider had informed him Di Tomasi was amongst the prisoners still not accounted for. How had he managed to get away? He must have had help. His frown deepened. That little rat, Manzello, had been telling the truth after all: Di Tomasi was in league with the partisans.

He pressed the intercom button. A nervous-looking corporal marched in and stood to attention in front of him.

'Any news on Di Tomasi?'

'No…yes, *Signor Maresciallo*.'

'Well, which is it?'

The man hesitated, then ventured. 'One of the *Carabinieri* stopped a motorcyclist, a member of the *Bersaglieri*. The man said he was on his way to Aquila. The odd thing was…'

'Yes?' prompted Scarpone impatiently.

'There was a woman riding pillion.'

'A woman, eh!'

Before the marshal could question the corporal further, the man volunteered, 'The *Carabiniere* said he was puzzled because the rider seemed a little mature to still hold the rank of *tenente*.'

All at once, things began to make sense: an earlier report of a dead dispatch rider stripped of his clothing; a pair of expensive shoes cast into the ditch; a wrecked motorcycle. But why had Di Tomasi returned to Rome? And why go to Aquila?

Again, the corporal volunteered information. 'The officer thought the man looked familiar.'

The marshal's face turned purple. 'Why didn't he arrest him?'

The young corporal looked increasingly uncomfortable. 'There was a lot going on at the time, *Eccellenza*. It was only afterwards …'

His superior cut him short. 'Did he recognise the woman?' Rising to his feet, Scarpone came round from behind his desk and paced the floor in front of the corporal, his hands clasped behind his back.

'No, *Signor Maresciallo.*'

The answer didn't please the marshal. 'Get out!' he shouted.

The corporal saluted smartly and made his escape, leaving the marshal scowling after him. Scarpone came to a decision. Pressing the intercom button on his desk again, he summoned his stenographer.

A young woman came in, armed with a notepad. Despite the urgency of the situation, Scarpone couldn't stop his gaze from sweeping over her. He'd slept with her on several occasions, and made a mental note to get her into his bed again. 'Take down this dispatch, then send it off immediately.'

'Yes, *Signor Maresciallo.*'

He started dictating. 'Double the road blocks on all routes west. Di Tomasi and his female companion must be picked up. Look out for a regulation *Bersaglieri* motorcycle.' An idea occurred to him and he softened his tone, speaking directly to the stenographer. 'Do you happen to know who this woman could be, Anna Maria?' He deliberately used her given name to evoke a sense of familiarity.

She glanced timidly up at him before replying. 'There was a woman once who called in asking about him. You may remember her. Of course, I'm only guessing but…' The marshal moved up behind her and slid a hand inside her blouse. She stiffened then choosing her words carefully, said, 'A striking woman with long black hair, name of …' She paused to think. 'I think it began with C.'

Livia Carduccio! Of course, the exciting beauty he'd bedded a couple of times. That was well over a year ago, before the German withdrawal from Tunisia, before Mussolini began to lose his grip. She'd appeared out of the blue and disappeared just as mysteriously. Now he understood why. The little strumpet had wanted to wheedle information out of him. How easily he'd been duped! A surge of anger coursed through his veins finding outlet in a vicious pinch to Anna Maria's nipple. She cried out, and he removed his hand from her breast without apology.

'Amend that dispatch,' he snapped. 'It should read: Di Tomasi and Livia Carduccio. That will be all.' Abruptly he dismissed her, but not before noticing with a touch of amusement the tears of pain that had sprung to her eyes. She would have a nice blue-black bruise to hide from her fiancé.

Pacing the floor, he thought through the significance of this new discovery. It put a different complexion on things. It tied Di Tomasi firmly in with the Resistance. Unconsciously, he chewed at the index finger of his right hand. Suddenly aware of the taste of blood, he drew out a handkerchief and wrapped it around the broken skin and returned to his chair to sit down heavily, resting his elbows on the desk, his head in his hands. His skull throbbed as he tried to work out what was in Di Tomasi's mind. What was the fucking idiot playing at? Did he really believe he wouldn't be picked up? He thumped a fist down on the desk and spoke aloud. *By God, I'll get the man.*

Nineteen

A child! Suppressing his astonishment, Vincenzo urged Livia into the sidecar, handing the bundle in after her. He turned into Viale delle Medaglie d'Oro, driving recklessly down the steep hill towards the city. A sudden explosion jolted his hands off the handlebars but he managed to regain control, cursing under his breath as the child's cries became screams of terror. Who was this child? What business did Livia have snatching a child from the Convent?

He continued on through the dust-obscured streets, taking the outer periphery. Grit stung his eyes, dust choked him. At last the thunderous bombing began to recede but the traffic out of the city had slowed to walking pace beside a trail of pedestrians stumbling along on the verge. He steered the bike between the vehicles but the sidecar impeded his progress. All at once, he felt Livia tug at his trouser leg.

'Vincenzo, there's a road block ahead.'

He swiftly assessed the situation. They were travelling at barely ten kilometres an hour and there were twenty or more vehicles ahead of them. Dare he risk facing the road block? He had outwitted the police once with his stolen uniform, but he wasn't sure he could do it again. And what if the police officer had become suspicious and reported the incident. Besides, this time, there was the child to consider.

All at once, an opportunity presented itself. Just ahead was a breach in the hedge just wide enough for him to drive through. Steering sharply to the right, he accelerated across the verge and drove onto a narrow farm track. The soldiers were too busy examining papers to pay attention to a stray bike.

Making for a small copse some six hundred metres ahead, he drove across the bumpy ground without thought for the discomfort of his passengers. Once in the shelter of the trees, he stopped and checked on them. Against a backcloth of orange flares and grey smoke, Livia was completely absorbed in rocking the child on her lap. He recoiled with shock. Why hadn't he realised at once? It was *her* child! He had seen that same glow of maternal love on Alice's face not so many years earlier.

The scene touched him, dissipating anger. Here was a vulnerable young woman, a different Livia to the one who'd followed him down to Lucania and made love with such passion; different to the Livia who had pointed a gun at his neck. The child's presence turned her into a stranger.

He frowned and said, 'Livia, we're not going any further until I get an explanation.'

She looked up, took off her beret and shook her hair loose. Tweaking back the blanket covering the child, she whispered with a ring of pride in her voice, 'This is my daughter, Isabella.'

Isabella! Vincenzo's heart convulsed. The same name as his own baby daughter, the baby who'd tragically died at only six months. This Isabella looked to be about two years old. He did a quick calculation, recalling that Livia had vanished from the partisan scene for a few months shortly after he'd got to know her. This must have been while she was pregnant. She'd reappeared at his Rome hotel almost a year later. He broke out in a sweat. One night of seduction in that camp above Florence! Could the child be his? He didn't want this, there was Alice, there was Beppe.

'Tell me about her,' he muttered, fearful at what he might hear. 'What was she doing in the Convent?'

'The nuns were looking after her.'

'Why didn't you look after her yourself?'

'How could I?'

'Where's her father?' he asked. He meant: *Am I the father?*

Livia leapfrogged over the question, saying sarcastically, 'I could hardly bring her on missions with me.'

He could barely stop himself from retorting: *surely your place was with your child, not the Resistance.* His mind was in a whirl. In his circle, mothers were there for their babies, even those wealthy enough to employ a nanny as he and Alice had done. He scrutinised Livia's face and, all at once, the difference in their ages became a barrier. It stretched not from a couple of

211

decades but to an entire generation. 'Why did you join the Resistance in the first place?' he snapped. Anything to cover his confusion.

'It's a long story.'

Again, he thought: *Am I the father?* He said, 'I'm listening.'

'Later.'

'Not later, now!'

She blinked in surprise at the force of his demand. 'There's no need to shout. If you must know, it was like this. I met Sergio at Padua University. His father wanted him to go to Salzburg University, mine wanted me to go to Bologna but we had both insisted on Padua, and so by chance, our paths crossed.' She stopped speaking.

Vincenzo's tension eased. So he wasn't the father! He wasn't sure whether he felt relieved or saddened. 'Go on,' he said more gently.

With a wistful expression on her face, she said, 'We fell in love, our first year was wonderful; then I fell pregnant. We told our families, naively believing that love conquers all. We thought they'd get over the shock, and be pleased for us.'

'And were they?'

Bitterness crept into Livia's voice. 'Sergio's father's a bigot, a Nazi sympathiser. That son of a bitch bullied Sergio into joining up even though he'd been given deferment for his studies.' She jutted her chin. 'We stood up to him. We planned to marry as soon as I came of age.' She paused, and spoke in a whisper. 'It didn't work out.'

'What happened?'

Livia gulped. 'Sergio was killed during his first month of active service.'

Vincenzo was shocked. 'I'm sorry, Livia, truly I am.'

She tossed her head. 'It's water under the bridge.'

'What about your parents? Surely they helped you?'

'They were consumed with shame; I was a bad influence on my younger brother and sister; "Get rid of the blasted thing," raged my father. How could I do that? How could I kill my unborn child?' Vincenzo tried not to show his feelings but Livia noticed his expression and, to his surprise, jumped to her father's defence. 'Papà would never suggest anything risky; he's got lots of connections; he would have paid for the abortion; it would have been perfectly safe, a qualified doctor in a decent clinic not some filthy backstreet midwife.' She paused for breath conscious that her story was garbled. 'I wouldn't hear of it, that's why they cut me off. Naturally, I had to drop out of university.'

Vincenzo felt puzzled. Why had she been so quick to jump to her father's defence after he'd been so hard on her? In his view, even her guilt didn't excuse her father's abandonment of her. He would never have abandoned a daughter of his like that.

'I don't understand,' he ventured.

'It was my fault, I let them down. We've always been a devoutly religious family, you see. But I'm not religious, not any more.'

'How did you manage?' he asked.

'Guido helped me and … '

'Guido!' interrupted Vincenzo. He'd always suspected their relationship to be more than platonic.

Intuitively picking up his mood, Livia shook her head. 'There's never been anything between us. He's a good friend, that's all, my *only* true friend. He pulled some strings, arranged for Isabella to be looked after in the Convent. His aunt was a nun there. It seemed the most practical thing to do. By pledging myself to the Resistance, I was assured of a roof over my head and my child was safe and … ' She hesitated, distress clouding her brow. 'The excitement…the danger kept me going.'

Vincenzo frowned in puzzlement. 'What made you decide it was time to collect her from the Convent? Despite the bombing, surely she's safer in the care of the nuns?'

Livia looked down and stroked the sleeping child's forehead. 'I couldn't leave her there any longer.'

'You could have waited until the fighting ended?'

She frowned with irritation. 'You don't understand.'

'Explain!'

Reluctantly, she went on: '*Suor'Augusta*, Guido's aunt, was looking after her. I trusted her; she was the buffer between the outside world and the grasping nuns. But she died of tuberculosis earlier this year.' Livia's words became almost incoherent. 'Without her that conniving Mother Superior would have taken Isabella from me. Don't forget, unmarried mothers don't have much say in these matters. They might have sent her to one of their orphanages or worse still ... ' Her eyes widened with animosity.' ... might have tried to indoctrinate her into the church, turn her into a novice. You've no idea how difficult it was for me to prise her out of their clutches.'

Vincenzo looked baffled. 'They wouldn't do that.'

'Oh but they would,' she insisted. 'Bearing a child out of wedlock, why, they consider me to be a whore!'

'But Livia, the Fascist Regime sponsors the expanding birth rate. Young mothers are afforded privileges to encourage them to enlarge their families,' he argued.

She shook her head vehemently. 'You don't know anything. Why do you think it took me so long in the Convent? I had to fight for Isabella. The Reverent Mother wouldn't even let me see her at first. In the end, I had to snatch her and run. That's why Isabella hasn't got any clothes apart from what she's wearing.' She broke off, then croaked, 'Can you believe that? I was driven to kidnap my own child!'

Vincenzo stared at her in perplexity. Why couldn't she be straight with him? He was certain she was hiding something more. Feeling enraged, he turned his face away from her and cursed under his breath. He would never understand the workings of a woman's mind.

'Did you know you were pregnant that time in Florence?'

She shook her head. He could see that she had told him all she was going to tell him, and although he felt sorry for her, he was angry too. He switched on the engine and stamped on the starter making the bike spring abruptly to life. Turning his attention to getting them all safely to Castagnetto, he rode on knowing that the farm track would eventually bring them out to another road. The sun began to shine and, beside him, he could hear Livia trying to soothe the child, who had woken up.

They hadn't gone far when the bike began to lose power until, to Vincenzo's dismay, the engine died. *Merda!* They were out of gas. Swinging his leg over the seat, he gave the vehicle a kick and began stomping up and down furiously. The situation was impossible. They were in the middle of nowhere without transport and with the added burden of a small child.

'What shall we do?' asked Livia. Since collecting her daughter from the convent, she had left all the decision-making to Vincenzo.

'How do I know.' He found her dependence on him irritating. What was the matter with her. She had always been the resourceful one, the one to come up with the ideas.

She lifted the child out of the sidecar and pulled herself up. 'At least we can have some breakfast," she said, reaching into her bag and drawing out half a loaf and a hunk of cheese.

'Where did this come from?' he demanded.

With a return of spirit, she laughed, 'Courtesy of our unfortunate biker friend. There's beer too and water for Isabella.'

Vincenzo experienced a tremor of shock. How could she be so casual about a man she'd killed in cold blood? He watched her break off a piece of bread for her daughter and tuck into a piece herself. He studied them both, feeling increasingly uneasy. He was trapped in an impossible situation. He knew it was up to him to get them out of it, but when he'd rashly entered into a love affair with this fascinating beauty, he hadn't bargained on ending up in a cosy family unit. The introduction of Isabella changed everything.

He came to a decision. Once he'd got them to safety, he'd end the affair. He had his own family to consider. After the war, Alice and Beppe would come home and life would get back to normal.

When they were ready to move on, Livia said, 'I'll have to carry Isabella.'

He shook his head. 'Let me take her.' But when he tried, the child's eyes filled with panic and she refused to leave her mother.

Livia made excuses. 'She's not used to men. The accountant, Don Luigi Pasquale is the only man who calls at the Convent. He's in a wheelchair. The sisters grow fruit and vegetables, they sell the produce to the locals but they're a closed order and they're not allowed to have dealings with the general public.

That's why Don Pasquale handles their business affairs. Apart from him, there's only Padre Sebastiano, who calls in each week to hear Confession.'

Vincenzo listened to her gabbled explanation without comment. He had come to realise that placing her baby in the care of the nuns had been her only option, but why remove her from their care at this point in time? And why had she kept the child's existence a secret?

The temperature soared. Livia removed Isabella's slippers and dressing gown, leaving her in her nightdress. '*Poverina*! She doesn't like the heat. The garden at the Convent is always cool and shady with lots of trees.' When the child started to snivel, she whispered, 'Shh Isabella.'

Isabella! Once again, the name brought a lump to Vincenzo's throat. It was a constant reminder of Alice and his life before the war. It seemed a cruel twist of fate that the child's name should be Isabella.

The going was slow with frequent rests. Isabella was now fully awake and, although Vincenzo offered to carry her many times over, she still refused to be parted from Livia. He was troubled about the blow Livia had received to her head during the collision. Could she hold out for much longer? To take his mind off these problems, he began to plan his next move with the Resistance, convincing himself that Guido would get in touch with fresh instructions from Claudia.

They turned into a field, and again Vincenzo tried to take Isabella, but she refused to be parted from her mother. As they trudged on in silence, he was reminded of the long rambles he used to have with Alice and the children. Here in the heart of the countryside, the War seemed far away. Birds sang, a gentle breeze stirred the long grass, daisies and buttercups bowed beneath their feet to spring back to attention in their wake.

Suddenly, the roar of engines shattered the calm. Vincenzo swivelled around and saw a convoy of military vehicles driving along the distant road.

'Up there!' shouted Vincenzo, pointing to a derelict barn. The building was no more than five hundred metres away beyond a field of sunflowers. Snatching the child from her mother's arms, he shoved Livia ahead of him. Crouching low, they scrambled through the sunflowers until, in her haste, Livia faltered and fell. Behind them, the roar of the vehicles grew louder.

Suddenly, the engines cut out. Vincenzo raised his head to check, and to his astonishment, he saw a woman signalling to them. He threw himself down between the sunflowers next to Livia. The child let out a frightened cry, forcing him to clamp a hand over her mouth. Beside him, Livia's eyes widened as they heard the sound of sticks thrashing through the sunflowers. Between the stalks, he caught sight of grey-green uniforms. These were the *Carabinieri* carrying out a search. They must have found the abandoned motorcycle.

He flattened himself to the ground, covering the child with his body, and squeezing the hand that Livia reached out to him.

Twenty

All at once, the thrashing stopped. Vincenzo heard mumbled voices, one of them a woman's. An order was shouted, swiftly followed by the roar of engines. They'd gone. Incomprehension followed relief. He started to get to his feet but a rustling in the sunflowers made him freeze. He looked up and met the gaze of an old woman.

'You're safe,' she said, holding out a helping hand to Isabella, but Livia made a protective grab for her child.

'Thank you for your warning,' said Vincenzo, anxious to show gratitude after Livia's brush-off.

The woman gave a toothless grin. 'You're welcome.'

'What made them leave?' he asked her.

She pointed to the east. 'I said you'd gone that way.'

'We can't thank you enough.'

'Come and have some refreshments,' she cackled.

Livia butted in. 'We haven't time.'

Vincenzo thought quickly. It would be churlish to refuse. Besides, they needed a rest. 'Thank you very much,' he said, overriding Livia's refusal, and giving her no choice but to follow him up to the farm. She didn't look happy about it.

The farmhouse was a run-down rambling place, hidden from the road by the barn. A chained-up mongrel bared its teeth and growled as they approached, prompting the woman to shriek something unintelligible at it before leading them into a dark, sparsely-furnished kitchen. A wooden shutter was nailed across the only window, a splintered crack allowing sufficient sunlight in to focus on a knotted oak table. It highlighted a coffee-stained beaker and a cracked plate, the latter sticky with the remains of an earlier meal. Crumbs and spilt food coated the table's surface. Livia gave a cry of alarm and jumped back, pulling her daughter with her when a rat appeared out of the darkness to scurry across the floor before vanishing into the shadows. The woman didn't appear to notice this unwelcome intrusion.

'Welcome, please make yourselves at home,' she mumbled, drawing out a wobbly chair from under the table.

Her traditional widow's weeds led Vincenzo to surmise that she was in her sixties or seventies. Strands of iron-grey hair straggled from a grubby scarf tied round her head, which was tied at the nape of her neck.

'Have you come far?' she asked.

'From down south.'

'Fleeing from those accursed fascists, eh?'

Livia looked up in alarm but Vincenzo sensed that they had nothing to fear from the woman. She was a humble peasant scratching a meagre living off the land.

Isabella stood beside her mother, sucking her thumb, staring in bewilderment. This was the first time that Vincenzo had taken a good look at the child. She was dark-haired like her mother with the same large brown eyes.

'The little one looks under-nourished,' said the woman. 'I'll get her something to eat.'

'She's already eaten,' cried Livia in alarm. When the woman turned away, she mouthed at Vincenzo, 'This house is disgusting. We must get out of here.'

Livia was right. The house *was* filthy. Throughout his eighteen-month exile to Lucania, he had never seen a hovel as squalid as this. Donna Caterina's house had been spotless and even Donna Teresa had taken pride in her humble cave-like dwelling, scrubbing her doorstep and polishing the furniture daily. He, too, wanted to leave but he was grateful for the woman's courage, and he couldn't bring himself to refuse her well-meant hospitality.

The woman seemed unconcerned by Livia's hostility as she put a coffee pot on the stove. Going to a cupboard, she brought out a hunk of bread, which looked several days old, and may have been chewed by molars other than human.

He shook his head and said, '*Gentile Signora*, please don't trouble yourself. We mustn't take your rations. We're most grateful for your warning, but we can't stay as we still have a long way to go.'

The woman looked crestfallen reinforcing Vincenzo's belief that to refuse her hospitality would seem, to her, an insult of the highest order.

She held up a carafe. 'Wine?'

Reluctantly, Vincenzo nodded. The consumption of a small beaker of wine would be preferable to the woman's coffee. She placed the caraffe in front of them. 'What about the child?' she asked.

'I'm still feeding her myself,' gasped Livia.

'Still suckling, huh?' The old woman nodded in approval and patted Isabella's head with a gnarled hand. The child cowered away, burying her face in her mother's shoulder.

Vincenzo and Livia gulped down the rough red wine and lost no time in making their departure.

'Thank you very much for your hospitality, *Signora,*' said Vincenzo. He drew some notes out of his pocket and offered them to her. The woman adopted a coy expression, but when he insisted, she snatched the notes from him as if afraid he would take her feigned refusal seriously.

Livia hurried away with Isabella, stopping at the gate to beckon him but Vincenzo had only taken a few steps when the woman called him back. 'Wait!' she called. 'Use this, it will make your journey easier.' She trundled an old wicker bassinet across the yard. 'Please take it,' she begged. 'I have no further use for it. My sons and grandchildren are far away.' She flung out an arm. 'Far away, in *Sud America.* They left before the War.' She shook her head as if talking to herself, mumbling, 'Couldn't go with them, couldn't leave my home. They left me here all alone.' She jutted her jaw belligerently and then fell to mumbling, '*Non importa!* I still have my animals.'

Vincenzo felt touched. What a sad figure she made, scratching a living off a run-down farm with no one to help her. Ignoring Livia's protests, he went back and took the pram from her. 'Many thanks, *Signora,* you're very kind.'

She gave a little bob and muttered, '*Che gentiluomo!*'

Livia was horrified when she inspected the bassinet. 'My God, I'm not letting Isabella ride in that!' she exclaimed indignantly. "What would people think if they saw us?'

This display of snobbery amused Vincenzo so much that he almost burst out laughing. It afforded him further insight into his lover's multi-facetted character. Smothering his amusement, he retorted, 'Don't be ridiculous, Livia, there's no one here to see us.'

She bit her lip. 'All right, but we'll have to give it a good wash first.' Her mood changed, and she said sheepishly, 'I was horrible to that old woman, wasn't I?'

"You weren't very polite,' he agreed.

'She was very brave. I should have thanked her. I don't know what comes over me.'

'Yes, you are a mixed-up person,' smiled Vincenzo, taking her into his arms and giving her a hug while Isabella stood staring at them, her thumb still in her mouth.

It was late evening by the time they reached Castagnetto. This suited Vincenzo. He wanted to get there under cover of darkness. On reaching the perimeters of the vineyard, he was not surprised to see that his villa was blacked out. His greatest wish was to spend the night in his own home, although common sense told him that this was risky. Still...just one night! But as they made their way along the lane, he began to feel alarmed. It was too quiet. He told Livia to push the pram into the vines.

All at once, the back door of the villa opened, throwing a finger of light across the lawn. Two uniformed figures stumbled out. The door closed, leaving the figures barely visible, but the men's laughter reached him as they exchanged a joke in a language which wasn't Italian.

Vincenzo clapped a hand to his head and muttered, 'My God, the Germans have taken over my villa!' Why hadn't he thought of this possibility?

'What shall we do?' gasped Livia, who had crept up behind him, leaving the pram hidden amid the vines.

He gave Livia a firm push. 'Get back!' He waited until the soldiers had relieved themselves against the wall, then watched them stagger back into the house. He felt disgusted. Were these men so ignorant that they weren't used to using internal plumbing? He beckoned to Livia. 'We've got to get rid of the pram.'

221

Livia lifted the sleeping child out of the pram, leaving Vincenzo to push it over to the river where, in the middle, the water was deep. It brought back memories. In defiance of his orders, he knew his sons used to swim in it. He'd never let his wife know. Shoving the bassinet down the bank into the water, he prayed it would sink to the bottom, but to his dismay, it started to float downstream. He yanked off his boots and jacket and rolled up his trousers before tentatively wading in and grabbing the pram by its handle, cursing himself for not having had the common sense to weight it down with stones. Snatching at an overhanging branch, he managed to hook the pram's handle over it, wedging it so that all but the handle was submerged. Clambering up the bank, he sat on an uprooted tree and put his boots back on.

'You took your time,' complained Livia when he rejoined her.

'Keep your voice down.'

'Where to now? We've got to find somewhere to hide before Isabella wakes up.'

Vincenzo cast her an exasperated glance. He felt angry with her. Why couldn't she have left the child in the Convent?

'You shouldn't have ditched the pram,' grumbled Livia.

'I had to, it was too conspicuous.' He glared at her. 'You've changed your tune. Earlier today, you didn't want to use it.'

They stood facing one another, both frowning. Suddenly, the compulsion to kiss her was too much for Vincenzo. Ignoring the sleeping child in her arms between them, he took her face in his hands and kissed her fiercely. She responded with the same passion and he knew *his* Livia was back. All at once, Isabella began to slip from her arms. Vincenzo caught her.

'What a mess I've got us into,' whispered Livia.

'We'll make it.'

'I do love you, Vincenzo, and I know I'm asking a lot of you.'

'No, darling,' he replied. 'You can never ask too much of me.'

They walked in silence with Vincenzo taking care to shorten his stride to match Livia's because he knew she was close to collapse.

'Where are we going?' she asked.

'To Grazia Elena's cottage,' he replied.

The night was still, with a sprinkling of stars. It was like many other balmy Tuscan evenings he'd experienced.

Livia plucked his sleeve. 'Listen!' she whispered.

He stopped. The sound of marching boots interrupted the peace of the countryside, faint at first but getting louder. 'Quick, into the bushes,' he mouthed at Livia.

Isabella stirred and uttered a gentle whimper. Livia clasped her daughter and shrank back into the shrubbery. Vincenzo followed her. A few minutes later, a dozen German soldiers marched passed them at a distance of no more than a few metres. They were heading for the village.

'We'll have to change our plan,' he said once the detachment was safely out of range.

'What d'you mean?'

'We can't go through the village, there'll be a curfew.'

'What are we going to do?' Livia sounded plaintive.

'There's a disused chapel half a mile back. It means retracing our steps.'

'But Vincenzo, surely it would be better to go on.'

He shook his head. 'I know the layout of the village, it's too risky.'

Livia gave an involuntary shiver and sank down to squat on the ground, her shoulders hunched over her child. He felt concerned. She hadn't got over the shock of the motorcycle accident; she needed rest. He prised the little girl from her mother and said gently, 'Come along, *amore,* it will be all right.'

Too exhausted to argue, Livia struggled to her feet and followed him back along the path they had taken earlier.

Half an hour later they reached the chapel. Vincenzo was relieved to find the door unlocked. He led the way to the vestry, and took a threadbare altar cloth out of a cupboard, spreading it out on the floor. Livia sank heavily down onto it.

Isabella woke up with the first light of dawn and started to grizzle. Livia gave a sleepy grunt and turned over. To keep her quiet, Vincenzo gave the child their last few drops of water.

'More!' she demanded, holding out the water bottle.

'I haven't any more.'

'I'm hungry,' she whined patting her stomach.

'We'll have breakfast soon but we have to walk a little way first.'

Isabella plucked at her mother's sleeve and, this time, Livia woke up. She seemed disorientated. 'What time is it?' she asked, rubbing a hand over her eyes.

'Five o'clock. We must get moving.'

Livia pushed her daughter aside and got to her feet, swaying slightly.

'What's wrong?' asked Vincenzo in alarm.

'I got up too quickly,' she replied but the words were no sooner out of her mouth than, she spun around and ran outside.

Vincenzo hurried after her. She was on the far side of the chapel, holding onto the wall and retching.

'Livia, what's wrong?'

At last she recovered. 'I don't know what came over me, it must be hunger.'

'Look, Mamma!'

Both Livia and Vincenzo gave a start. Isabella had climbed up the ridge behind the chapel and stood pointing at something. Livia rushed over and swept her up into her arms. 'Damn you, Vincenzo, why didn't you keep an eye on her? She could have fallen over the edge.'

But Vincenzo was more troubled by what Isabella had pointed at. In her concern for her child, Livia had failed to notice what was going on in the valley below.

'Get back!' he snapped, pulling mother and child clear of the ridge.

'What's the matter?'

'Didn't you see? There's a German unit in the dell and a newly constructed building. Could be an arms depot.'

Livia clapped a hand to her mouth. 'Oh God!'

'I wonder what the Germans have got planned for the village,' muttered Vincenzo under his breath.

They collected up their belongings and made their way down the other side of the hill. At that early hour, it was easy to mingle with the farm labourers making for the fields. Still wearing his purloined uniform and with a two-day stubble on his chin, Vincenzo felt confident that he wouldn't be recognised. They would probably think he had been assigned to escort the woman and child to a camp.

From time to time, he glanced at Livia, and felt alarmed. Her face was drained of colour, she could scarcely place one foot in front of the other. He would need to get his doctor friend, Stefano Amato, to take a look at her as soon as possible. He stopped to transfer Isabella to his shoulders. The little girl had grown used to him now and no longer fretted to be carried by her mother.

He was worried about off-loading Livia and Isabella onto Grazie Elena. She was no longer a young woman and her eyesight was failing. But without contact with Claudia and Guido, where else could he take them?

Grazia Elena was in the yard feeding the chickens. When Vincenzo opened the gate, she glanced up in alarm, not recognising him in the Bersaglieri uniform. He called her by name and she dropped the bowl of chicken feed and clutched a hand to her throat.

He rushed over. '*Madonna mia,* I didn't mean to startle you.'

At the sound of voices a teenage girl ran out of the house. 'Who are these people, Grandmama?'

Grazie Elena soon got over her surprise. 'It's all right, Giuliana,' she said. 'It's the count.'

The girl gasped in astonishment. 'But why...?' Then realising that Livia was about to collapse, she helped her into the house. 'What's the matter with her?'

'I think she's got concussion. Go and fetch Dr Amato,' said Vincenzo, as he assisted Livia into a chair.

Snatching up a shawl, Giuliana ran out of the house.

'Mamma!' cried Isabella, holding out her arms to her mother, but Livia was too exhausted to respond.

Grazia Elena gave the child a reassuring hug. 'Don't worry, little one, your mamma will be all right. What happened to her, *Signor Conte?*' she asked.

Vincenzo described the motorcycle accident and their flight from Rome but was spared from going into too much detail by the arrival of Stefano Amato, who confirmed Vincenzo's suspicions that Livia had a slight concussion. 'Give her a week or two and she'll be as good as new, she's young and healthy,' he said.

As Vincenzo escorted him to the gate, he asked, 'Who is she?'

'A friend.'

'The child? You're not ... ?'

'Of course not,' retorted Vincenzo.

'How did you meet her?'

'Through mutual acquaintances.'

Amato eyes narrowed. 'What are you mixed up in, Vincenzo?'

He took his friend by the arm and explained, 'I found out more than I bargained for when I went up to Padua three years ago. Livia is part of that.'

The doctor gave a shrug and said, 'I warned you. Take care! Remember your wife and son in England.'

'How could I forget them!' snapped Vincenzo hotly.

'Forgive me, Vincenzo, I'm sure you know what you're doing.' In an endeavour to restore peace, he went on, 'Don't forget, the woman will need at least a couple of weeks' rest.'

The two men parted company amicably, but Vincenzo knew that Amato's interest had been aroused and he wondered how long he would be able to keep his curiosity at bay.

Vincenzo soon realised that he'd been right to bring Livia and Isabella to Grazia Elena's house. His old housekeeper was only too delighted to accommodate them. After a hastily prepared meal, Livia went to bed while Giuliana took Isabella out to play in the yard.

'I'll need to get hold of some clothes,' he said when he was alone with Grazia Elena. 'I've nothing but this uniform to wear.'

She looked puzzled. 'Where did you get it?'

'It's a long story,' he replied, hoping she wouldn't press him. The last thing he wanted was to explain the episode of the dead policeman and Livia's part in it.

'There's one of my late husband's suits in the wardrobe. I dare say it will fit you, but it's not what you're used to.'

He thanked her, then went on to explain that the three of them would need to stay under cover for a while.

'Will Giuliana be discreet?' he asked.

Grazia Elena looked indignant. 'My granddaughter can be trusted.'

For the next few days things remained quiet, but calm was broken when one day, towards the end of July, Giuliana called them all into the house.

'Come in and listen to this,' she shouted.

They all rushed in to hear a special News Bulletin on the wireless. The newsreader gabbled with excitement as he made his announcement: 'Benito Mussolini has been ousted as Prime Minister and most of his Cabinet have been deposed. General Badoglio has taken over as leader of the government and the former dictator has been imprisoned on the Island of Ponza.'

He went on to explain that all political dissidents would be released. Grazia Elena's eyes lit up as she clasped her employer's hands and cried, 'What wonderful news! You'll be safe now.'

The newsreader gave a list of other officials who had been booted out of government. Scarpone was not among them. This did not surprise Vincenzo. The marshal was conniving and had a talent for covering his back.

Livia's return to health brought restlessness. 'I hate being cooped up here with nothing to do,' she complained. 'I'm well enough to go down to the village now. You never know, I might be able to find out about that arms depot.'

Vincenzo was appalled. 'Don't be ridiculous, Livia, it's too dangerous. The Germans will get suspicious. If you're challenged, how will you explain your presence here?'

'I'll say I'm a relative of Grazia Elena staying with her for a few weeks.'

He tried to reason with her but Livia was insistent, and much to Giuliana's indignation, she insisted on taking over the day-to-day food shopping. But it wasn't long before Giuliana's resentment disappeared. Admiration began to overlay hostile acceptance, due mainly to Livia's colourful descriptions of the big fashion houses in Milan, and the dance halls and cinemas in other northern cities that she had frequented before the War. This was a fantasy world far beyond Giuliana's reach, and she loved to hear about it.

Livia also befriended Aldo Comolli, the owner of the village café, telling Vincenzo how much they both hated the Germans. She wanted to take Isabella down to meet Aldo but he managed to talk her out of that. He felt troubled because, although the café proprietor was a good man, he was garrulous. He could easily let something slip, and he didn't want them to be forced to flee the village. The discovery of the arms depot made it essential for him to stay in Castagnetto until he could make contact with the cell.

Isabella settled in well. Vincenzo found a length of rope and rigged up a makeshift swing on the tree in the yard, and Giuliana took on the task of keeping her amused.

'Higher, Giuliana, higher!' cried the little girl as she swung back and forth below the branches.

Livia instinctively trusted Giuliana, welcoming the attention she gave Isabella. Vincenzo soon realised that although she adored her daughter, Livia was not cut out for motherhood. She even agreed to the child's bed being moved into Giuliana's room.

They had still not been able to contact Claudia, and Vincenzo was losing patience. He and Livia viewed the news of Italy's capitulation with mixed feelings. Surrender changed the status of the occupying Germans from defenders to oppressors, making the villagers even more jittery. They all listened to Grazia Elena's old wireless and learnt that British and American troops had landed at Salerno and Taranto. In private, Vincenzo and Livia discussed the issue of the arms depot, voicing their concern about the vulnerability of the village.

'What are the Krauts planning?' questioned Livia. 'Maybe they'll retreat.'

'I'm sure they won't give up easily. It's my guess they'll forge on down to Rome. Castagnetto is right in their path, the village could end up being the arena for a bloody battle.'

Twenty-one

One night Guido turned up. He explained that he'd waited until things had cooled down before coming to look for them. A drink at Comolli's bar had led him to Grazia Elena's cottage. Vincenzo experienced a shiver of dread. How easily Guido had learnt their whereabouts! He'd warned Livia not to confide too readily in Aldo Comolli.

Grazia Elena and Giuliana were wary of Guido. 'He looks like a gypsy,' Vincenzo heard Grazia Elena say. 'Why is the count consorting with such a vagabond?' She did, however, reluctantly agree to let Guido bed down in the barn.

The three partisan members talked into the night. When Guido learned about the armament depot he looked alarmed. '*Dio!* That's bad news...but, wait a minute, now that Mussolini's been arrested and the pressure's off, why don't you go up to your villa, Vincenzo? You could say you've only just got here, try to win the commandant's friendship. He's not to know you're an escaped dissident.'

'That's a splendid idea!'

'How good is your German?' asked Guido.

'I spent a year in Berlin before joining the army.'

'That could prove useful.'

'What about Scarpone, you said yourself that he may still be looking for you?' protested Livia.

'I'm not worried on that score,' rejoined Vincenzo, forgetting his own earlier misgivings. 'He'll have lost interest in me by now.'

'You should be, Vincenzo,' she insisted. 'Mussolini may have fallen, but that bastard's still in office.' When Guido shot her a surprised glance, she finished lamely, 'It could put us all in danger.'

Vincenzo quickly dismissed her concern. 'Guido's right, a tête-à-tête with the commandant could reveal something.'

'It's a really stupid plan,' argued Livia. 'Why don't we ....'

Guido lost impatience. 'Keep out of this, Livia.' He turned to Vincenzo. 'How do the villagers feel about the Germans?'

'They're tolerated, not welcomed. Most people are barely civil to them and the Germans themselves practically ignore the villagers.'

Again Livia interrupted them. 'There you are! He won't see you. Why don't we just blow up the arms depot?'

'Shut up, Livia!' snapped Guido.

'I have to try,' said Vincenzo in a more kindly tone.

'You're not equipped for this sort of play-acting,' she persisted.

Vincenzo grinned. 'You didn't see me in my school play. I was the star turn.'

Making light of the situation didn't help.

'It's absurd!' cried Livia. 'Scarpone only has to hear you're back and he'll send his men up here to arrest you. Let me go up to the villa instead of you. It's easier for a woman. Why, I guarantee I shall be able to twist that Kraut Commander round my little finger!'

Vincenzo's face clouded with anger. He thumped the flat of his hand on the table and shouted, 'Certainly not!'

Guido broke in to the argument. 'Maybe that's not such a bad idea.'

Livia's eyes flashed triumphantly. 'What did I tell you? Leave it to me, I'll find out all we need to know. I can charm the socks off that son-of-a-bitch. It worked with Scarpone, and he's far more intelligent than that over-weight Kraut.'

Angrily, Vincenzo sprang to his feet and grabbed Livia by the shoulders. 'You're not going anywhere near that fat bastard.' Ignoring Guido's presence, he shouted, 'What you did before must never happen again.' He shook her violently, thrusting his face into hers. 'D'you hear me?'

Livia struggled free, turning to Guido for support, but he looked dumbfounded. After a moment, he said, 'Maybe Vincenzo is better equipped to handle this, Livia,. After all, he speaks German, and besides, he's got a genuine excuse to visit his own villa.'

Vincenzo nodded. 'It's settled.'

He looked at Livia, aware of how she hated losing an argument, and he wasn't surprised when she spun on her heel and left the room, slamming the door behind her.

Later that night in the privacy of their room, she was full of remorse.

'I'm so sorry, *amore mio*,' she whispered. 'Forgive me for losing my temper.'

Forgive her? He always did.

'Please don't do this,' she begged.

'There's no other way.'

She started to argue but Vincenzo's expression hardened, letting her know that it would be useless to protest.

After Livia had fallen asleep, Vincenzo lay awake. He brushed his fingertips along the length of her lustrous hair and kissed her lightly on the cheek, asking himself how she managed to arouse so many conflicting emotions in him. With Alice he had been content. They had had minor squabbles of course, but Alice had never deliberately stoked his anger. Theirs had been a comfortable relationship, lacking drama. With Livia it was different. She took delight in fuelling his emotions, making him feel deliriously happy one minute, driving him insanely jealous the next. He never knew where he was with her; he knew only that he would kill for her.

He fell asleep, waking early the next day to plan his move. In two days time after Guido had found some decent clothes for him to wear, he would go up to his villa explaining that he had just arrived from Rome. He would say that he had hitched a lift as far as Castagnetto because his own car was out of commission. It was a long shot. He knew how suspicious the Germans were.

Livia was unusually subdued the next day. After the evening meal, she excused herself early with, 'I'm off to bed, good night.'

After she'd gone, embarrassed by their earlier display of emotion in front of Guido, Vincenzo muttered, 'She's still angry with me.'

'My friend, keep away from her, she's trouble.'

'I thought you were her friend,' replied Vincenzo, somewhat taken aback.

'I am, but you're also my friend and I repeat, she's trouble.'

Vincenzo stiffened. 'I'm well aware of her shortcomings,' he retorted.

Next day Livia listened to the two men making their plans. She longed to shout out: *Stop it you fools, your plot won't work!* She blamed Guido for encouraging Vincenzo in the madcap scheme.

She studied her lover, trying to analyse why she adored him. Other men she had dated had been younger, and better looking, so what was it about this middle-aged man that so entranced her?

During their discussions, Vincenzo and Guido seemed to have forgotten her. She hated being ignored. Eventually, she flounced out of the room, praying that Vincenzo would follow her, but he didn't. An hour later, she went down again to find the men still absorbed in discussing their plan.

She drew up a chair between them and announced loudly, 'I've had an idea.'

Vincenzo brushed her aside. 'Not now Livia.'

Again, she tried to butt in but they waved her away. She clenched her fists in frustration, realising that collecting Isabella from the Convent had changed her lover's view of her. He no longer saw her as the brave Amazon. She was now a mother, to be protected and kept in her place.

'Listen!' she shouted.

Guido looked up angrily and, much to her astonishment, Vincenzo pushed back his chair and, taking her by the elbow, pulled her to her feet and marched her to the door.

'Everything's under control, Livia,' he said with constrained patience.

She tried again. 'Why won't you listen to what I've got to say? It's Isabella, isn't it? You would have involved me if we hadn't collected her from the Convent.'

'You have to think of your daughter, Livia,' replied Vincenzo.

'Damn it, I should have left her there at the mercy of those nuns.'

Pulling away from him, she ran upstairs, tears of anger and frustration coursing down her cheeks. Damn them! She'd show them how impossible their scheme was. Vincenzo may have been successful spying on his colleagues at the Fascist Headquarters but he wouldn't be able to coerce information out of a high-ranking German officer. She waited until Grazia Elena and Giuliana had gone to bed before creeping quietly along the corridor to Giuliana's room, pausing on the landing to listen. The men's voices reached her from downstairs interspersed by the occasional guffaw of laughter as they sat drinking.

She eased open the door to Giuliana's room and held her breath. The occupants didn't stir. Giuliana and Isabella were enjoying the untroubled sleep of youth. She couldn't resist going over to kiss Isabella's cheek.

Creeping to the wardrobe, she quietly searched through Giuliana's clothes, freezing in alarm when the girl gave a shuddering snore. The bad moment passed. Turning her attention back to her task, she picked out a cotton skirt and a colourful blouse. Closing the wardrobe door quietly, she crept out of the room.

Back in the bedroom she shared with Vincenzo, she hurriedly made some alterations to the garments, chopping off several centimetres from the skirt, sewing the hem with large untidy stitches. She wasn't an able seamstress. The blouse had a ruched neckline and would serve as it was. Footwear was a problem. Giuliana's feet were a size smaller than hers and the only shoes suitable were a pair of red ankle-straps. She'd found them hidden at the back of the wardrobe and suspected they had been concealed from Grazia Elena, who wouldn't have approved of them. If she felt a tweak of conscience at stealing the teenager's clothes, she quickly dismissed it. After the War, she would take her to Milan and buy her whatever she wanted. She deserved that. Giuliana had been very kind to Isabella.

The skirt, knee-length now, was a little tight round the hips. She smiled to herself. What a surprise Vincenzo would get when she broke the news of her pregnancy. She'd been dying to tell him, but had decided to wait until the awful business of the munitions depot had been sorted out.

After applying lipstick and mascara, she pinned her long hair back from her face with a tortoiseshell clasp. The peasant-style blouse showed off the swell of her breasts. Satisfied with her appearance, she crept downstairs and left the house.

It wasn't easy finding her way down to the village in the dark, but she reached the street without mishap. The windows of Comolli's café were blacked out, but she could hear music and voices coming from inside. A knot of fear tightened in her stomach as she rehearsed her performance in her head. A drunken soldier stumbled out of the café nearly knocking her over, and she almost lost her nerve.

He gave her a slurred apology in German and disappeared down the deserted road, reminding her that a curfew was in place for the villagers. Taking a deep breath, she pushed open the swing door and went inside. A hush fell over the café as all eyes turned in her direction. Soldiers of various ranks were sprawled at tables littered with beer bottles. Behind the bar, Aldo Comolli hesitated in polishing a beer mug. He gave her a warning frown but she ignored him.

'Well, boys, who's going to buy me a drink?' she asked in broken German. She'd picked up a smattering of the language from her erstwhile fiancé, Sergio, who had been bi-lingual.

With girls in short supply, several men jumped to their feet, jostling one another to get to the bar. The village women refused to fraternise with their so-called allies, and following *Il Duce's* downfall, it was even worse. Now, the German soldiers were seen as oppressors.

Livia had heard them discussing the German occupation. 'They're supposed to be allies but they behave like conquerors,' she'd heard one woman complain.

'It's outrageous,' another said. 'The commandant has no right to put his men in the villa. It's belonged to the Di Tomasi family for centuries. Why doesn't the Count come home and turf those Aryan beasts out?'

She'd smiled to herself. What would they think if they knew Vincenzo was living less than a kilometre away? She'd heard the men, troubled by the number of soldiers in the vicinity, speculating on what the commandant's plans were. 'Why don't they move the platoon on? There's nothing here for them?'

Livia had her sights set on one particular officer. He sat alone, a lean, blond-haired man with thin lips and pale blue eyes. She'd seen him in the commandant's company and knew that he was the Platoon's Second in Command. He was a loner and didn't mix with the other officers. She felt his gaze on her, sensed his lust, concealed behind indifference in front of the men of lower rank.

She accepted a couple of drinks and began to feel a little dizzy remembering, too late, that she'd not been able to drink alcohol during her first pregnancy. Ignoring the warning signs, she flirted outrageously, bantering with the men in her terrible German, mocking them when they took a stab at Italian.

Aldo Comolli came over and cleared the empties from the table, muttering in her ear: 'Go home before it's too late, *Signorina.*'

She smiled sweetly back at him and shook her head. Later in the evening, the blond officer signalled to her but Livia ignored him. She knew how to tease a man. Three quarters of an hour later, they left the bar together. The lower ranks watched them leave, some sneering behind their officer's back. On her way out, she snatched up a bottle of Cognac and, pointing a finger at her escort, called out, 'Put it on *his* tab, Aldo.'

She allowed the man to support her as they made their way around to the back of the building, telling herself that this was part of her plan. In truth, she may well have fallen without his arm to lean on. Her legs felt weak, her vision blurred.

The officer led her into a barn adjacent to the café. He released his gun holster, and started to unbuckle his belt. Reality hit her. She'd slept with many men; she'd been free with her favours; she wasn't ashamed of it. This was different. Panic rose. Stalling for time, she said flippantly, 'Don't be in such a hurry, tell me your name first?'

'It's not important.'

'I can't go with a *complete* stranger,' she retorted.

He gave a mirthless smile and said, 'Johan Fleischer.'

She had watched him knock back a large quantity of beer and whisky, yet he seemed sober. This man was not going to be easy to trick into giving away information.

Showing bravado, she laughed and said, 'I don't like that name, I shall call you *Cazzone*.' She hoped his knowledge of Italian didn't extend to vulgarities. 'Want another drink,?' She flourished the Cognac bottle in front of his face.

He wrenched it out of her hand and flung it down. The bottle hit a scythe leaning against the wall and broke, its contents trickling across the straw between their feet. He grabbed her by the shoulders and pushed her down to the ground.

Livia tried to maintain control. 'Hey, what's the hurry?' she giggled. 'Tell me about yourself first.'

'Shut up!'

She tried again. 'What's the rush?'

His brows drew together and he muttered something incomprehensible under his breath. Fear almost crushed her. Things weren't going to plan. He pushed up her skirt and yanked off her cami-knickers, tearing the seam.

'There's no need to be rough,' she cried.

He fell on top of her, wresting the breath from her lungs, crushing his mouth to hers. He smelt of antiseptic, like a hospital ward. She closed her mind to what happened next.

His lust satisfied, he rolled off her and started to get to his feet. She felt utterly humiliated. She had failed. Johan Fleischer was neither intoxicated nor infatuated. The tables had turned on her. He had used her. Her lips stung, her body felt sore, her heart pounded. She had learnt nothing. This man was going to walk away leaving her to drown in the aftermath of useless sacrifice.

Despair made her reckless. She reached up and tugged at his legs as he pulled up his trousers. Taken by surprise, he let his trousers drop to his feet. He stooped to recover them, cursing angrily. Livia acted swiftly. Before he had time to straighten up, she caught him off-balance and shoved him backwards onto the straw. Snatching up the smashed Cognac bottle, she knelt over him and thrust the broken glass close to his throat. He reached for his gun holster but she kicked it away.

Her danger forgotten, Livia regained the courage she had shown in the hills above Florence.

'What are the commandant's plans for the village?' she demanded.

He didn't reply. She jabbed him with the jagged bottle.

'Out with it. We know about the arms depot, but what do you intend to use those weapons for?'

Still he refused to answer.

Getting angry, she jabbed the bottle again, drawing blood. 'What are you Nazi pigs planning to do to our village?'

His pale eyes bored mercilessly into hers, and she could sense his alarm even though he appeared fearless. He replied in immaculate Italian, 'I knew what you were up to all along.'

Despite his defenceless position, it was as if he had the upper hand. Livia fought to maintain her resolve, jabbing the broken bottle at him again, drawing more blood.

Fleischer gave an arrogant laugh. 'What does it matter, the village will soon be inaccessible. You'll all die of starvation or be blown sky high.'

'What d'you mean?'

'We're laying a minefield around the village. No one will be able to get in or out.'

'I don't believe you.'

She felt his torso tauten. He was looking for a chance to throw her off. Pressing her knees more tightly into his sides, she jabbed the bottle again.

'The village will serve as an ambush for those fucking Brits and Yanks. They won't get past us.'

She realised he was playing for time. Clearly, he didn't believe she had the guts to kill him. Her thoughts flew back to the hidden arsenal; even Vincenzo hadn't known how extensive it was. This momentary lapse of attention cost Livia dear. It gave the German his opportunity. He snatched at her wrist and twisted it. She managed to wrench her arm free while keeping hold of the broken bottle. Drawing up her leg, she rammed her knee into his groin. He cursed, his upper body curling towards her in a reflex action, but the strength of his grip had weakened her wrist. Pain destroyed her concentration.

Fleischer reached for her neck. Summoning all her remaining strength, Livia brought her arm down and drove the broken bottle into his throat, slicing the jugular. His eyes became blank and he slumped back onto the straw. Livia watched horrified as, with a gurgle, blood pulsated from his windpipe to soak Giuliana's favourite blouse.

The blood-spattered bottle slipped from Livia's fingers. Bile rose to her throat and she vomited uncontrollably over her victim's body. Stumbling to her feet, she stood frozen to the spot as Fleischer's legs gave a final convulsive jerk.

Sober now, she forced herself to follow her training regime: conceal the body and escape from the scene as quickly as possible. Somehow, she managed to drag the German's body to the back of the barn and cover it with straw. Then she pushed a wheel-barrow across the floor and up-ended it on top of the corpse.

The silk blouse was beginning to stiffen as the blood dried on it. With a shudder, she stripped it off and put on the cardigan she had brought with her. Carrying Giuliana's red shoes, she went to the well behind the barn and tossed the stained garment into its depths. After a final check, she staggered blindly in the direction of Grazia Elena's house, panting as she clambered up the hill on bare feet.

Her head throbbed and she had a stitch in her side. Nausea rose and receded in her throat. She had to get back before Vincenzo discovered she was missing, but first of all, she must stop off at the pump and wash away the German's stink.

Despite the horror she'd experienced, she felt elated. Vincenzo wouldn't have to risk his life. She had the information they needed, now all they had to do was to contact Claudia and bring in reinforcements.

It was a dark night and she had difficulty in finding her way. She heard a rustle in the bushes: an animal? She felt a blow on her shoulder, knocking her to the ground. Her spine scraped the rough terrain as someone dragged her along by the legs. Her head bumped on a rock, and she passed out.

When she came to, Livia was disorientated. She'd been blindfolded and tied to a chair with her hands fastened behind her back.

'She's come round!'

The voice spoke in Italian. Relief flooded over her. Italians, not Germans! She could explain what she had done. She opened her mouth to speak, but her words were blunted by a slap to her jaw. Tears sprang to her eyes, remaining unshed behind the tightly tied scarf. The pain extended from her jaw, up the side of her cheek to the top of her head. Again, she tried to gasp out a protest but her words were cut short by another slap. Her teeth rattled.

She heard them muttering among themselves, made out the word 'traitor'. Could they mean her? Then she recognised the voice of a woman she'd seen in the village. This was better. She could appeal to a member of her own sex. She went to speak again but a blow to the side of her head sent her reeling to the floor. She landed on her side and realised that her legs were also tied to the chair.

The discussions continued, but more quietly, and she couldn't make out the words. The side of the chair pressed against her leg, her shoulder ached, the nerve-ends in her wrists cried out for release. The group fell silent. Someone came over and righted the chair. The blindfold was whipped off. Thank God! They had realised their mistake. They would release her now.

Light from a lantern blinded her. Someone lowered it. She blinked and saw that she was in a shepherd's hut. Her captors stood in a group staring at her. There were half a dozen old men, a teenage boy and two women. She went to open her mouth but her jaw wouldn't function. Incapable of speech, she shook her head vehemently, pleading her innocence with her eyes. No one spoke. The minutes ticked by.

Suddenly, one of the women came to life. Striding over, she stopped directly in front of Livia and, leaning forward, spat in her face. 'Collaborator!' she shrieked.

Livia flinched as the spittle trailed down her cheek. She found her voice and cried out: 'Stop, for pity's sake, I'm not a collaborator, let me go.'

The woman laughed and spat again. Turning back, she jerked her shoulder to the others. 'What are you waiting for?'

Livia stiffened in panic, and her eyes widened as she glimpsed the flash of steel. Another women came towards her, a cut-throat razor in her hand.

Without uttering a word, the second woman grabbed a handful of hair, tugged it to one side and chopped if off. Livia gave a piercing scream. The woman chortled and continued to shave off her crowning glory while Livia struggled and shouted in protest.

The men shuffled their feet uneasily. 'Can't you shut her up?' one muttered.

'With pleasure.' A piece of rag was rammed into Livia's mouth.

The men's reluctance seemed to incite the women. While one wielded the razor, the other grinned triumphantly. Livia kicked her heels against the legs of the chair. Why wouldn't they listen to her? Resistance was useless, and she realised that these people weren't interested in whether she was innocent or guilty. All that mattered to them was that they had found an outlet for their hatred of the German interlopers.

She recalled the kangaroo trial of Angelo Bernadini up in the hills above Florence. His accusers had refused to give him a chance to defend himself. *He was guilty*, she shrieked to herself, *I am innocent*. All she could do was watch in abject dismay as her beautiful locks cascaded to the ground around her feet.

Blood trickled down from her forehead where the woman had carelessly nicked her scalp. She felt nauseous and swayed.

'Hold her!' snapped the woman.

A gnarled hand gripped Livia's shoulder, the nails digging painfully into her flesh. Blood filled her mouth, soaking the rag. The left side of her jaw began to swell and she knew that several teeth had become dislodged.

Their task finished, the women stood back to survey their handiwork; the men clustered behind them. One of them scooped up a handful of hair and threw it in her face. With a toss of the head, the first woman spun on her heel and marched away. The other woman followed her.

The men started muttering uncomfortably among themselves. 'What next?' she heard one of them say. The reply was too mumbled to catch. After a few minutes, they slunk away, taking the lantern with them.

Livia wasn't sure how long she remained there. It could have been hours. From time to time, she slipped into semi-consciousness to jerk awake nearly toppling the chair over. Bile rose to her throat, almost choking her. If only they'd removed the gag! She forced herself not to panic.

Then she heard a noise. Someone was coming into the hut. It was Vincenzo! Three silhouetted figures came into view. Not Vincenzo! Before she had time to register what was happening, one of them strode over and hacked at the cords tying her to the chair. Her fingers were numb but she managed to pull off the gag, spitting out a mouthful of blood and babbling, '*Grazie, grazie.*'

She tried to stand up, wobbling uncertainly. The man who'd cut her free stood barring her way. She began to feel alarmed. His manner wasn't friendly. His gaze travelled up and down her body displaying undisguised lust.

'Let me go,' she babbled. 'Please let me go.'

He threw back his head and guffawed. 'What do you think, Diego, shall we let her go?'

Without waiting for his companion's reply, he grabbed her by the shoulders and threw her to the ground. The chair toppled over beside her. Before she could regain her feet, he released his trousers and stood astride her. Spitting out a globule of chewed tobacco, he dropped to his knees, pushing her skirt up over her thighs, snarling, 'Collaborator! Fraternise with the Nazis, would you?'

'No!' she screeched, vehemently shaking her head, but he laughed at her denial.

She fought him, scratching his face and tearing at his hair. Her legs felt weak, her arms stiff. He smelled of cheap alcohol and stale sweat. Her thoughts flew back to her encounter with the German. No hospital odour this time round, no hint of carbolic. Her strength ebbed away. Yielding to her fate, she closed her eyes and prayed to God for mercy.

The man got up, gave the thumbs up to his companions and growled, 'Who's next?'

Livia opened her eyes. A figure loomed over her. This time, she flopped helplessly under her attacker's weight as once again, she was subjected to rape. The man's rough woollen trousers rubbed against her thighs as he grunted obscenities in her face, his eyes glinting cruelly. Done, he moved away, leaving her gasping for breath.

A third figure was shoved towards her. *Jesù*, not again! But she saw that this was a mere youth. He drew back, shaking his head as if mesmerised.

The others taunted him. 'Come on, Son, this is your chance to lose your virginity.'

The boy didn't move.

One of the men nudged him. 'Get on with it. She's a tasty piece of work.'

The other chortled, 'Well, she was before those she-devils got hold of her.'

'No!' begged Livia.

The skinny teenager looked down at her, terror in his eyes. With a gulp, he turned tail, pushing his way between his companions to run out of the hut. Livia clenched her fists. They would kill her now.

A golden glow shone onto the wall. Dear God, the angels were coming for her! The two men exchanged a nervous glance. 'Better get out of here,' one muttered. They bolted for the door.

Livia lay on her back on the straw, numb with shock. The nightmare was over! God had sent the dawn to save her.

Without warning, an agonising pain shot through her abdomen. Rolling onto her side, she clutched her arms across her stomach and drew her knees up to her chest, screaming as the pain intensified. This was the worst nightmare of all. She was losing her baby. The pain eased, then worsened. It eased again. Somehow, she managed to get to her feet and, doubled over, staggered towards the door of the hut, lured by the golden ray of hope streaming in.

Another stab of pain brought her to her knees. In horror, she felt the blood gush from her body and knew that if she didn't get help soon, she would bleed to death. Between bouts of pain, she crawled outside, into the autumn morning. She heard the sound of a tractor in the distance and prayed that someone would come up to the hut. No one did.

Twenty-two

The search for Livia didn't begin until after ten o'clock next morning. On going to bed the evening before, Vincenzo had assumed that because Livia was still annoyed with him, she had slept on the camp bed in Giuliana's room He asked the teenager where she was.

The girl shrugged. 'I don't know.'

He went outside and found Isabella playing with a kitten that had strayed into the yard. When she saw him, she called out, '*Ciao Babbo*!' and held out her arms to be lifted up. Since their arrival in Castagnetto, she had lost her shyness. She was a pretty little girl with a pleasing personality, and seeing her play with Giuliana's old dolls made him reflect on the sad passing of his own little Isabella. He no longer stopped her from calling him Babbo. Secretly he was pleased.

When he went back into the house, he found Grazia Elena looking puzzled.

'What's the matter?' he asked.

'Giuliana says someone's taken some of her clothes.'

'Perhaps Isabella's been playing in the wardrobe?'

'She's not tall enough to reach the handle.'

'Maybe Livia borrowed them. Have you asked her?'

'We still can't find her.'

'Perhaps she's gone down to the village.'

Grazia Elena shook her head. 'I would have seen her pass the window.'

Giuliana appeared in the doorway. 'Where can she be?'

Where indeed? But there wasn't time to speculate because Guido rushed in. 'Vincenzo, I think you should see this,' he called out.

Vincenzo followed Guido towards the village, where his companion stopped to point at a high-heeled shoe half hidden behind a rock. Vincenzo experienced a tremor of shock. It wasn't the shoe that drew his attention; it was the traces of blood on the rock itself.

The two men followed a trail of flattened bushes off the beaten track until they came upon the matching shoe. Vincenzo picked it up and stared at it in disbelief. He examined the blood speckled grass, afraid of what he might find in the undergrowth. Clearly, something awful had happened. Dear God, let it not be Livia!

'This way!' shouted Guido.

Vincenzo scrambled after him up the rough track until they reached a shepherd's hut. Guido got there first. 'Vincenzo, come quickly!' he yelled. 'I've found her.'

Gasping for breath, Vincenzo rushed to join him, stopping to stare in horror. Livia was sprawled on the ground, Giuliana's blue cardigan rumpled across her shoulders. Her arms were flung out as if she were making a last despairing plea for mercy. He gulped back the bile of nausea. Her head had been roughly shaven. In places the razor had nicked her scalp leaving dried spots of blood between tufts of remaining hair. It was a grotesque sight. His gaze travelled over her. Her trunk and legs were soaked with blood.

He flung himself down beside her, propped her head on his arm and turned her face towards him. She gave a low groan and her eyes flickered open.

'Get help!' shouted Vincenzo, but Guido was already racing down the hillside. 'Who did this to you, my love?' he croaked.

She tried to speak but faltered, closing her eyes again. 'Hold on, *amore*, help's on its way,' he whispered. A knot of anger tightened in his chest. What had those German bastards done to her?

'Isabella?' Livia's voice was barely audible.

'Isabella's safe, she's with Giuliana.'

Livia's lips moved again, breaking the crust of dried blood around her mouth. He took a handkerchief out of his pocket and gently wiped her face. She flinched and whispered, 'I'm so sorry, darling, I ... '

He stroked her cheek, finding it difficult to speak. Hatred for the German invaders swelled in his heart, but this was not the time to give voice to it. This was the time for expressions of tenderness, not hatred.

'I love you so much.' He sensed her words rather than heard them. She gave the hint of a smile and went limp. He thought she'd passed out but, all at once, her eyelids fluttered open again and she murmured, 'Isabella ... look after her ... ' Her head lolled back on his arm.

'Don't leave me, my darling,' he whispered hoarsely.

Guido and Stefano Amato approached, the latter panting heavily as he climbed the steep hill. Like him, the doctor was a middle-aged man, unused to excessive exercise.

'Hurry up, Stefano!' he shouted. He looked down again at Livia, but her eyes stared blankly up at him.

At last Dr Amato reached him. 'Let me see her.'

Vincenzo shook his head as he slid the palm of his hand across Livia's eyes, and murmured, 'It's too late.'

'Let me see.'

'No, Stefano!' He couldn't prise himself away. Not yet. While he cradled her in his arms, she belonged to him; she was still his warm, vibrant lover.

He heard Guido say, 'Leave him, *Dottore*, let's take a look inside the hut.'

When they'd gone away, he spent several minutes gazing down at Livia's battered body, too shocked to take in the grim reality. When Guido and Stefano came out of the hut, he placed her gently on her back with her hands across her chest.

Getting slowly to his feet, he faced them and asked, 'What did you find in there?'

'You'd better come and see for yourself,' replied Guido.

Inside the hut, he followed his friend to a toppled-over chair stained with blood. His gaze focused on the sliced through ropes still attached to it. A glance down made him shudder with revulsion. He was standing on a mass of dark hair. Stooping, he picked up one of the tresses and, with a tortured howl, pressed it to his lips.

Guido shook his head sorrowfully. 'We can only guess what happened,' he said, taking Vincenzo's arm and urging him outside to where Stefano Amato was bending over Livia's body.

'If only we'd found her earlier,' muttered Vincenzo.

Amato straightened up to face him. 'She wouldn't have survived; she'd lost too much blood.' He cast the count a shrewd glance and asked, 'What dreadful thing are you involved in, Vincenzo?'

When the count failed to reply, the doctor gave a resigned shrug and, taking Guido aside, said quietly, 'The poor creature's been gang raped and badly beaten.' Adjusting his monocle, he turned and asked Vincenzo. 'Did you know she was pregnant?'

'No!' Dear God, why hadn't she told him?

'Yes, my friend, three, maybe four months.'

Guido shuffled his feet, glancing around anxiously. 'We must get her back to the house. We don't want the villagers getting wind of this.'

Jolted into action, Vincenzo stooped to lift Livia's body. As he did so something fell out of her cardigan pocket. He picked it up and saw that it was a button from a German officer's uniform. Hatred rose like a shaft of steel in his chest. Knuckling the button in his fist, he took a silent oath that he wouldn't rest until he had exacted revenge for the horrendous murder of the woman he loved.

He carried Livia down the hillside, refusing assistance from his companions. Back in the house, he laid Livia on the couch. Showing discretion beyond her years, Giuliana suppressed her tears and quietly took Isabella outside to play, leaving her weeping grandmother to offer the men a shot of cognac.

Grazia Elena and the doctor cleaned Livia up and changed her clothes, but Vincenzo still couldn't bring himself to look at her body. The kindly woman had even taken the trouble to place a lace kerchief over her shaven head.

He paced the floor in glowering silence. Shock had changed to clinical rage. He now knew what he would do.

'Sit down, Vincenzo,' said Guido. 'We have to talk about this.'

'There's nothing to talk about,' snapped Vincenzo. 'It's down to the Krauts.'

'I'm not so sure,' Guido demurred.

'Who else would do a thing like that?'

'The Germans wouldn't have shaved her head.'

'What do you mean?'

'A shaven head rings of punishment, not torture. This could be the work of someone closer to home. Livia may have been mistaken for a collaborator,' suggested Guido.

'What bloody nonsense! I've got proof it was a German, haven't I?' Vincenzo unclenched his fist and thrust the button at the other man.

'We should keep an open mind in case … '

'What the hell are you getting at? Are you suggesting that someone in the village did this to Livia?'

Guido gave up, realising that it wasn't the right time for such a discussion.

The next day, they buried Livia in a plot on the hillside. Padre Ferdinando, who had officiated at Enzo's funeral almost four years earlier, conducted the service, discreetly refraining from commenting on the count's unexpected return to the vicinity. The grave was a short distance from the house, marked with a pile of stones and a simple wooden cross.

After the burial, Vincenzo went to the bedroom he had shared with her. Her belongings were scattered everywhere. With a wistful smile, he recalled telling her off for being untidy. He scooped up a discarded blouse. Her scent was still evident. Her bag lay on the floor. With trembling hands, he emptied its contents onto the bed. An assortment of personal items fell out: a leather purse, a cracked mirror, a comb with a couple of teeth missing and a headscarf. As he touched the last item, something dropped onto the counterpane. It was a silver chain with a pendant attached to it. He picked it up, then with a frown, crushed it in his hand. Now he understood why Livia had snatched Isabella from the nuns. He opened his hand, and pressed the pendant to his lips. Destroy it; he had no other choice.

He slumped down onto the bed, his head in his hands, the trinket still trailing between his fingers. *Livia, what have you done?* Pressing his fists to his forehead, he gave a howl of anguish as he pictured his lover in defiant mood. Even when faced with dire consequences, she would thumb her nose at the enemy. Arrogant and headstrong -- that's when he desired her the most. He was racked with remorse. Why had he rejected her so savagely when she'd tried to prevent him from going up to the villa? She'd paid for his brush-off with her life.

Dio Santo! What about Isabella? The only thing he could do for Livia now was to protect her daughter.

Grazia Elena watched the count closely, recalling his reaction to his son's death four years earlier. She would never have been able to accept his relationship with Livia, but nevertheless, she shared her employer's pain, encouraging him to talk about his son in England, reflecting on how much Beppe would have grown in the intervening years.

'He's thirteen now,' said his father. 'I won't recognise him when I see him again.'

Grazia Elena gave a laugh. 'Of course you will,' she said. 'Oh, what a happy day it will be when you're all together again. You and the countess will move back into the villa and all will be well.'

At the mention of the countess, a cloud gathered on the count's brow. 'Things will never be the same again,' he said.

'They will,' declared the old woman. 'You will put this terrible time behind you and live once more as a family.'

He didn't reply and she knew in her heart that it was impossible to turn back the clock. Things had changed, the count himself had changed. When he and Livia had arrived, bringing with them a little girl called Isabella, she had experienced a tremor of shock. The coincidence was disturbing. She saw the count grow more and more fond of Isabella and knew that while the little one lived with them, Livia's memory would never fade. She prayed that a relative of Livia's would turn up to claim the child.

The news of the murder sped through the surrounding villages and it wasn't long before word got around that the count was back. This enticed the villagers up to Grazia Elena's house, making it vital to keep Isabella out of sight. To keep busybodies away, Vincenzo took to going down to the village on a regular basis. He took coffee and cognac at Comolli's Bar, chatting to the bartender, but despite his amiability, Comolli remained tight-lipped over the events of that evening, refusing to speculate on what had followed. It seemed that nothing would draw him out. Vincenzo respected him for this, and it reinforced his conviction that the Germans were responsible for Livia's death.

'It's time I went up to the villa to see the commandant," Vincenzo announced one morning. 'Clearly Livia found out something, that's why they killed her.'

Guido was more cautious. 'Wait!' he warned. 'Wait another week. You may not be welcome there at the moment.'

'I can't wait,' cried the count. 'We need to know what's happening with the arms depot.'

Guido placed a hand on his shoulder. 'Be patient, my friend. Your emotions are still too raw. Besides, the Krauts are edgy; one of their officers is missing and you won't get anything out of them until they find him.'

After a few days, the commandant ordered a house-to-house search for Fleischer, maintaining that he must have been taken hostage. Rumours of proposed reprisals spread through the village, but when a couple of soldiers who'd been at Comolli's that evening came forward to report that Johan Fleischer and the girl had left together, the search was dropped. Vincenzo drew his own conclusions: the German Authorities feared that Fleischer had drunk too much, lost his temper and killed her, then deserted his post rather than face a Court Martial. Under these circumstances, the commandant would be only too keen to hush up the officer's disappearance.

News began to filter through that the Germans now occupied Rome. 'The Krauts have freed Mussolini,' Guido told them. 'They're setting him up in government somewhere on the banks of Lake Garda.'

This worried Vincenzo. If *Il Duce* came back to power, what of Scarpone? Now that his presence in Castagnetto was common knowledge, the marshal might decide to send a squad up to arrest him. He cast a glance through the window at the little girl playing outside. Something had to be done about her. He would have to ask Claudia to arrange for her evacuation to somewhere safe.

Then they learnt that Italy had joined forces with the Allies against Germany. 'We can't delay my visit to the commandant any longer,' Vincenzo said to Guido and, this time, his companion agreed.

Fortuitously, the decision was taken out of their hands. Since Livia's death, the count's presence in the village had become known, prompting the German commandant to invite him to dinner. The call was more of a summons than an invitation, infuriating Vincenzo.

'Things couldn't have worked out better,' laughed Guido. 'Since he's the one to have made the first move, he can't suspect you of trying to spy on him.'

Returning to his old home as a visitor was an unpleasant experience for Vincenzo. As he stepped across the threshold, his feelings were ambivalent. On the surface, nothing appeared to have changed; the place was spotless, the officers quartered there had clearly respected his property. He was greeted deferentially, if somewhat formally, by a sub-lieutenant, and ushered into the commandant's presence.

Commandant Karl Reinhardt was a thickset man with thinning hair and close-set eyes. He was full of haughty bonhomie, speaking poor Italian with a stilted accent. Vincenzo replied courteously, suppressing his amusement at Reinhardt's grammatical errors as he made a point of apologising profusely for taking over the villa.

'Now that you've returned, count, you must move back in. I'm afraid I'm unable to vacate the premises, but provision will be made for you in the East Wing.'

Vincenzo held up his hands in mock protest, although he knew it would be foolish not to take up the commandant's offer, and before the evening was out, he intended to agree to move back. However distasteful returning to the villa in such circumstances might be, it was a God-given opportunity for him to snoop around and find out what was going on.

Reinhardt went on. 'The West Wing's been turned into a hospital, you know.' The West Wing housing the nursery and school room! Vincenzo bit back his anger. The commandant's next observation took his breath away. 'I understand you were obliged to spend some months down south under house arrest. You must have found this bothersome.'

'The time passed quite quickly.'

'It was all a mistake no doubt, but I'm sure you won't want to risk incarceration a second time. Marshal Scarpone assures me the whole episode was nothing more than an unfortunate misunderstanding.' So the commandant was in contact with Scarpone! The commandant went on, 'The marshal seemed surprised that you'd left the area without authorisation. However … ' He gave a hearty laugh. 'Wasn't it Cicero who said, *Laws are silent in times of war.*' He stood up and gestured to the door, ushering his guest into the large dining room. 'Come my friend, it's time for lunch.'

On entering the dining room, Vincenzo nearly turned on his heel and walked out. Alice's favourite table-cloth was spread over the Rosewood table with the best wine glasses and silver laid out. But what irked him most was seeing the exquisite crystal glass candelabra they'd chosen together whilst on honeymoon in Venice taking pride of place in the centre of the table. Whenever the door opened its three candles flickered, reflecting diamond patterns on the wall opposite. As he took his seat, he found himself gripping the edge of his chair to stop himself from giving vent to anger. How dare these barbarians make free with his most treasured possessions! He could almost hear Alice's outrage at such an imposition.

They were joined for lunch by two of the commandant's aides, especially chosen because of their knowledge of Italian. The conversation was formal. Vincenzo sensed the discomfort of the two subordinates and felt sorry for them.

The sumptuous meal stuck in his throat. Over the past nine months, he had become accustomed to a simple diet. Down in Lucania, Donna Caterina had done her best with the limited rations at her disposal and, since lodging with Grazia Elena and her granddaughter in Castagnetto, the meals were even more meagre. Rations intended for two were being shared between four adults and a child. If it hadn't been for Grazia Elena's chickens and Giuliana's efforts with the vegetable patch, they would have starved.

But this wasn't his entire reason for a poor appetite. With every gulp of wine, he tasted again the nausea he had tasted when he'd set eyes on Livia's battered body; with every bite of meat, he chewed again the hard kernel of hatred he'd chewed at the moment of that fateful discovery.

Reinhardt mentioned his business interests, politely enquired about the intricacies of the wine growing industry and enthused on the beauty of the countryside. His main topic of conversation, however, was Renaissance Art, a subject on which he considered himself to be an expert, talking at length in his appalling Italian about the paintings in the Pitti Palace. The progress of the War wasn't mentioned. Vincenzo endeavoured to bring the subject up on several occasions, but his host played dumb and cleverly directed the conversation back onto neutral territory. Coffee was about to be served, when there was a knock at the door.

'Come,' called out Reinhardt, looking annoyed.

A nervous-looking corporal came in and spoke softly into his superior's ear. '*Was?*' snapped the commandant. His features were white and taut as he listened to the corporal's message. Throwing down his napkin, he jumped to his feet, barking orders at the two officers seated at the table. They responded instantly, pushing back their chairs and marching out of the room.

Belatedly, Reinhardt remembered his guest. Turning to Vincenzo, he said in Italian, 'You must excuse this unseemly behaviour, *Signor Conte*. I'm afraid something urgent has cropped up and I must ask you to leave at once.'

At the door of the villa, they shook hands, the German's impatience to be rid of him apparent in the nervous darting of his eyes. 'You must come again.' It was a meaningless formality. There was no further mention of him moving back in.

Vincenzo couldn't wait to get away. The commandant, in his egotism, had failed to consider the possibility that his distinguished guest spoke German. In fact, Vincenzo had understood every word. The news he'd overheard had shocked him even more than it had shocked his host. All the way back to Grazia Elena's he worried about its possible repercussions.

Guido was in the kitchen. He'd dozed off in front of the stove, his chair tilted against the wall, his feet resting on the table. He leapt up when Vincenzo entered the room, sending the chair crashing to the floor.

'Well, comrade, did you learn anything useful?' he asked eagerly.

'Pour me a drink!'

Guido poured out a jigger of cognac. It was several seconds before Vincenzo could bring himself to impart his news. At last, he said, 'They've found Johan Fleischer, the missing officer's body, in that old barn behind Comolli's café. He was stabbed in the throat.'

Guido looked up sharply. '*Merda!* '

'This could bring reprisals,' said Vincenzo. 'But Reinhardt's a proud man, he might prefer to hush up the affair.' He frowned and went on. 'There's something I don't understand. Was Livia killed before or after Fleischer?'

Guido chewed his lip thoughtfully. 'Maybe someone from the village saw Fleischer attacking her, then followed him down the hillside and took revenge.'

'But who?'

'We'll never find out. The villagers will close ranks.' Guido placed a hand on Vincenzo's shoulder and said, 'You look exhausted, comrade, get some sleep, and we'll talk in the morning.'

But next day, there was no time for discussion because Vincenzo was again summoned to the villa. The commandant was not so congenial on this occasion, and the preliminaries were cut short as he glowered at the count and said, 'Since news filters down to the village pretty rapidly, I expect you've heard what's happened, *Eccellenza*. A German officer's been found murdered. This is a very serious crime. I need to be sure that I can count on you to help solve it.'

'I don't see how I can help.'

'You're influential in this part of the world, the villagers confide in you. Report back to me the minute you learn anything, the merest rumour. Do I make myself clear?'

When Vincenzo remained silent, the German hammered his desk with a knuckled fist and shouted in German, 'The culprit *must* be found.'

Vincenzo pretended incomprehension whereupon Reinhardt shouted the same thing in Italian,

'I couldn't agree more, especially as this is the second homicide in the village.'

'The second?'

Deliberately keeping his voice level, Vincenzo went on, 'The young woman, who was left to bleed to death up on the hillside.'

'Oh yes, I'd forgotten. A sad affair.'

The count opened his hand and showed Reinhardt the tunic button. 'This was found next to her body.' It seemed obscene to talk about Livia as if she were a casual stranger. The German reached for the button, but Vincenzo snatched it away. 'Was there, by any chance, a button missing from Fleischer's uniform?'

The colour rushed to the commandant's face. 'Certainly not. That button must have been planted there.' He gave an embarrassed cough. 'It's not difficult to obtain such an item if you know where to look.'

He'd unsettled the commandant. Good! Perhaps now, he'd think twice about delving too deeply into the mystery of Fleischer's death. The meeting ended abruptly with Reinhardt pleading important business to attend to.

As he saw Vincenzo out, he said, 'By the way, count, I'm afraid I must ask you to hand over your house keys.' Vincenzo stiffened, his instinct being to refuse. Reinhardt gave an amiable shrug, as if being asked to forfeit them were a normal occurrence. 'Orders from above. Annoying I know but I'm sure you understand. It's just a precaution.'

Angrily, Vincenzo yanked his bundle of keys from his pocket and rammed them into the commandant's outstretched hand. His mood was black as he hurried back to the Grazia Elena's house. When Guido heard the news he, too, was angry but *his* anger was focused on the commandant's anomalous reaction to the button incident. Pacing up and down, his hands linked behind his back, his head thrust forward, he made Vincenzo run over the sequence of events, again and again.

'Producing the Fleischer's button knocked Reinhardt off balance, it's my guess he'll hush the whole thing up.'

'On the contrary, he'll demand retribution,' argued Guido.

Vincenzo shook his head. 'Reinhardt knows one of his men is responsible for Livia's death. He won't want it becoming common knowledge that a crime against a civilian has been committed.'

'When have the Krauts ever been averse to murdering civilians?' scoffed his companion. 'I've heard reports from France that when a pair of lovers broke the curfew, Reinhardt had the boy shot and, not content with that, ordered a whole row of houses to be destroyed as well.'

'Livia was stalked, raped and murdered. It can't be classed as a war crime.'

'She broke the curfew.'

The two friends argued it out for a further ten minutes, but when no agreement could be reached, they parted company in disgruntled humour. Guido vanished for the rest of the day, leaving Vincenzo to spend time on his manuscript. The women deliberately kept out of their way. Grazia Elena busied herself with some darning, sitting in her rocking chair in the yard to watch over Isabella, while her granddaughter went into the village to queue for bread.

Giuliana returned looking flustered, her basket empty. Panting for breath, she burst in on Vincenzo and gasped, '*Signor Conte* ... come quickly. The Germans have locked up all the men from the village.'

Twenty-three

The two men exchanged a look of alarm. 'When did this happen, Giuliana?' asked Guido.

'First thing this morning just as the men were setting off for work. Soldiers burst into their houses.'

Vincenzo tried to calm the girl, taking her gently by the elbow, he walked her to the door, saying, 'Go back to the village and reassure the women, we'll sort this out.'

'But…'

'Don't fret, Giuliana, it's probably only a routine investigation.'

The girl looked unconvinced. Composing herself, she gave him a weak smile, picked up her basket and left the house.

After the door had closed on her, Guido said, 'Get up to the villa, comrade, see if you can diffuse the situation.'

'That's easier said than done.'

'Tell that son of a bitch Livia killed his damned officer.'

Vincenzo clenched his fists. 'Blame Livia, you're not serious?'

Guido raised an eyebrow. 'Think, my friend, she *could* have done it. You found the Kraut's button in her pocket.'

Vincenzo couldn't disguise his astonishment. Could Livia have killed the man? He shook his head. It was impossible. Or was it? She'd killed that motorcyclist without compunction.

Guido went on. 'Either Livia takes the blame, or the villagers do. It's a plausible explanation; one that Reinhardt might buy.' Vincenzo couldn't bring himself to speak. Guido's voice jolted him back. 'A stab wound to the throat smacks of Livia's hand. One of the Krauts must have seen her and taken revenge. He won't come forward. Taking matters into his own hands would get him into serious trouble with his superiors; you know what they're like about discipline.'

Livia's image rose graphically in Vincenzo's memory. On their last night together, she'd looked so beautiful, so appealing as she'd begged him not to approach the commandant. He shouldn't have brushed her off so cruelly. He blamed himself for her death, and for the situation in which they now found themselves. He should have lied; he should have told Livia that they'd dropped the idea of going up to the villa; then gone there afterwards without telling her.

His hesitation angered Guido. 'Get up there, Vincenzo, what are you waiting for?'

Reinhardt received him courteously. '*Eccellenza*,' he said, ' To what do I owe the pleasure?'

Vincenzo ignored his host's invitation to be seated. Instead, he went to stand opposite the German, addressing him across the polished mahogany desk, the one that had belonged to his father and his grandfather before him.

'*Signor Comandante*,' he began. 'I've been told that you've locked up some of the villagers.'

The commandant's thick lips twitched. 'It was unavoidable, I'm afraid.'

'What's happened to justify such an arrest?'

Reinhardt adopted a grave expression. Rubbing his hands together, he replied, 'One of your villagers is responsible for killing a German officer. We've questioned them but no one is prepared to admit to the crime. Locking them up will undoubtedly unleash someone's tongue.'

'What if they're innocent?'

'Innocent?' Reinhardt gave a scathing smile. 'Who else could have done it? Surely, you're not suggesting it was … ' He clapped his hands together and laughed. 'One of my men? Why, that would be a convenient solution, wouldn't it? No, *Signor Conte*, this is down to one of the villagers. And mark my words we'll get to the bottom of it. Someone will squeal. They'll soon get fed up with being cooped up: no food, no water, no ablutions.'

'That's outrageous!'

The German stared at him, mouth grim, eyes hard.

Vincenzo decided to make an appeal to his better nature. 'You realise what this means to the village, don't you? This is a vital time of year for the farmers; the women can only do so much … '

'The women are confined to the village boundaries until further notice,' snapped the commandant.

'You can't do it! The harvest needs gathering in, the livestock feeding; they'll lose their livelihoods.' The commandant's triumphant expression told him he'd allowed himself to fall into a trap.

'A confession will break the deadlock.'

It was now or never. 'If I tell you I know the identity of the killer, will you let the men go?' said Vincenzo.

Reinhardt's brows arched. 'You know the culprit?'

Vincenzo nodded. 'Let the men go and I'll give you the name.'

The German let out a hearty guffaw. 'Do you take me for a fool?'

'I thought you wanted the matter sorted out quickly.'

Reinhardt frowned. 'Is it one of the men held in custody?'

'I'm not telling you until I have your guarantee of safe passage for the innocent.'

'That's asking too much. How can I agree to anything when I have no idea what you're going to offer me?' Reinhardt stroked his chin. 'Give me the name first; then I might be prepared to make a commitment.' His chest swelled as he went on, 'The Third Reich is renowned for its sense of justice.'

Vincenzo confronted the arrogant figure, fighting down the urge to grab him by the throat and throttle him. He knew he'd aroused Reinhardt's curiosity. Dare he appeal to the German's elevated image of himself? Would snobbery override the man's baser instincts?

'I'm sure we can talk this over rationally, *Signor Comandante*,' he said. 'You're a man of education, of culture, would I insult you by making false claims?'

Flattery did the trick. 'Very well, I agree,' replied the other man after a moment's hesitation. Pressing the intercom button, he gave the order for the men's release.

The die was cast. Vincenzo loathed himself for what he was about to do. It felt like betrayal. He tried to tell himself that Livia, herself, would have applauded his actions. But would Reinhardt believe him? He would never be able to live with himself if his explanation fell on deaf ears. He met the

German's mocking gaze. 'Johan Fleischer was killed by Livia Carduccio.'

Saying her name brought a rush of nausea. She was dead, the woman who had entered his life so fleetingly yet changed it so dramatically. The temperature in the room seemed to plummet as the commandant took in this news.

'Who is she?'

'Was.'

'Ah...the woman, whose body was found on the hillside. What makes you think it was her?'

'The button I showed you...'

The commandant looked puzzled. 'Tell me, how did *she* die?'

Vincenzo gave a swallow. 'She died of her injuries; her body showed evidence of a struggle. Fleischer must have put up a fight.'

The commandant gave a snort of disbelief. 'That doesn't ring true.'

Vincenzo felt hope slipping away. 'I wouldn't lie to you.'

'Maybe not, but you've made a mistake. For one thing, a woman could never have committed such a hideous crime.'

Thinking of Livia, the count replied, 'In certain circumstances, she could.'

The commandant levered his bulk out of his chair and came round to the front of the desk, stopping barely a foot away from Vincenzo. Rocking back on his heels, he clasped his hands behind his back, and said, '*Signor Conte,* you are mistaken.' With a hoot of laughter, he spluttered, 'You've been listening to gossip...gossip, that's all it is. You Italians are all alike.'

Vincenzo felt desperate. Dear God, this act of betrayal must not be for nothing. 'Do you doubt the word of a fellow army officer?' he demanded.

The commandant brushed him aside with, 'My dear fellow, your army days were over years ago.' Taking a handkerchief from his pocket, he wiped his red-rimmed eyes. 'A woman? No, *Eccellenza* ... ' He pronounced the title sarcastically. ' ... your little ruse didn't work. Such loyalty is commendable. I'm afraid the men must remain where they are.' He spoke into the intercom, countermanding the order.

He wasn't going to keep his word. It had been a gamble and it had failed. Vincenzo opened his mouth to speak, but the squeal of a telephone curtailed his protest. Reinhardt answered the call, speaking in German. Vincenzo heard the line crackle and guessed that it was long distance, from Berlin perhaps.

'Certainly *Herr General*, we'll be honoured. I'll wait for the details of your arrival. The next few days, you say.' A pause. 'I understand perfectly. Everything will be ready for you.'

So an important official was visiting the base. Eichmann?

The commandant replaced the receiver and turned back. 'I must ask you to leave now, *Eccellenza*.'

'About releasing the men ... ?'

'I've made my decision. Much as I regret penalising the villagers, I cannot let the murder of one of my officers go unpunished. This is a serious crime.' Reinhardt thumped the desk with his fist 'The perpetrator must be brought to justice.'

Justice, thought Vincenzo. Where's the justice in locking up an entire village?

As he escorted him to the door, Reinhardt once more donned a courteous manner. 'You have a charming village, *Signor Conte*, the villagers are fine people. My men have been happy to mingle with them ... ' He shook his head pensively. ' ... this unfortunate matter has changed things. Your attempt at providing the answer is commendable. I understand your motive, but I'm certain that a woman couldn't have killed Johan Fleischer.'

Vincenzo loathed having to demean himself. 'Please, commandant, reconsider. I swear to you, it's the truth.'

Reinhardt gave a thin smile, and wagged a finger in his visitor's face, '*Non, mon ami, ce n'est pas la verité*'

Ordinarily, this side-step into French would have amused Vincenzo, but the circumstances stamped out hilarity. He burst out angrily, 'You can't accept my explanation because it isn't what you want to hear.'

'Calm yourself, *Eccellenza*. Consider this, the woman's body was found days before Fleischer went missing. She couldn't have had anything to do with it. No, this heinous murder is down to one of the men from the village.'

To discourage further argument, he opened the door and ushered his visitor out, leaving Vincenzo to reflect on how conveniently he had twisted events to suit himself.

By the time he reached the cottage, Vincenzo's fermenting anger had reached eruption point. He burst into the kitchen, startling the occupants. Grazia Elena read the expression on his face and hurriedly ushered her granddaughter out of the room.

Guido got to his feet. 'So, comrade, things didn't go well,' he said.

'The son of a bitch beat me at my own game,' snarled Vincenzo. 'He's got more brains than I gave him credit for.'

'Did you find out anything useful?'

'Reinhardt wants a scapegoat. He's under pressure from above to retaliate for this murder. To him, it's a matter of pride.'

'That's what I thought. Did you find out anything else?'

'There's a VIP coming down from Berlin. Eichmann perhaps? That's put pressure on him to clear up this domestic matter quickly.'

'Could the visit be something to do with the arms depot?'

'I'm certain of it. On my way back I did a spot of reconnaissance. Since Fleisher's murder Reinhardt's reduced the number of sentries on duty at the depot. He must have deployed them to search for his missing officer and now, of course, he's posted some men outside the vestry. This works in our favour. With only two sentries on duty, we can take them by surprise, break into the arsenal for Semtex and blow up the villa while Reinhardt and his cronies are asleep. It's perfect.'

'Wait a minute! It's not as simple as that. Do you know anything about explosives?'

'No, but you do,' rejoined Vincenzo.

'To make a success of it, we have to plant a bomb *inside* the villa.' Guido jabbed a finger at him. 'How do we do that? You said that Reinhardt has confiscated your keys.'

Vincenzo grinned triumphantly. 'There is a way. There's a disused well to the rear of the villa. It was abandoned years ago when the water became contaminated after a fox drowned in it.

Some hundred feet down, there's a small door set in the wall about sixty feet below the level of the cellar. From this door, there's a narrow passage leading up into the cellar beneath the kitchen. A trap door opens into an alcove next to the pantry.' He refrained from voicing his qualms that with the autumn rains, the door in the well could have become submerged. He went on. 'You can gen me up on how to plant the Semtex and prime the detonator…'

Guido raised a dissenting hand. 'Wait! Am I not to be involved in this?'

'You don't know the layout of the house.'

'You can fill me in.' He narrowed his eyes and, after a pause, said quietly, 'Your home will be destroyed.'

Vincenzo cast him a contemptuous glance. 'A minor sacrifice.'

'You're prepared to do this?'

'Of course.' It was easy to agree, but what would it feel like when the villa had been destroyed?

'Maybe we should contact Claudia and wait for back up,' suggested Guido.

'There's no time. Reinhardt's edgy. He could order the men to be shot. Besides, we don't want him tightening up his security again. The fewer people involved in this the better. We can't afford to wait.'

Guido slapped the palm of his hand down on the table. 'In that case, let's draw up our plans.' He slid an empty wine carafe to one side. 'This is the villa. We'll approach the depot from here?'

'No,' disagreed Vincenzo, shuffling coffee cups and tumblers around the table.. 'This is a better route.'

For a while, each man remained wrapped in thought. Vincenzo spoke. 'We make our move tomorrow night, agreed?'

The exhilaration Vincenzo felt at having laid their plans soon evaporated. That night, in the loneliness of his room, he consumed three quarters of a bottle of whisky. He had reached his nadir. Suddenly everything seemed hopeless. The plan was too audacious. Even Guido had voiced his misgivings. He recalled the Florence fiasco and had to admit to himself that the current plan was even less well prepared than the assassination attempt had been. Should they call it off before it was too late?

He woke next morning with a hangover, but with the coming of the day, his uncertainties were swept away. He deliberately avoided contact with the others, seeking to shed his hangover and clear his mind.

At nightfall, the two men met outside the barn which was Guido's temporary abode. This makeshift accommodation had never brought complaint from Guido, who was well used to such hardship.

Both men were wearing black and carried short-handled knives. They approached the arsenal in silence. The sentries weren't expecting trouble. They were standing close to the wall of the arms depot, sheltering from the heavy rain under their waterproof capes. It was over in seconds. Taken by surprise, the unfortunate guards slumped to the ground, blood spilling from their throats. Guido pounced on the bodies, delving into the men's pockets until he found some keys. A streak of lightning lit up the sky as they shunted their victims into a nearby ditch, where they landed with a splash.

Guido gave a smothered laugh. 'The weather has been kind to us. Thunder will drown out our movements.'

But the heavy rain bothered Vincenzo. It could bring a rise in the water level of the well.

The lead-lined door of the bunker opened with a groan. Vincenzo went inside and flashed his torch. It revealed tier after tier of ammunition: guns, grenades, mines and explosives.

Guido drew in his breath in astonishment. 'My God, I didn't expect anything like this.' He moved to a safe built into the wall, his eyes glinting. 'What have we here?'

'Another flash of lightning reminded Vincenzo of the oncoming storm.' Leave it, Guido, there's no time. It will take hours to work out the mechanism.'

Guido wasn't to be put off. 'I did a bit of safe breaking before the War. It's a tough one but I'll crack it,' he said, starting to finger the dial.

Lightning flashed more frequently, thunder louder, rain beat a tattoo on the roof.

'Leave it!' snapped Vincenzo. 'If the water rises too high, I won't be able to find the door in the well.

'I'm nearly in,' retorted his companion. 'Collect the explosives we need.' He waved his hand towards the back of the building. 'I saw grenades over there. Is there Semtex?'

'Yes, I've found it, but hurry up!'

'Bring some of that Semtex over here.'

'Christ no! Do you want to send the whole place up?'

'I know what I'm doing.'

Vincenzo ran to stand behind his companion. Bringing out his knife, he placed it close to Guido's neck. 'Don't think about it,' he warned.

Guido either didn't hear him or chose to ignore him. '*Madre mia*, I've cracked it! No need for the Semtex after all,' He spun around triumphantly, stopping in amazement when he saw the knife. Bursting out laughing, he said, 'What the devil are you doing, comrade?'

With a snort of irritation, Vincenzo returned the knife to its sheath, while Guido reached into the safe and pulled out a cardboard tube, emptying out its contents. It was a detailed plan of the village and the roads leading up to it. There was a document with it. He thrust it at his companion. 'What does it say?'

'It's a plan to mine the area around the village in the event of Monte Cassino falling to the Allies. It confirms what I overheard during my visit,' replied Vincenzo. 'Reinhardt sees himself as a one of the Fatherland's saviours.'

Guido roared with laughter. 'That inflated Frankfurter! So that's his game.' He grew serious. 'Time to get on with the business in hand.' He re-rolled the map pushing it back into its cardboard tube and returning it to the safe. Reaching into his pocket, he brought out a waterproof bag and put the Semtex inside it.

During the time spent in the bunker, the storm had worsened. The torrential downpour soaked them in minutes, blinding them as they tried to make an inspection of the well. A grid had been fixed over the top of it, a precaution, Vincenzo recalled, that Alice had insisted upon after Enzo had daringly descended into its depths, urging his brother to join him. Wisely, Beppe had refused to follow. The grid was rusty and came away easily. Guido tested the ladder. It rattled against the wall of the well. He shone his torch. Clearly, the water was rising fast.

'I'll go instead,' announced Guido.

Vincenzo was tempted to let him. Guido was years younger than him and much fitter. He shook off his misgivings. If the villa was going to be blown up, he would be the one to do it. After a short argument, he won the day with his insistence that he knew the layout of the villa.

Guido gave in gracefully, slapping his shoulder and saying, 'Fair enough, but follow my instructions to the letter when you prime the detonator.'

Vincenzo nodded, listening intently while his companion ran over the details again. Guido clasped his hand. 'Good luck, my friend!'

Twenty-four

Vincenzo tested the rope tied round his waist, and using the rusting ladder for guidance, he felt his way down. Some of the rungs gave way under his feet to fall with a splash into the murky depths, but the rope held. The water level had risen considerably, and Vincenzo guessed that the stream feeding the well had become dammed with autumn leaves. It happened when the overflow from the stream gushed upwards to meet the torrential rain pouring down from the heavens.

The water lapped at his feet, then crept up to his shins. His teeth began to chatter. This was worse than he had imagined, but there was no turning back. By the time he reached the hidden door, the water was almost up to his knees. He gave Guido the thumbs up.

The ancient lock to the door was rusty and the key almost slipped from his numb fingers but, after much prodding and poking, it responded. Vincenzo threw his weight against the door but it wouldn't budge. Clutching the rope and with knees lifted, he swung himself out and back, propelling his feet against the door. It still wouldn't budge. He repeated the action several times until at last the door swung inwards with a splintering groan.

The recoil left Vincenzo spinning crazily on the end of the rope. At last he was able to steady himself, but his grip was beginning to falter and he felt dizzy. Once he'd regained his equilibrium, he hoisted himself onto the threshold, letting go of the rope. The door creaked as he tried to shut it, and he realised that it was broken beyond repair. With water slopping over his feet, he felt for the jagged wall recalling that, according to legend, during the turbulent medieval era, the entrance had been used as an escape route for anti-papal members of his family. He gave an ironic grimace. It was being put to use again in the twentieth century!

His flashlight revealed a steep flight of flagstone steps. He tried to visualise the layout of the secret passageway. Would he still be able to gain access to the cellar? Shining the torch upwards, he climbed the mossy steps, using the wall to stop himself from losing his balance. At the top he ducked under a stone archway to find himself in the cellar. It appeared undisturbed, with the vintage wine he had been hoarding until the War was over still securely stored on a rack close to the ceiling. He had planned to open it to celebrate Alice and Beppe's homecoming. The blade of doubt sliced into his chest. Was he right to destroy the villa?

The bad moment passed. On going to the trap door leading up to the kitchen, he got a shock. The door was rusty and refused to budge. He found Mateo's tool box in the corner and with the use of a chisel, tried again. This time, the trap door shifted enough for him to shine the torch through a narrow gap. To his dismay, he saw that a piece of furniture had been dragged over the trap door: the heavy oak dresser, crammed with china and glassware!

Merda! What now? He clenched his fists and swore with frustration. He was trapped. All this effort for nothing. He looked back at the archway leading down to the well door and gave a shudder. Would the water have reached the door during the fifteen minutes he'd spent in the cellar?

He punched the wall, grazing his knuckles. There must be a way. He inspected the obstruction again, and this time, saw that the opening was only partially covered. He gave the trap door another push and realised it had become wedged against one of the dresser's feet. Thankfully the only sound he could hear was the low hiss of the wood-burning kitchen stove. Standing on a stool, he pushed his arms through the narrow gap and with his cheek pressed against the ceiling, he managed to move the dresser along a few centimetres. His muscles ached with the effort, but after a short rest, he tried again and managed to move it another few centimetres. Racked with pain, he inched the dresser along until the gap was large enough for him to wriggle through.

He stood in the kitchen panting for breath, flexing and unflexing his fingers and shoulders to relieve the tension. A glance at his watch told him there no time to lose. Twenty-five minutes had elapsed since he'd entered the building. He crept into the hall, glancing across at the elegant staircase and gave his head a shake, closing his mind to the consequences of his actions.

His gaze came to rest on a clock placed on the table at the foot of the stairs. A wedding present from his father-in-law, Robert McPherson-Corke, it was a fine timepiece with a pleasing chime, manufactured in London during the eighteenth century. It's uniqueness lay in the melody played on ten bells every three hours. He knew the commandant had kept it wound up because he had heard it chime on his visits to the villa. At that time, he would have given anything to seize it. Now, it was to be the ultimate sacrifice. Casting sentiment aside, he followed Guido's instructions, disciplining his trembling fingers to prepare the detonation. The next toll of ten bells would be the clock's last.

A noise from the upper floor made him shrink back into the shadows. A light came on. He sucked in his breath and waited for exposure. No one came down the stairs. As he waited, memories flooded his mind: recollections of Alice and Enzo and Beppe, of birthday celebrations, of Christmas festivities, of dinner parties with friends. These unheralded images summoned up unbridled anger, unseating caution. He fingered the knife in his pocket and dwelt on the pleasure it would give him to steal in on Reinhardt in his slumber and drive the blade into his heart.

The flushing of a lavatory brought him to his senses. Once the upstairs light had gone out, he darted across the hall to unlock the front door and make his escape. A shock awaited him. The door was not only bolted but it was locked from inside and the key was nowhere to be seen. He glanced furtively towards the stairs, hoping that no one else would need the bathroom. He quickly rationalised the situation. He would have to leave by another door, but a hurried inspection told him that every single door had been securely locked, the keys removed. Hurrying back to the kitchen, he swept his torch around the room to find the service door also locked, and the pantry window tightly shuttered with a heavy padlock keeping it in place.

The only other possibility was the coal chute in the room next to the kitchen. The door was locked but he remembered the spare key Grazia Elena kept tucked away on the lintel above the door. His spirits lifted when he discovered it was still there. Flashing the torch around the blackened coal bunker, he saw with alarm that heavy army equipment had been stacked up against the chute, blocking the opening. Reinhardt had made the villa into an impenetrable fortress. There was no alternative other than to go back through the cellar.

Things got even worse. When he squeezed through the trap door, he was horrified to find his feet sloshing in water. The level was rising faster than ever. With a gulp of dismay, he remembered the men camped at the back of the house. Someone must have shifted the protective dyke Matteo had erected to divert the flow.

All at once, he heard footsteps in the hall above. Reinhardt's voice reached him: 'How could anyone have got in? Search the place! Find the intruder!'

Vincenzo didn't stop to listen. Someone must have noticed his wet footprints on the tiled hall floor. Dragging the trap door into position, he splashed across to the stone archway and shone his torch into the void before wading into the freezing water. Tucking the torch into his belt, he took a deep breath and dived into the narrow shaft, feeling his way to the bottom with his hands.

His legs scraped against the jagged walls, his eyes stung as he tried to pierce the darkness. He twisted his body first one way and then the other trying to locate the doorway. The door itself had been forced open by the incoming surge of water. It took all Vincenzo's strength to combat the torrent. His lungs screamed for air. Would he ever get out? When his head eventually broke the surface, he floundered in the water, arms and legs flailing, gasping for breath.

Once the air had revived him, he groped for the rope, panicking when he couldn't locate it. Guido must have pulled it clear. Unaware that he was trapped, his companion would be waiting for him at the appointed meeting place. Treading water, he felt his way around the slime-covered wall of the well, searching for the ladder, only to discover that he was caught in a section where the rungs had broken away. Close to despair, he envisaged his life slipping away. Snatching the flashlight from his belt, he found that it still worked and on shining it round the well he saw that Guido had not pulled the rope clear. It had become snagged on the jagged wall not more than a couple of feet above his head. Summoning his remaining energy, he pressed his feet against the wall and tried to propel himself upwards to grab the rope. It slipped through his fingers and he sank into the water. He tried again and again until he managed to get a grip on the rope and haul himself up.

Using the rusting rungs as a guide, he climbed up the rope, but his fingers were so numb that he found himself sliding down again. He yelled Guido's name but there was no answering call.

At last, he reached the top of the well and clambered out, collapsing onto the muddy ground. The wind swirled around him, gusting wildly one minute only to lapse the next. During these interludes, the rain gained momentum, unleashing its venom like a startled rattlesnake. Regaining his breath, he got to his feet and ran towards the vine terraces. Exhilaration fed power to his aching limbs. Everything except his heart was silent. It thumped against his ribcage in time with his father-in-law's clock.

Suddenly a momentous force threw him forward, the earth shuddered under him, a tumultuous roar reverberated into the night. He lay on the ground, his head covered by his arms while the explosions went on and on. When, eventually, they subsided, he waited several seconds. Scrambling to his feet, he started to run towards the agreed meeting place. He felt intoxicated. He'd done it. His ears still rang from the blast yet through the confusion, sounds of shouting reached him.

Reason told him to distance himself from the scene as quickly as possible, but the urge to look back was too strong. He needed to applaud his achievement, to pay homage to his old home.

He stopped and turned. In the distance, silhouetted figures ran around wildly, screams rent the air. Flames leapt into the sky, spotlighting the sheeting rain. Debris peppered the lawn, reminiscent of playthings discarded by his children in years gone by. He shook his head to rationalise his thoughts. But success was inebriating, it couldn't be suppressed. He'd outwitted those German bastards. Their polished jackboots would no longer defile his beloved home. Livia's murder had been avenged. She would have laughed at that, shared in his triumph. The purpose of the exercise -- the release of the imprisoned men and the abortion of the commandant's plan to mine the village -- was temporarily forgotten.

Revenge was heady. He yelled in exaltation. All at once, another explosion rent the air. The blast propelled him backwards. Rocks and masonry shot up. His eyes widened with horror as a piece of twisted girder hurtled directly towards him. Impact was unavoidable. The breath was wrenched from his lungs and he passed out.

Twenty-five

Vincenzo opened his eyes but felt nothing. He was floating. In what? A swimming pool; the sea? Memory returned: the icy water of the well.

He tried to sit up, but collapsed back. Water trickled between his fingers. He realised that he wasn't floating, but lying in a muddy stream. Lifting his head, he smiled wryly at the strange angle of his right leg. A broken leg! Was that all? A few weeks in plaster. Stefano would sort it out. He sank back exhausted.

The next time he opened his eyes, someone was peering at him from a distance. Slowly, the blurred face came into focus. 'Give me a hand, Guido, I don't seem to be able to sit up.' With these words, he passed out again.

Days and nights merged. His friend, Dr Stefano Amato, came to see him; Giuliana and Grazia Elena appeared at his bedside, but he was too exhausted to pay them any attention. He heard them talking in hushed tones. One morning, he woke up with his head feeling clearer. Giuliana was there.

She smiled, 'You look better today. Would you like to be propped up so that you can take some broth?'

He nodded.

Giuliana disappeared from the room, returning with Guido and between them, they lifted him into a semi-sitting position. Grazia Elena came in carrying a tray. She sat down on the chair beside his bed and, much to his embarrassment, started feeding him.

'I can do it myself,' he protested but one attempt made him realise just how weak he was. A pain shot through his leg.

Later that day Stefano Amato came. 'How are you, my old friend?' he asked. 'You look better than you did last time I saw you.'

'I hope you've come to tell me I can get up,' said Vincenzo.

The doctor shook his head. 'Not yet, I'm afraid. But now you've gained a little strength I can examine you properly.'

'What's to examine?' asked the count. 'I know my right leg's broken.'

'Your right leg's on the mend, it's the left one I'm concerned about.'

'It hurts like hell. Can't you do something about it?'

'Not until I've examined you.'

Giuliana came in and lifted the lower end of the protective sheet from the cradle set up over his legs.

'I want to see the damage,' grumbled Vincenzo.

'That's not a good idea.'

'I want to see for myself.' Ignoring the pain, he summoned all his willpower to hoist himself up onto one elbow. Before Giuliana could stop him, he snatched the sheet away.

His right leg was in a splint. His gaze shifted to his other leg, and he recoiled with shock. It finished several centimetres below the knee. Bone jutted through mutilated flesh; the dressing covering it was soaked with blood. With a low moan, he closed his eyes and sank back onto the pillow.

'I told you not to look,' said Amato.

Vincenzo opened his eyes again. 'Why the hell didn't you tell me?' he demanded.

'You didn't give me the chance.'

For the duration of the examination, the patient remained silent. When it was over, he asked, 'Did *you* remove it?'

Amato heaved a sigh and said gently, 'It was blown off in the blast.' The blast! Now he remembered: it must have been that massive piece of girder which had hurtled towards him. He heard Stefano's voice again. 'I'm going to try and get you into hospital?'

'How? The hospitals are bursting at the seams with war wounded. Can't you patch me up?'

Amato picked up his pipe and tried to light it. 'I can't hide the truth from you, Vincenzo.' He tapped the bowl with his match box, struck a match and tried again to light the pipe. 'You may need further amputation. The stump is inflamed, there's risk of gangrene.'

Vincenzo glared at him. 'You're a surgeon, you do it.'

'My hands aren't steady, I no longer perform operations, you know that!'

'I want you to do it.'

'My friend, I can't. This type of surgery needs to be done in a hospital theatre with all the necessary equipment.' He sucked at the stem of his pipe and inhaled.

Vincenzo's scowl deepened. 'What's the matter, lost your nerve?'

Amato didn't take offence. 'You should be in hospital,' he insisted and, without waiting for further protest, turned and left the room.

After Stefano had departed, the others left Vincenzo alone, giving him time to digest the extent of his terrible injuries. Why did the phantom leg give him so much pain? Despair crushed him. He thumped the counterpane with balled fists. Was he to end his life a useless cripple, stumbling along on a wooden leg, smoking endless cigarettes and drinking more than was good for him simply to allay the boredom of inactivity?

His thoughts flew back to his Army days. He recalled seeing a fellow officer sprawled on the plains of Abyssinia. He had lost both legs. The man had stared up at him with glazed eyes, silently entreating him to put an end to his misery. He relived the terrible moment when he had withdrawn his revolver from its holster, feeling his palms sweat against its tortoiseshell butt. He'd focused and pressed his finger to the trigger but, knowing that the medics were on their way, he had been unable to complete the deed. The man had shrieked profanities after him as he'd walked away. He had died in hospital two days later.

The recollection revived feelings of guilt. How cowardly he'd been not to finish the job. Yet he knew in his heart that nothing would ever induce him to kill a wounded man when there was still a chance of life. With these memories flickering through his mind, he fell asleep.

Four hours' sleep restored rationalisation. He awoke to find Grazia Elena sitting beside his bed. She was knitting a small garment in multi-coloured wool. It was some time before she realised he was watching her. She rested her knitting needles in her lap and said, 'So you're awake.'

'What's that you're knitting?' he asked, adding with mock sarcasm, 'Don't tell me it's a sock for my stump.'

The old woman burst out laughing. 'I see you haven't lost your sense of humour. Actually, it's a cardigan for the little one.'

'Isabella? How is she?'

'Missing her mother of course, but Giuliana looks after her very well.'

'I'd like to see her.'

'All in good time.'

'Is Guido still here?'

'No, he's gone up north.'

Ah, thought Vincenzo, Guido's made contact with Claudia at last. Later in the day, Stefano Amato called and filled him in with what had happened on the night of the explosion.

'You're lucky to be alive, my friend. Guido carried you all the way down the hill. You were in a terrible state, wouldn't have lasted another hour.'

'I haven't had a chance to thank him.'

'He'll be back.'

He tried to lever himself up in the bed and grimaced. 'The pain gets worse, not better.' Ashamed of his show of irritability, he asked, 'What happened after the explosion?'

'Chaos! All the officers were killed, the men were thrown into panic.'

'Was there talk of reprisals? And what about Eichmann's visit?'

'It appears the German High Command were too busy negotiating with that bumbling fool, Badoglio, to worry about our insignificant little village. The visit must have been cancelled. The remaining troops were re-grouped and sent down to Monte Cassino.'

Vincenzo frowned. 'I can't believe they'd let this pass.'

'The Germans put the explosion down to a freak accident, a lightning strike. There was a second explosion, you know.'

'A second explosion?'

'It narrowly missed sending the whole arsenal up. The guards on duty were blown to pieces in the blast.'

Vincenzo frowned. The poor fellows were already dead.

'What about the weapons?' he asked, wincing with pain.

'That's enough talking. You're tired; take some rest I'll try and get you into hospital. That leg must be sorted out. There are no ambulances, but I have just enough petrol left to drive you there. We'll talk about it tomorrow.'

'Stop fussing. Go on with your story, what about the weapons?'

Stefano heaved a resigned sigh. 'The departing Germans took most of the heavy artillery with them, but they left in such a hurry that some of the explosives and small arms got left behind. Guido called for back-up, and your friends in the Resistance moved in quickly to clean the place out.'

'All this happened while I was unconscious.'

Amato smiled. 'Yes, my friend.'

'What happened then?'

'It was a tense few days. Padre Ferdinando released the men from the church and they went into hiding. The women locked themselves in their houses. Even after the Krauts left it was days before they would venture out. They were terrified of retaliation. Eventually, things got back to normal and the men resumed work in the fields. But everybody was on the alert, and they kept their children close by them.'

Vincenzo spoke bitterly. 'The Krauts were going to mine the road through the village. They were going to sacrifice Castagnetto.'

Amato nodded. 'Guido told me. The village has got a lot to thank you for, my friend.'

'Guido Ottone and Livia Carduccio were the authors of the plot.'

'That's not what the villagers believe.'

'What d'you mean?'

Giuliana came in carrying a tray with Vincenzo's supper on it, interrupting the conversation.

Stefano Amato got up to leave. 'I'll call again in the morning and we'll talk about getting you to hospital.'

The next day, Claudia came down to Castagnetto. She called in to see him and, in her customary manner, came straight to the point. 'Sorry about the loss of your leg, Vincenzo.' She might have been talking about the loss of a pet dog. 'We can't ask for your help any more and, even if we could, you couldn't go back to Rome while Scarpone's still in office.' She paused, apparently marshalling her thoughts. 'I must admit, I had my doubts about you at first. Guido and Livia persuaded me to keep you on. They were proved right. You've done a good job and we're grateful.'

Vincenzo felt so angry he could hardly bring himself to speak. What right had this woman to pass judgement on him, to decide whether he would be of further help to the cell?

'If you need somewhere to stay, away from the War, you could go up to San Baldino,' she suggested. 'My father runs a smallholding there; he's getting on a bit and could do with some help. He's hopeless with paperwork. It's a peaceful little community, the perfect spot to help you put the pieces of your life back together again.' He opened his mouth to protest, but then she said something which astounded him. 'Your stump will heal, I'm not so sure about your heart.'

Turning abruptly, she went out of the room, leaving him speechless.

The day after Claudia's departure, he woke up feeling disorientated. Perspiration trickled down his forehead, he could barely focus. A tiny corner of his mind knew he was bordering on delirium, but he felt too weak to resist it. He was back in Donna Caterina's house with the boy, Rocco, leaning over the bed and leering at him with that terrible harelip. All at once, Rocco vanished and a woman's figure appeared. 'Livia!' he called, straining to make out her features as she drew close. *Why is she wearing a black veil?* He reached out to snatch at the veil, but her figure spiralled away into the distance.

It was light when he woke up again. He couldn't figure out the day or the hour. Giuliana was sitting in a chair by the window, doing some mending. He could see her perfectly clearly. When she heard him stir, she got up and hurried over. 'How do you feel?'

'Not too bad,' he lied.

Soon afterwards, Stefano Amato came to examine him. 'Your leg's causing concern, Vincenzo. I'm afraid I can't get you to hospital as the Florence road's blocked following last night's raid.'

'What raid? I didn't hear anything?'

The hint of a smile touched Amato's lips. 'You were on another planet,' he replied. He went on, 'If we leave things as they are there's a serious risk of gangrene. I shall have to do a further amputation myself. Do you agree?'

'Dammit! You know I do.'

'Giuliana's making preparations for surgery,' Amato went on to explain but his patient didn't hear him. He was back in the freezing water of the well.

Once again, Vincenzo came round to find Giuliana at his bedside. She made the sign of the cross, gasping '*Grazie a Dio!*', then rushed out of the room, returning with the doctor.

'It was touch and go,' said Amato, nodding his head thoughtfully.

'It's done!' Vincenzo was astonished. 'How much did you take off?'

'Not too much. Don't worry, you've still got your knee. I did a tidying up job, fashioned an 18cm posterior skin flap, had to make certain that no rough bone areas remained, pulled down the tendons ... '

'Spare me the gory details.'

Amato grinned. 'I thought you wanted to be kept well informed.'

'Not *that* well informed. What are my chances?'

'We'll have to see how things go but, at the moment, they look good.'

Time passed and Vincenzo's wounds began to heal but the agony went on, endless days and nights of excruciating pain interspersed with brief episodes of relief. He learned from Amato that Guido had rejoined Claudia in the north, and that life in the village had settled down, but he was taken aback one evening, when his friend said, 'This is only a brief visit, Vincenzo. Now that I'm satisfied you're on the mend, I shall be leaving for Milan. My sister's terminally ill, I must go to her.'

Vincenzo felt let down. Stefano Amato had been his mainstay throughout the difficult weeks of his recovery, not only as his doctor, but he had also kept him abreast of the progress of the War. Grazia Elena and her granddaughter were diligent in their care of him, but they had no interest in events outside their village. They lived from day-to-day, scraping a living, their thoughts focused on survival. They listened to wireless reports, but didn't really comprehend the significance of the Soviet advances on Poland, the D Day landings or the Allies' liberation of Athens. When in October 1944 Rommel committed suicide, they raised their eyebrows: who was this man? On another occasion, when he asked Giuliana to question Padre Ferdinando on the latest news from Rome, she returned with such a garbled version that he decided it was better to remain in ignorance rather than be misinformed.

The hours stretched endlessly ahead of him until, one day, Grazia Elena agreed that he was well enough for Isabella to come to see him. Accompanied by Giuliana, the little girl came nervously into the room. He wondered how she would react. After all, it was weeks since she'd seen him. When she saw him sitting in his chair, a blanket across his knees, she wrested her hand from Giuliana's and ran across the room to fling herself at him. Somehow he managed to restrain the scream of agony which sprang to his lips; tears of joy mingled with tears of pain.

Giuliana rushed over and lifted the child off. 'You mustn't do that Isabella, your Babbo's been hurt.'

'Leave her, she wasn't to know,' gasped Vincenzo.

Isabella asked innocently, 'Have you fallen over and hurt yourself?'

'I'm afraid so. I've hurt my leg.'

'You'll have to learn to hop. I can hop. Look!' She started to demonstrate, urged on by the applause of her audience. For the next hour, she sat at the foot of his chair, chatting excitedly about the games she had been playing with the stray kitten Giuliana had eventually been persuaded to let her keep.

The next few months were the worst Vincenzo had ever experienced. After his initial relief at surviving the explosion, he was filled with desolation. Yes, he had survived, but at what cost? The bleak cloud of reality weighed heavily on his shoulders. He saw his future looming: a crippled old man confined to a wheelchair.

Life offered one ray of happiness: Isabella. She came to see him daily and when the onset of spring brought improvement to his general health, he spent even more time with her. Out in the yard, she would toss her ball at him, giggling merrily when he reached out for it, almost toppling out of his chair. He had never played with his own children. Work had kept him busy, and Grazia Elena and Alice had taken on the task of keeping Enzo and Beppe amused. Even Matteo had spent more time with the boys than he had.

He grew to love the little girl, recognising in her, a loneliness akin to his own. She had a vivid imagination, involving him in her fantasies. He played the role of papà to her dolls, of prince to her princess, of magic genie to her Aladdin. He read her stories and nursery rhymes. She danced for him, she sang for him, she was her mother's child, a constant reminder of Livia, and he adored her.

Until now, events had been a roller-coaster, leaving no time to grieve. In this period of convalescence, there was plenty of time. Livia had died, their unborn child had died with her. He had never loved any woman as he had loved her, no one could ever replace her. Her memory shone like a beacon. When he closed his eyes, he saw again her challenging smile, heard afresh her teasing voice; her scent lingered in his nostrils. He lusted after her, dreamt they made love, only to wake up in an agony of despair.

He would lay awake in the small hours, angry at being unable to get out of bed, unable to expunge frustration by pacing the floor. The return of his energy needed an outlet. He used his mind, forcing himself to plan ahead. The War would soon be over. His wife and son would return home to find the villa in ruins. He glanced down at his legs. Would Alice be able to cope with a crippled husband? Would Beppe, at almost fourteen, fit into the rural life of Tuscany? His son was an English schoolboy now, cared for by his English mother and grandfather, destined, he felt sure, for a place at Oxford or Cambridge. Beppe, the introverted scholar, Enzo the daring exhibitionist -- how he missed them both! This cranial activity plunged him back into despair.

One day, Giuliana brought up a subject he didn't want to talk about. 'If you want to live a normal life,' she said. 'You'll need an artificial leg.'

'Of course I won't,' he protested, refusing to look further into the future than the next day.

To fit a false leg was to admit defeat. He preferred wheeling himself about in a clapped-out wheelchair purloined upon the death from bronchitis of the old widow, Olga Papini, in late January. This way, he saw himself as a convalescent, halfway to recovery.

One day in June, Giuliana rushed into his room, crying, 'The doctor's back.'

This was good news. Vincenzo had missed his friend, as had the villagers who, in his absence had been obliged to walk some seven kilometres to see the nearest doctor.

On his arrival, Grazia Elena and Giuliana hovered at the door eager for the latest gossip from Milan. They were disappointed when Vincenzo asked them to leave. 'Isabella can stay,' he said, smiling kindly at their indignation. Obediently they withdrew, looking hurt.

'Was that necessary?' asked Stefano Amato.

Vincenzo nodded. 'I have something important to tell you.'

'What is it?'

'Hmm ... ' Vincenzo cleared his throat. 'I've decided to die.'

'What?' Losing his customary calm, Amato leapt to his feet, frowning with concern. 'No, my friend, don't do it, suicide is a terrible sin.' He knuckled his fists. 'Believe me, things are never as bad as they look. You'll recover; they'll fit you with an artificial limb. One day, you'll walk again.'

Vincenzo couldn't help feeling amused by his friend's reaction. 'Calm down, Stefano, and let me finish. I'm going to die as far as the rest of the world is concerned.'

'How?' Amato sat down again, shock lingering in his eyes.

'Nobody outside the village knows I survived the blast. As far as everybody else is concerned, I've disappeared. I'll not be missed.'

'Not be missed? What nonsense!'

Vincenzo laughed. 'My dear, loyal, old friend, no one's interested in me. I'm finished. I've thought this through and made up my mind. I shall put my affairs in order and vanish.' He leant forward and fixed Amato with a piercing stare. 'Will you help me?'

'Help you? What can I do? I've never heard anything so far-fetched. What about Alice and Beppe?'

'They'll be better off without me. After the requisite number of years, Alice will be able to claim her inheritance and Beppe will be set up for life.'

Vincenzo grinned as the doctor got up to pace the floor, stepping carefully over Isabella's dolls, which were strewn on the rug.

'You can't erase yourself from the face of the earth,' he bellowed.

'With your help, I can.'

Amato's eyebrow shot up. 'Forget it, there's no way I'd falsify a death certificate.'

Vincenzo gave a shrewd smile. 'This is war, laws don't apply any more. My medical records could get *mislaid*.'

'Don't be ridiculous!' Amato's indignation grew. 'My dear friend, your housekeeper and her granddaughter know you're alive. Can you trust them to keep their mouths shut? And what about the villagers? There's been a constant stream of enquiries since the explosion.'

'What did you tell them?'

'The truth, that you're not yet ready for visitors.'

Vincenzo looked triumphant. 'There you are! They'll think I didn't recover from my injuries...that I had a setback; gangrene set in or I suffered a heart attack. You can make something up. I shall move out secretly under cover of darkness.'

'You're out of your mind. No one will believe a cock and bull story like that. You've gone mad; the medication I gave you has mangled your brains. Either that or you've been drinking?'

'Under the watchful eye of those two guardians of the wine cellar!'

'I'm going to call the women in to hear this.'

'Don't!' Vincenzo spoke so sharply that Isabella looked up in alarm. He hastened to reassure her. 'It's all right, little one.'

Amato went to the door. 'I insist.'

Vincenzo gestured to him to sit down. Leaning forward in his wheelchair, he spoke calmly. 'Stefano, what I've got in mind is perfectly feasible, but I need your help. Can I rely on you or not? Does forty years of friendship count for nothing?'

'Go on,' mumbled Amato, still troubled.

'I shall add a codicil to my Will and backdate it by a year - to July 1943 - the month Livia and I arrived in Castagnetto. I'll need you to witness it.'

'That's illegal? I can't put my signature to an illegal document.'

'Not even for your oldest friend? What difference does a month or two make? Surely I can count on you, Stefano. You must send the Will to my partner in the law company for safekeeping. Tell him nothing except that you've heard I'm missing, believed dead.'

'And the second witness?'

'Grazia Elena of course.'

'But she can hardly see.'

'Precisely!' Vincenzo gave a chuckle. 'She'll sign anything I ask her to.'

'I can't let you do this.' Amato's face was purple with outrage. 'It's fraud. And there's the child to consider? Are you going to abandon her?'

'Certainly not! Don't you see, I'm doing this for Isabella.'

'What do you mean?'

'I'm taking her with me.'

'Taking her with you?'

'Yes, I'm adopting her, unofficially of course.'

'You're madder than I thought. Where do you intend to go?'

'To the Dolomites.'

'It's too dangerous. Those mountains are a rabbit warren of revolutionaries. If they're not fighting the Krauts, they're fighting one another.'

'Not where we're going. Claudia has offered us accommodation on her father's smallholding. It's in a sleepy hamlet. We'll be quite safe there.'

'And what are you going to live on, Vincenzo? Your bank accounts have been frozen.'

'I have funds in a safe deposit box in Zurich. I shall need your help with that too.'

The doctor raised surprised eyebrows. 'You sly old fox.' He shook his head contemplatively. 'Finance apart, it's not fair to drag the child away from Grazia Elena and Giuliana, the two people she's grown to trust.' He got up and went to look out of the window. After a few minutes silence, he turned and said, 'Don't do this, Vincenzo, I implore you, don't do it.'

Vincenzo remained unperturbed. 'There's nothing here for Isabella. At the moment she's happy, but have you thought about what will happen after the War when Giuliana's young man comes home and they get married? Will her bridegroom want to take on somebody else's child? As for Grazia Elena, she's much too advanced in years to look after her.'

'Why don't you send her back to the Convent?'

Vincenzo experienced a rush of anger. '*Merda!* What do you take me for? I can't send her back there. They'd recruit her as a novice...' His words petered out.

'Why are you being so pig-headed. Disappear if you like, but return the child to the nuns.'

Vincenzo lost his temper. 'For Christ's sake, Stefano, Livia would never forgive me.'

Isabella looked up startled at the mention of her mother's name. Seeking to reassure her, he said quietly, 'Come here, little one.'

She dropped her doll and ran over to slip her hand into his. 'What's happening, *Babbo*?'

He smiled, gently squeezing her hand, and said, 'Did you hear that, Stefano? Did you hear her call me *Babbo*?'

'I only thought ... ' began Amato weakly.

'*Madre di Dio!* It's out of my hands. Can't you see, it's not a case of me adopting Isabella, *she* has adopted me.'

'Don't get carried away, it's probably because you were the first man to show her any affection, plus the fact that her mother trusted you.'

'Precisely,' he said. 'Her mother trusted me and Isabella, herself, chose me to be her papà. I shall bring her up as my own daughter. Livia would have wanted that.' He had made up his mind and no one, not even his oldest friend, was going to talk him out of this.

The doctor shook his head. 'Vincenzo, my friend, you're overlooking something.'

'What's that?'

'You're not fit enough to make such a long journey.'

Vincenzo brushed him off. 'Needs must, now that Scarpone has forged a nice little niche for himself in the Badoglio Government, he might decide to settle an old score.'

'What old score? What are you talking about?'

Briefly Vincenzo explained how, years ago, he'd humiliated the young, up-and-coming Scarpone in front of Alice.

'*Madonna!* Surely ... '

'He arrested me on the flimsiest of evidence, sent me down to Lucania for two years. He knows Livia was a member of the Resistance.'

Amato frowned in puzzlement. 'I don't understand.'

'Guido's sources learnt that the bastard's still on the lookout for me, that he knows about my connection with Livia and the Resistance. If he's checked on Livia, he'll know about Isabella. When he learns I'm dead, he might decide to take revenge.'

'No decent man would take revenge on a child.'

'Scarpone is not a decent man. Can't you see, Stefano, for the child's sake we must leave as soon as possible.'

'I still think she'd be better off with the nuns.'

Vincenzo frowned. 'No, Livia would turn in her grave if I let her go back there.'

'All right, I'll go along with it,' agreed Amato at last.

Vincenzo heaved a sigh of relief. 'Good man! I knew you wouldn't let me down.'

Twenty-six

Rome

Eduardo Scarpone levered himself off the young girl beneath him. He heard her let out her breath as she pulled the sheet over her naked body. Climbing out of bed, he went to the bathroom, relieved himself and ran the bath water. When he returned to the bedroom, she was curled in a foetal ball, almost hidden by the bedclothes.

Stupid little tart, he sneered. He'd a good mind to fuck her again. She wasn't much fun: submissive, impassive, not like that elusive beauty Di Tomasi had vanished with. She'd been alive, exciting, innovative. This reminder of Di Tomasi darkened his mood. *Merda!* How he'd like to get his hands on the toffee-nosed bastard!

Seized with frustration, he grasped the covers and dragged them off the girl. She shuddered, looking up at him with frightened eyes. 'No! Please, not again.'

'What are you complaining about? I put money in your pocket, food in your belly...or would you prefer to rejoin the ladies of the night on the Appian Way?'

Without giving her a chance to reply, he grasped her thighs and spread her legs. Launching himself on top of her, he smothered her scream by biting her lips. Her blood tasted hot and sweet. Squeezing her wrists, he yanked her arms above her head, pressing his full weight down onto her under-nourished frame. He forced his tongue deep into her mouth, drawing back momentarily when he heard one of her ribs snap. The sound that should have arrested him, drove him on. Her feeble struggles to free herself amused him. She was powerless. Serve her right! If she couldn't respond with passion, he would make do with terror.

He squeezed his eyes tightly closed, moving rhythmically, lost in a symphony of carnal desire. His lust spent, he relaxed. Her blood on his lips sickened him now. He let go of her arms. She didn't move. As he wiped a hand across his mouth, he saw that her eyes were wide open, accusing him, condemning him. Filled with revulsion, he rolled off the bed and stood staring down at her. 'Stop gawping at me, you skinny little hussy!' he shouted.

The bath water! Hurrying back into the bathroom, he turned off the tap just as the water began to lap into the overflow. At the wash-hand basin, he dashed cold water over his face, shaking the drops out of his hair, and wiping steam from the mirror so that he could study his reflection. He'd gone too far. It was Di Tomasi's fault. The man had incensed him, made him lose control. He slapped the damp tiles with the palm of his hand. What did it matter anyway? The girl was nothing but a useless little trollop. He stepped into the bath and luxuriated in the steaming water.

Afterwards, he cleaned his teeth and had a leisurely shave to give the girl time to pull herself together and leave. He'd left money on the bedside table for her. But when he went back into the bedroom, she was still there.

He crossed to the bed and looked down at her. Her mouth was open. Blood had gathered on her lower lip, oozing between her teeth. Enraged, he slapped first one side of her face and then the other. Her head flopped from side to side like that of a rag doll, spilling blood onto the pillow. Her wrists showed signs of early bruising; he could see a mark where her rib had cracked. Her legs were still wide apart, one drawn up and twisted awkwardly, the other stretched out straight with the foot pointed, like a ballet dancer.

Dear God, the broken rib had punctured her lung! What the hell was he going to do? He couldn't think straight, all his military training, his sense of discipline, had deserted him. He felt like the little boy he used to be when he'd lived in the seminary with the monks. If only Father Paolo were there to tell him what to do! Then it came to him. This was a portent, a sign that he must move on.

He was cool-headed now. Going to the drinks cabinet, he grabbed a bottle of whisky and took it into the bathroom. He dipped his arm into the tub and released the bath plug to let some of the water run out. He didn't want the bathroom flooded when he plunged the girl in. Then he returned to the bedroom and lifted her off the bed. She was as light as a feather-filled eiderdown. Half-starved, her torso was skeletal, her shoulder blades protruding like wings. As he carried her, her arms and legs hung flaccidly, but her eyes seemed to bulge from their sockets.

He slid her to the floor, propping her upright against the wall. He would have preferred to close her eyes, but for his purpose, it was better if they remained open. It wasn't easy pouring whisky into her mouth. Her head kept dropping forward, so that most of the alcohol spilt onto the floor. The room began to reek of whisky. At last, he was satisfied that she seemed sufficiently inebriated. Placing his hands under her armpits, he hauled her up until he could slide her into the bath. A horrendous gurgling sound rose as she sank to the bottom. He stood back and surveyed his handiwork.

Now what? The Police would find her and write the incident off as accidental drowning. They wouldn't spend too much time looking into the death of a drunken whore. These days they had more important things to do. Of course, they'd want to question him, but that didn't matter because he wasn't going to hang around. He would disappear, using one of the many aliases his underworld contacts had provided for him. He was ready for change. How he hated the new liberal regime! His loyalty had always lain with Mussolini. Staying with Badoglio's government had been merely for expediency.

He put on a civilian suit, carefully tied his tie in a Windsor knot and inspected himself in the full-length mirror. Nature had been kind to him: a tall, handsome figure with a striking profile and cold blue eyes, he fitted perfectly into *Il Duce's* upper ranks. He tried to keep his packing to essentials, but couldn't resist including his dress uniform. A last look around his spacious office with its en-suite bedroom and bathroom, gave him a few regrets. Would his accommodation in the Fascist Leader's new location in Salò be as lavish?

All at once, he felt a surge of excitement. Mussolini's headquarters on Lake Garda were merely an interim measure. The Nazis had recognised *Il Duce's* importance, rescuing him in order to set him up in power again. It *would* happen, and he would be part of the neo-Fascist Government. But first of all, he had a mission to fulfil. Di Tomasi may have been declared *missing presumed dead*, but he was certain the man was still alive. The grudges against him had accrued. There had to be retribution.

Straightening his shoulders, he faced the mirror again and gave the Fascist salute before picking up his suitcase and leaving the room. He'd already forgotten about the girl.

Twenty-seven

Several days later, Guido came down to Castagnetto in a battered old Fiat, ready to drive Vincenzo and Isabella up to Padua. When they started out Isabella thought the journey was exciting, but she soon became tearful. For Vincenzo it was an ordeal. His good leg ached, his stump throbbed.

'We've found you decent lodgings with a nice old couple. Totally reliable, utterly discreet,' Guido assured him. 'They've been running a halfway house for years, but it's not going to be easy with the child in tow; you'll have to keep her quiet. Anything unusual could arouse curiosity from the neighbours.'

Vincenzo felt a shudder of alarm. What was he doing, taking over the protection of a child when he couldn't even take care of himself? He smothered his misgivings and said, 'I wouldn't want to get these people into trouble. Perhaps we should go straight up to San Baldino?'

Guido shook his head. 'You'd never make it. You'll need to rest before you embark on the journey up the mountains. Besides, you're not much good to anybody until you get fitted with a false leg.' He gave a wry grin. 'Just you wait and see, old Orazio will expect you to earn your keep. Claudia's charity doesn't run to hangers-on. She suggested you stay there because she needs someone to help out on the farm, not the heavy work mind, but the old boy's illiterate and since his nephew was called up earlier in the year, there's no one to manage the place. Those bastards north of the border think nothing of ripping him off.'

'He sells to the Austrians?'

'Certainly! For those rascals, war in Europe hasn't happened. Theirs is a local conflict, been going on for decades.'

'So border disputes don't stop them trading with one another,' muttered Vincenzo. 'It's a crazy world.'

They drove on in silence until Guido drew to a halt at the rear of a large block of flats. 'Wait here,' he ordered. 'I'll make sure the coast is clear.'

He came back, and in the gathering dusk, smuggled the illicit pair into a tiny apartment. Vincenzo recognised the building as one of Mussolini's hair-brained schemes thought up during the thirties to provide accommodation for the masses. Utilitarian, the walls were thin and offered little privacy.

Their stay did not go smoothly. Despite Guido's assurance that they were trusted by the Resistance, their hosts seemed ill-at-ease. It didn't take Vincenzo long to realise that Isabella was the bone of contention. Her presence made them nervous. He found himself frequently shushing her. She became fretful, constantly asking for Giuliana. In Castagnetto, she had enjoyed playing in the open air; here she was confined to a small room. Vincenzo tried to keep her occupied, involving her in his attempts to walk along the corridor on his new artificial leg, but this exercise was so painful that he soon lost patience and gave up.

The straps he was obliged to wear in order to keep the leg in place caused chafing, resulting in sores, not only on the stump but also around his waist and on his shoulder, where the straps were too tight.

Too young to understand his black moods, the little girl started throwing tantrums. The situation snowballed with her screams having to be drowned out by the old couple's ancient gramophone being played at full blast. This, in turn, brought a hammering on the walls from next door.

Before Vincenzo had fully regained his strength, the pair had no choice but to face the hazardous journey up to the Austrian border where Orazio Fabbri lived.

Before their departure, Claudia came to see them. 'My father's lost without my cousin, Nico,' she explained. 'He came to help out shortly after my mother died. He was only fourteen but he was a real worker.'

'I thought things weren't going too well at the farm,' said Vincenzo.

Claudia cast him a surly look. 'That wasn't Nico's fault. There were two bad winters in succession.' She frowned, smarting at his unintended criticism of her cousin. 'Let's see if *you* can do better.'

Vincenzo bit back a riposte. Claudia had deliberately overlooked the sizeable sum he'd put at her disposal. It was this financial pledge that had persuaded the cantankerous Orazio to agree to take them in. He recognised that father and daughter were cast from the same mould. From the outset, he'd known she was only helping him *disappear* because it gave her a chance to line her own pocket, and he was certain she was keeping some of the money back from her father. With his poor head for figures, it was unlikely Orazio would be any the wiser.

Before they left, however, she did come up with one of her surprises. 'I've arranged for someone to measure you for a new prosthetic.' Noticing Vincenzo's expression of scepticism, she went on, 'Don't worry, this will be different. The young man's completely trustworthy. As a matter of fact, he was at university with your son.'

'A friend of Enzo's?'

Claudia smiled. 'Yes, Guido's nephew, Oscar.'

Oscar, the student Enzo had sacrificed his life for! So he'd completed his studies after all. Guido had never mentioned his nephew since their conversation in the trattoria in Padua way back in 1940. Vincenzo was touched. This must be Oscar's way of repaying the debt.

Claudia went on. 'He works at the hospital, says he can get hold of one of the latest models, the best available. It's made of aluminium and it will be much lighter and more comfortable than the one you've got now. I'll smuggle it up to San Baldino for you.'

Vincenzo found it difficult to speak. *Smuggle it up?* That meant it was stolen property. Claudia must have made the Oscar connection. To refuse the offer would be to insult Guido's nephew. Besides, despite his earlier rejection of an artificial limb, he knew he couldn't manage without the new leg. 'That's kind of you, Claudia, and please thank Oscar for me. How much will the leg cost?'

She hesitated momentarily, confirming his suspicions. 'Hmm, a contribution to *The Cause*?'

The communists! He'd always known that Guido and Claudia were political animals, their loyalties swinging well to the left. He was faced with a moral dilemma: stolen property, a contribution to a cause he didn't support? Oscar was taking a risk because of what had happened to Enzo, but Claudia's part in this was political. Again, he was tempted to reject the offer, but such a decision could have repercussions. Claudia knew too much about him to risk offending her and he couldn't jeopardise Isabella's safety.

'How much?' he asked.

Guido drove Vincenzo and Isabella up to San Baldino on a sultry summer's evening. After the child had been settled in bed, the two men took their leave of one another.

'Well, *mio amico*, this is it,' said Guido as they shook hands at the edge of the smallholding. 'The end of the line, eh?'

'Until this evil War is over,' replied Vincenzo.

Guido heaved a deep sigh. 'Once it's over, you and I will follow different paths. It's inevitable.'

Vincenzo knew there was no arguing with that. He could go along with his companion's line of thinking up to a point, but he couldn't bring himself to embrace communism. The two men shook hands, and without another word, Guido got into the car and drove off.

After Claudia brought the new leg, Vincenzo learned to walk with more confidence, gradually stepping out without the aid of a stick. He resumed his writing. He had brought his draft manuscript with him although the reference books he needed had been left down south with Donna Caterina. One day, he intended to retrieve them.

He felt happier than he had done for years. High up in the mountains among the goats and the hens, in the company of a bad-tempered old man and a sweet-natured little girl, he began to pick up the threads of his life. Occasionally, as Guido had predicted, a minor fracas would break out between locals from the border areas, but such disturbances were usually provoked by family feuds and had nothing to do with the War.

The child was his pride and joy, and he dreaded the day she would be old enough to go to school, the nearest of which was some seven kilometres away. He hoped by then he would be capable of driving again since he didn't trust Orazio behind the wheel of a car. The old man was too fond of the bottle.

Whenever he thought about his past life, it was without regret. Stefano Amato had been a true friend, arranging matters exactly as he had requested. To all intents and purposes, Count Vincenzo Di Tomasi had passed on.

From time to time, Claudia visited her father. A female version of her anti-social parent, she stomped around the smallholding inspecting and criticising. Her presence disturbed all three of them. Father and daughter were always at loggerheads, ranting and raving at one another in a dialect unintelligible to Vincenzo. However, Claudia did bring news, albeit out-of-date news.

The winters were hard, but the summers were a joy, and as he watched his adopted daughter grow from a charismatic toddler into a pretty little girl, he thanked God that he had made the decision to disappear.

One April day in 1945, Claudia drove up in a borrowed jeep. Braking sharply in the yard, she leapt out of the vehicle, shouting, 'We did it, we got him at last.' Waving her arms jubilantly, she rushed across the yard. 'They've strung him up in Piazza Loretto, him and his vile bitch, Clara Petacci. May they both rot in hell!'

They got drunk that night, all three of them, drunk on Orazio's homemade gin, drunk until they slumped into a stupor, unaware of the wide-eyed child who crept out of bed to come and see what all the fuss was about.

Less than a month after Mussolini's assassination, the War in Europe ended. Over the following months, the locals saw the return of their young men and Vincenzo began to worry that once Orazio's nephew was demobbed, the old man would tell them to leave. If Claudia returned as well, the house would be at bursting point. He could, of course, afford to purchase a home for himself and Isabella. There were plenty of funds in the Zurich Account but he hated the prospect of upheaval, and decided to leave the matter in abeyance.

There was another reason for his reluctance to move out. Despite Orazio's disagreeable manner and Claudia's interfering nature, he liked the Fabbri's. They were down-to-earth people who said what they thought and were unencumbered by the restrictions of accepted social behaviour. He recognised that he, himself, was a changed man. What had been important before he lost his leg had, afterwards, become totally inconsequential.

Isabella was now four years old. Vincenzo was pleased by the way she'd settled in. She loved helping Orazio feed the chickens and delighted in sitting beside him on a milking stool while he milked the solitary cow. Vincenzo watched fascinated as a strong link grew between the two of them. The old man was belligerent, easily roused to anger. Caught in the path of his wrath, it was wise to move out of reach since he didn't hesitate to lash out with his fists or his walking stick. With the child he was as gentle as a nursemaid, and she adopted him as a grandfather, calling him *Nonno Orazio*.

She didn't mind giving his prickly chin a goodnight peck and she wasn't averse to slipping her tiny fingers into his work-worn hand. At first, afraid that he would frighten her, Vincenzo had been alarmed when, after imbibing too much cognac, the old man flew into a drunken rage. To his surprise, Isabella would, without prompting, slip quietly out of the room to return hours later and sit at Orazio's feet to listen to his wildly exaggerated stories.

During the spring and summer months Vincenzo became increasingly adept on his artificial leg and started taking short walks in the meadows. Isabella often went with him. She enjoyed picking wild flowers, and it gladdened his heart to see her take an interest in the flora and fauna. She pointed out birds and he was often able to name their species for her.

Then one day, just as the little girl was stooping to pick another flower, a man's voice startled them both. 'We meet again, *Signor Conte*!'

Vincenzo knew the voice. 'Scarpone!' he gulped.

The marshal stepped out from between the trees. He was wearing his fascist dress uniform, but it didn't have the crispness of a high-ranking officer. The tunic was crumpled and only partly buttoned, the trousers stained, the jack boots smeared with dust.

'Surprised to see me?' he sneered.

'What are you doing here?'

'I came to see you.'

Without warning, the marshal reached into the holster at his waist and drew out a Buretta.

Vincenzo's heart convulsed as he felt Isabella slip her hand into his. 'For God's sake, Scarpone, put that damn thing away,' he snapped.

'Got you worried, huh?'

'This is ludicrous. Put it away,' repeated Vincenzo. Without wresting his gaze from that of Scarpone's, he shoved the little girl behind him and said, 'Run home, Isabella.' She didn't move. Again, he pushed her, but still she resisted.

The revolver in Scarpone's hand remained steady. 'I've come for you Di Tomasi,' he said. 'This is the moment I've been waiting for. You're an enemy of the State, you deserve to die.'

'The War's over, Scarpone.'

The marshal gave a frenzied laugh. 'It is for you.'

The man's mad, thought Vincenzo, he's trapped in a time warp. With the child still close by him, Vincenzo knew he must keep a hold on the situation. Whatever happened, this maniac must not find the telling pendant, still hidden in the back of his pocket watch. He never had been able to bring himself to get rid of it.

'How did you find me?' he asked, striving to keep his voice even..

Scarpone gave a smirk. 'I was on to your little game, I knew you weren't dead. It's taken me a while, but at last I've tracked you down.' He was so involved in self-congratulation that, momentarily, his concentration wavered.

Vincenzo snatched the opportunity. Ignoring the encumbrance of his prosthetic limb, he shook off Isabella's clasp and took a stride forward only to stumble on the uneven ground and fall to his knees, twisting the artificial leg under him. The pain was excruciating.

Scarpone roared with laughter. 'Shall I shoot you like the cowering dog you are or shall I let you get up, and try to make a run for it?'

Vincenzo struggled to his feet, limping as the throbbing in his leg intensified. He backed away, again placing himself in front of the traumatized child. 'Don't shoot,' he said. 'Let me send her home.'

Scarpone gave a crazy laugh. 'Do you take me for a fool? She'll raise the alarm.' A puzzled expression creased his brow. 'Who is she anyway?'

So Scarpone didn't know of Isabella's existence! All these years, he'd been worrying unnecessarily on that score. He decided to play for time. 'She doesn't understand; she's not old enough to call for help.' He had to protect her. Could he persuade this arrogant madman to let her go, to let them both go? He drew in a breath. Life was precious. He desperately wanted to survive; he wanted to see Isabella grow up; and yes, despite the rejection of his past life, he wanted to see Beppe again.

He tried once more. 'The War's over, Mussolini's dead, the Fascist Government has fallen. What's the point of committing murder? The country's beginning to rebuild itself; you can be part of it.'

Fury exploded across the marshal's face. His eyes flashed. 'Fascism will rise again. Long live *Il Duce*!' He pointed the revolver once more, his finger on the trigger.

In a split second, Vincenzo was aware of two things: a searing pain in his shoulder and the sight of the butt of Orazio's shotgun crashing down on Scarpone's head.

He dropped to his knees, clutching his shoulder, his mind consumed with only one aim: to protect Isabella. With blood gushing from his wound, he threw out his right arm to pull her to the ground, but couldn't reach her. Scarpone started to come round, and made a grab for his revolver.

'Get down, Isabella!' shouted Vincenzo. The child stood frozen to the spot.

The marshal got unsteadily to his knees and reached again for the gun, but Orazio kicked the Buretta out of his reach. Raising his shotgun, he levelled it at the marshal and fired. Scarpone's head exploded. Isabella's scream shattered the air. Shocked into life, she threw herself into Vincenzo's arms and buried her head in his jacket.

Vincenzo gasped for breath. He lay on his back with the child on top of him. His good hand brushed her head and he found her hair sticky with his blood. He tried to move, but his stump was twisted beneath him. He fought giddy waves of unconsciousness. Through a haze of unreality, he saw Orazio toe Scarpone's body aside.

The old man seemed unperturbed by the situation. 'Can you make it back to the house?' he growled.

Vincenzo nodded and croaked. 'Yes. Take the child.'

Orazio tried to pull Isabella away but she clung to Vincenzo's jacket, her tears mingling with his blood.

'Lend me a hand,' said Vincenzo, as he struggled to stand up.

Despite his advanced years. Orazio was strong. He hauled him to his feet. 'You're losing blood,' he said testily and, taking off his cloth cap, he wedged it under Vincenzo's jacket to stem the bleeding.

Once he'd steadied himself and adjusted his false leg, Vincenzo put his good arm around Isabella's waist, lifted her up and carried her like a small parcel down the hill to the farmstead.

By the time they reached the house, the initial numbness of his wound had worn off, sending a searing pain around the damaged area. But this was nothing compared to the throbbing in his stump. In the kitchen, he lowered Isabella to the floor. She was still reluctant to leave him, pressing herself against him, and eyeing the old man's shotgun anxiously.

'Orazio, put that damned shotgun down,' snapped Vincenzo. 'You're frightening the little one.'

'Eh, yes,' mumbled the old man. He locked the weapon in his gun cabinet and said, 'I'll go down to the village and find Claudia.'

'Get her here quickly, we've got to get rid of Scarpone's body,' said Vincenzo, fighting to remain conscious now that the effects of the gunshot wound and the damage to his stump had started to take their toll.

Vincenzo was dozing when Claudia arrived.

'Let me take a look at that shoulder,' she said.

Her competence at tending his wound impressed him. 'Where did you gen up on nursing?' he asked.

She gave a short laugh. 'In the field. You learn a lot by watching medics at work.' She finished applying the dressing. 'You're lucky, it's only a flesh wound. The bullet went clean through. So long as there's no infection you'll be as good as new in a week or two.' Going to the cupboard, she pulled out a piece of sheeting and folded it into a triangle to use as a sling. She noticed him grimace as her knee brushed his leg, and asked, 'Is the leg troubling you?'

'It's nothing to worry about.'

'I think I'd better take a look,' she insisted.

She rolled up his trouser leg and gave a gasp. 'That looks nasty, you ought to see a doctor.'

'Stop fussing! Just put a dressing on it and give me something for the pain.'

Even though Claudia handled the wound tenderly, he had to fight faintness. When she'd finished cleaning it up, she gave him one of her rare smiles and said, 'You're a brave man, Di Tomasi.' She left the room, returning with a cloudy liquid in a glass. 'Drink this, it'll help you sleep.'

'What is it?' he asked suspiciously.

She grinned. 'Don't worry, it isn't a poison.' He sniffed it, made a face and gulped it down. 'You'll sleep now,' she said with conviction.

He frowned. 'What about Scarpone?'

She waved aside his concern. 'Don't worry, Papà's already dug a hole for the bastard. We'll tip him into it before the night's over.'

'How did he manage to track me down?'

She shrugged. 'Who knows? I heard he'd been on the run for some time. Badoglio's Government put him on their black list. We've saved them the trouble of hunting him down.'

'But they won't know that,' laughed Vincenzo.

Claudia raised an eyebrow. 'Ironic, isn't it?'

Twenty-eight

The next day, Vincenzo had time to reflect on the previous day's events. Scarpone was dead. The marshal had been responsible, albeit indirectly, for his son's brutal killing. But revenge did not have the sweet taste he craved. Orazio had pulled the trigger, not him.

During the following weeks, his anxieties dropped away. Isabella was no longer in danger. Perhaps she never had been, he thought ruefully, recalling his surprise when Scarpone hadn't known the child's identity; perhaps the fears he'd harboured for so many years had been groundless. He got out his pocket watch and polished the dial with a handkerchief. It had stopped the day he'd forced the trinket inside it.

His stump never did heal properly and he was seldom free from pain. During the winter months he suffered from arthritis; in the summer, heat rash. Nicotine and alcohol eased his discomfort, but they didn't improve his general health. He developed a rasping cough, his blood pressure soared and he experienced palpitations, although he kept this to himself. Inactivity made him introspective. He found himself thinking about Beppe more and more.

Isabella would sometimes intrude on these nostalgic thoughts. '*Babbo*, why don't you come out and play with me?' or 'Let's go for a walk.'

Vincenzo invariably replied, 'Maybe tomorrow *bellina*.'

Her bottom lip would tremble but she never insisted.

How beautiful she was! Studying her expressive face, Vincenzo began to wonder whether he had been right to bring her to this isolated spot. She was lonely. It was a strange childhood for such an animated little thing.

There were times when, however tired he felt he couldn't refuse her requests for his company. He didn't want to go out because he knew the cold winter wind would make his stump ache when he came back into the warm room; in hot weather, perspiration would aggravate the slow-healing sores on his stump. He would shake aside his anticipated discomfort. A double cognac would fix it.

Over the years, the smallholding began to fall into disrepair. Orazio was now in his eighties and, although still agile, he was unable to do the heavy work. He drank excessively, became noisy and belligerent, giving Vincenzo cause for alarm when he reeled from one side of the room to the other without noticing whether the child was in his way or not. Things got so bad that he seriously considered breaking his cover and returning to Castagnetto. Fate intervened.

One morning, Vincenzo woke up to find the house freezing. Icy air blasted under the ill-fitting bedroom door, a gale howled up the stairwell. It took him ten minutes to attach his artificial leg, ten minutes of misery. After all this time, and despite the convenience of the aluminium prosthetic, he still felt hampered by his disability.

He limped downstairs to find the door to the yard wide open. Snow covered the threshold. He swept it out and shut the door before looking around for signs of Orazio. There were several empty flasks and bottles on the floor and on the table. He went to the foot of the stairs and called out to the old man. When there was no reply, he crossed to the window and rubbed the frosted pane with his sleeve. Orazio was nowhere to be seen.

Isabella appeared at the foot of the stairs, wrapped in a blanket. She shivered and asked, 'What's the matter, *Babbo?*'

'Nothing, darling, go back to bed. I'll call you when I've got the fire going.'

'Where's *Nonno Orazio?*

'In bed, I expect.'

She shook her head. 'His door's wide open and his room's empty.'

Vincenzo put his arm around the child's shoulder and said, 'He must be outside fetching wood for the fire, I'll go and look for him. Go back to bed now.'

Reluctantly, she turned and tip-toed upstairs, stopping half way to look back anxiously.

Vincenzo pulled on a coat and muffler and went out into the yard. The wind blew fiercely, sweeping the snowflakes into mini vortices, freezing his breath and forcing him to grit his teeth in the face of its ferocity. He found Orazio several metres from the house. He was laying face-down, his body covered by a blanket of snow. His outstretched fingers still clutched a beer bottle.

The old man was dead. His watery eyes stared sightlessly at the cattle trough ahead of him. Snow had gathered in the caverns of his mouth, hiding his remaining teeth, discoloured by a lifetime of heavy smoking. His trousers were soiled, the ground beneath him stained with vomit. He had not been an attractive figure in life; in death, he was repugnant. Yet Vincenzo couldn't restrain the knot of sadness rising to his throat. In his way, the old man had been kind to them, and in lucid moments, he had been an amusing companion with his far-fetched tales of local feuds and 'goings-on'. Isabella, too, had taken to him. Isabella! It was vital that she didn't see the old man in this state.

He glanced back over his shoulder. At least fifteen minutes had passed. To a child fifteen minutes was a lifetime; she would be calling for him, or worse, she would come to the kitchen door.

Bracing himself against the gale, he struggled over to the cowshed and tugged the door open. He had to make several journeys across the yard with the empty bottles Orazio had discarded. Under his feet, the snow had impacted, becoming treacherous.

'*Menaggio!*' He slipped and cursed his artificial leg. The foot wouldn't respond as he needed it to. The black mongrel tied up on a piece of rope outside the kitchen door rushed towards him barking. Ruthlessly, he kicked it. 'Get out of my way!'

The wooden shed door flapped in the wind as if made of canvas. Vincenzo was afraid it would be wrenched off its hinges. He propped it open with a plank of wood, and went back for Orazio. It took all his strength and willpower to haul the body into the shed. He dragged it to the far side and hid it under some straw, certain that it would be safe from predators until he could contact Claudia. In the yard, falling snow had already begun to cover the impression made by the old man's body.

He went back inside the house, and while lighting the fire, tried to invent an explanation to satisfy Isabella.

The old man's death drew Claudia back to the smallholding. Since the end of the War she had become a leading light among the local communists, her voice heard at rallies throughout the north-east. Vincenzo wondered whether, in view of her political interests, she would want to sell the place and move on. Instead, she decided to make the farm her bolt hole. She arrived unannounced bringing in tow a woman in her mid-twenties.

'My cousin, Nico, won't be coming back,' she sniffed. 'He's going to continue his education; wants to be an accountant. It doesn't matter, Sofia's going to help out.'

'How do you do, *Signorina*?' muttered Vincenzo as the newcomer extended a limp hand for him to shake. Alarm bells rang in his head. This woman was a soft, city-bred individual, not the type to cope with the hard graft of farm work.

'But Claudia, who'll do the heavy work?' he asked.

Claudia shrugged off his concern. 'I'll do most of it. If it gets too much, I can call on one of the local lads to help out. You can manage the running of the farm while Sofia does the cooking and the housework.'

Five-year-old Isabella, listening on the sidelines, started to fidget. Slipping a hand into that of her adopted father, she whispered, 'But there aren't enough bedrooms, *Babbo*, where is Sofia going to sleep?'

This brought a nervous giggle from Sofia and a hard stare from Claudia, who muttered, 'Your father will explain.'

The household settled into a routine. Claudia worked in the fields, and Vincenzo looked after the management of the smallholding. Isabella grew fond of the feather-brained Sofia, and managed to win the affection of *Il Capo*, as they all secretly referred to Claudia. Thanks to the little girl's endearing personality, the two women frequently vied with one another for her attention, a situation which amused Vincenzo.

One autumn day, Guido paid them a surprise visit. After warm greetings and nostalgic reminiscences between the two friends, he revealed his reason for coming. 'I bumped into Dr Amato in Milan recently.'

'Stefano! How is the old codger?' exclaimed Vincenzo.

'He's well, but I'm afraid he gave me sad news. He told me he'd had a letter from your partner in the law practice, umm…'

'Giacomo Tobino,' prompted Vincenzo.

'Yes … sadly Tobino learnt your wife was killed in an air raid during the London Blitz.'

For a moment, Vincenzo was stunned. 'Beppe?' he gasped.

Guido placed a hand on his shoulder. 'He's fine.'

'Grazie a Dio!'

Guido's voice dropped to a mumble. 'I'm so sorry to be the bearer of bad news. This must be a terrible shock for you.'

Vincenzo realised that his friend was eyeing him oddly. Embarrassed, he forced himself to behave like the grieving husband. 'Did she suffer?'

'I don't think so.'

'What was she doing in London?'

'Who knows?'

'It never occurred to me that I would out-live Alice.'

The news should have been devastating, but somehow it failed to touch Vincenzo. Guido might have been reporting the death of a passing acquaintance. Alice was from a different lifetime, Livia had seen to that. Livia! The anguish he'd experienced at her death had sunk him into a bottomless pit. Her magnetism had extinguished his love for Alice.

'It's a tragedy for a boy to lose both parents.' Guido spoke through his meanderings.

Recovering from bewilderment, Vincenzo muttered, 'Poor Beppe, how dreadful for him.'

'Isn't it time for a reunion?'

Vincenzo flinched, but refused to swallow the bait. Guido went on, 'The lawyer asked Dr Amato whether he had ever received proof absolute that you were dead.'

Alarmed, Vincenzo gripped the arms of his chair. 'What did he tell him?'

'He said he had no definite information.'

Vincenzo relaxed, indebted to his friend for keeping his promise and perpetuating the lie. At all costs, he wanted to keep to the charade of his demise; it was too late to change things. Ignoring Guido's advice to come out into the open, he asked him to arrange for Stefano Amato to send funds to Donna Caterina to enable her to take Rocco to the States for treatment, explaining that this had been a codicil to his Will. This kindly act produced the return of his books from Lucania, in a parcel addressed to the count's son, since Donna Caterina was under the impression that he was dead.

With research information to hand, Vincenzo resumed work on his social history. But the news of his wife's death had unnerved him. He suffered pangs of guilt, longed to mourn for her, yet all he could conjure up was the image of a dear friend. It was unsettling to look back, and remember that before the onset of hostilities he and Alice had been perfectly happy together.

Isabella continued to delight him. Her warm personality filled the house. She never complained about the tasks allotted her. Her laughter would ring out, lifting his spirits when he felt low. They spent many happy hours together with Vincenzo making the child giggle with his imitation of Claudia when she was in one of her black moods. He would strut awkwardly across the room on his artificial leg, head thrust forward, hands laced behind his back, a glowering frown on his brow.

The child would suddenly panic. 'Stop, *Babbo*, I think Claudia's coming. She'll kill you if she sees you mimicking her like that.'

As time went by Claudia became a parody of her father, dressing in baggy trousers and ill-fitting jacket, her cropped hair once jet black was now iron-grey and thinning. Her eyesight had started to fail and she was forced to wear spectacles. She imbibed alcohol like a man although, fortunately, was more capable of holding her drink than her father had been.

It was an eccentric household. After Isabella had gone to bed at night, Vincenzo would retire to his room to work on his manuscript, leaving the two women by the dying fire. They appeared to have nothing in common yet, despite the belittling treatment dished out by Claudia, Sofia hung on to her partner's every word, never challenging her authority.

Twice a week, Claudia attended one of her meetings, and on these occasions, Sofia took to encouraging Vincenzo to join her in the kitchen. The first time took him by surprise. She knocked at his door and called, 'Vincenzo, come down and keep me company. I've made a special cake for you.'

He tried to decline, but Sofia insisted and eventually, out of politeness, he felt obliged to join her. On seeing the cake placed in the centre of the table between a bottle of wine and two glasses, he felt awkward. How was he going to disentangle himself from the situation? Since losing Livia and suffering the loss of a leg, he had considered himself an old man, unfit for entry into the mating game. Besides, it had never occurred to him that Sofia's sexual inclinations swung both ways.

'I'm so glad you've decided to come down,' gushed Sofia, pulling out a chair. 'Here, take a seat.'

Vincenzo hesitated. 'Do you think this is a good idea?' he ventured.

She picked up the bottle and poured some wine. 'Don't worry, Claudia doesn't need to know.'

'I am feeling rather tired,' he muttered, starting to get up.

Sofia plucked at his sleeve. 'Please don't go. I need to talk.' Reluctantly, he retook his seat. Sofia blushed and whispered, 'I love Claudia so much. Do you think she really cares for me?'

This was unexpected. Relief rushed through him. He'd wrongly interpreted her intentions. Sofia was truly troubled; she wasn't about to flirt with him. He listened patiently while she poured out her heart, realising that loneliness and insecurity were at the root of her problems.

From then on, Sofia regarded him as a kindly uncle, sharing her qualms and her dreams with him. The intense love she felt for Claudia resurrected his own sense of loss, making him suffer again the emotions he'd suffered after Livia's death. At that time, he'd been unable to sleep properly, waking after only a couple of hours to toss and turn, imagining her suffering at the hands of those German bastards. '*She's been raped at least twice,'* Dr Amato had told him. *'And beaten; then to lose her unborn child ...'*

My child! thought Vincenzo. But Livia had left him a legacy in the shape of a little girl and he knew, in the depths of his soul, that Isabella had been his salvation. But for her, he would have given up years ago. She adored him, and he convinced himself into almost believing that she was, in fact, his biological child. He had lost contact with his son, but he would always have his daughter. She must never learn the truth.

He contemplated her future. What would become of her once he was no longer around? Claudia could not be relied upon to step in since she was older than he was, and certainly not interested in becoming a parent. The soft-hearted Sofia was younger and more suited to motherhood, but he knew that if anything should happen to her intrepid bed partner, she would fall to pieces. He considered writing to Giuliana to see if she could offer help, but thought better of it.

The years rolled on and by the summer of 1959, his health began to deteriorate. He was in his mid sixties but he looked far older. Working on his manuscript became a chore rather than the pleasurable occupation it had once been. Claudia grew impatient when he made mistakes with the accounts.

'Really, Vincenzo,' she snapped. 'Why don't you pay more attention?'

On one occasion, when he slipped up badly, costing the business a considerable loss, Claudia's vitriolic diatribe was worse than any he had heard during his entire time with the Resistance. Generally, she met crisis with stoic resilience, but this time, she became infuriated. The shouting brought Isabella hurrying into the room. On seeing how distressed her father was, the teenager rushed over to Claudia and demanded angrily, 'What do you think you're doing? Get out and leave my papà alone. Can't you see how upset he is?'

Afterwards, the woman had the grace to apologise to the young girl and the pair talked things over calmly, deciding they had no choice but to entrust the day-to-day running of the smallholding to Sofia, with Claudia and Isabella doing the accounts between them.

'That's not necessary,' protested Vincenzo, although secretly he was relieved to be rid of the responsibility. Swelling and soreness in his stump were an ongoing problem, and heavy smoking and lack of exercise had also undermined his health. Eventually, despite his protestations, Isabella insisted on calling in the local doctor.

'Emphysema is difficult to treat,' he explained to the concerned girl. 'There's little I can do, except ease your father's suffering.'

After he'd departed, she tearfully related his diagnosis to Claudia, who took it upon herself to confront Vincenzo. 'I'm going to contact your son in England,' she announced. 'You can't hide from the world any longer.'

Vincenzo panicked. 'No,' he croaked. 'Beppe's better off without me. Let him continue to believe I'm dead. He's got Alice's family in England. Besides, he may be married by now.' He stopped for breath, unused to gasping out more than a single sentence at a time. 'And what about Isabella? She may not take kindly to meeting a brother she knows nothing about.'

Claudia spoke with brutal honesty. 'Nonsense, Vincenzo, you owe it to your son to get in touch. Give him time to say goodbye to you. As for Isabella, when you go she'll be all alone, let her have an opportunity to meet her long-lost brother.'

Vincenzo felt too ill to prolong the argument, and worn down by her persistence, he reluctantly agreed to let Claudia telephone his brother-in-law, Arthur McPherson-Corke, in Harrogate.

PART IV

Missing presumed dead

Twenty-nine

In 1950 Joe gained a First in Mediaeval History. He returned to Harrogate for the summer, spending a few weeks helping out in his uncle's office. Although he'd written her several letters, he hadn't heard from Patricia. Consequently he was taken by surprise when, on leaving the office one evening in late July, he found her waiting for him. She took his arm. 'Are you pleased to see me?'

He nodded, a wide grin spreading across his face.

'Congratulations!' she said. 'You got a First, that's terribly good, isn't it? I don't know much about degrees and things but a First must be good. You're awfully clever, Joe.'

He blushed, brushing aside her praise with, 'Let's go to Betty's for tea.'

'Betty's is a bit expensive, isn't it?'

He patted his pocket. 'I've just been paid.'

When they reached the tea rooms, Patricia put out her left hand to push the door open and he noticed her wedding ring, a reminder that she was a married woman. The waitress ushered them to a table, and he realised it was too late to change his mind. He told himself there was nothing wrong with having a cup of tea with a friend, but a tweak of conscience made him resolve that when they left Betty's, he wouldn't wait around. He would see Patricia to her bus straightaway.

Once seated, Patricia slipped off her cardigan, letting it hang over the back of her chair, and smiled at him in that delightfully fresh way of hers. 'How have you been?' she asked.

'Fine, and you?'

'All right, I suppose...' She paused, then burst out, 'I want to leave Roger.'

'Leave him?' Fighting confusion, Joe forced himself to play the role of sympathetic confidante. 'Don't be hasty. Maybe you can sort out your problems.'

Patricia shook her head, oblivious to the shock she'd given him. 'Trouble is, if I do, I've nowhere to go.'

'Why don't you go back to your mother?'

'I can't do that,' she protested hotly. 'I can't give Mum the satisfaction of saying *I told you so!* She hated Roger from the word go, said he was two-faced, said he couldn't be trusted. I don't want her throwing *that* back in my face.'

So her mother had seen through Roger! This surprised Joe because, according to her daughter, the woman was an empty-headed flirt who, since the death of Patricia's father, had drifted from one unstable relationship to another. 'You could at least stay with her until you find a place of your own,' he suggested lamely.

'How am I going to find a place of my own on my wages?'

'I thought the sales assistant job was better paid.'

'It is, but it's still not enough.'

Lowering her gaze, she fell silent, fiddling with the cutlery. Why is she so negative, wondered Joe. 'Does Roger want a separation?' he asked. She shook her head, so he went on, 'Are you sure it's what *you* really want?'

'Yes.' She felt for his hand and whispered, 'Joe, you're the first person I've told.'

Acutely aware of the pressure of her fingers in his hand, Joe frowned and said, 'I hate the thought of you being unhappy, but you must think this through.' Hoping his inner turmoil wasn't showing, he continued to play his neutral role even though his heart was thumping against his ribcage and his brain was posing unanswerable questions. Was she really unhappy with Roger or was she just bored with married life? Whatever the reason, he told himself, once she was free, there was hope for him.

The waitress took their order. When she'd gone, Patricia changed the subject. 'Tell me about yourself,' she said, flipping open her napkin and spreading it across her lap. 'I want to know everything that's happened since we last met. I suppose you've got to find a proper job. You won't want to stay in that dreary old office now that you've got your degree.'

'I'm staying on at Oxford.'

'What?' Patricia looked dismayed. 'Why?' Then she brightened up. 'Oh I see, they've offered you a teaching post.'

Joe smothered a smile. 'I'm taking another degree: History of Music. I've taken up the violin again.'

Patricia's mouth dropped open. 'But Joe, you'll never earn any money while you're a student.'

'Money isn't everything.'

The arrival of the waitress with their tea brightened the atmosphere. Over muffins dripping with butter, they discussed the latest Hollywood films and he listened while she enthused about Frank Sinatra.

'He was over here recently,' she said. 'But Roger wouldn't let me go to his concert. He said the tickets cost too much. Roger's ever so mean.'

Joe asked her whether she'd ever been to see an opera but she pulled a face.

'One day, I'll take you down to London and we'll go to the Royal Opera House at Covent Garden.'

'Covent Garden? Wow, I'd like that,' she exclaimed. 'I once saw a Variety Show at the Palladium, would it be like that?'

He reached for her hand and said, 'Not exactly, but I know you'd love it.'

By the time he got around to asking for the bill, Joe was once again completely besotted by Patricia. He watched her every movement, basking in her sparkling smile.

On leaving Betty's, he forgot all about his resolve to see her to her bus.

'I don't want to go home yet; Roger's not in so I shall be all alone,' she said.

'Would you like to come to the pictures with me?'

She wrinkled her nose. 'I'd rather go dancing. There's a new dance hall opened up not far from here. We could try it out.'

Joe was in heaven. It was mid-week and the place wasn't too crowded. The band played slow numbers and they danced close together, Patricia's head resting on his shoulder, his face buried in her hair. During the strains of the last waltz, he took courage and began whispering endearments in her ear. She smiled coyly, brushing her lips against his cheek. He felt as if his heart would explode. The evening had been magical.

'I'll see you to your bus,' he said as they left the dance hall.

She dimpled mischievously and said, 'The last one's gone, we'll have to get a taxi.'

In the cab, Joe put his arms around her, their lips meeting in a tentative kiss as the cabby discreetly turned his attention to the road, whistling softly under his breath. Joe's pulse raced. How many times had he imagined what it would be like to kiss her! They got out in front of her block of flats and he paid the taxi driver. The evening had cost him half his week's wages but it was worth it. He would pay out a month's salary for another evening like this.

'Which floor do you live on?' he asked.

'The second.'

He hugged her again, kissing her more fiercely than ever.

'You can come up if you like, Roger's away.'

His puritanical side was shocked, but her inviting eyes and the touch of her hand was enough to persuade him that there could be no harm in it if she was intending to leave her husband anyway. At the door, he hesitated but she pulled him inside.

'There's some gin in the drinks cabinet,' she said, kicking off her shoes. 'Make yourself comfortable.'

While she padded into the kitchen to look for glasses, he couldn't rest and wandered around the room, covertly inspecting things, mindful that this was a part of her life into which he should not pry.

She came back and poured the drinks, setting them down on the coffee table before going over to a gramophone and selecting a Bing Crosby record. Returning to the sofa, she patted the cushions. 'Come and sit down next to me.'

He sat down, deliberately leaving a space between them, but she moved closer. He kept reminding himself that she was someone else's wife. On the wall opposite, hung a framed photograph of Roger in his leather biking gear, holding aloft a silver cup. Joe reached for his drink, gulping it too quickly. Patricia giggled and placed a hand on his knee. The pressure of her fingers eradicated everything else from his mind. He couldn't bring himself to look at her: she was too desirable. He blinked as Roger's display of motorcycle trophies next to his photograph seemed to magnify. Was Roger throwing down the gauntlet *in absentia?*

Patricia wriggled even closer, and he caught a waft of her perfume. Her leg pressed against his as she chattered on about a romantic film she'd seen recently but her words made no sense to him. It was as if she were speaking a foreign language. All at once, she encircled his neck with her arm and whispered, 'You seem preoccupied, Joe, what's the matter?'

'Nothing,' he spluttered, slapping his tumbler down on the table and spilling most of its contents.

She placed a finger under his chin, turning him to face her. It was no good. He had no choice: he would have to accept Roger's challenge and face the consequences. Taking Patricia in his arms, he pushed her gently down onto the sofa, pressing himself on top of her. She stared up at him with wide blue eyes, the tip of her pink tongue peeping out from between even white teeth. Somehow, they slipped off the sofa onto the floor, hurriedly stripping off their clothes. This is meant to be, surely this is meant to be, he thought.

Afterwards, they lay side-by-side, their perspiring bodies sticking to the cold linoleum. The hearthrug had somehow been kicked away. Joe blinked up at the ceiling, conflicting emotions churning inside him. He was awash with love for her. He turned his head, and she smiled at him, her gaze sweeping down her own body, inviting him again. She was as beautiful as he had imagined; her perfect skin pale and smooth; the fine curls at her groin a match for the blond locks on her head. He gulped down a moment of shame. Patricia had been the one to take the initiative because he was the virgin, not her.

'Let's go to bed,' she whispered.

'What about Roger?' With a gulp of panic, Joe scrambled to his feet and snatched up his trousers.

'He's not due home until lunch-time tomorrow.'

'All the same ... ' he started to say.

Patricia jumped up, and grabbing his hand, led him into the bedroom. Laughing at his awkwardness, she pushed him back onto the bed and said, 'Don't tell me you didn't enjoy it just now!'

'Oh Patricia,' he exclaimed, reaching up to pull her on top of him. 'That was the most precious moment of my life.'

She laughed again. 'There are more precious moments to come.'

She woke him in the morning with a cup of tea, standing at the end of the bed in a thin cotton night-gown, through which he could see her neat figure.

'What time is it?'

'Seven o'clock. Don't worry, there's plenty of time.'

'I've got to get to work,' he said. 'And what about Roger?'

'I told you, he's not due home until lunch-time.'

Joe's imagination raced. Suppose Roger got home early! Ignoring the tea, he went in search of his clothes, dressing hurriedly, his face flushed with apprehension. She went with him to the door, standing on tip-toes to kiss him.

'I'll meet you outside the office one day next week,' she said. 'That is, if you want me to.'

'Of course I do,' he stuttered. Still straightening his tie, he ran down the stairs, passing a young man on his way up. At the main entrance, Joe stopped and listened. A door opened and he heard Patricia say, 'Hello Roger, you're early.'

Joe and Patricia continued to meet secretly for the whole summer. When he told her he had to return to Oxford, she was inconsolable, weeping all the way to the station, and promising to find ways of visiting him without Roger knowing.

'When do you plan to leave him?' asked Joe.

'I'm going to start looking for a better paid job next week,' she assured him. 'Then when I've saved up a bit, I shall move out.'

'You *are* going to divorce him, aren't you?'

'Divorce costs a lot, you know. Those lawyers charge the earth. Where am I going to get that sort of money from?'

She was right, of course. During the train journey, Joe chewed over the problem. She could never earn enough. He told himself he didn't mind, he would take care of her under any terms. The argument, however, wasn't convincing. He wanted things to be legal; he wanted to marry her.

Patricia phoned him regularly. He lived from one phone call to the next and was delighted when she told him she'd been given promotion. *They've put my wages up quite a lot,* she wrote. *And I'm going to move into a bed-sit with a girl from work.* But that was as far as it went. He sent her money for the fare so that she could visit him in Oxford, and she came frequently, staying at the cheap boarding house she'd stayed in before. The landlady obligingly turned a blind eye when he sneaked out in the morning. Whenever Joe mentioned the word *divorce*, she started crying, saying that she would never be able to get away from Roger.

'What's he doing now?'

'How would I know?'

'Is he still living at the flat?'

'I think so.' She pouted, then tossed her head and said, 'He's found himself a new girlfriend, but I don't care.'

This unsatisfactory arrangement lasted until Joe graduated with yet another First Class Degree.

'I'm so proud of you, Joe,' she said gaily on the day of his Graduation.

He showed her off to his companions, sometimes experiencing a twinge of embarrassment when her chattering became a little too frivolous. It was time for him to look for a teaching post and when one came along in a public school in Surrey, he was delighted. What could be better than living in a leafy suburb? One thing troubled him. Would Patricia agree to go with him?

He was about to broach the subject when she delivered her news.

'My divorce becomes absolute next month, darling.'

'Your divorce!' Joe couldn't believe his ears. 'How did you manage that?'

She gave a teasing smile. 'I kept it secret because I wanted to surprise you. Roger wants to marry Cynthia so he came up with the incriminating evidence; paid for it all too.' She flung her arms round Joe's neck. 'I shall soon be a free woman.'

He picked her up and swung her, his heart beating a tattoo of happiness. What could be better? A new job, money in his pocket at last and, to cap it all, Patricia as his wife.

Things didn't go according to plan. Once free, despite the close rapport they had developed over three years, Patricia seemed reluctant to tie the knot.

'Do you love me?' demanded. Joe.

'Of course I do, darling,' she replied. 'But I'm not sure I want to get married again yet.' She looked serious. 'I'm not into babies and all that stuff, you know.'

'That's all right,' he said. 'There's plenty of time for all that. Just promise me you'll think about it.'

She looked down at the floor and whispered, 'Maybe.'

Before taking up his post, he went to see his uncle and aunt. After dinner, he and Arthur went to the study where his uncle lit up his pipe. Lately, Joe had grown close to Arthur, who seemed to like him more than his own sponging sons. Even Aunt Thelma had changed her attitude now that she realised he had no intention of taking over the house.

He told his uncle about Patricia. 'Maybe once she's seen how nice it is living in the Home Counties, within easy reach of London's big shops, she'll agree to marry me,' he said.

'You can't hurry her, Joe. After all, she's already made one mistake. You can't blame her for wanting to be certain this time. Give her time,' advised Arthur gently.

Joe clasped his hands to his head, lowering his gaze to the floor. 'I'm getting impatient,' he moaned. 'After all, we've known one another for years.'

'Perhaps, if you bought a house in Surrey Patricia might be tempted to settle down. D'you need money? This house is yours to sell. You shouldn't worry about us, you must think of yourself.'

Joe looked up, startled. 'I wouldn't hear of it,' he said.

'You know, Joe, you could always go back and claim your estate in Tuscany,' suggested Arthur.

'What's the point?' Conscious of his uncle's scrutiny, he sighed and said, 'Maybe, I'll go back one day; when the time's right.'

He wasn't sure he wanted to go back. After learning of his father's death, he had emotionally disassociated himself from his Italian roots.

Thirty

Joe went down to Surrey alone. Patricia kept changing her mind about joining him, but in the end, the purchase of a house in a quiet avenue in Godalming, persuaded her to join him.

Much to his delight, she also changed her mind about marrying him and, on a sunny afternoon in late autumn, they tied the knot at the Registry Office in Harrogate with only Uncle Arthur, Aunt Thelma and Patricia's best friend, Eileen, present at the ceremony. He was a little disappointed that she didn't invite her mother, whom he had still not met, accepting the excuse that she had gone to Scarborough with her latest fancy man.

Thanks to his grandfather's generosity, Joe still had a little money left over from his mother's trust fund and now that his education was complete, what was left of it was his to use as he saw fit. He decided that the following Easter, he would take Patricia away on a belated honeymoon. When he broke the news to her she was delighted.

'Where are we going, Joe?' she cried. 'I hope it's somewhere exciting. Let me guess! Torquay, Scarborough?'

He grinned. 'Neither. We're going to Italy.'

'Italy! Isn't that where you come from?' He felt a twinge of irritation. She could be surprisingly vacuous sometimes! Surely she knew he was half Italian, he'd never made any secret of it! But her excitement bubbled over, and when she threw her arms round his neck and kissed his face all over, his annoyance melted away. She smelled so sweet and the downy skin on her arms as it touched the nape of his neck was as soft as a kitten's fur. He couldn't believe that he had won the heart of such a beauty.

She drew back, and placing the tip of her finger on his chin, giggled, 'I know, you're taking me to that magical place with all the canals and gondolas, what's it called ... ' She paused to think, then cried triumphantly, 'I know, Vienna, no Venice!'

His expression betrayed his dismay. 'Another time,' he mumbled. 'This time, I thought you'd like to visit my old home in Tuscany.'

'Tuscany? Is that a *big* town?'

He laughed, and said, 'Wait there, I'll fetch the atlas and show you.' Returning with the atlas, he pointed out Castagnetto and she asked, 'Is that where we'll be staying?'

'No, we'll be staying in Florence.'

'Florence?' she repeated, then giggled. 'For a moment I thought it must be one of your relations. Will I like it?'

'Of course you will. It's a wonderful place.'

The journey over to Italy was trying. Patricia felt sea-sick on the ferry and grew bored on the long train journey through France and Switzerland, grumbling about lack of leg room. By the time they reached the spectacular stretch of the journey through the Valle d'Aosta, she had fallen asleep. Despite his irritation at her niggling complaints, Joe wanted to wake her up so that she could share the wonder of the views with him. He twisted his head to look down lovingly at her blond head nestled against his shoulder, and decided not to disturb her. She looked more like a child than a twice-married woman. Once, her eyes fluttered open, and she smiled sweetly up at him, then she slipped back to sleep, her lips slightly parted, her chest gently rising and falling.

The choice of destination had been an impulsive decision. When his uncle learned of it, he voiced his reservations. 'Is that a wise choice, Joe? It could be upsetting for you, might bring back painful memories.'

'You were the one who suggested I go back there.'

'Not under these circumstances. You should go on your own initially.'

'Patricia will love seeing the old place just as much as I will,' came Joe's disgruntled reply.

'I'm not so sure,' muttered Arthur doubtfully, but Joe chose to ignore his uncle's reservations.

Patricia was impressed by the city of Florence. On their first day, dazzled by Joe's enthusiasm, and his knowledge of the history and paintings, she allowed him to show her around, not moaning that her feet hurt or that it was too hot. He had splashed out on their hotel accommodation, choosing a medieval palazzo situated in the historic part of the city.

'This is so romantic, darling!' she cried. 'Why, it's like living in the olden days!'

The room was high-ceilinged; filmy curtains fluttered at the window because Patricia insisted on opening the wooden shutters so that they could lie in bed and admire the night sky punctured by a million stars.

Enthralled by the magic of her surroundings, she lost her habit of flitting from one subject to another, of planning their next move so that enjoyment of the present was lost in dreams of the future. She seemed in awe of him. They made love several times in a big four-poster bed, its springs creaking beneath their exertions.

However, as his uncle had predicted, returning to Tuscany was upsetting for Joe. He woke up early on the first morning, got up and stood gazing out of the window at the street below. The town was just coming to life with shopkeepers opening their shutters for the day, and office workers and shoppers making their way to wherever they had to go, some on foot, others on bicycles. Cars frequently hooted causing Joe to reflect on the impatience of the Italian character in comparison to that of the English.

He could vaguely remember what Florence had been like during Mussolini's regime, when fascist flags hung over every building and the stamp of marching feet was commonplace. In peacetime, the ancient buildings showed no signs of the oppression and foreign occupation that his father must have experienced.

Patricia woke up and came to stand beside him. 'I can't wait to go shopping,' she said. 'I simply must have a look around those wonderful markets.'

'I'd like to visit Castagnetto today,' he replied.

She wrinkled her nose. 'Oh Joe, can't we go shopping today. I want to buy a real leather handbag.'

Now that he was within reach of his native village Joe couldn't wait to visit his father's villa and vineyard. He wanted to retrace his old steps and seek out Grazia Elena and Matteo. Until they'd actually set foot in Italy, he hadn't realised how much the trip meant to him. After all those years in England, he still felt Italian. Castagnetto was his home; he felt drawn to it.

'We can do that tomorrow,' he said.

She pouted. 'It's different for you. You've been here before, but I want to see everything.' She threw out her arms. 'I want to buy lots of nice things.'

Joe shook his head. 'We're going to Castagnetto today. I've already enquired about the buses; there's one leaving at 9.30. If we hurry we can catch it.'

Patricia agreed with bad grace, complaining during the bus ride that the seats were uncomfortable, that the wooden slats dug into her back. She was, however, enchanted when the hilltop town of San Gimigniano came into view. 'Can we go up there?' she exclaimed.

Joe squeezed her hand, pleased that she seemed in a better mood. 'Later in the week,' he promised.

The bus stopped in the village. Joe asked what time the last bus for Florence left.

'*Le cinque*,' the driver informed him before making his way across the road to a café.

'*Cinque*? Doesn't that mean five o'clock?' gasped Patricia. 'Surely there must be an earlier one.'

'Five o'clock will be fine,' replied Joe.

The village hadn't changed much. The houses were in need of a touch of paint, the awning outside the only café was torn and faded, the church tower was pitted with what Joe surmised to be mortar shells. Apart from that, everything looked just as he remembered it. A couple of women standing outside the latteria stopped their gossiping to stare at them with undisguised curiosity.

'Where to?' demanded Patricia. 'There doesn't seem to be much going on here.'

'It's a sleepy little village.'

'Sleepy! It looks dead to me.'

Joe took her hand. 'Come on,' he said, 'I'll show you where I grew up.'

As they left the village, Patricia chatted non-stop about their proposed shopping expedition for the next day. Joe kept silent. Encapsulated in a world of nostalgia, he hardly heard a word she said. His surroundings looked familiar, yet unfamiliar. The woods seemed denser, the fields more undulated, the river narrower than he remembered.

He tried to recall the days following the news of Enzo's death, but the memories became superimposed by an earlier recollection. He stopped at the spot where he and his brother used to lark about in the water during the long hot summers. Their mother had forbidden them to swim there, but they did anyway. Enzo, always the daredevil, and nine years his senior, encouraged him to take risks. His brother's taunts flooded back:

'Come on Beppe, what are you waiting for?'
'But Enzo, Mamma will be furious with us.'
Enzo dives in and as his head breaks the surface, he shakes the water out of his hair and says, 'She'll never know.'
'She could find out.'
'Don't be such a baby.'
His brother's jibe cuts deep. Enzo is his hero and one day, he wants to be just like him: just as tall, just as clever, just as brave. He strips off his clothes and dips his foot into the water. It strikes cold because the sun never penetrates the overhanging trees. No one, not even Enzo knows how deep the water is.

He plunges into the inky depths after his brother. The drop seems interminable. Undergrowth brushes his limbs; a sinewy frond wraps itself around his neck. Seized with panic, he claws it clear, kicking out with his legs in his desperation to surface. Emerging at last he gasps for air.

Enzo is poised naked on a fallen tree trunk on the bank, his head thrown back in laughter, his arms spread wide. A mythical god! His mop of fair hair inherited from their English mother has been bleached almost white; his chest is sun-tanned. His skin doesn't go lobster red like so many of Alice's compatriots.

'Come on, Joe.'
He'd forgotten all about Patricia. 'Coming.'

She went on ahead, and he was about to turn away, when his attention was drawn to the far bank. The handle of an upturned pram had become wedged under the exposed roots of a tree. Had the river not been low, it would never have come to light. He stared at it, raking his memory, wondering whether it was the one his nanny used to push him around in. No memory surfaced. Patricia called him again, so he hurried after her.

She took his hand. 'How much further?'

'Not far now.'

As they walked along the gravel road, a mixture of excitement and trepidation swept over him. His eyes lit up when he saw that the tree house was still intact. Stopping beneath it, he fancied he could hear the operatic arias he'd once played on his old wind-up gramophone, and felt an almost irresistible urge to climb up into the tree house. Parts of the platform still looked sound. He gave the rope ladder a tug, only to have it come away in his hand. Perhaps he could climb the tree. It wouldn't be difficult; the lower branches were strong. He stole a glance at Patricia. How she'd jeer at him. *Joe, don't be such an idiot!*

She tugged at his sleeve, looking grumpy . 'Come on, I can't wait for ever to see this wonderful villa of yours. I thought you said it wasn't far.'

Leaving the shelter of the copse they followed the track between the neglected vines. And there it was!

'Wow!' exclaimed Patricia, her eyes shining. 'That's some villa! Can we go inside?' Joe let go of her hand and raced across the grass, to stop abruptly in front of the villa. He flung out his arms in horror.

'What's wrong?' gasped Patricia as she ran to catch up with him. When he didn't reply, she cried out impatiently, 'Joe, what's the matter?'

When he turned to face her, the shock in his eyes made her gasp in astonishment.

'Can't you see?' he shouted. 'Can't you see that it's nothing but a shell; my home has been razed to the ground.'

In that moment, he wanted to hit Patricia. How could she not see that daylight was streaming through the windows; that the front facade was intact, yet there was nothing behind it? He felt as if he had lost a loved one. His cherished home was nothing more than a skeleton, its windows empty eye sockets peering out of a skull.

Moved to comfort him, Patricia slipped an arm through his and whispered, 'How terrible for you. It must have been bombed during the war.'

Her compassion made it worse. Shaking her off, he strode around to the back of the house, stepping in through what remained of a french window. The atmosphere was static. Rotting furniture and disintegrating brickwork stood erect like gravestones. Outside, the changing seasons had induced nature to repair war's destruction by producing an abundance of grass and wild flowers. Inside, decomposition had stamped its mark: blackened walls smelt of decay; crumbling architraves cast desolate shadows across weed-punctured mosaic floors.

'This is creepy,' muttered Patricia, catching him up again. She stood close to him, not from compassion this time, but from a need for reassurance.

Joe ignored her. Lost in memory, he saw the rooms as they used to be, with pictures on the walls, cushions on the sofas, shutters at the windows. Placing a hand on the curved banister rail, he looked up at the central staircase, which had once led to his bedroom. Now it led nowhere. A vast brick chimney breast stood proudly upright between shattered walls. He could almost feel the heat from the roaring fire where, on wintry evenings, the family had gathered.

His gaze turned to the short flight of stone steps leading down to the kitchen, still intact although slippery with moss. He ventured down, and saw that the large range on which Grazia Elena had cooked so many meals was still there. Its door hung open on one hinge, its once meticulously polished surface, was dented and rusty. He ran a finger over the scorched kitchen table sending a shower of ashy dust down onto his shoes.

He gulped down grief and disappointment. How could it have come to this? Going back into the hall, his gaze traced the layout of the downstairs rooms, then travelled up to the ruined storeys above. He couldn't trust himself to speak.

Beside him, Patricia tapped an impatient foot. 'Come on, Joe, there's nothing here. Let's go!'

He nodded, and turned his face away so that she couldn't see his tears.

Thirty-one

'Well,' said Patricia as they trudged back to the village. 'It might have been a splendid house once but it isn't now.'

'It's all down to those Nazis,' muttered Joe in a choked voice.

Patricia slipped her arm through his. 'Never mind, Joe, it's not as though you'd ever want to come back and live here.'

He nodded his agreement and patted her hand, trying to make light of his disappointment, but the dilapidated state of the house, and the discovery that the vines had been left to go wild had been a bitter blow. His thoughts turned to Grazia Elena and Matteo. Would they still be around? Even as a little boy, he'd thought of them as old: Matteo with stooped shoulders and a balding pate; Grazia Elena, plump and white haired, carrying with her a hint of embrocation. He remembered asking Enzo why Matteo had hairs growing out of his nostrils.

His brother had burst out laughing. 'Old men get to look like that, Beppe, you will too, one day.'

For once, he'd been ready with a riposte. 'What about you, Enzo? You're older than me, you'll be like that before me.'

'Not likely!' snorted Enzo. 'I won't live that long. I'll die while I'm still in my prime.'

Those remembered words, so cruelly brought to fruition, brought Joe a shudder of anguish, causing him to clench his fists and quicken his pace.

'Slow down, Joe, I can't keep up with you,' complained Patricia.

'Sorry darling.'

With an effort, he controlled his feelings, turning to smile at Patricia when she kissed his cheek, and by the time they reached the café, he had recovered from the bad moment. The proprietor directed them to a window table and handed them a menu.

'What would you like?' Joe asked Patricia. 'There's Spaghetti Bolognese or Risotto.'

She pulled a face. 'Not that foreign stuff. Can I have egg and chips?'

The rotund, red-faced proprietor smiled amiably, waiting patiently for Joe to explain that the choice was limited. Finally, he spoke. 'Perhaps *la bella signorina* would like some bread and cheese and olives with a green salad,' he suggested.

Patricia waited for Joe to interpret for her, brightening up when she realised that the other occupants of the café were staring at her, that she was the focus of attention.

She dimpled. 'That will do nicely thank you, but without the olives.'

Joe beamed proudly. How he loved her when she allowed her ingenuousness to shine through!

The proprietor backed away, then stopped. '*Signore*,' he said, addressing Joe. 'Don't I know you?'

It had never occurred to Joe that he would be recognised. He'd left Castagnetto a nine-year-old child; he was now a twenty-four year old man. He felt abashed. His father had been a count, the most important man in the region and now, since Vincenzo's death, he was entitled to claim the title. Legally, in fact, he was count Giuseppe Di Tomasi.

Patricia had intuitively understood the question. 'You should do,' she said proudly. 'My husband used to live in that big villa.'

The proprietor snapped his fingers. 'I knew it. *Dio mio!* You're young Beppe Di Tomasi. *Il Conte!*'

This announcement produced uproar. Several men got up from their tables and came over to shake Joe's hand, talking excitedly.

'You're the image of your father!' exclaimed one of them. 'For a moment, I thought you *were* him, although I knew it couldn't have been.'

Joe introduced his wife, and in turn, they complimented Joe on the *bellissima signora*. Patricia accepted this flattery with a guileless smile. More men and a couple of women joined the group.

The proprietor introduced himself. 'My name's Aldo Comolli, don't you remember me, *Signor Conte*?'

'Indeed I do,' exclaimed Joe. With a flash of recognition, the years fell away as he saw again Aldo Comolli as he had known him when he was a little boy: slimmer, with a full head of hair.

In benevolent fashion, Comolli produced *espressos* for everyone and opened a bottle of grappa. Patricia watched the assembled company pick up their tiny coffee cups and gulp back the contents, followed by the same routine with the aqua vita. She followed suit and nearly choked. Everyone laughed, though not unkindly, and one of the women offered her a handkerchief with which to dry her streaming eyes.

'These people are so nice,' Patricia whispered to Joe, and he grinned contentedly.

When the men had gone back to work, Aldo Comolli came over again, drew up a chair and sat down with them. Two elderly women and the bus driver were left, the latter having fallen asleep over the table. Quite unashamedly, the women continued to eavesdrop.

'I remember your father very well, *Signor Conte*,' said Comolli.

With a frown of embarrassment, Joe replied, 'Please don't address me as count, you knew me as a little boy, call me Beppe or Joe.'

The man shrugged. 'As you wish.' Smoothing a hand down his long striped apron, he went on reflectively, 'Your father died a hero.'

'A hero?' gasped Joe.

Comolli looked surprised. 'You must have been told.'

'No.'

Joe was astounded that the man knew the circumstances of his father's death when, according to Uncle Arthur, the Italian Authorities could only come up with *missing presumed dead*.

Comolli went on. '*Ahimé*, those were terrible times. The German commandant's plan was to mine the village, cutting off the Allies' advance. Your father put a stop to that. Then the Resistance moved in and sabotaged the armament depot.' He scratched his bald pate and frowned as he reminisced. 'We had no idea there was a partisan cell in our midst ... that's what caused the blunder over the Carduccio woman.'

'Who?'

'Livia Carduccio, she was a member of the Resistance.'

'How does my father fit in to all this?' gasped Joe.

'Your father was very courageous…'

Joe was feeling more and more perplexed. Patricia shifted impatiently beside him, muttering, 'Isn't it time we left?'

Realising that she couldn't understand a word of their conversation, he apologised, 'Sorry darling, I won't keep you waiting long. I just want to talk to Aldo for a bit longer.'

Turning back to Comolli, he continued in Italian, 'I don't understand, surely my father wasn't involved with the Resistance?' When Comolli didn't reply, he pressed him further. 'How was he killed? Tell me what happened.'

'He blew up the villa, killed the German officers inside. ' Joe's thoughts raced - so Babbo blew up the villa himself! He heard Comolli's voice again. 'But he was badly wounded, left for dead. Resistance Members rescued him, took him up to the north. Sadly, he didn't survive. Maybe it was just as well since that bastard, Scarpone, was after him.' Scarpone! Joe delved into his memory, striving to make sense of what he had just heard. Comolli supplied the explanation. 'He was one of Mussolini's most prominent advisers. A nasty piece of work.'

'How did Scarpone get to know about my father's involvement?'

Comolli shrugged. 'Who knows? Old man Matteo maintained it was that accountant fellow, Manzello. Your father sacked him after he found him fiddling the books. All I know is that your father went to Rome on business, and shortly afterwards, Scarpone sent his henchmen up to search the villa. They ransacked the place, threatened Grazia Elena. She never got over the grilling they put her through. That's why her granddaughter, Giuliana, came to Castagnetto to look after her.'

Joe was so involved in Comolli's story that he didn't even notice when Patricia got up and left the café.

'This doesn't make sense,' he said. 'The Allies didn't reach Sicily until 1943.'

'That's right. Before that, your father was exiled to Lucania for nearly two years.'

'Exiled?'

'Scarpone's men found revolutionary material in the villa. Manzello must have planted it there. The count didn't come back here until the summer of '43. He brought the Carduccio woman with him.'

'Who *is* this woman?'

Comolli cast a glance around the café and lowered his voice. 'She was a bit of a mystery. Apparently, she helped him escape from a prison train.'

'So he wasn't officially released from exile, he escaped?'

Comolli nodded.

'What connection did the Carduccio woman have with my father? What happened to her?'

'Hmm …'

Comolli seemed reluctant to reply and, out of the corner of his eye, Joe saw the eavesdropping women lean eagerly forward. He decided not to pursue the issue for the moment. Changing the subject, he asked, 'Does Grazia Elena still live in the same cottage?'

'Yes. Why don't you go along and see her?'

'We will. And Matteo?'

'He passed away soon after the war ended.'

He got up to leave with Comolli accompanying him to the door. Patricia stood tapping her foot impatiently under the awning outside. On the threshold, Comolli asked, 'When are you coming back to claim your land, *Signor Conte?*'

This re-introduction of formality embarrassed Joe. 'Beppe, please,' he insisted. After all, Aldo Comolli had ruffled his hair and offered him boiled sweets from a big jar behind the counter when he'd called at the café before the War. He went on, 'I don't know about claiming my title.' He reached for Patricia's hand. 'I'm an Englishman now, with an English wife and a job in an English school.'

'What a shame!' sighed Aldo Comolli. 'Our village needs esteem after what happened.'

'What d'you mean?'

'The woman, Livia Carduccio, poor soul!' he muttered.

Joe was even more baffled. Why did the woman's name keep cropping up? Now that they were a safe distance from the prying ears of the women he felt able to question the patron, but the squeal of a telephone cut short his enquiry. Comolli politely shook hands with them both, excused himself and hurried back inside the café.

Patricia tugged at Joe's sleeve. 'Come on,' she said. 'It's already half past two and our bus leaves at four thirty.'

Joe hesitated, he dearly wanted to know more, but Patricia was right. Time was getting short. His enquiries would have to wait if they were to fit in a visit to Grazie Elena.

As they made their way up the steep hillside to her house, Patricia kept complaining about the heat. 'Is it always like this?' she groaned.

'Summer's worse. In August, the temperature reaches 40º.'

'What's that in pounds, shillings and pence?' pouted Patricia, the charm she'd displayed in the café giving way to bad-temper.

Joe tried to brush off her sarcasm. 'Absolutely boiling!' he replied with a grin.

Two children were playing under the trees outside Grazia Elena's house. They looked up with shy curiosity at the strangers.

'What are they staring at?' sneered Patricia.

'I don't suppose they see many strangers.'

Joe went to the beaded curtain hanging across the open entrance door. His heart beat fiercely, his face felt flushed and he found himself rubbing sweaty palms down the sides of his trousers. He was about to confront his old life; it was a terrifying prospect.

He jangled the bell and a stocky, dark-haired woman in her late twenties came to the door. She was dressed in black with a colourful apron tried round her waist. In her hand, she held a ladle dripping liquid. A voice from within called, 'If it's Father Ferdinando, Giuliana, tell him to come straight in.'

The young woman scrutinised them for a few moments, then demanded, 'What do you want?'

'Good afternoon, *Signora*,' replied Joe. 'I've come to see *Signora Polaski*.'

The woman looked at him suspiciously. 'I'm her granddaughter. Can you tell me what you want with her?'

'I'm an old friend.'

'She has no old friends,' retorted the woman defensively. 'Gianni, Luisa, come here!' Her children ran over to stand beside her. With her arms protectively around them, she again addressed Joe. 'Tourists aren't welcome here. Now, if you don't mind, I have work to do. *Arrivederci.*' She started to close the door.

To Joe's surprise, Patricia stepped forward. With a friendly smile, she held out her hand and said, 'Let me introduce myself. I'm Countess Di Tomasi and this is my husband, Count Di Tomasi.'

This announcement astonished both Joe and the young woman for, although Patricia had spoken in English, her meaning had been abundantly clear. The woman's mouth dropped open in surprise. Regaining her composure, she shooed the children back into the garden and invited the visitors in. 'I'm so sorry, *Signor Conte*. I'll speak to my grandmother at once,' she said apologetically.

From the other room, Joe heard a murmured exchange of words. The woman came back. 'My grandmother will see you but you mustn't stay long. This is a great shock for her. She's a very old lady and her heart's not strong. Ten minutes, no more.'

'I shall take care not to tire her,' replied Joe.

Reassured by his cordiality, the woman showed them into a gloomy room. It took time for Joe's eyes to become accustomed to the semi-darkness. A tremulous voice reached him. '*Signor Conte!* How is this possible? They told me you were dead.'

Joe went over to the woman, who was seated in a squeaky rocking chair. He understood at once the reason for the shaded room. Her eyes were opaque. He took her hand and gently squeezed it. 'You're thinking of my father. Grazie Elena, I'm Beppe.' He felt her hand shake and she reached out with the other hand to touch his face, tracing his features with her fingertips.

'Beppe,' she gasped. 'It really is you!'

Joe and Patricia stayed with Grazia Elena for nearly an hour. The old lady insisted that she wanted to hear all Joe's news, weeping when he told her his mother had been killed in an air-raid, saddened to learn that his grandfather had also died.

'I remember him well,' she declared. 'Such a typical English gentleman! And your poor mamma -- to die so young.' She squeezed Joe's hand. 'Poor child, left with no one.'

'I still have my Uncle Arthur and his family,' he assured her, omitting to mention the ongoing friction between himself and his cousins. Even in adulthood, Leslie never missed an opportunity to make derogatory remarks about him in front of Patricia, and until he started courting the daughter of a prominent businessman, Ronald had been unable to hide his envy of Joe's academic achievements. Their impending engagement pleased his Aunt Thelma who had always cherished high hopes for her eldest offspring.

Recalling Giuliana's warning about her grandmother's heart condition, he waited patiently for the right moment to question her about his father.

'How long did my father stay with you?'

'Several months. It was a terrible time. The Germans took over your father's villa and every evening those foul-mouthed soldiers got drunk in Comolli's bar. I don't know how the poor man put up with it. His wife stopped serving in the evenings. She's dead now, of course, lost her will to live when both their sons died in North Africa.' Grazia Elena wiped a tear from her eye.

'Carlo and Giorgio!' Joe was shocked. He remembered the curly-haired twins who'd been his brother's constant companions before Enzo went off to university.

In the middle of her story, Grazia Elena dropped off to sleep, leaving Joe wondering what happened next. He left the old woman to rest and joined Patricia, who was sitting under a tree, thumbing through a woman's magazine she'd brought with her.

'We mustn't miss the bus, Joe,' she said. 'Don't forget you said you'd take me shopping when we get back to Florence.'

'Eh, yes,' he replied absentmindedly. 'Where's Giuliana?'

'She muttered something about going into ... ' She wrinkled her nose. ' ... *i campi*.'

'The fields? Which direction did she take?'

Patricia pointed a beautifully manicured finger. 'That way. Don't lose track of time, Joe. Promise?'

He strode off under the burning sun until ten minutes later he caught sight of Giuliana's red spotted headscarf. She was raking the earth in readiness for planting. Her two children were playing hide and seek. Since their arrival, there had been no mention of her husband. Perhaps he, too, had been killed in the War, thought Joe, realising immediately that her children were too young for that.

The young woman looked up at his approach. 'You'll find it too hot out here,' she stated. 'You English are unused to the heat. Why don't you go and sit in the shade with your wife?'

'I'm Italian,' he corrected her.

'I hope you didn't over-tire my grandmother.'

'Of course, I didn't. She fell asleep half way through telling me about my father. Perhaps *you* can carry on with the story.'

Giuliana shrugged, and turned back to her task.

'That's hard work for a woman,' he observed.

She straightened up, leant on the rake handle and wiped the back of her hand across her forehead. 'I can manage. I'm only staying here to look after my grandmother. My husband's gone to work in Switzerland. Once the old lady goes, we'll join him.'

'About my father, can you tell me anything?'

'Not much, only that he died as a result of his wounds.'

'You must know more.'

The girl gave a dismissive shrug and continued her raking.

Joe began to get annoyed. 'If *you* don't tell me, I'll have to ask your grandmother again,' he said sharply.

This had the desired result. She stopped raking and pointed to a tree stump, saying, 'I could do with a break, let's go and sit over there. Have you got a cigarette?'

'Here.'

They both lit up, and the young woman inhaled deeply. She blew a smoke ring and said, 'The count was very badly wounded in the blast when the villa got blown up.'

'I know he was responsible for that, but what happened afterwards?'

'His partisan friends took him away. He was too weak for us to take care of him. Dr Amato did all he could.'

'Tell me about the Carduccio woman.'

She gave a sniff. 'The count turned up out of the blue, bringing her with him. It must have been July '43'

'Who was she?'

Giuliana shrugged. 'Your father met her through the Resistance. He brought her to us because she'd been injured in a motorcycle accident -- had concussion -- so I took charge of Isabella.'

'Who?'

'Isabella, Livia Carduccio's daughter, poor little mite.'

The day had almost reached its zenith and, despite his assertion that the heat didn't bother him, Joe was sweating profusely. Isabella! His head began to throb as he tried to come to terms with what Giuliana had told him. Comolli hadn't mentioned that the Carduccio woman had a child.

'How old was the child?'

'About two. Livia wasn't the maternal type so she was more than happy to let me take care of her.' Giuliana sighed. 'Such a lovely little girl.'

'What happened to her?'

'Who knows? She disappeared at the same time as your father. I think the partisans must have handed her over to her relatives.'

'Joe!' Patricia's voice reached him across the meadow. 'Look at the time, if we don't leave now we'll miss our bus.'

'Coming, darling,'

Giuliana took a last drag on her cigarette, threw away the stub and got to her feet. 'Must get back to work.'

Joe had one last question to ask. 'Was my father close to this woman?'

The colour rose to Giuliana's cheeks. 'They were fairly close,' she replied.

He had to know. Swallowing hard, he grunted, 'How close? Did they share a bed?'

Giuliana's blush deepened. 'Yes.'

Joe did a quick calculation: summer 1943; that meant both his parents were being adulterous at the same time. He was sickened by the discovery. Was Livia's daughter his half-sister? The throbbing in his head intensified. How could Babbo call this child Isabella knowing how devastated Mamma had been at losing their own Isabella?

'Joe, come on!' called Patricia.

'Sorry, darling.'

He took his leave of Giuliana and hurried back to the house.

'Just look at the time, Joe,' grumbled Patricia. 'You're so thoughtless.'

With a toss of her head, she started walking down the path, turning impatiently when he said, 'I must say goodbye to Grazia Elena before we leave; wait by the gate.'

The old lady was just waking up. Joe thanked her for her hospitality but didn't question her further. She seemed to have forgotten their earlier conversation because she kept repeating that she wanted to hear all his news. Sadly, he recognised that she was slipping in and out of senility. Fighting back tears, he kissed her cheek and whispered, 'Bless you!'

The bus was waiting outside Comolli's café. They climbed in and, once again, Patricia moaned about the hard wooden seats. Joe tried not to let her grumbling bother him, telling himself that he had a beautiful wife and a rosy future.

He squeezed her hand and said, 'Never mind, darling, we'll be back in Florence soon, and this evening I'll take you out for a special dinner.'

Patricia cast him a winsome smile. 'And tomorrow, we'll go shopping all day long,' she whispered. 'Remember, you promised.'

'For as long as you like,' he assured her.

Patricia fell asleep for most of the journey, her head resting on his shoulder. He heaved a sigh, telling himself that the past was now dead and buried. But try as he may, Joe was unable to completely shed his despondency. Giuliana's bombshell had maligned his father's memory, just as the discovery of the signed copy of 'Lady Chatterley's Lover' had done to that of his mother. His head started to throb again. The visit had been too brief. He felt cheated. A lot had happened during the years of separation. There was so much he needed to know, things that might explain his father's behaviour. If there'd been more time, he was convinced that Giuliana would have opened up to him.

Arthur had been right. He should have come back to Italy on his own.

As the bus approached Florence Patricia woke up and chattered cheerfully about their proposed shopping expedition. Her gaiety revived Joe's spirits. If Patricia was happy, then so was he. After she had changed into a dress she had bought especially for their holiday, they went down to the hotel restaurant where the *maggiordomo* showed them to a secluded side table. A three-piece orchestra began playing Neapolitan melodies and it wasn't long before Patricia had caught the eye of the guitarist.

'This is lovely, Joe,' she crooned, reaching for his hand and giving it a squeeze, while still managing to give the guitarist a coy glance. 'You are clever to choose such a super place.'

When the waiter brought the menus, she looked perplexed. 'But it's in Italian. I can't understand a word of it.'

Joe smiled proudly at her. 'Never mind, darling, I'll choose for you.' He consulted the menu. 'I think you'd like the *Tagliolini agli Asparagi* to start with.'

Patricia frowned. 'It won't be terribly foreign and spicy, will it?'

'Of course not.' Joe turned to the waiter. 'What local dishes do you recommend for the main course?'

'The *Arrosto di Maiale* or *Filetti di Merluzzo alla Fiorentina* are both very good and, of course, there's always the *Bistecca*.'

Joe dutifully translated for her and Patricia settled for the fish. He chose the steak and selected a local wine. Patricia made no secret of her appreciation of the good-looking waiter's attention, smiling sweetly up at him when he refilled her glass. Although, over the years, Joe had become accustomed to her flirting, he still found it difficult to control his jealousy. At times like these, he recalled his brother and wished that he had been blessed with Enzo's looks and personality. Keeping a tight rein on his emotions, he told himself that her flirtations were harmless and that, later on, he would have her all to himself.

Back in their room, she sank down onto the canopied four-poster, exclaiming, 'Oh darling, I feel like a princess!' And after they'd made love, she became even more voluble. 'Darling Joe, that was incredible; it's never been so good. I love you so much; I never knew you could be so romantic.'

He studied her in the half light, listening to the distant strumming of a guitar and marvelling yet again that such a beautiful woman could be his. He reminded himself that he was Italian. Weren't Italians the world's greatest lovers? His confidence grew. At last, he had exorcised his wife's unspoken innuendos that he wasn't as good as Roger.

Thirty-two

On their return home to Godalming, Joe felt proud and pleased when Patricia extolled the delights of her first visit abroad, outrageously embellishing their excursions to her friends. For the next year and a half, he felt himself to be in paradise. He had finally won his bride's heart. He wasn't even too troubled when Patricia waved off his suggestion that it would be nice to start a family with, 'Oh Joe, there's plenty of time for that. We're having fun, let's not spoil things with dirty nappies and sleepless nights.'

He refused to acknowledge to himself that their idyllic life was due to his willingness to accede to Patricia's every whim. When she overspent, which she frequently did, he could never hold on to his annoyance because she would cuddle up to him and whisper how sorry she was, her eyes brimming with tears. After a spell of bad-temper, she would delight him with her gaiety as she skipped and sang her way around the house, describing her plans to re-decorate the bedroom or to re-landscape the garden.

In the spring of 1956, Joe received a letter from Giuliana telling him that Grazia Elena had died. The news was not unexpected, but it saddened him. The old lady had been there for him during his formative years, and his memories of her were fond ones. Her granddaughter invited him to the funeral, but even after a year and a half, Giuliana's revelations, on top of his disappointment about the villa, were still painfully raw and he couldn't face going back to the scene of such heartache. He excused himself by pleading pressure of work.

Giuliana's letter coincided with the receipt of another letter, offering Joe a professorship at Boston University starting in September. It was a prestigious position and he couldn't wait to break the news to Patricia.

'The USA!' she cried, throwing out her arms with alacrity. 'Wow, won't my friends be envious. Just wait till I tell them!' She wrinkled her nose. 'Where exactly is Boston?'

'New England, it's on the East Coast,' he replied, relieved that she was so enthusiastic. He failed to notice until much later that she hadn't bothered to congratulate him on his achievement, that her sights were focused only on how this new adventure would affect her.

They sold the property in Godalming and, on a farewell visit to his aunt and uncle, Joe signed over his claim on the house in Harrogate. On the way home, Patricia took him to task

'What made you do that, Joe?' she complained. 'That's our inheritance you've given away. That spiteful old cow doesn't deserve anything, and as for those beastly cousins of yours, if they're too lazy to make their own way in life, then it's their own fault. Why, the only time they visit their parents is when they're after a handout.' She shook her head with exasperation.

'They're not so bad,' replied Joe, although privately he was inclined to agree with her about his cousins. 'In any case, the house by rights belongs to Arthur.'

'How do you figure that out?'

'He's my grandfather's heir. Morally I have no right to the house.'

'But it's the old man's decision. He didn't leave it to your uncle, he left it to you.'

'Only with the proviso that I give it back when I become reunited with my father.'

'But you haven't become reunited with him,' snapped Patricia. 'Oh Joe, you do try my patience sometimes!'

Joe shrugged. 'Grandpa believed I would be one day. Leaving me the house was only a precaution.' He smiled wryly to himself. Robert McPherson-Corke had not trusted his daughter-in-law. With the passing of the years, Joe understood that by putting the property in *his* name he had tied Thelma's hands. This way, she had no choice but to treat him kindly during his remaining study years. He patted his wife's arm. 'Don't worry, darling, we can manage perfectly well without the extra money. Going to the States will open up all kinds of opportunities to us.'

Patricia was an immediate hit in Boston. Her peaches and cream complexion and her English accent charmed everyone. At first, she seemed content, but by the following spring, she began complaining that campus life was boring, and that she missed her old friends, pleading with Joe to go home for a visit.

'Wait until the summer vacation,' he suggested.

She pouted, then wriggled up to him and murmured, 'Let me go now. Who knows, we might want to start a family by the summer.'

This proposition coming from Patricia gladdened Joe's heart. At last, she was willing to settle down and think about motherhood!

'Of course you can go. I'll book you a flight at Easter.'

Patricia threw her arms round his neck and kissed his face all over. 'Thank you, thank you, darling,' she cried. 'I knew you'd agree.'

She went home for two weeks, a long lonely two weeks for Joe. He couldn't believe how much he missed her. On her return, he went to the airport to meet her, carrying a large bunch of red roses.

'What did you bring those for?' were Patricia's first words. 'They'll be dead by the time we get home.'

'They're still in tight bud,' he protested, his joy at seeing her dampened.

Patricia's visit to England destroyed Joe's fragile happiness. From then on, she was offhand with him, barely polite to his colleagues, and unwilling to socialise with the other campus wives. When he brought up the subject of a baby, reminding her of her comments before the trip home, she shrugged him off. 'Did I say that? I don't remember.' He put her behaviour down to homesickness vowing that, next time, they would make the trip home together.

It was during the first semester of his second year at Boston that Joe really became worried about Patricia. She mooned about the house, refusing to make an effort and befriend the wives of the other professors.

'They're old and boring,' she complained.

Then there was an unexpected change. In 1958 Patricia joined a drama group. Joe was surprised because she had never shown any interest in acting. What was more surprising was that by Christmas she had become one of the leading lights. The new Patricia brightened Joe's life. Things were almost as good as they had been back home in Godalming. But her involvement in the group snowballed until she was out nearly every evening.

One day, he challenged her. 'Surely you don't have to rehearse so often, darling, after all the next performance isn't for a few months.'

She looked at him sharply and snapped, 'I enjoy rehearsing. Why do you resent me enjoying myself?'

'I don't.'

'You do, you know how I hate living here.'

'You loved it when we first came.'

'Well, I don't any more. I hate campus life, I hate all those fuddy duddies we have to mix with. The drama group's the only thing that keeps me sane. Besides, I'm the star. Don't you want me to do well?'

'Of course I do, but I miss you, Patricia. Don't go out this evening, stay home with me. I'll open a bottle of wine and cook your favourite meal.'

Patricia pulled a face. 'Not that French thing, *Coq au Vin*! It's the only thing you know how to cook.'

'I thought you liked it.'

'Well I don't.'

With a frown, she picked up her bag and flounced out of the house, slamming the front door behind her.

Joe was both furious and disappointed, but his initial anger swiftly diminished. He felt hurt. They had exchanged heated words before, but Patricia had never left without making it up. He spent a miserable evening planning a reconciliation, yet even the soothing music from his collection of operatic areas failed to lift his spirits. When Patricia got home, she was clearly tired, and he hadn't the heart to confront her, telling himself that the next day would be soon enough.

The following morning, when he mentioned the argument Patricia was sweetness itself. 'Oh darling, I *do* want to spend more time with you, but how can I?' Her delicately pencilled eyebrows rose in dismayed perplexity. 'You know I'm playing the lead. I've got loads of lines to learn.'

'I'll help you with your lines,' he offered, clasping her wrists enthusiastically. 'I'd like that.'

Patricia gave an indulgent smile. 'Honestly darling, my friend in the drama group knows the role inside out, she's better at coaching me.'

Joe felt snubbed. He continued to protest, but had to curb his indignation when Patricia got upset.

'Don't be like that, Joe,' she cried, tears beginning to well in her eyes. 'You sound like my mother. She was always checking up on me, didn't want to let me out of her sight...' She blew her nose on a tissue and finished sulkily, 'Just because we're married, it doesn't mean I have to tell you everything. I'm entitled to my little secrets.'

What secrets? thought Joe. He had never kept anything from her so why would she want to hide anything from him? After that, things went from bad to worse until, one Friday, she stayed out all night. When she hadn't returned by eleven o'clock, Joe was frantic. Pushing aside pride, he rang all her friends and acquaintances. No one had seen her. He remembered that she kept the names and telephone numbers of her fellow actors in an address book -- one of her little secrets -- and until now it had never occurred to him to look at it. Fear for her safety overrode discretion; he searched the house for the address book, but couldn't find it.

He called the local police precinct and, although the desk sergeant was sympathetic, he was unable to help.

'Your wife's only been gone a few hours,' he said. 'Phone back tomorrow if she doesn't come home, but I shouldn't worry, she's probably stayed over with a friend.'

The conversation helped to put things into perspective. That was the explanation: rehearsals had run late and Patricia was staying with one of the girls from the show. He consoled himself with a bottle of whisky, but was unable to drag himself upstairs to bed, settling instead for a blanket and a pillow on the sofa. Waking, stiff and hung-over the next morning, he was about to telephone the police again when she walked in.

She frowned with irritation on seeing the bedding on the sofa and demanded, 'Why did you sleep down here when there's a perfectly good bed upstairs?'

No apology, no concern. Joe's temper flared. Grasping her by the shoulders, he shouted, 'Where the hell have you been? I've been sick with worry...'

'I stayed with Susan, I told you I was going to.'

He shook her roughly. 'No you didn't.'

She wriggled herself free and snapped, 'Yes I did, you never listen to what I tell you.'

Swivelling on her heel, she ran upstairs and started running the bath water.

Joe flopped down on the sofa. *Had* she told him? He could be doing her an injustice. He'd been working hard lately, giving extra tuition, maybe he had forgotten. With a sigh, he went upstairs and knocked on the bathroom door.

'Go away!' she shouted.

'I'm sorry, Patricia,' he said. 'Can I come in?'

There was silence, then he heard her say softly, 'Are you truly sorry?'

'Of course I am. I must have forgotten you'd told me.'

'Come in then.'

The room was filled with steam and the aroma of lavender. Patricia was in the bath, steeped in water crowned with bubbles. She reached out a hand to him and whispered, 'Get in with me, Joe.'

He gave a sigh. It seemed that all was forgiven.

For the next few months, their lives continued along the same lines. Patricia's performance in 'Blythe Spirit' was heralded as outstanding by the local press. Much as he loved her, Joe felt this was an exaggeration. On stage, as in real life, she over-acted. But who was he to criticise her? He adored her, and took pleasure in immersing himself in her reflected glory. Besides, now that the show was over, and the group had taken a break for a couple of months, he would see more of Patricia. She couldn't fall back on the excuse of rehearsals.

For a few days, things looked up. While he was teaching, Patricia set about tidying the house, cleaning the windows, re-hanging their clothes in the wardrobe, re-arranging the drawers. He came home one day to find her weeding the flower beds.

'Wow, you've been busy,' he said.

She replied cheerfully, 'Somebody had to do it.'

The next day he arrived home to find the house empty. He took a shower then went downstairs, and helped himself to a beer from the fridge. He saw the note as he shut the fridge door. Frowning, he pulled it off. It was very much in Patricia's style, the phrases flowery and self-indulgent. He read the words with disbelieving eyes. She stressed how unreasonable he was to expect her to fit into campus life; she couldn't bear it any longer; she had met someone else; his name was Bill, they had been seeing one another for ages; her new man was marvellous; he reminded her of Roger. *He reminded her of Roger!* Joe read the note several times, feeling that the sheet of paper must surely ignite under his burning scrutiny. Patricia had never been the perfect partner, she had been selfish, she had been moody but, as far as he knew, she had never been unfaithful.

How wrong he had been! Seated at the kitchen table with the can of beer in front of him, he felt a complete fool. He'd been cuckolded. His face reddened as if the contents of Patricia's letter were emblazoned across the skyline for the whole world to see. With a sweep of his arm he sent the can flying across the room. Beer formed a frothy puddle on the table, dripping to the floor to form yet another. Lowering his head onto his arms, he let out a wail of despair. *He reminded her of Roger!*

In the weeks following Patricia's departure, Joe hardly slept. He performed everyday tasks in a trance. His colleagues uttered consoling phrases: *you're better off without her; you'll soon find someone else.* He wished they'd leave him alone, but he was too polite to tell them to mind their own business.

Sadie, his cleaning lady was even worse. 'That little cutie don't know where she's well off,' she ranted, vigorously polishing the dining room table. She flicked the duster. 'Most gals would give their eye teeth for a fella like you and a house like this. She'll come running back, you mark my words!'

That Patricia would see sense and come running back was Joe's fervent hope, but it didn't happen. He found it difficult to concentrate. He dreamt about her at night, he thought about her all day. He only had to pass a florist to be reminded of how much she loved roses, a pet shop window conjured up a picture of her drooling over a Labrador puppy, and Elvis Presley's rendering of *I need your love tonight* was guaranteed to bring a tear to his eye. Months passed without a word from her.

The year ended and the new term began. A dedicated tutor, Joe loved his subject and it was no hardship for him to stay on late at the university, coaching students. At home, he left books and newspapers laying about; dirty cups and glasses stayed on the coffee table. After showering, he dropped his towel on the bathroom floor; he left the top off the toothpaste. Clutter disguised his loneliness. It was also an act of rebellion. Patricia would have scolded him for it.

When Sadie came into clean, she tutted, 'I know it aint none of my business but I don't get it. How come ya living in such a mess?'

He looked at her over the top of his glasses and grunted, 'Don't fuss, Sadie, a bit of untidiness doesn't bother me.'

In a moment of anger, he moved his clothes into the spare room, and told Sadie to give the master bedroom a thorough vacuum. Then he drew the curtains and locked the door in a bid to convince himself that this would expunge any last hope he entertained of Patricia's return. The tactic didn't work. He could rid her presence from the house, but he couldn't rid her memory from his heart.

He dreaded coming home in the evening. The silence of failure greeted him at the front door. Restless nostalgia filled the long, lonely night. Tossing and turning in the darkness he would ask himself over and over again what he'd done to drive her away. This nocturnal ritual of soul-searching didn't provide the answer and he would wake in the morning feeling tired and irritable. He would nick himself shaving and swear at his own reflection, despising the image facing him.

His anger exploded into hatred when he overheard a conversation between two of his students. 'What's the matter with old Thomas these days?' asked one.

'Haven't you heard?' replied the other with a chuckle. 'His wife's run off with an actor.'

The first student burst out laughing. 'Shite! What a sucker! I always thought they were an odd couple; she's a tasty bit of skirt, far too classy for him.'

They moved out of hearing, but Joe had heard enough. The memories flooded back: the shame at being called an *eyetie*, the indignity at being ridiculed for his *funny accent*, the humiliation at being jeered off the cricket field, and now, two-timed by his wife. His brother's image flashed across his mind: Enzo would have confronted these obstacles, no woman would have cheated on Enzo. Why should *he* put up with it? He resolved to put his life in order.

The next evening, his Uncle telephoned him from England. Joe's spirits sank. Now he'd be forced to tell Arthur that Patricia had left him. He wasn't ready for that. Yet even as these thoughts flashed through his mind, he realised that he was about to take the first step towards a new life. He braced himself to break the news. Arthur didn't give him the chance.

After the conventional exchange of pleasantries, he said, 'I've got good news.'

'What is it?' Joe clutched at his uncle's words, grateful for this momentary reprieve from revealing his failed marriage,

'I've had a phone call from Italy,' Arthur paused. 'Joe...your father's alive.'

Joe gripped the receiver. This was extraordinary news. 'But the Italian Authorities said he was dead!' he stuttered.

'They made a gigantic cock-up.'

His uncle went on speaking, but Joe was locked in the memory of what Giuliana and Aldo Comolli had told him, and didn't listen. His father had died a hero back in 1943. He'd died to save the village.

He found his voice. 'It's a practical joke, Uncle, someone's got a warped sense of humour.' For a moment, it crossed Joe's mind that it might be one of Patricia's pranks, but he quickly dismissed the notion. She couldn't, she wouldn't do that. Besides, she wasn't bright enough to think up such a trick.

'It's no joke, Joe, it's genuine. The woman who phoned should know because he lodges in her house.' Lodges? Had Papà lost his fortune? 'He's asking for you. Get over there as quickly as possible. He'll want to meet Patricia.'

'I can't go.'

Arthur sounded astonished. 'Why not?'

'No,' muttered Joe, as if speaking to himself.

'You *must* go. I'll give you the details.'

'No!' retorted Joe and put the phone down.

He sank down on the bed and stared at the floor between his feet. He couldn't take in this new turn of events. After the disturbing visit to Castagnetto in 1954, he'd deliberately erased his father's image from his mind. To have it resurrected so unexpectedly five years on left him feeling disorientated. He was slowly coming to terms with life without Patricia. The last thing he wanted was more emotional turmoil. Patricia! He hadn't told his uncle about Patricia.

That night, he dreamt about her, the usual dream: her running off in the distance between two men. He could never catch them up.

The door bell woke him. He thought he was still in the dream until the continued buzzing penetrated his subconscious, urging him out of bed. Snatching his bathrobe off its hook, he ran downstairs on bare feet, stopping in the hallway with a jolt. Through the glass panelled door was the outline of a figure, a figure he recognised. He opened the door.

'Hello Joe.'

Patricia looked fetching in a turquoise knee-length linen suit, white lacy gloves with frills at the cuffs and a small leather bag swinging from her shoulder. She was dressed for a lunch party. It seemed odd at 7.30 in the morning.

He stared at her in disbelief. She appeared to have lost a little weight and her hair was done differently: twisted into a French pleat and fastened with a tortoiseshell comb. She looked breathtaking. Reflecting on her surprise arrival later, he was amazed at how much detail he had absorbed during those first few minutes.

'Hello Joe,' she said again. 'Aren't you going to welcome me back? My suitcases are in the taxi. You'd better get dressed and bring them in.'

A bald head thrust out of the cab window. 'Hurry up, lady, I can't wait here all day.'

With a start, Joe recovered his powers of speech. 'What are you doing here?' he demanded.

Patricia looked somewhat miffed and announced, 'Darling, I've left Bill, I've come home.'

Frowning, Joe replied, 'You can't come waltzing back here just as you please.'

Her blue eyes widened. 'You don't mean that, Joe.'

'I do,' he croaked. 'Go back to Bill.'

'You can't turn me away, this is my home.'

She took a step forward, but he crossed the threshold with his arms spread, barring her way. 'Not any more.'

With a nervous giggle, she picked up the vanity case by her feet. 'Don't be a tease, darling.'

He stiffened. Here was the woman he'd cherished, the woman he'd yearned for. Why wasn't he welcoming her back? Her winsome smile, once captivating, was now irksome. He wanted to take her by the wrist and shove her into the waiting taxi. He had never experienced such anger, his nerve-ends juddered with it. During his childhood his cousins had provoked him, his aunt had infuriated him, his mother had disappointed him, but he had never been stirred into giving full vent to his temper.

He glared at his wife, his fists clenched so hard that the nails were digging into the palms of his hands. 'Go back to the taxi, Patricia.'

'I can't, I haven't any money to pay him.'

'Here!' He snatched up his wallet from the hall table and thrust a bundle of notes at her.

The tears welled in her eyes. 'You're not being fair, Joe, I thought you'd be pleased to see me. I'm truly sorry about what happened, I promise to be a good and faithful wife from now on.'

'It's too late.'
'What d'you mean? Too late. Why?'
'It's over, I want a divorce.'

He couldn't believe the words were coming out of his mouth. The situation was farcical. What a trio they made! Patricia doled up to the nines, Joe himself clad in nothing but a bathrobe and a bald-headed taxi driver getting angrier by the minute?

'Come on, lady,' shouted the latter.

Without turning, Patricia flapped an impatient hand in the cabbie's direction. 'Okay, okay.' Cringing under Joe's icy stare, she choked in panic, 'Stop playing the fool, Joe. At least, let me in so we can talk about this.'

A week ago, Patricia's surprising return would have gladdened his heart, but last night his uncle's telephone call had unearthed a far deeper emotion. His father was still alive. What could be more important that that? He understood now. Despite the passing of the years, the revelations, the heartaches, he wanted a reunion with Vincenzo. There was no putting it off. He would phone his uncle for the details and book a flight to Italy. Patricia's return had clarified his thoughts. She no longer mattered.

He felt liberated. It was as if a veil had been lifted from his eyes. He opened his wallet again and thrust more money at her. 'Get out of here, go and find yourself somewhere to stay. I'm leaving for Europe tomorrow. We'll talk about a divorce when I get back.'

PART V

Like Enzo

Thirty-three

By the time he landed at Milan Airport, Joe was sick with apprehension. Over the years of his exile he had not forgotten his native language, but the words did not slip easily off his tongue and he felt strange being back in the country of his birth. He hadn't seen his father for twenty years and, despite the fact that Vincenzo had been hailed a hero in Castagnetto, he couldn't rid himself of the disappointment of discovering that he had taken a lover the minute his family had left for England. He wondered how he was going to face up to the reunion.

Claudia Fabbri met him at Bolzano Station, a copy of *La Stampa* tucked under her arm for identification purposes. He had visualised a rotund motherly figure. This woman was a far cry from that. Small and skinny with a swarthy complexion, she gave the impression of having spent her life on the brink of starvation. Although her face was prematurely wrinkled, her gait spoke of energy and physical strength. She greeted him brusquely, extending a sinewy hand for him to shake. Before he could stop her, she picked up his overnight bag and strode ahead of him out of the station to a rusty Fiat parked opposite the entrance.

He enquired after his father, but she didn't give a straight answer. 'It's a long time since you last saw him. How old were you when you left for England, nine, ten?'

'Nine,' he replied.

Heading into the traffic, they lapsed into silence. Claudia drove aggressively, grunting impatiently if impeded by other vehicles. When a taxi driver cut in front of her, she stepped on the accelerator, catching him up at the traffic lights, where she lowered her window, leant out and shouted, '*Che fai, testa di cazzo?*' The man made a vulgar gesture and roared off the minute the lights changed. '*Merda!*' she burst out. 'I'd like to give that son of a bitch a piece of my mind.'

Joe was shocked. In his cocooned academic world, women didn't swear. Even Patricia, who would become extremely voluble when it came to an argument, had never resorted to using foul language.

They took a circuitous route, fraught with hairpin bends, but these seemed to bother Claudia less than the city traffic jams.

As they navigated the mountainside, she said, 'Your father's been grumpy lately. His stump gives him a lot of pain.'

'His stump?'

Claudia didn't mince her words. 'He lost a leg in the fracas at Castagnetto.'

Joe bit back his shock. 'This was when he went missing?'

'Yes. There's something else you should know.'

'What's that?'

'You have a sister. You'll meet her; she's devoted to your father.'

'Isabella!' Joe hadn't forgotten her, but he'd assumed she'd be living with her mother's family.

'You know about her?' Claudia seemed surprised.

Briefly, Joe explained about his visit to Castagnetto in 1954. 'How old is she?' he asked.

'Just turned 18.'

The rest of the hair-raising drive was covered in silence, giving Joe time to contemplate on what might lie ahead. His emotions were in turmoil. He hadn't anticipated meeting his half sister, and felt resentful of her presence. Had she been living with his father all these years, sharing her days with him, enjoying his affection?

As they entered San Baldino, he noticed the Austrian influence, all road signs being displayed in both Italian and German. Claudia drove through the village to continue yet higher up the mountain. At times, he feared the clapped out vehicle wouldn't cope. Eventually, they rounded a bend into a tiny hamlet where Claudia slammed on the brakes, throwing him forward to bang his head on the windscreen.

'This is it,' she said, smiling for the first time. 'I'm glad you've come, but be warned, your father will be very different from the way you remember him.'

'Have you known him long?' he asked.

'Since 1940.'

The door of the house opened and a young woman appeared. She ran towards Claudia and threw her arms around her neck, hugging her tightly. Joe felt a knot of panic. Could this be Isabella? But when he got a better look at her, he saw that she was too old to be his sister, nearer his own age in fact. Claudia introduced them. 'This is my friend, Sofia,' she said. 'Come along in, Beppe.'

'Call me Joe,' he butted in. 'Everyone does.'

Claudia nodded and led him into the house. 'It's probably not what you're used to,' she said. 'But it's home to us.'

Joe saw that the house was basically furnished, although an attempt had been made to modernise the kitchen. It was very different from his old home in Castagnetto, and he wondered how and when his father had fallen on hard times. Why hadn't he gone back to Tuscany instead of settling in this remote and inclement hideaway in Trentino? Claudia disappeared into another room, leaving him with Sofia, who offered him a beaker of red wine, and tried to make polite conversation in a dialect he couldn't understand.

Claudia came back accompanied by a teenage girl. 'This is your sister, Isabella,' she said.

The girl stepped forward to greet him, a hesitant smile playing at the corners of her mouth. 'It's a pleasure to meet you,' she said shyly.

Joe was taken aback. In his reluctance to acknowledge his half sister, he had refused to conjure up her image. Now, here she was in flesh and blood, forcing him to accept her as a real person.

He shook her hand, English style, unable to bring himself to greet her with a kiss on the cheek in the Italian manner. She looked surprised, but quickly recovered her composure. 'Papà is awake now. Would you like to go in and see him?'

Joe followed Isabella into his father's bedroom. Vincenzo was propped up in bed with an abundance of pillows behind him. His breathing was stertorous, his skin sallow and marked by liver spots, his thatch of wavy hair, snow-white. Joe felt riveted to the spot. His feet wouldn't budge. He ran his tongue across his dry lips, unable to force words from his mouth. Vincenzo made the first move. Easing himself up, he held out his arms. 'Beppe, *figlio mio*, come here!'

The sound of his father's voice brought tears to Joe's eyes. Vincenzo Di Tomasi may have grown old in body, but his voice remained as strong and positive as ever. Shedding the years, the young man flew across the room and hugged his father as he had done when he was a little boy. When they eventually drew apart, he saw that Isabella had discreetly left the room.

Father and son talked for half an hour on general subjects, each treading carefully, afraid of touching a nerve.

At last, Vincenzo said, 'It must have been terrible for you when your mother died. Such a tragedy! What was she doing in London?'

Joe had been dreading this question. 'Visiting friends,' he said guardedly.

He avoided answering more questions because his father suddenly grew tired and needed to rest. This short dialogue set the pattern for the remainder of his stay, and he learned the details of his father's War years in abbreviated snatches. He was shocked to hear the truth about how his brother had died.

'I always knew Enzo's death was no accident,' explained Vincenzo. 'How I regret not listening to my boy. His views may have been exaggerated, but they had substance. If I'd discussed them with him, maybe I could have warned him of the danger he was putting himself in.'

Joe listened in amazement to his father's account of his exile to Lucania. 'It was the calm before the storm,' he said, giving a more detailed account of Giuliana's 1954 version. Vincenzo grinned. 'You didn't know about the door in the well, did you, my boy?'

Joe shook his head.

Vincenzo gave a chuckle. 'Enzo did, but after I caught him trying to clamber into it, I had the well covered over.'

'I was shocked to find the villa destroyed,' said Joe.

'I always imagined it would be yours some day.'

When he grew too exhausted to talk, Joe told him about his own life in Harrogate disguising the circumstances surrounding his mother's death, and making light of his miserable school days.

'You've done well, son,' gasped out Vincenzo. 'I knew you'd make Oxbridge, and I had every faith in your grandfather to see you through.' He stopped speaking, his face grey as he fought for breath. Joe rushed to the door and called for help. Isabella came at once and ran over to the bed. 'Give me a hand!' she cried.

'Is he going to be all right?' asked Joe anxiously. 'Hadn't we better call the doctor?'

'It's not necessary,' replied Isabella. 'Papà's tired, that's all.'

Together they hoisted the old man up against his supporting pillows, their hands brushing behind his head. As his laboured breathing eased, Vincenzo closed his eyes and sank into sleep. The girl's fingers entwined themselves in Joe's. 'Thank you for coming,' she whispered. 'It means so much to him.'

Joe met her gaze and experienced a frisson of emotion. How could he be resentful of this slip of a girl, who clearly adored his father, caring for him with unselfish love! Her lips parted in a smile, revealing a row of small even teeth, then she dropped her gaze and withdrew her hand to straighten the bed covers.

After a few days, Joe summoned up the courage to ask his father about Isabella's mother.

'Livia?' Vincenzo's eyes clouded. 'She tried to winkle information out of a German officer, but the tables were turned on her. She died a horrible death. I'd rather not talk about it.' Vincenzo closed his eyes, a signal for Joe to leave him alone.

Joe felt guilty for causing his father pain. Clearly, he'd been deeply in love with Livia Carduccio. He found it confusing. For years he'd borne a grudge against his parents for the apparent ease with which they had both disregarded their marriage vows. With hindsight, he realised that separation from her husband at a time when she was grieving for Enzo had been very difficult for his mother. Maybe, seeking comfort in the arms of a lover had been the only way she could deal with the pain.

His thoughts switched back to Vincenzo. Joining the Resistance had catapulted his father into danger and intrigue, far removed from the comfortable existence he had enjoyed before the War. Joe heaved a troubled sigh. This was not the reunion he had imagined. It was distressing for both of them, yet he knew he had been right to make the journey to San Baldino.

Joe seldom left the room during the first two days, reluctant to distance himself from Vincenzo. His father's days were numbered. Each time he watched him close his eyes, he waited anxiously for him to open them again. There were so many questions he needed to ask him. He ran them through in his mind: *Why did you leave it so long before contacting me? Are there any more skeletons in the cupboard? Why did you call your daughter Isabella?* This last question puzzled him more than the others.

The women came in to see the invalid from time to time: Claudia bossy, Sofia twittering, Isabella devoted. Each of them tried to persuade Joe to take a break from his bedside vigil. On the third day, Isabella's persuasive powers prevailed.

'Come and keep me company while I feed the chickens,' she suggested. 'Papà will sleep for at least a couple of hours.'

He followed her down the narrow staircase out into the farmyard, and while she scattered maize feed, he studied her. She was beautiful. Slender and graceful, she moved with a light step, her body tilted over the basket she carried. Her thick dark hair fell loosely to her shoulders obscuring her face. His heart gave a jolt when she lifted her head, shook back her hair and looked at him with the sweetest of smiles. Basking in her warmth, he smiled back and realised that despite the sad circumstances of his return, he felt incredibly happy.

'Would you like to go for a walk when I've finished?' she asked.

'I'd like that very much.'

They walked up a hill until the ground began to flatten out into a small plateau, where Isabella stopped and said, 'I'd like to show you my favourite view.'

Joe followed her gaze.

'It's magnificent, isn't it?' she murmured.

'Breathtaking.'

She came to stand close to him. 'I'm so glad you came, Beppe.' Smothering a giggle, she added. 'Would you prefer me to call you Joe?'

'Yes.' It was a reflex response. Fleetingly, he recalled the resentment he'd felt at being ordered to change his name when he started at Monksmede, and wondered why he was now turning down the opportunity to revert to his old name.

'Are you still at school?' he asked her.

'I start university in September.'

'Where?'

'Florence, I shall be able to visit Castagnetto. What a pity you don't live there? Have you ever thought of moving back?'

Joe shook his head.

'I suppose, your wife, being English, wouldn't want to live there.'

'Patricia and I have split up,' he replied curtly.

'I'm so sorry, Joe.' She reached for his hand. 'I didn't mean to be indiscreet.'

'It's water under the bridge now.' Anxious to get off the subject of his marriage, he asked, 'What are you going to do at university?'

'Art and Design.' She noticed they were still holding hands and edged away, saying, 'We'd better get back.'

Further talks with his father revealed little more although Joe felt sure he had not heard the whole truth. One thing still bothered him. 'Why did you let the Authorities proclaim you *missing presumed dead*?' he asked.

'I'm glad you brought the subject up, son,' gasped Vincenzo. 'It's time to set the record straight.' He paused for breath between each sentence. 'I'll get Claudia to contact the Authorities tomorrow.'

'I just want to know why you chose to disappear.'

'I needed time to adjust,' gasped out Vincenzo. 'To get over Livia's death, to adapt to my disability.'

Livia! His disability! Yet again Joe felt the cruel rod of rejection. 'What about me? Had you forgotten my existence?' he demanded.

Vincenzo's breathing grew more rasping, Joe called for help, red-faced with embarrassment when Isabella and Sofia reprimanded him for tiring his father. He stayed in San Baldino until Vincenzo's condition started to improve, but was afraid to question him further for fear of provoking another attack. He took daily walks in the hills with Isabella.

'You know, Joe, I only learnt of your existence from Claudia,' she told him.

Joe looked shocked. 'D'you mean, Papà didn't mention me?'

She shook her head. 'I found that awfully strange.'

'Unnatural,' replied Joe, a bitter edge creeping into his voice.

Isabella immediately jumped to her father's defence. 'He probably didn't want to burden you.'

'Burden me?'

'Yes, you know, he didn't want to become dependent on you.'

'He didn't seem to mind becoming dependent on you, Isabella.'

She ignored this and said, 'He's never got over the loss of his leg. Of course, I don't remember much about him before he lost it. I was only little, but I think he was quite different then.'

Joe was impressed by Isabella's maturity. For a teenager, she seemed very philosophical about caring for their father. He realised that, like him, she must have had a very lonely childhood.

They continued talking and discovered they had much in common. The eleven-year difference in their ages seemed to shrink with each passing day.

Joe could barely bring himself to leave, aware that this could be the last time he'd see his father. 'I'll come back later in the year,' he promised, but he knew it would be difficult to take another vacation during term time.

His farewell from Claudia and Sofia was formal. He thanked them for their hospitality, knowing that, in reality, they were both glad to see the back of him. He'd been an inconvenience, a disruption to their daily routine.

Isabella came to say goodbye while Claudia was revving up the Fiat's old engine. She took his hand, and led him out of sight. 'I'm so sorry you have to leave, Joe, I hate goodbyes.'

Her expressive eyes welled with tears. 'Promise you'll come and visit me in Florence.'

'I will if I can,' he said. 'But it's a long flight from the States and I can only come during the school holidays.'

'I understand,' she replied. 'And I do hope things work out for you ... with your wife, I mean.'

He realised with a jolt that Patricia was the last person on his mind. The pretty young girl standing in front of him dominated his thoughts. Her fingers tightened in his. 'I'm so glad we get along, Joe. I was afraid I wouldn't like my half-brother or that he wouldn't like me.' She wrapped her arms round his neck and kissed him on the cheek before spinning around and running back into the house.

Throughout the flight back to the States, Joe brooded on what he had learned. He was glad his father hadn't lied to him about his love for Livia, but it irked him that he had invented his own demise without considering how much this would distress his son. But more than anything, he felt hurt that Vincenzo had never again mentioned Alice.

On arrival at Boston Airport, his thoughts switched to Patricia. Did she really want to come back to him? Maybe she'd turned over a new leaf. For a week, he rode on this fantasy, but a few days later, he received a letter from her demanding a divorce. She'd made it up with Bill, she explained, and they wanted to get married.

Joe's anger was unbounded. He felt humiliated. How could he have imagined that Patricia would change? Unable to still his restlessness, he drove into the countryside at high speed, stopping eventually, to go into a Drive-In. He watched the movie, a can of beer in one hand, a hamburger in the other. The next day, he could recall nothing about the film, not even its title. But the episode brought him to a decision: he would do the gentlemanly thing and grant Patricia a quickie divorce on the grounds of *his* adultery. A swift clean cut was preferable to a suppurating sore.

While waiting for the decree nisi he withdrew into himself, refusing kindly-intentioned invitations from sympathetic friends, shutting himself away in the evenings to listen to his favourite operatic arias. Joe's last memory of Patricia was her effusive farewell outside the Court Room in Reno when she blatantly kissed him on the lips, begging him to stay in touch.

'Don't forget, darling,' she sang out gaily. 'You're my bestest ever friend. You always have been and you always will be.'

With these words ringing in his ears, he saw her hurry away on the arm of her new husband-to-be, turning as she got into a waiting cab to blow him a final kiss.

The following year, Joe returned home to Yorkshire. Arthur met him at the airport. 'I was sorry to hear about the divorce,' he said.

Joe shrugged. 'I'm a loner, always have been.'

'You're still young, Joe and there are plenty more fish in the sea.'

'No, Uncle, I don't think marriage is for me.'

'Where are you staying?'

'I've booked into a hotel for a couple of nights, then I'll have to start looking for something more permanent.'

'You're welcome to stay with us,' said his uncle. 'There's plenty of room now that the boys have moved on. The house is really too big for your aunt and myself.'

The offer was tempting. Ronald was now married to his wealthy heiress and working in her father's shipping company on Tyneside, and Leslie was away on safari in Southern Rhodesia. A character-building exercise, his exasperated father called it.

But after considering the options, Joe politely declined Arthur's invitation. Although this meant living in digs, he couldn't bear the prospect of his Aunt Thelma's frequently repeated *I told you so*. She had never trusted Patricia and, for once, Joe was obliged to concede that she had been right.

Depression settled upon him. He felt as if his life had come to an end. Despite Patricia's selfishness, he couldn't condemn her completely. There had been moments of indescribable joy in their marriage, and he didn't doubt that if he were to have his time over again, he would still ask her to marry him.

Lack of motivation prevented him from accepting a suitable lecturing post, although he wasn't short of offers. Aunt Thelma phoned him, remonstrating: 'You've got to pick up the threads of your life, Joe; the sooner you get back into a routine, the better you'll feel. Besides, if you keep turning down opportunities, they'll run out.'

He knew his aunt was right and he began to sift through the offers.

Thirty-four

During the month following Joe's visit, Vincenzo grew weaker. He feared he would never see his son again and, with this fear in his mind, he clung to his adopted daughter, knowing that within a few weeks, she too, would leave him when she started at university. She frequently read to him from the newspaper since he could no longer concentrate on the written word. Work on his manuscript had long ago been set aside. It had been a labour of love for half a lifetime, and it saddened him to think that it would never be completed.

He began to relive the past. Omitting the war years, he would muse about happier times with Alice and the boys. Sometimes the past and the present would merge: Isabella was his real daughter -- she hadn't died in infancy. On one occasion, he confused the young woman by describing the other Isabella. 'Such a beautiful baby with lots of blond hair and huge blue eyes.'

'But my hair's dark and my eyes are brown, Papà.'

Jolted out of his reflections, Vincenzo hurriedly replied, 'All babies are born with blue eyes.' This slip alarmed him. How easily he could have given the game away!

He talked to Isabella about his joy at the reunion with Joe. 'I'd like you two to keep in touch when I've gone. I know I haven't got much longer,' he said.

'Don't talk like that, Papà. You'll get better.'

He shook his head. 'There's another long winter ahead.'

'Stop it!' she scolded him. 'I can't bear it, I can't bear to think of you no longer being here for me.'

'The inevitable has to be faced,' he persisted. 'That's why I want you to keep in touch with Joe. Write to him from Florence.'

'I will Papà,' she promised and, on her first visit home after starting at university, she said, 'I wrote Joe a long, newsy letter and he replied by return of post.'

'Could you read it to me?' asked Vincenzo.

Initially, Isabella seemed only too pleased to read Joe's letters aloud but, over the ensuing months, she became more reluctant to share them with her father. Misgivings began to form in Vincenzo's mind. 'You two write to one another quite frequently, don't you?' he commented on one occasion.

Isabella looked surprised. 'I thought that's what you wanted.'

Her response was innocent enough, but when a blush crept to her cheeks Vincenzo became uneasy. Surely his adopted daughter couldn't be falling in love? It was unthinkable: she believed Joe was her brother. And when she broke the news of Joe's divorce, he felt even more alarmed, and he realised that by concealing the truth, he could be denying happiness to the two people he loved the most.

For weeks he agonised over his dilemma. The only person who knew the truth was Stefano Amato; even Claudia was unaware that Isabella wasn't his real daughter. He tried to sweep his concern aside. Isabella would get over it. After all, they were only writing chatty letters to one another.

'Joe's left the States and gone to live in England,' she told him. 'He's planning to come and see us.'

Vincenzo's heart lifted. He'd feared he would never see his son again. But his inner conflict escalated. The lie he had perpetuated began to sicken him. Should he run the risk of losing Isabella's trust by telling her the truth? His tortured mind wouldn't let go of the memories, and it was with perfect clarity that he recalled the moment he had found the pendant among Livia's things...

He'd assumed it was a St Christopher, but on closer inspection, he'd seen that it was, in fact, the Star of David. Unable to believe his eyes, he'd turned it over, and with the aid of a magnifying glass, read: *To Livia, on your eighth birthday, from your loving Papà.* The rest of the inscription was in Hebrew: '*Yevarechechà Adonai veyishmerecha*', words he'd recognised as those of the Rabbi's opening benediction. A friend from university had worn a similar pendant. They'd lost touch after the young man had emigrated to the States at the first signs of antipathy towards the Jews.

The discovery had shocked him. Always disparaging of religion, he had taken Livia for an agnostic, especially since her daughter had been in the care of the nuns. He had imagined that, like him, she had been brought up a Catholic. Snippets of conversation had begun to make sense: her fear of the Fòssoli Concentration Camp; her rush to take Isabella from the Convent when Jews were being rounded up and dispatched to Germany; her intense hatred of the Nazis. The irony was, that in good faith, her companions had given her a Christian burial!

At night, he was consumed with unanswered questions. Why hadn't she told him she was Jewish? Why hadn't she told him about the baby she was expecting? Time and again, he relived the terrible discovery of her torn body in the doorway of the shepherd's hut.

Now, as then, grief persuaded him that the pendant together with the uniform button, were proof that a German had been responsible for her death. She'd tried to wheedle information out of one of the Nazi officers. It was a plan that had gone horribly wrong. The officer must have known she was Jewish. When he'd tried to arrest her, she'd put up a fight. Faced with the prospect of incarceration, she would not have gone quietly. Even now, one thing still mystified him. If *he* hadn't known about her Jewish origins, how had the Germans known? An informer? A rival with a score to settle? A nosy neighbour? The nuns? It was common knowledge that many of the clergy had been fascist sympathisers.

He recalled his first impression of Livia. Proud! Challenging! For a dreadful moment, he pictured her being carted off to Fòssoli, manhandled into a dormitory with other women. Didn't the Nazis shave the heads of Jews in Concentration Camps? Her defiance must have provoked the officer trying to arrest her into pre-empting the shaving policy.

Later that day, when Isabella came to see him, he asked her to hand him his pocket watch.

'It doesn't work, Papà,' she reminded him.
'I know.'
'Would you like me to get it repaired for you?'
'No thank you.' He yawned. 'I'd like to sleep now.'

Isabella kissed his cheek. 'I'll leave you then. Sweet dreams!'

After she'd gone, he prised open the pocket watch and took the trinket out of its hiding place. It had been there for sixteen years. Unable to bring himself to dispose of it, he'd tucked it into the back of the watch, telling himself that one day, he would give it to Isabella. Overcome with emotion, he pressed the pendant to his lips, just as he had done all those years ago.

Guilt weighed heavily on his mind. Had the day of reckoning arrived? Isabella would wonder why he hadn't told her before. Inner torment drained his remaining strength. All these years he had cheated Isabella. He had never told her that her mother was Jewish; he had never shown her the *Star of David* pendant. He hadn't told her that her real father had been killed during the war. He had always intended to reveal the truth when she was old enough to understand, but each passing year had made making the revelation more difficult.

He returned the trinket to its hiding place, then drifted into a restless sleep, to wake up with the conviction that it was now too late to tell her. Emphysema and diabetes had taken their toll. He hadn't the strength or the courage to risk losing Isabella's love during the remaining days of his life.

Gusty October came and went, foggy November followed, the December snows arrived. Isabella talked more and more about Joe. 'I'm trying to persuade him to look for a teaching post in Italy,' she announced one day. 'You'd like that, wouldn't you, Papà?'

Indeed he would, but he knew the time had come to set the record straight. He would reveal the truth, but he would do it posthumously. That evening, he asked Sofia to bring him a pen and some paper.

'Don't tire yourself,' she advised. 'If you want to write a letter, I'm sure Isabella will do it for you. Let me call her.'

He waved Sofia away, gasping out, 'Don't trouble her. I want to do this myself.'

Next morning, Sofia found him dead, a half-written letter on the floor beside him. It was addressed to Stefano Amato.

Thirty-five

Joe flew over to Italy on the first available flight. Isabella met him at the station in Bolzano. She looked pale.

'Papà didn't suffer,' she hastened to assure him. 'But it's odd, he passed away in the middle of writing a letter.' She strode ahead of him to Claudia's old Fiat and, unlocking the door, said nervously, 'I only learned to drive last month; this is the first time Claudia's let me use the car.'

Joe hid his concern. How would she cope with the snow-covered hairpin bends? In the event, she proved to be a competent driver, and he felt more comfortable with her than he had done with Claudia. On arriving at the house, she took him in to see the coffin, and to Joe's relief his father looked at peace. In fact, Joe had to acknowledge that he looked more like the papà he remembered.

'The funeral's been arranged for tomorrow,' said Isabella. 'It doesn't give you much time to settle in, but I thought under the circumstances, you would rather...' At a loss for words, she gazed at him, her eyes filled with tears.

Impulsively, Joe slipped his arm around her and said gently, 'I understand.' Weeping softly, Isabella responded by burying her head in his shoulder. Seconds later, embarrassed by the moment of intimacy, they sprang apart and Joe found himself saying, 'There'll be a lot of things to sort out afterwards, Papà's effects, financial matters, letting people know.'

The burial took place at the cemetery in San Baldino. Joe wondered whether his father would have preferred to be interred in Castagnetto, but it was too late to change the arrangements, and he didn't want to upset his sister. Organizing the funeral must have been distressing for her.

It was a bitterly cold day. A blustery breeze sent wintry clouds scudding across the sky to reveal startling patches of blue. Underfoot, the snow was crisp and dry. White vapour preceded each member of the funeral party as they panted their way up the mountainside to the graveyard. It reminded Joe of a long-forgotten dragon story his mother used to read to him when he was a little boy. He turned to look at Isabella. She was sobbing silently into a handkerchief. Reaching for her hand, he gave it a gentle squeeze.

Claudia had invited a small gathering of local people to the bar of San Baldino's only hotel. Joe and Isabella dutifully thanked everyone for their condolences. At last, the gruelling event was over and the four chief mourners returned to the farmhouse.

Claudia and Sofia went to bed early that night, leaving the two young people alone. As they talked about Vincenzo, Isabella shed a tear or two. Her grief intensified his own. He had barely got to know his father again, only to lose him.

'What are you going to do?' he asked. 'Will you come back here during the holidays?'

She shook her head. 'There's nothing for me here now. Claudia and Sofia are very kind, but they don't really want me around. I shall move all my things down to Florence.' She smiled sadly. 'What about you?'

'I've got to find a new post,' he said. 'I've wasted a lot of time since leaving the States. It's time to get on with my life.'

'I'm sorry your marriage didn't work out, Joe.'

'Don't be,' said Joe emphatically. 'Patricia and I were never meant for one another. I think I always knew that.'

Isabella looked down at the floor. 'I think unfulfilled love is so sad,' she murmured shyly.

'Oh my, what a romantic little sister I've got!'

'Don't tease me,' she protested. Lifting her head, she met his gaze. 'Joe, why don't you come back to Italy?'

He felt touched that she wanted him to return, but his dream of coming back to his place of birth had been abandoned years ago. Giuliana's revelations had dampened his enthusiasm. He frowned thoughtfully. Things were different now.

His sister went on eagerly, 'You could easily find a position in Florence. They're crying out for English-speaking professors. And besides, if you came back you could finish Papà's book.'

'I don't know about that,' gasped Joe. 'I've never thought of myself as a writer.'

'Oh Joe, you could do it if you set your mind to it. And think how much it would have meant to him!'

'I'll give it some thought,' replied Joe uneasily.

All at once, she jumped to her feet and exclaimed, 'I almost forgot. Look!' Delving into her pocket, she brought out a sheet of paper. 'Do you remember I said Papà was writing to someone the night he died. He never finished the letter. It's very mysterious. I don't understand it.' She looked up enquiringly, her dark eyes wide. 'Do you know anybody called Stefano?'

'I don't think so,' he said slowly. He took the sheet of paper from her and read the words aloud: *My dear Stefano, I sincerely trust that you are alive and well. It pains me that we lost touch over the years, and I never thought I would be writing to you in this vein. The truth is, old friend, you were right all along. I should never have cut myself off from the world and from my son. Beppe (or Joe as he now calls himself) has suffered because of my misguided actions.* At this point Joe found the writing almost indecipherable. He frowned and then read on. *As for Isabella, I now realise she must be told the truth...* the letter stopped there.

'What does it mean, Joe?' cried Isabella. 'What must I be told?'

'I've no idea. Did Papà ever mention this man over the years?'

She shook her head. 'I don't think so.'

Joe tapped his forehead with a knuckled fist. 'Just a minute! There was a friend of Papà's who sometimes came to visit us when I was little. He was a doctor. He came to see us once when I had the measles.'

'We must find him,' cried Isabella.

Joe put the letter down on the table, saying with a catch in his voice, 'I suppose I now have the right to claim my title.'

'Oh Joe,' cried his sister. 'How exciting! Will you expect me to curtsey?'

On this light-hearted note, they parted company, but Joe spent a restless night, tossing and turning in his father's bed. On his first night there, sheer exhaustion had guaranteed him a full night's sleep. The second night was different. Fond recollections were interspersed with bitter recriminations. Now that Vincenzo had gone, he felt cheated. It was as if his father had deliberately snatched his adolescence from him. Why had he hidden himself away all those years?

Next morning, he got up feeling tired and angry. When Isabella again suggested that he return to live in Italy, he brushed her aside with, 'Why should I do that? There's nothing here for me now.'

She'd turned away looking crushed, and he felt ashamed of himself. Yet, how could he return to Italy with all its harrowing memories? After that, there was little opportunity to talk to his sister. Isabella had to get back to Florence and he had a plane to catch. At Bolzano Station they parted awkwardly, and as he gave her a farewell hug, he felt her body stiffen.

Isabella watched the train pull out, her eyes glazed, her mouth set in a straight line. When it had disappeared from view, she turned and left the station. The tears she'd been holding back began to flow. Blindly, she ran across the road to the car, wrenched open the door, and got in. Resting her folded arms on the steering wheel, she gave way to despair.

What had made Joe turn against her? Days earlier, despite the sadness of the occasion, they had been able to chat about their papà, share their memories, laugh about them. They had puzzled over the mysterious unfinished letter together. Bleakly, she re-ran their conversations, but could still not fathom the reason for Joe's change of mood. She recalled how irritated he'd seemed when she had suggested he should come to live in Italy. Had she put too much pressure on him? Did he think she was looking to him for financial support? Her cheeks reddened through her tears as she remembered an Americanism she'd heard. He thought she was after a *quick buck!*

A tapping on the car window startled her. It was Sofia. 'Let me in,' she mouthed. Isabella opened the passenger door for her and, after dumping her shopping on the back seat, Sofia climbed in. 'You poor thing,' she exclaimed, putting an arm around the unhappy girl's shoulders. 'You're missing your dear papà.'

Locked in the arms of the kindly Sofia, Isabella gave vent to her grief.

There was a pile of post on the doormat when Joe got home: a couple of bills, a special offer from Readers' Digest, a receipt for a settled account and an offer of employment from a prestigious public school in Edinburgh.

He had attended a second interview for the post shortly before leaving for Italy, and had intended to accept the job should it be offered to him. He re-read the letter. They needed a response immediately. This posed a dilemma, and when his uncle telephoned to enquire how the funeral went off, he found himself discussing his problem with him.

'They want me to start in the Spring Term,' explained Joe. 'That gives me less than a month to sort out papà's papers, and you know how slow those bureaucrats in Rome can be.'

'I don't understand,' said Arthur, sounding puzzled. 'You can make phone calls as easily from Edinburgh as you can from Harrogate.'

Joe hesitated before replying, unwilling to reveal his inner conflict. 'Isabella suggested I look for a job in Italy, apparently they're crying out for English teachers in Florence.' Masking his real reasons behind practicalities, he went on, 'There's the financial side to consider, the drop in salary would be considerable.'

'Your father may have left you some money.'

'I don't think so. You should see the way he was living. Everything of value must have been confiscated by the fascists. As for the villa, it's a mere shell, and the vineyard's completely run down. Don't you remember, I told you about it? All I'll have in the way of an inheritance is the title, and a lot of good that will do me!' He gave a bitter laugh. 'Patricia's the only person who would have been impressed by that.'

'If you really want to go back, you'll find a way, Joe.'

'Not without money,' replied Joe. 'I haven't worked for months. I've been living on my savings. The divorce cost me a fortune.'

'What about the money you got from the sale of your house in Godalming.'

'Patricia took care of that too.'

'Don't lose heart, my boy,' said Arthur finally. 'Things will work out for you.'

That evening, Joe wrote a letter of acceptance to the school in Edinburgh. He stuck a stamp on the envelope and propped it up on the mantelpiece. The decision was made. He'd always liked Scotland. This could be his chance to make a fresh start.

He posted the letter on the way to the newsagents to buy his morning paper. On the way back, he passed the pillar box, pausing to stare at it. Somewhere in there lay the letter containing the key to his future. He shrugged and walked on, then stopped abruptly, overwhelmed by a rush of regret. He didn't want to go to Edinburgh; he wanted to return to Italy, he wanted to start a new life back in the country of his birth. But most of all, he wanted to be close to Isabella.

A post office van drove past him, slowing down to stop beside the pillar box. Joe looked over his shoulder and watched the driver get out, his collecting sack ready. On impulse, he sprinted back along the road, dropping his newspaper en route.

'Wait!' he called out.

The postman looked up enquiringly, holding out his hand for the letter he thought was about to be posted.

'I've made a mistake. There's a letter in there I didn't mean to post,' panted Joe.

'Sorry, once a letter's been posted, I can't hand it back,' replied the man.

'It's vital I get it back, I can tell you the address.'

'Can't do it, chum, it could cost me my job.' The postman turned away, unlocked the box and reached inside.

'I've only just posted it so it'll be right on the top.'

The postman shook his head. 'It's against the rules.'

'This is a matter of life and death!' persisted Joe. Retrieving the letter had by now assumed monumental importance.

The postman turned to face Joe, and said tetchily, 'Didn't you hear me? I said it could cost me my job.'

'It could cost me my life,' announced Joe dramatically. 'There it is!' He pointed and, before the man had time to react, leapt forward and snatched up the nearest envelope.

'Give it here!'

Joe backed away, holding the envelope out of reach. 'This isn't it, but I'll not give it back until you hand over *my* letter. Don't worry, I'll help you look for it.'

With a disgruntled frown, the postman decided to break the stalemate. 'Okay, what's the address?' he demanded. 'I hope you realise this is well out of order.'

Joe reeled off the address. He felt giddy with excitement. He'd never done anything this impulsive in his entire life. At school, he'd obeyed the rules, stood in line, handed in his homework on time. When teaching, he'd followed the curriculum to the letter, had never been known to miss a lecture. Now, here he was being irresponsible and daring. Like Enzo!

'I've got it.'

The postman held up the letter and Joe snatched it from him. 'Thanks, thanks so much,' he mumbled, hurrying away.

'Hey, wait a minute! What about the other letter.'

'Oh sorry,' gasped Joe, retracing his steps and thrusting the envelope into the postman's outstretched hand.

'You've made me late for the rest of my round,' grumbled the other, adding for good measure, 'You're lucky I didn't call the police.'

With a grin of triumph, Joe jogged back along the road, tearing up the letter as he went and scattering the scraps to the winds. Whistling *La donna è mobile* under his breath, he paused briefly to scoop up his discarded newspaper.

Joe spent the next few weeks corresponding with the authorities in Rome. Uppermost in his mind was his claim to the family vineyard in Castagnetto. He was informed that there could be a long delay on the legal side because his father's former partner in the law company had emigrated to the States. They were having difficulty in tracing him. Joe was able to produce the death certificate issued by a doctor in San Baldino but the Registrar insisted on contacting the signatory of the original document issued in 1943, which stated that the count was *missing presumed dead.*

'Who is the signatory?' asked Joe when finally he managed to make contact with the Registrar by telephone.

'Dr Stefano Amato,' came the reply. 'Do you know where he is now?'

'I'm afraid not.'

'Without Dr Amato's verification that your father didn't actually die in 1943, we can do nothing.'

Joe began to lose patience. 'Why not?'

'Our records are incomplete.'

Once more, his enquiries got him nowhere. Time was slipping by with February looming, and Joe was getting desperate for money. He would have to get a job, any job. But his return to Harrogate had convinced him that he really belonged in Italy. Making Castagnetto his home became an obsession, plans began to take shape in his mind. He would realise his boyhood dream. Procrastinating officials, unseen obstacles would not stop him. Opposition fired his determination. He would rebuild the villa and re-establish the vineyard with or without financial support.

In April, infuriated by the bureaucrats in Rome still dragging their heels, Joe packed up his belongings and, with just a few pounds in his pocket, flew to Florence, where he booked into a cheap pensione close to the *Ponte Vecchio*. He decided to surprise Isabella, and a discreet telephone call to the university gave him the information that her last lecture of the day finished at four o'clock.

She came out of the building with a group of friends. His gaze rested on her for several minutes before she saw him. She was wearing blue jeans and a hooded anorak and her dark hair was tied back in a ponytail. A bulging bag hung from her shoulder and there was a bundle of books under her arm. She was chatting animatedly and didn't see him approach.

'Excuse me, miss, may I carry your books?' he asked with a grin.

She twirled around in surprise, dropping the books as she flung her arms about his neck. 'Joe, how marvellous to see you!'

Her delight almost overwhelmed him. Eventually, she released him and turned to her friends. 'This is my brother, Joe.'

They nodded politely, and after exchanging a few words, went on their way.

'Let's go for a drink,' he suggested as they both stooped to retrieve her books.

She smiled her agreement. 'Oh Joe, I'm so pleased you're here.'

'Me too,'

They chose a table outside a café and Joe ordered *Amaretti* and lemon tea. He couldn't help noticing how hungry his sister was. 'Would you like some more?' he asked.

She looked somewhat embarrassed then admitted, 'Yes please. This is the first thing I've eaten today.'

'Why's that?'

She looked down at her hands and murmured, 'I guess I wasn't hungry until now.'

Not wishing to further embarrass her, Joe called the waitress and ordered more tea and a large slice of *Torta di Mela*.

'Tell me all your news,' said Isabella, tucking into the cake. 'I can't wait to hear what you've been up to.'

He told her about rejecting the job offer in Scotland, and about his lack of progress with the release of his inheritance, mentioning the need for verification from Stefano Amato.

'Why, that was the man Papà was writing to when he died!'

'Yes, I know, but how do we find him?'

'We could advertise.'

'He may be dead.'

'Don't be such a pessimist!' scoffed Isabella.

Joe grinned. 'Let's start in Castagnetto. Are you doing anything at the weekend?'

'I'm free on Sunday.'

'Good, if we catch the early bus we can be there by midmorning.' Joe heaved a sigh. 'You know, back in '54, I vowed I'd never go back there, now I've decided I want to make Castagnetto my home.'

Isabella's eyes glowed with interest. 'Truly?'

Joe nodded, taking time to study her face. 'You look happy,' he said. 'You're obviously enjoying university life. Have you got a boyfriend?'

'Sort of.' Joe felt a wrench at his stomach. She hurried on. 'It's not serious. What about you, have you met anybody?'

Joe rocked back in his chair. 'Me? Who would look at a loser like me? No money, no job, no prospects.'

'Don't put yourself down, Joe.'

He looked at her sharply. She meant it. She admired him. He felt flattered.

After leaving the café, he escorted her back to her digs, a small rented room on the fourth floor overlooking the Gherardesca Gardens. 'This is nice,' he said. 'My digs in Oxford weren't nearly as good as this.'

Isabella wrinkled her nose. 'Trouble is, my landlady's awfully strict. She won't allow visitors.'

'Why didn't you say so?' said Joe, his innate respect for rules and regulations rising to the fore. 'I'd better leave. I'd hate to get you into trouble.'

'Don't be silly. You're my brother. That doesn't count.'

That evening they went to a nearby trattoria.

'Do you like pasta?' she asked.

'Of course I do.'

'But weren't you brought up on roast beef and Yorkshire pudding?'

'We didn't get much roast beef during the War.'

'Fish and chips?'

'Sometimes, as a treat,' laughed Joe.

'Tell me what it was like living in England?'

He described life with the McPherson-Corke's, making light of his loneliness, joking about his unruly cousins.

'You lost your mother when you were quite young, didn't you, Joe?'

'Not as young as you were when your mother died.'

'I never really knew her, but Papà said she was very beautiful.'

'Like her daughter.'

A blush rose to Isabella's cheeks. 'You're teasing me.'

'I meant it. You're the most beautiful girl I've ever set eyes on.' The words were out before he could stop them.

She narrowed her eyes and said curtly, 'More beautiful than your ex-wife?' Her reply startled Joe. What was he thinking of, flirting with his half-sister? She spoke again. 'I'm sorry I shouldn't have said that; you don't want to be reminded of Patricia.'

The evening ended awkwardly, and they parted with a handshake at the door of her digs.

'You *are* coming to Castagnetto on Sunday, aren't you?' he asked.

'I said I would, so I will.'

'You don't have to.'

She was immediately on the defensive. 'Don't you want me to?'

He shrugged, unable to find the words to restore their relationship to the way it had been before. 'Of course I do. I'm going to catch the nine o'clock bus from *Piazza della Stazione.*'

He walked back to his lodgings with his head bowed and his hands shoved deep into his pockets. Coming back had been a mistake. Isabella was his sister, the feelings he harboured for her were indecent. At home in Harrogate, he hadn't acknowledged these sentiments as anything more than brotherly affection. He knew now that what he felt was far stronger: he was in love with her.

The next day, Joe got up early and made his way to *Piazza della Stazione*. The bus was waiting at the terminus so he boarded it, sitting at the back and gazing despondently out of the window. There was no sign of Isabella. He was convinced she wasn't coming; he'd frightened her off with his misplaced compliments.

On leaving England, he'd been positive that his decision to return to his native land had been the right one. Now, he was beset with doubts. How foolish he'd been to relinquish the job offer in Edinburgh! So keen was his feeling of regret that had the bus not filled up, with passengers standing in the aisle, he would have got off and hurried back to his lodgings to pack up and leave Florence. It was hot in the crowded bus. He rolled up his shirt sleeves and wiped his forehead with a handkerchief. The driver climbed aboard, and switched on the ignition.

'Wait!'

The driver slowed down and pressed the button to open the doors. All heads turned to look at the latecomer. Isabella got in, her shoulder bag swinging off her arm, her face pink from having run across the square. Joe's spirits soared, his misgivings forgotten. Leaping to his feet, he pushed his way to the front of the bus. 'You've come!'

She nodded, pushing a lock of hair back from her face. The bus pulled away from the kerb, and they were thrown against one another as it lurched around a corner, his bare arm coming into contact with hers. She giggled and clutched his wrist for support. The touch of her fingers made his flesh tingle; he caught a waft of her perfume and felt intoxicated. The bus lurched again, and their foreheads almost touched. He stared into her dark eyes and saw...saw what? Her expression was unfathomable. He found it disturbing.

The bus had almost emptied by the time they reached their destination. It stopped outside Comolli's Bar where the remaining passengers and the driver got out and went inside the café.

'Let's have a cup of coffee first,' suggested Joe. 'Then we can go on and take a look at the villa.'

Aldo Comolli, who'd put on even more weight in the eight years since Joe had seen him, was busy behind the bar. He greeted his customers jovially, exchanging a joke or two with the bus driver. When he saw Joe, his mouth fell open. 'My, my, so you've come back, welcome *Signor Conte*!'

Joe grinned with genuine pleasure when Comolli came round from behind the counter and took him in a bear-like hug.

'It's good to see you, Aldo,' he said.

'And where is the beautiful contessa?'

'In America.'

'America huh! So that's where you live now.' He smiled at Isabella, looking somewhat puzzled, and said, 'Aren't you going to introduce me to this young lady?'

'Of course, I'm sorry. This is my sister, Isabella.'

Looking puzzled, Comolli took Isabella's hand and kissed it gallantly. 'A pleasure, *signorina*. Please take a seat. A drink? It's on the house.'

When Comolli went back behind the bar, Joe turned to Isabella. 'He didn't seem to know about you.'

'I never came down to the village,' she explained. 'Papà wouldn't let me. I suppose he thought it was too dangerous with all those German soldiers milling around.' She sighed. 'He was always over-protective. After all, they were only ordinary conscripted men with families back home in Germany.'

Comolli returned with two campari sodas and a dish of olives. He sat down at their table, and Joe took the opportunity to ask about Stefano Amato.

'Does the doctor still live in the village?' he asked.

'The good doctor!' Aldo Comolli raised bushy eyebrows and gave a shrug. 'He left Castagnetto years ago, I don't know where he went. He had a sister in Milan, but she died.'

'Was he married?'

'Widowed; I believe he has a son.'

'Is there anybody in the village who would know where we could find him?'

The bartender frowned thoughtfully, then shook his head. 'It's all so long ago. Anyone who might have known him has long since died or gone away. I'm sorry, I can't help you.'

They'd drawn a blank. Joe felt disappointed.

'Never mind,' said Isabella. 'Let's go and look at the villa.'

'The tree house is still here!' exclaimed Joe, as they approached the property. He strode ahead to stand underneath it, pointing up at it's high branches. 'I spent many happy hours hiding up there when I was a little boy.'

'It's special for you?'

'Indeed it is.'

Joe experienced a surge of nostalgia. Eight years ago he'd entered the ruins of the house he'd grown up in with the woman he'd intended to spend the rest of his life with. He frowned at the memory. Patricia had not been interested; her thoughts had been on the shopping expedition planned for the next day. With hindsight, he saw how shallow she was. Had he really loved her or had it been mere infatuation?

Isabella felt for his hand and pulled him across the threshold. The place had fallen into further decay, with grass and weeds growing over all exposed areas. The once splendid staircase was covered in moss, birds were nesting in the walls.

'It must have been magnificent,' sighed Isabella. Releasing her hand from his, she ran into one of the rooms. 'Let me guess, this is the dining room?'

'Yes.' Joe pointed. 'And that's a little side room where my mother liked to sit and read.' With a flash of recall, he saw again Enzo's coffin resting on its bier in the window recess, the morning sunlight rising behind it.

'You can re-build it.' Isabella's excitement transmitted to Joe.

'I would like to think so,' he murmured.

'Yes Joe, you can come and live here, restore the vineyard, make it into a thriving business again.'

Excitement brought colour to her cheeks. If only he could share her naive certainty! But the reality added up to *money* and, as yet, he had none. His earlier determination to rebuild the villa and vineyard seemed to have trickled away, and he found himself making excuses.

'I don't know about that. I have to think about the future. The divorce was expensive; Patricia's alimony is costing me a fortune. I've got to start earning a living. I ought to go back to England and look for a job.'

Isabella's face crumpled. 'No! You're the only family I have.' She grasped his hand and squeezed his fingers. 'Don't abandon me.'

He shook her off as gently as he could. 'It's no good, I can't stay in Italy. Even with financial backing, re-building the villa and restoring the vineyard would be a mammoth task. I've no experience in these things and without funds, it's impossible.'

'But there may be some money. Now you're here, why not go down to Rome and see one of the partners in person? It's easier to resolve problems face to face. I'm sure there'd be someone in the company who would be able to help you.'

He shook his head and said curtly, 'The bus will be leaving soon, we must get back to Comolli's.'

On the way back to the village, Isabella insisted. 'You can't leave Italy without even trying to find out.'

At first he argued, but eventually, worn down by her persistence, he agreed to take the train down to Rome the next day.

Thirty-six

Joe came out of Rome Termini Station and took a taxi to a modest hotel in *Via Calabria*, where he off-loaded his suitcase and went out again. There was no point in wasting time. Following Isabella's advice, he didn't telephone the law company in advance. 'Surprise will give you the edge,' she'd said. 'They won't be able to fob you off.'

He took his father's valid death certificate and his own passport, as proof of identity, and walked the short distance to *Via del Quirinale*. The offices of *D'Onofrio, Cacioppo* & *Brazzi* were well-appointed; the receptionist seated behind a large electric typewriter looked somewhat officious.

'None of the partners will see you without an appointment,' she stated. 'If you give me your name, I can book you in to see Signor Brazzi one day next week.'

'That's no good, I'm afraid,' said Joe. 'I need to see someone today.'

Joe felt his irritation rising when the girl pursed her lips and cast her eyes ever so slightly heaven-wise. 'Tch, tch,' she said. 'That's impossible, Signor Brazzi is tied up all day. He's a very busy man.'

'What about one of the other partners?'

'Both our senior partners are in meetings.' She squared her shoulders. 'An appointment is essential. Do you want me to fix you up with one or not?'

Joe glanced up above the girl's head. 'That's my grandfather,' he said, pointing at a brass plaque screwed in place on the wall. The receptionist twisted around to look at the plaque, which named the founders of the company back in 1906. 'My name is Count Giuseppe Di Tomasi.'

'Show me proof of identity,' she scoffed.

Joe produced his British passport, which she flipped open at the first page. Her confidence restored, she looked up and said, 'This says you're Joseph Thomas.'

'During the War I was sent to live in England. My headmaster made me anglicize my name. Here's my birth certificate.'

Still unconvinced, she slid the documents back at him across the polished desk with the words, 'These don't prove anything.'

Joe drew out the death certificate. 'This might.'

She took it from him, frowning in puzzlement. A door opened and a man of about his own age came out. Noticing the girl's confusion, he came over and asked, 'Is there a problem, Rosina?'

Joe took to the man at once. He had a pleasing and unhurried manner. The receptionist explained. 'This gentleman insists on an immediate appointment. I'm only following Signor Cacioppo's instructions. He said clients must make an appointment at least a week in advance.' She shot a hostile glance at Joe, but conceded, 'Although this does seem to be a rather special case.'

'May I see that document please.'

She handed over Vincenzo's death certificate. 'I don't understand, Signor Brazzi, this gentleman says he's the deceased's son but he has a different name.'

Joe proffered a hand to shake. 'Joseph Thomas aka Count Giuseppe Di Tomasi.'

The lawyer glanced at the name on the death certificate. Meeting Joe's gaze, he said, 'You'd better step into my office, sir.'

Joe sat down in a comfortable armchair and waited while the other man took his seat behind a leather-topped desk. His hopes rose. After months of time-consuming correspondence and unsuccessful telephone calls, it seemed someone was prepared to listen to him.

Brazzi spoke. 'Perhaps you'd better explain what this is all about.'

Joe explained why he'd been brought up in England. He went on to describe the reunion with his father, and the circumstances surrounding his death. He also described the difficulties he had encountered with the authorities in Rome, including the problems in tracing his father's old partner, Giacomo Tobino.

'Giacomo Tobino is my uncle,' said Brazzi. 'He retired to the United States some years ago. Went to live near the Canadian border. He doesn't keep in touch. He must be well over eighty now. The last I heard was that he's suffering from senile dementia. That may explain the difficulty you've had in contacting him.' An amused smile twitched at the corners of his mouth. 'As for my partners, I'm afraid they're rather old-fashioned. I'm the new boy on the block and I don't always get a say on what's going on.' He heaved a resigned sigh. 'I'm biding my time, they're both due for retirement in a year or two.'

'I see,' smiled Joe, warming even more to the man facing him. 'Is my father's Will in your safekeeping?'

'I'm sure it is.' Brazzi pressed a button on his desk and spoke into the intercom. 'Rosina, please go down to the basement and look for the files on Count Vincenzo Di Tomasi.'

'Signor Cacioppo told me not to leave Reception unmanned.'

Joe smiled as the lawyer drew in a deep breath. 'I'm overriding those instructions,' he said calmly. 'If anybody comes in they can ring the bell on your desk and one of the typists will attend to them. And, by the way, cancel my two o'clock appointment with Mr and Mrs Donato.'

The intercom clicked off and he turned back to Joe. 'I'm afraid this may take some time, would you care for...' He paused, then continued with a twinkle in his eye. '...what I believe the English call, a spot of lunch?'

When the two men returned to the office, there was a pile of dusty folders on the desk.

'This looks promising,' smiled the lawyer. 'Why don't we split the files. You look through that lot, I'll take these.'

They spent the afternoon, scrutinising the yellowing pages. The hours ticked by and it was six o'clock before anything useful came to light.

'Here we are!' Brazzi gave the desk a triumphant slap with the palm of his hand. He twisted the file round for Joe to read. It contained a letter from Dr Stefano Amato addressed to Lorenzo Brazzi's uncle, dated 1943. Attached to it was the Last Will and Testament of Count Vincenzo Giuseppe Luigi Di

Tomasi. The letter informed the law company that the Count was *missing presumed dead* after an explosion at his villa in the village of Castagnetto.

Joe's grin reached from ear to ear. 'I can't thank you enough,' he said. 'Let me take you out to dinner to celebrate.'

The lawyer glanced at his watch. 'Thank you, but I must get home to my family,' he said. 'Come back tomorrow and we'll go through the finer details.'

The next day brought more surprises. Brazzi greeted Joe enthusiastically. 'I've uncovered a few things,' he said.

'Good news?'

'Good and bad,' replied the lawyer. 'Your father's estate is tied up in investments and property. You can, of course, sell some of it off, but there are no immediate funds at your disposal.' His eyes twinkled as he added, 'You have a considerable interest in this company, although I imagine, since you're not a lawyer you may wish to pull out.' He proceeded to reel off a list of Vincenzo's business interests, all of which would incur lengthy negotiation to unravel.

Joe was dumbfounded. Brazzi went on to explain that most of his father's fluid fortune had been lost with the destruction of the vineyard. 'Although,' he explained. 'Over the years, he transferred considerable sums of money to an unknown account. Do you know anything about it?'

Joe shook his head. 'To tell you the truth, Lorenzo, I'm a simple soul, not at all money-orientated. Making a fortune has never been my top priority.' He gave a grim smile. 'Although, of course, it was *always* at the top of my ex-wife's list.'

Brazzi thumbed through the files in front of him. 'After your father's reported demise, my uncle looked into the whereabouts of this secret account, but came up with nothing. I'll set up another search if you like.' He leant forward over the desk. 'Think back, Joe, did your father ever mention foreign investments or a Swiss Bank Account?'

Joe shook his head. 'No. Oh dear, I was hoping to rebuild the villa and the vineyard; for my half-sister,' he added hastily.

'Your half-sister?'

'Yes, my father had a mistress… Joe felt his face begin to flush. 'A woman he met during his association with the Resistance.'

'Your father was involved with the Resistance?'

'My papà wasn't a communist,' Joe hastened to explain.

Brazzi laughed. 'The War's over, Joe, people are more liberal these days, although I must admit, this may explain a lot of things. How old is your sister?'

'She's 18. She's studying art at the University of Florence. The vineyard would give her a steady income because, let's face it, working as an artist can be very unstable. I don't want her being hard up. Her allowance ceased with Papà's death and she's been getting by on very little money.'

'Well,' said the lawyer. 'The account number must be amongst your father's things, I suggest you go home and take a good look through them.'

'We made a thorough search when we were looking for Dr Amato's address,' replied Joe.

'Amato's address? I may be able to help you with that.' Lorenzo Brazzi plucked a card from an index card system on his desk and handed it to Joe. 'This is the doctor's last known address. Of course, he may have moved on since then.'

'Thank you very much, I'll look him up,' said Joe.

He spent the train journey back to Florence staring out of the window, deep in contemplation. He knew what he wanted to do. Once funds were available, he would rebuild the villa and the vineyard. The restoration work could be placed in the hands of local builders and vine-growers. He would return to England and supervise the work from there and, once Isabella finished her studies, she could make the villa her home.

'Is it good news?' demanded Isabella when Joe called to see her the next day.

'I don't know about good,' he replied. 'But you were right. Going to Rome saved a lot of time.'

When he didn't explain further, she burst out, 'What happened? For goodness sake, Joe, don't keep me in suspense.'

He chose his words carefully. He didn't want her getting carried away by enthusiasm. 'I've located Papà's Will.'

'Oh Joe, that means you'll inherit.'

'Not so fast! There are drawbacks.' He went on to describe his meeting with Lorenzo Brazzi, deliberately keeping his voice even. 'All Papà's assets in Italy are tied up. Lorenzo says it will take years to free them, but he thinks there's money in a Swiss Bank Account.'

Isabella's eyes lit up. 'You'll be able to rebuild your villa after all.' When he responded with a frown, she demanded, 'Tell me the down side.'

'Lorenzo Brazzi doesn't know the entry code. I can't get at the money.'

Isabella looked defiant. 'That won't stop you. If you go in person to the bank with proof of identity, they'll release the funds to you.'

Joe's mouth twitched with amusement. 'It doesn't work like that, *tesoro*.' The tender word passed his lips unintentionally, prompting hesitation. What was he saying? Isabella was his sister, not his sweetheart.

A perplexed frown puckered Isabella's brow, but Joe soon realised it was nothing to do with the endearment he'd let slip. 'Maybe that's what *Papà* was writing to Dr Amato about. He must have realised I can't finish my course without funds.'

'What d'you mean?'

'I've used up all my savings. I can't afford food and board let alone study expenses.'

Joe looked alarmed. 'How have you been managing?'

'I've been working in a shop in my spare time and my friends have helped me out, but next term I'll need new books and materials.'

'Why didn't you write and tell me?'

'I didn't want to worry you. Besides, what could you have done? You were between jobs yourself.'

This was true. Joe felt a tweak of conscience. Here he was, jobless in Florence, when he could be settled in a teaching job in Edinburgh receiving a regular salary.

Isabella broke into his thoughts. 'We must get hold of that money so that you can rebuild the villa. It's your inheritance, Joe, you can't let it go.'

He caught her hand, touched by her concern. 'It's yours too, you've as much right to it as I have.'

She shook her head. 'No, you're the legitimate heir, I'm only a...a love child.' As she turned away, he caught a glimpse of the blush that rose to her cheeks.

To ease the tension building between them, he said, 'Brazzi gave me Amato's last known address.'

Isabella's eyes lit up. 'What are we waiting for? Let's write to him!'

'I will, but don't build up your hopes too much, he may have moved away, or even died.' He drew a piece of paper from his pocket. 'It's not far from here. '

'We could go and see him. This is so exciting. I can't wait to hear what he's supposed to tell me.' She ran across the room, pulled open a drawer and took out their father's letter.

'I think we ought to write and warn him of our visit, not just turn up on his doorstep,' Joe advised her.

Two weeks later when there was no reply from Dr Amato, Joe began to lose hope. The doctor seemed to be the only link to the funds stashed away in Switzerland. Isabella remained optimistic, finding encouraging words. 'Write again. Suggest a date for a visit. That may prod him into replying.'

When the second letter brought no response, she said, 'We'll just have to go and knock on his door. Even if he's moved, someone there might know where he's gone.'

'He's probably passed over.'

Isabella refused to accept this pessimistic view. 'There might be a perfectly plausible reason for him not being there. Besides, he may have relatives, sons or daughters.'

To placate his sister, Joe agreed to visit the house in Borgo San Lorenzo, although he felt certain it would be a waste of time. As they boarded the bus to go there, he checked that she'd remembered to bring their father's letter with her.

She looked at him scornfully. 'As if I'd forget it!'

But the trip proved disappointing. The house was locked up, all windows shuttered. Suppressing a sob, Isabella muttered, 'I so much wanted to meet Dr Amato, I wonder what he is supposed to tell me.'

The visit destroyed her hopes. On the way back, she hardly spoke a word. On reaching her digs, Joe felt reluctant to leave her alone. He cast her a covert glance, reminded that learning the meaning of their father's unfinished letter was more important to her than the discovery of the missing code numbers. He tried to comfort her, saying with more confidence than he felt, 'I'll think of something. Don't worry, we'll catch up with him eventually.'

When she still looked downcast, he put his finger under her chin and tipped her face up towards him. She looked so young, reminding him that she was eleven years his junior.

'I know I'm being silly,' she whispered. 'But somehow I feel it's important.'

Once again, he caught a waft of her perfume as her dark hair brushed against his cheek. His hand tightened on her arm as she drew closer and, without knowing how, he found his lips touching hers. Starting as a gesture of affection the kiss somehow became more meaningful. Before he could stop himself, he was kissing her fiercely. And she was responding.

Abruptly, he leapt away from her, gasping, 'I'm sorry, I'm so sorry,' mortified by what had happened.

The expression on her face was one of astonishment, but it swiftly changed to alarm. 'Oh Joe, this can't be!'

The shock of their moment of intimacy made his cheeks burn. He knuckled a fist and pressed it to his forehead. He had to leave, he put distance between them. Curt words spilled from his lips. 'I must get out of here.'

'I don't understand…'

'I need to make a phone call.' He snatched up his jacket and hurried to the door.

'Wait!' cried Isabella, hurrying after him. He ignored her and taking the stairs two at a time, dashed out of the building.

The next morning he called her, and after an awkward exchange of greetings, said, 'I'm leaving for England.'

'Come and see me before you go,' she begged. 'Meet me for coffee at that café near your pensione.'

He could hear the tremble in her voice, and replied hoarsely, 'There's not time.'

'Have you booked your flight?'

'Not yet, but I'm going to take the first one available.'

'Let's meet for half an hour, Joe.'

His grip on the telephone tightened, and he found himself shaking his head vehemently although he knew she couldn't see him. 'We can't meet again, Isabella.'

'You can't abandon me. What about our enquiries? Please, Joe, you've got to help me find Dr Amato. It's so important to me.'

Joe fought to keep his emotions under control. 'I'm not abandoning you. I'll see you're all right. I'll get a job and send you money regularly so that you can continue your course.'

All at once, Isabella lost her temper. 'To hell with my course! I don't want money from you, I want you to stay. I want you here in Florence.'

Joe had never heard her so assertive. She had always appeared gentle and sweet-natured. This forceful side was new to him. He tried to explain. 'Don't you see, we can't let this happen.'

Isabella's voice rose. 'It won't happen again, we were carried away by the moment. It was a foolish impulse. Stay, Joe, please, I can't bear you to leave, please don't go!'

Joe's emotions were in turmoil. He was in love with her. If he didn't leave, things would get out of hand. It was better to hurt her now than to cause her greater heartache further down the line. 'I have no choice,' he said, adding more gently, 'You'll come to understand that it's for the best. Take care, Isabella. I'll write to you.'

Replacing the receiver Joe stood for several minutes thinking about their conversation. Had he been too hard on her? Meeting her once more could do no harm. He frowned. No, it was too late. Picking up the phone again, he dialled the airline and booked his ticket home for the following day.

It was an evening flight, giving him all day with nothing to do. He checked out of the pensione, leaving his luggage in the hallway for collection later, and spent the day walking the streets. Skipping breakfast and lunch, he stopped occasionally to drink an *espresso* and a *grappa* at a bar. At four o'clock he returned to collect his bags.

Tied to the handle of his hold-all was a note from Isabella. It was brief: *Stefano Amato has been in touch; please, please come with me to see him. Isabella.*

For several seconds, Joe stared at the note, then he looked at his watch. It was nearly time to check in. He would phone his sister from the airport saying that his flight was about to take off. He picked up his bags and went out into the street to hail a taxi.

Thirty-seven

Isabella paced the floor of her room. She tried phoning Joe, but the pensione proprietor told her he had paid his bill and checked out, adding that he'd left his bags in the hallway for collection later.

She went to the pensione and waited beside his luggage for two hours, missing an important lecture. But a two o'clock interview with one of her tutors couldn't be shelved. She left it until the last minute, running all the way to the university with little time to spare. Before leaving, she scrabbled in her bag for paper and pencil, writing Joe a note and tying it to the handle of his hold-all.

As she elbowed her way through the afternoon shoppers, she told herself that if he didn't respond, she would never bother with him again. The kiss had alarmed her too, but she was positive she could push the incident aside. If *she* could do that, why couldn't he?

Her interview didn't go well. She couldn't concentrate, and her tutor became impatient. She left his rooms feeling despondent. Everything was going wrong. It would have been better if Joe had never returned to Italy. He was right, they were playing a dangerous game. What if things got out of hand? Incest! The very word appalled her. Back in the sanctuary of her room, she allowed her emotions to gush forth.

She loved Joe; he was her brother. But he didn't seem like a brother. Was it because she had only known him for a couple of years? If they had grown up together as siblings normally did, would her feelings have been so intense? She gave an involuntary shudder. Only a pervert would fall in love with her brother!

A rush of panic engulfed her. There was another possibility. Perhaps she had made a fool of herself, mistaken affection for passion. In that case, why would he be in such a hurry to leave? Earlier in the day, she'd phoned the airport to enquire about his flight. She glanced at her watch, and began to regret leaving the letter; perhaps there was still time to retrieve it.

She sank onto a chair and, with her arms folded across her body, rocked in an agony of indecision. She wanted Joe to go with her to see Dr Amato. Anger overrode despair. Surely it wouldn't hurt him to do this one last thing for her! The contents of Vincenzo's letter had troubled her. She was truly nervous about meeting the doctor on her own. She consulted her watch again. Joe must be boarding the plane now.

The taxi drew up outside his sister's digs and Joe got out, hauling his hold-all after him. He knew that what he was doing was madness. He would miss his plane; he would be obliged to find another room for the night; he would be faced with emotional upheaval yet again when he saw Isabella. Notwithstanding this, he felt as if he was on an unstoppable downhill ride, and the only option was to go with its momentum.

He rang the doorbell and Isabella let him in. 'Joe! I thought you weren't coming.' Her eyes lit up but she stood back as if afraid to get too close. 'Dr Amato phoned me; he's invited me up to his house for drinks this evening.' Her brow furrowed anxiously. 'You will come with me, won't you?'

'That's why I've come back. What time is he expecting you?'
'Six o'clock.'

He glanced at the clock and saw that it was already ten past five. Good, that gave no time for inconsequential dialogue. 'We'd better get going,' he said. 'Can I leave my bags here?'

After a poor attempt at light conversation, they fell silent. Joe noticed that Isabella sat well away from him on the bus seat. They got off and walked the short distance to Dr Amato's house. It looked more welcoming this time. The shutters were open and the place had an air of occupancy. A middle-aged woman answered the door and invited them to wait in a large cool sitting room with french doors opening onto a courtyard garden.

Dr Stefano Amato came in, preceded by a small brown and white dog, which barked madly as it circled their legs, its tail wagging furiously.

'Don't worry,' said the doctor when Isabella looked nervous. 'He's not vicious.'

Having ascertained that the newcomers were friendly, the little dog ran out into the courtyard.

'Do sit down. I'm sorry I haven't answered your letters, I've been staying with my son in France,' said their white-haired host, moving about the room with the aid of a silver-knobbed walking stick. 'Can I offer you a drink?'

The niceties dispensed with, he smiled and sat down opposite them. Addressing Isabella, he said, 'I was sorry to hear about your father. We were great friends, Vincenzo and I.' He shifted his gaze to Joe and asked, 'Is this your boyfriend?'

Clearly, the man had not recognised Joe, and his mistaken assumption made both his visitors give a guilty start.

'No, this is my brother, Joe,' gasped Isabella. "You may remember him as Beppe.'

'Beppe! Well, this is a surprise. So you're called Joe now."

"Yes, I've been Joe since I was nine."

"Well, well, I'm delighted to see you've met up with one another. Does this mean you saw your father before he died?'

'Yes,' replied Joe. 'But sadly, only once, in '59. Papà died last year.' He felt the anger rising as he studied the quietly spoken old man. If the doctor had got in touch with him in England, he would have been re-united earlier. All those lost years!

Noticing Joe's irritation, Amato said, 'Vincenzo swore me to secrecy and there was no way I would betray an old friend. How did you trace me?'

Joe explained how he'd called on *D'Onofrio, Cacioppo & Brazzi* in Rome, and learned that the way in which his father's fortune was tied up was complex. 'I had hoped to rebuild the villa, but Lorenzo Brazzi says it's going to take a long time to release monies; possibly many years,' he explained. He spread his hands. 'Without funds, I can do nothing.'

A broad smile spread across the doctor's lined face. 'There are funds,' he said. 'And I can give you access to them. You *will* be able to rebuild the Estate.'

Isabella wriggled excitedly. 'There you are, Joe, what did I tell you?'

Amato went on. 'Your father entrusted me with his Swiss bank account number in case he should pass away before me.' He heaved a sigh. 'What a pity I never got to see my old friend again. He suffered so much. Tell me, was the end sudden?'

'It happened sooner than anticipated,' replied Isabella. 'But I think he died peacefully.' Delving into her bag, Isabella brought out Vincenzo's letter. 'Papà started writing to you, but never finished the letter,' she explained. 'That's why we got in touch. We thought you ought to see it because there's a bit of a mystery about it. Perhaps you'll understand what Papà was trying to say.'

The doctor took a pair of reading spectacles out of his pocket and studied Vincenzo's last words. With a frown puckering his brow, he read aloud, '*As for Isabella, she must be told the truth*....I see.'

The girl leant anxiously forward in her chair. 'Can you throw any light on it?'

The old man looked up from the letter and studied them as if deciding what to do. 'You're fond of one another, aren't you?' he said at last.

'Of course we are.'

'And you've kept in touch with one another?'

'Yes, we've been corresponding ever since Joe's first visit,' replied Isabella.

'Did your father know this?'

What a strange question, thought Joe, exchanging a puzzled glance with his sister.

'Of course he knew. It wasn't a secret. He was pleased. After all, he drew us together,' said Isabella.

'For many years, he kept you apart.,' stated the doctor.

Joe resented Amato's claim. What right had the man to pass judgement? He gave voice to his indignation. 'Papà must have had his reasons: the shock of losing his leg, the separation from my mother and me, not knowing what had happened to us. Clearly, he was afraid we wouldn't accept his terrible disability. He must have lost the will to live. How was he to know it wouldn't have made any difference to us?'

Amato waited patiently for Joe to finish. 'I disagreed with your father's decision,' he said gently. 'But he was adamant. He thought it would be best for everyone concerned. He swore me to secrecy, and I'd never betray a friend.'

Joe experienced a rush of guilt. What had prompted him into giving vent to such a diatribe? The doctor was only expressing his concern. A lump rose in his throat as he glanced at Isabella. It would have been closer to the truth to conjecture that Vincenzo had lost the will to live when Livia died.

'Another drink?' Joe and Isabella both shook their heads at their host's offer. 'I have a rather long story to tell you,' he went on.

The evening shadows gathered as Stefano Amato described Vincenzo and Livia's courage and suffering throughout the summer of 1943. During the telling of the story, Joe realised that his father had omitted a great many details from his own explanations.

'They were both so brave,' murmured Isabella.

'Indeed, they were.'

'Did they ever find the German soldiers responsible for my mother's death?'

Dr Amato hesitated before replying. 'I was hoping you wouldn't ask me that?' he said. 'But since you are both intelligent young people who want to know the truth, I shan't keep it from you. Years later I learnt ... ' He paused and closed his eyes as if marshalling his thoughts. 'The appalling truth is, Livia was killed by the villagers.'

'What?' cried Joe and Isabella together.

Unconsciously, Stefano Amato placed his hands together as if in prayer, looking down at the carpet under his feet. 'On that fateful evening, Livia went down to Comolli's Bar intending to try and wheedle information out of one of the German officers. She told no one of her plan.' He diverged a little. 'The villagers, especially the women, were suspicious of her: a beautiful, young woman appearing in their midst! Livia was different, more sophisticated than they were, a woman of the world. They envied her, and they hated their men-folk ogling her.' He shook his head and looked up. 'I digress ... a Nazi officer was killed that night. No one knows for sure whether Livia killed him, but old Comolli did see them leave the bar together.'

'Surely she would have told Papà what happened?' burst out Joe.

'Vincenzo never saw her again.'

'I don't understand,' whispered Isabella.

'She was accosted on the way back to Grazia Elena's cottage. We found her dying in the doorway of a shepherd's hut. Her head had been shaved.'

'Oh no!' Isabella buried her face in her hands and began to sob. 'She had such beautiful hair.'

Joe turned to stare at her. 'You do remember her.'

She nodded without replying.

The doctor went on. 'Your father wouldn't accept that the villagers had done that to her, but peasant women are strong-minded. It wasn't difficult for them to convince the old boys and the teenagers -- don't forget, most of the working men had gone off to War -- into believing that Livia was a collaborator.'

Joe cast their host a warning glance, as he reached out a hand to touch Isabella's.

Dr Amato cleared his throat and said, 'Ahime! Those were terrible times. She died as a result of their maltreatment. Once they learned the truth, the villagers mourned for her. Their shame cast a shadow over Castagnetto, a shadow that has only lifted with the arrival of a new generation. What they did was cruel and wicked. Collective guilt has been their punishment.' He paused, moved by Isabella's distress and Joe's concern.

'This has come as a terrible shock,' said Joe.

Amato nodded. 'There is one more thing you should know, and I think this could be welcome news.' He took off his glasses and rubbed an eye. 'I believe the words in Vincenzo's letter refer to what I'm about to divulge.'

Joe felt a cold shiver run down his spine. What more revelations could there possibly be? He squeezed Isabella's hand.

Amato spoke slowly. 'You two are not related.'

Joe released the girl's hand and sprang to his feet. 'What do you mean?'

The old man smiled. 'Isabella, my dear, Vincenzo was not your real papà. Your real father died early on in the War.'

'But, but ... '

Joe sat down again as the doctor held up his hands to curb the girl's questions. 'After your dear mother died Vincenzo decided to bring you up as his own daughter, and when the opportunity to move up to San Baldino arose, he looked on it as destiny. You see, your real father was from that region.'

Amato fell silent, studying his visitors over the top of his glasses. Joe stared back at him. 'Are you certain about this?' he asked, his voice sounding strange to his own ears.

'Absolutely.'

Joe felt for Isabella's hand again, repeating her name in his head. Isabella! The same name as his real little sister. What an odd coincidence?

'I believe this news has pleased you, despite the shock,' observed the doctor.

'Hmm, it will take time to digest,' replied Joe. Practical thoughts were racing around his head. 'As I understand it, *Dottore*, you falsified my father's death certificate. This could get you into trouble if the truth came out. How do you feel about that?'

'At my age, I'm not worried,' replied the doctor.

'But you could be struck off.'

Dr Amato began to laugh. 'My dear Joe, my days as a practising physician were over a long time ago. Do you think I'd care if they decided I should be struck off?' Still chuckling, he shook his head. 'Besides, I didn't sign a death certificate, I merely signed a document suggesting that your father was *missing presumed dead*. The only crime I committed was to allow the world to believe Isabella was Vincenzo's daughter.' He got to his feet, walked over to a large desk by the window and, unlocking one of the drawers, took out an envelope. Returning to Joe, he said, 'This is the code you need. I'm sure you'll make good use of your father's legacy. Now please excuse me. I'm an old man and I tire easily. Come and see me another time. It's been a real pleasure to meet you both.' He picked up a small hand bell and rang it. 'My housekeeper will show you out.'

The pair walked to the bus stop in shocked silence. When the bus arrived, Joe followed Isabella to sit by the window at the back. She didn't speak, keeping her gaze firmly fixed on the passing countryside.

Joe longed to touch her hand. From time to time, he stole a glance at her, longing to ask her what she was thinking. Did she feel betrayed by the lie his father had perpetrated over the years? He couldn't tell, her expression was inscrutable. Intuition told him to leave her alone.

Isabella felt as if she were in a trance. She had spent two days fretting over a forbidden relationship problem, which didn't exist. Anger at her stepfather's deception alternated with relief. The jolting bus nudged misgivings to the surface of her mind. What were Joe's feelings now there was nothing to stop them dating? Had that moment of passion been a mere whim? Sometimes the unattainable was more attractive than the attainable. Would he still insist on flying back to England? She studied his reflection in the bus window, desperately wanting to reach out and touch him. He looked stony-faced. She couldn't guess what he was thinking.

On reaching Florence, Joe said, 'With a bit of luck my room might still be available.'

'You can ring from my digs,' said Isabella, but when he went to the pay phone in the entrance hall and started dialling the pensione, she plucked at his sleeve and whispered, 'You don't have to leave. You could stay here tonight. My landlady still thinks you're my brother.'

'That's not a good idea.'

'Why not?'

He realised she was speaking in earnest and said quickly, 'You know why.'

'Please Joe,' she begged.

He shook his head.

With a little pout, she let go of his sleeve and went to sit on the bottom step of the stairs.

He felt angry. She was making it difficult for him. Didn't she realise, this was as much a shock for him as it was for her? He needed time. He loved her so much, but he couldn't believe she could be serious about him. All he wanted to do was to take her in his arms and kiss her. His associations with women had never been easy: his mother had rejected him, his aunt had despised him and his wife had betrayed him. What could this beautiful young woman want with a loser like him? Pointedly averting his gaze, he continued dialling. The receptionist informed him that his room was still available.

Finishing the call, he turned round to see Isabella running upstairs to her room. When he joined her, she was sitting on the bed, her hands clasped in her lap, her gaze downcast. He could see she was close to tears. Was she feeling embarrassed by her earlier insistence? Her next words negated this conjecture.

'What's come over you?' she muttered. 'I thought you loved me but it was all pretence, wasn't it? You were putting on an act in honour of Papà's memory. You don't really care for me at all.'

'No, Isabella, you've got it all wrong,' he protested hotly. 'What Dr Amato told us today was a bolt out of the blue. We need time to assimilate the news. Let's not rush into anything we might later regret.' He meant that *she* might later regret, but he didn't want to say as much. 'I'm going back to Harrogate tomorrow.'

'Why, Joe?'

'It's the sensible thing to do. We both need time to think.'

She sprang to her feet and flung her arms round his neck, crying, '*I* don't.'

He grasped her wrists and held her at arms-length. 'I must leave, Isabella. I'll write to you and... ' He ran out of words.

She lowered her head into her hands and burst into tears. Wrenching himself away from her was the most difficult thing Joe had ever had to do.

He collected his luggage and ran down the stairs, his heart thumping madly as he tried to unravel the confusion in this head. He needed to exercise caution. More than a decade older than Isabella, it was up to him to slow down the helter-skelter of her emotions. He was sure of *his* feelings, but was she sure of hers? If they let passion lure them into a love affair there would be no going back.

That night, Joe lay awake, mulling over the meeting with Stefano Amato, analyzing his father's actions. Vincenzo tried to repay Livia by adopting Isabella. Yes, that was it. His father had faked his demise because his lover had died instead of him.

He got up and paced the room in bare feet. However irrational Vincenzo's feelings of guilt had been, Joe believed that as his heir, these shackles of guilt had transferred to him; ergo, it was his task, as her 'stepbrother' to assume responsibility for Isabella. He balled his fists in frustration. It was better to hurt her than to give way to sentimentality.

At six thirty, Joe left the pensione. It was a Monday morning and the town was preparing itself for the working week ahead. He went to the nearest bar, ordered a coffee and a croissant, and then hailed a taxi to take him to the airport, prepared to wait for as long as it took to find a seat on a flight back to England.

Landing at Heathrow late in the afternoon, he took the next train up to Harrogate and booked into a hotel. Exhausted, he slept soundly for more than eight hours, waking with the certainty that his future was mapped out: he would remain in England and resume his career as a lecturer.

After breakfast, he telephoned Lorenzo Brazzi in Rome and told him about Dr Amato's surprise revelations. He went on to describe his plans for the villa. 'Don't worry about the cost, I've located the mystery bank account. There are plenty of funds. Just make the arrangements without involving me. I want the house and vineyard restored to their former grandeur. Use local labour as far as you can, and I'd like you, personally, to take on the responsibility of seeing that the work is done properly.'

'I take it you'll be coming over from time to time to inspect it for yourself?'

'I'm not planning to. Listen, Lorenzo, I'm relying on you. When it's finished, I want you to hand over the deeds to Isabella.'

'That's extremely generous of you considering she's not related to you after all.'

'She deserves more, but this at least will secure her future. Once the paperwork has been sorted out, do me a favour, write and tell her what I've done.'

'Don't you want to tell her yourself?'

'It would be better coming from you.' A knot tightened in Joe's chest. How could he ever explain to a third party how tortured he felt! He went on curtly, 'Please give me a ring as soon as you've put things in motion.'

A few days later, he telephoned his uncle at his office and arranged to meet him for a drink.

Thirty-eight

Arthur greeted Joe warmly. 'It's good to see you,' he said as they took a seat at a table in the Red Lion.

'The feeling's mutual,' replied his nephew.

'What can I get you?'

Joe held up a restraining hand. 'Let me, what's your poison these days?'

'A pint of Worthington's would go down well, thanks.'

When Joe returned with the drinks, his uncle asked, 'What brings you home? I thought you'd gone for good.'

Joe heaved a sigh. 'Changed my mind.'

"Oh?' Arthur's bushy eyebrows rose in surprise. "Have you got a job lined up?'

'Not yet.' He paused. 'I'm thinking of completing Papà's social history before taking up a new post.'

Arthur looked approving. 'Your father would have liked that, but what about money? Unless you manage to get a publisher to give you a big advance you're going to find yourself hard pushed for cash.'

Joe gave a chuckle. 'I'm not exactly impoverished any longer.'

'So you got through to the authorities at last?'

Joe nodded and, before his uncle could bombard him with questions, he asked, 'How are Aunt Thelma and the boys?'

'Very well,' replied his uncle. 'I'm a grandfather now. Ronald and Shirley produced a baby boy three weeks ago.'

'Congratulations! How about Leslie?'

'Not much change there,' replied Arthur. 'He can't stick at anything, chucks his job regularly. His latest scheme is to join an archaeological dig in Southern Turkey. When will the boy sort himself out?'

'At least he's seeing a bit of the world,' replied Joe in Leslie's defence.

"I suppose so, but your aunt frets about him. Never a day goes by without her bewailing his lack of direction.'

"He'll settle down one day.'

"I hope so. By the way, your sister's phoned up nearly every day, why didn't you leave her a forwarding address?'

Joe felt his face redden. 'Umm! I was coming to that,' he said gruffly. Briefly, Joe relayed the sequence of events during his sojourn in Italy.

'What an extraordinary story,' exclaimed his uncle. 'But I would have thought this was good news, given your fondness for Isabella.'

Joe felt even more uncomfortable under his uncle's scrutiny. 'It is good news, but don't you see, despite the changed circumstances, a closer relationship would still seem immoral. Besides, in the light of what we learnt from Dr Amato, Isabella must surely blame my father for her mother's death.'

'Did she say something to make you believe that?'

'No, not exactly.'

'Why not ask her?'

'How can I?'

'You must. It's plain from her phone calls that she truly cares for you.'

'She's just being kind. She's a very caring person.'

Arthur looked exasperated. 'No, my boy, her feelings are genuine. Why, I'd swear on my grandson's head that she bears you no grudge! Go back and sort it out with her.'

'I can't, I've arranged for Lorenzo Brazzi to supervise the rebuilding work. It will be a wonderful home for her once she's finished university. She can set up a studio there and exhibit her paintings.'

'Do you think she's talented?'

'Definitely!' replied Joe enthusiastically. 'She's also studying the restoration process of fine arts. I know she'll do well.'

Arthur slowly shook his head. 'You're a fool, Joe Thomas. Wake up to reality. Go back to Florence and propose to her.' He rocked back in his chair and added with a laugh. 'I'll buy Thelma a new hat for the wedding.'

Joe parted from his uncle in a state of bewilderment. Was it possible that Isabella really loved him? For several days, he pondered over Arthur's observations, then decided to write to Isabella. His innumerable attempts all ended up in the waste paper basket. At last, he opted for the chatty approach, describing how he was getting on with his father's manuscript, and mentioning his meeting with his uncle. She replied by return of post, a charming letter, which spilled over with her delightful personality. The correspondence between them continued with neither of them referring to their final meeting.

Weeks went by. He rented a flat in the centre of town and settled down to work in earnest on the manuscript. Isabella's lengthy epistles kept coming until, one day, a package arrived. It contained his father's gold pocket watch. There was a brief note included: *Dear Joe, I thought you would like to have your papà's watch. It doesn't work, but I'm sure you could get it repaired. Arrivederci Isabella.*

Isabella had found the watch tucked away in the pocket of Vincenzo's old Harris tweed jacket. Feeling nostalgic one day, she had taken the jacket out of her wardrobe and held it up to her face. It was rough against her cheek, reminding her of the beard he'd grown during the last months of his life. The smell of his tobacco still lingered on it. She knew she ought to get the jacket cleaned, and give it away to some worthy cause, but she couldn't bring herself to part with it.

The pocket watch fell out of a hole in the lining. She picked it up and saw that the case was scuffed, the dial yellowing. Clearly, it had been handled frequently. She was surprised because, as far as she knew, Vincenzo had never bothered with it. Only once, when he was feeling low, had he asked her for it. After she had brought it to him, he'd sent her out of the room.

She had forgotten about the incident. In fact, over the years, he'd annoyed her by pestering her for the time of day. One year, she'd bought him a wristwatch for Christmas. When he hadn't put it on, she'd felt hurt and asked him, 'Don't you like it?'

'Of course I do, but you shouldn't waste your money on an old man.'

'Don't be silly Papà,' she'd replied. 'I love buying you things.'

Nevertheless, he'd never worn it. She'd brought the matter up on another occasion, only for him to answer, 'The strap makes my wrist itch.'

'Have you *never* worn a wristwatch?' she'd asked him, feeling irritated.

'Never.'

'I'll change it for a pocket watch.'

'Don't do that,' he'd retorted and, despite her obvious disappointment, he'd never worn the wristwatch.

She wiped the back of the pocket watch with a handkerchief and noticed an inscription. Using a magnifying glass she saw that it had been a present from Alice to her husband on their first wedding anniversary. That's why she had decided to send the watch to Joe.

Thinking about Joe brought a mixture of sadness and anger. She had kept up the correspondence with him in the hope that he would eventually decide to return to Florence, or at least, come over for a visit. In her letters, she had opened her heart to him, writing flowing descriptions of her day-to-day life, expressing her ambitions for the future. His replies had been curt and unrevealing. At first, she had put it down to pressure of work. After all, he was putting a lot of effort into finishing Vincenzo's manuscript. But as time went by, she felt more and more estranged from him. Posting off the watch was an attempt to draw them closer. If he didn't open up to her when he received it, she would stop writing to him.

Joe was delighted to receive his father's watch. He remembered it well, could picture Vincenzo consulting it. He'd known he treasured it by the way he'd smiled at Alice when she'd caught him polishing it. The watch wasn't going and wouldn't wind when Joe tried it. He wrapped it up and put it into a drawer resolving to get it repaired at some future date. But despite being touched by Isabella's thoughtfulness, he felt troubled by her accompanying message. It was not her custom to be brief, but exams were looming and he assumed she was studying.

However, after three weeks without a letter, he began to worry and wrote asking her to reply by return. All he got back were a few words of greeting on a postcard posted while she was on a day trip to Pisa with some friends. He was in torment. Her letters had kept him abreast of progress with her studies, and of the company she was keeping. After a particularly restless night, he could bear the uncertainty no longer, and the next day, he took a taxi to the airport and booked himself on the first available flight to Florence.

He made his way to her digs only to be told by the landlady that the *signorina* had gone away for the weekend. Disappointment swept over him. His imagination began to run riot: she was with a boyfriend, she had fallen in love. It wasn't study that had kept her from writing to him, she had been out enjoying herself in the company of a young man nearer her age. He felt a wrench in his gut. The jealousy he'd felt when Patricia had fallen for Roger was nothing compared to this.

He had the rest of Saturday and the whole of Sunday to kill, and rather than spend time in Florence, he took the last bus of the day to Castagnetto. Aldo Comolli greeted him warmly. 'Welcome, *Signor Conte*!' he said, reverting to formality.

After a few friendly words, Joe asked, 'I need somewhere to stay, Aldo, have you got a room available?'

The man shook his head. 'Unfortunately, my sister-in-law has come for a visit. She's here for the week.' He paused to consider. 'Wait a minute! You could always stay up at Grazia Elena's old place. It's been empty for quite a while. The keys were left in my care in case anybody wanted it for a holiday let.' He laughed. 'It's a bit basic for most holidaymakers -- these days they expect all mod cons -- but you're welcome to use it if you're not too fussy.'

'Perfect!' exclaimed Joe

Comolli disappeared behind the counter to return with a set of keys. 'By the way, a couple of men have been here, surveying the villa. There's talk of the vineyard being restored with the work being allocated to local craftsmen. Is this true?'

Joe nodded, pleased that Lorenzo Brazzi had set the wheels in motion. He left the bar and trudged up to Grazia Elena's cottage in the gathering dusk.

Joe woke in the morning to the sound of church bells. Sunlight streamed in through the window. He rigged up a makeshift shower in the back yard, shivering as he towelled himself dry. There was nothing to eat or drink except for a bar of chocolate he had bought at the airport and water from the tap outside.

He took a chance, and drank from it, running off the rust residue first. Lunch would have to be at Comolli's bar since, being Sunday, the village grocery shop would be closed.

To stop himself dwelling on what Isabella might be doing, he went up to the villa to see if restoration work had been started. Donning shorts and a polo shirt, he climbed the hill, stopping by the low stone wall, which encircled the property, before strolling on to stand under the tree house. To a small boy, the tree had towered over everything. It had been his empire, his domain, a place where he could hide from everybody.

All at once, he experienced an overwhelming urge to relive his childhood fantasies. He glanced up wondering whether the floor planks of the tree house were still strong enough to hold his weight. The adrenaline surged through him. Like a schoolboy bent on a daring prank, he threw aside caution and clambered onto the lower branches, scratching the palms of his hands and scraping his knees as he reached for a foothold. Once level with the floor of the tree house, he wrapped both arms round the trunk and gingerly hauled himself up onto the rotting platform. One of the planks began to crack before splintering under the weight of his foot, leaving a wide gap. Hugging the tree-trunk, he steadied himself and surveyed the vineyard and the surrounding countryside.

'Joe!' Startled, he nearly lost his grip as his foot shot through the broken platform. 'Careful Joe!'

He looked down on Isabella's upturned face. She smiled at him, dimples indenting the corners of her mouth. 'Can I come up there?'

'It's not safe.' Joe's heart thumped as though he had been running a marathon. Was she really there or was she part of his fantasy?

'I'm coming anyway,' she retorted and, dropping her shopping basket, started to clamber up. He reached down and pulled her by the hand, not relinquishing his grip when she finally arrived at his level. 'What a wonderful view,' she cried. 'Is that an old well I can see beyond the house?'

'That must be the well Papà made his escape from.'

'What's that over there?'

'It must be the ruins of the armament depot Dr Amato told us about.'

Isabella gave a shiver. 'How Papà must have suffered!' Joe slid her a sideways glance. Vincenzo would always be her papà.

They climbed down and stood beneath the tree looking at one another.

'I was worried when you stopped writing,' he said.

'There seemed little point in carrying on when you'd made it clear you didn't intend to come back.'

'I thought ... ' He tried to sound unconcerned. 'I thought perhaps you'd got a boyfriend.'

Isabella tossed back her head. 'I've been too busy for that, studying and all.'

'I can't believe that. You're too attractive not to have some young man chasing you.'

She blushed. 'There has been someone but ...'

He felt a tug of jealousy. So he'd guessed right; there was a man in her life. He gave a swallow and asked, 'How did you know I was here?'

'Aldo Comolli told me you'd rented Grazia Elena's cottage.'

'He phoned you?'

She smiled shyly. 'No, I come here nearly every Sunday when the weather's nice.'

Joe couldn't hide his surprise. 'Why?'

She shrugged. Speaking seriously, she said, 'The lawyer phoned to tell me what you'd arranged about the villa but I can't accept it, Joe. The estate is yours by rights. I'm not even an illegitimate Di Tomasi.'

Joe frowned. He didn't want to be reminded of his father's deception. Isabella looked sad. He didn't like that, he told himself he wanted her to find happiness with her young man. But that wasn't true; he wanted her to find happiness with him. He had to draw their meeting to a close before it became too embarrassing.

The noon church bells rang out, reminding him of his hunger. He hadn't eaten properly since the previous day. Before he could use this as an excuse to return to Comolli's, Isabella picked up her basket and said, 'I've brought a picnic. Share it with me. I always bring enough for two, just in case.'

Joe looked puzzled. 'In case of what?'

Again, she blushed. 'In case you turn up.'

Joe experienced a rush of sheer joy. It was gone in a flash, countermanded by those irritating doubts. They sat down on the grass and Isabella unwrapped the food.

'This is really good,' said Joe, biting into a fresh bread roll filled with Parma ham and salad. Sharing the picnic helped to re-establish normality.

Tweaking a black olive from a small china bowl, Isabella asked, 'What are your plans now? Are you going to stay in England?'

'I don't know.'

'I suppose you've come back to inspect the work.'

'I thought I ought to, but they haven't started yet. Comolli said a couple of surveyors have been up here.' He studied her face as if seeing it for the first time, and tried again to persuade her to accept his offer. 'Please make this your home, Isabella.'

She wrinkled her nose. 'It's a big place for someone like me, besides, I told you, I can't.'

'One day, you'll get married and have children. It's a perfect home for a family.'

'I know.' Looking down, she started to pluck at a patch of daisies.

Joe couldn't take his gaze off her. She was so slim and youthful in pedal pushers and a T-shirt, her dark hair tied back in a ponytail with a blue ribbon. He picked up another bread roll and buttered it, offering it to her. She shook her head and, without explanation, jumped to her feet and ran across the grass, disappearing inside the ruins of the villa. Joe dropped the roll, and followed her.

He found her leaning against the wall, staring up at the broken staircase. Her face was flushed and tears stained her cheeks. 'Why did you come back?' she demanded. 'Stop tormenting me, leave me alone!'

Right again! She *did* blame his father for her mother's death.

He went over to her, not knowing what to say. She sniffed and wiped a fist across her eyes. Joe pulled a handkerchief from his pocket and handed it to her, saying evenly, 'Come back and finish the picnic.'

She stamped her foot. 'Damn the picnic!' Seconds passed, broken only by Isabella's suppressed sobs. All at once, she clenched her fists and shrieked, 'Why are you being such an idiot? Why do you keep coming and going. I don't want your stupid hand-outs. Don't you understand, I love you. Either get out of my life forever or...or...' She gave a deep-throated sob, her words dying to a whisper. 'Don't keep me hanging on like this.'

What did she mean? Joe couldn't trust his own ears. He felt the colour rush to his face. Did she really love him? He reached out and drew her close, murmuring in Italian, '*Ti voglio tanto bene, tesoro; ti amo.*' His words echoed around the shell of the building, a dozen declarations of his love. 'I hardly dared hope, considering the age difference, the bizarre circumstances of our meeting ...'

'To hell with the age difference! What does that matter?' Stunned by her forcefulness, he stared at her not knowing what to say. 'Oh Joe, how can you humiliate me like this?'

'Humiliate you? Oh my darling ... ' His words petered out as he held her in his arms.

She hid her face in his shoulder and gave way to more tears. Joe stroked her hair, almost moved to tears himself and, as her sobs subsided, he tilted her chin upwards and said, 'Will you marry me and live here with me?' The answer shone in her eyes.

As they drew apart, she gulped, 'I must look awful.'

'Dry your eyes, then let's go and finish off our picnic.'

Taking her hand, he led her out of the villa across the grass towards the tree house. Halfway across the garden, Joe looked back, visualising his home as it had once been. How amazing! He'd entered the ruined villa a despairing soul, only to come out of it the happiest man in the world.

Isabella squeezed his hand. 'How long will the re-building work take?'

'About eighteen months. Enough time for you to finish your studies.' He turned his gaze up to the tree above their heads. 'But I'm going to start repairing the tree house straightaway.'

Epilogue

1965

Three years have gone by. The villa has been rebuilt and Joe and Isabella have moved in. The vineyard has begun to flourish. On the birth of their first child, sentiment prompts Joe to take his father's pocket watch to an old Jewish watchmaker in Florence.

'It was my Papà's, but it's never worked,' he explains to the grey-bearded man. Feeling particularly garrulous due to his elation at the arrival of the newborn, he goes on to confide, 'My wife's just given me a son and I'd very much like the watch repaired so that I can pass it on to him in good working order.' As the words spill out, he feels foolish. It will be years before his son is old enough to tell the time.

The hint of a smile touches the watchmaker's lips. 'It probably only needs cleaning. Come back next week and I'll have it looking as good as new.'

On his return, the watchmaker greets him eagerly. 'Oh *Signor*, I've been waiting for you to come back.'

Surprised, Joe raises an eyebrow. 'Why's that?'

The old man unwraps the timepiece from a soft cloth. 'As you can see, I've given your father's watch a good clean.'

Joe inspects it, well satisfied with the result. The chasing looks as good as new. Smiling, he says, 'Thank you, you've done a fine job.'

'I found out what made it stop.' The watchmaker's eyes gleam mischievously.

Joe makes a guess. 'A broken spring, a loose coil?'

'Nothing like that. When I opened up the back, I found something inside.'

Joe's intrigued. 'What is it?'

Reaching into a shallow drawer, the old Jew brings out a pendant attached to a silver chain. He holds it up for Joe to see before placing it carefully on a piece of velvet. '*This* was what stopped it. I've polished it up for you.' His black eyes peer enquiringly at Joe over the top of rimless spectacles.

'Why, it's the Star of David!' gasps Joe. 'Are you sure it was in my father's watch?'

'Positive.'

Joe inspects the pendant again. 'There's an inscription on the back but I can't make out the words.'

'Would you like me to take a look?'

'Yes please.'

Removing his spectacles, the old man picks up his watchmaker's eyeglass and, squinting under the light of a desk lamp, mutters, '*Yevarechechà Adonai veyishmerecha*'.

'That sounds like Hebrew!'

'It is.'

'Do you speak Hebrew?' asks Joe.

'I studied it for my Bar Mitzvah many years ago. It means: *May God bless you and keep you safe*. And there's something else, a name...'

Agog now, Joe presses the palms of his hands on the counter and leans forward, asking impatiently, 'Can you decipher it?'

The watchmaker brushes a hand down his beard, clearly enjoying the interest his find has evoked. 'It says, *To Livia from your loving Papà.*' At Joe's gulp of astonishment, his eyes narrow shrewdly. 'Ah my boy, I can see it means something to you now.'

'Yes indeed!' Joe is gripped by excitement. So this is why his father went to such pains to conceal Isabella from the Nazis! 'Thank you, thank you so very much. This will mean such a lot to my wife,' he gabbles, fumbling in his wallet for money to pay the watchmaker.

And that is why Joe and Isabella's son is named Vincenzo Aaron Moisè.